THE**MONDAY**GIRL

THE GIRL DUET
PART ONE

JULIE JOHNSON

COPYRIGHT © 2016 JULIE JOHNSON
All Rights Reserved.

No part of this book may be used or reproduced in any manner whatsoever, including Internet usage, without written permission of the author, except in the case of brief quotations included in critical articles and reviews.

This is a work of fiction. Names, places, characters, and events are fictitious in every regard. Any similarities to actual events and persons, living or dead, are purely coincidental. Any trademarks, product names, or named features are only used for reference, and are assumed to be property of their respective owners.

COVER DESIGN BY JULIE JOHNSON

To every boy who thinks
this book is about him.

"Cool Girls never get angry;
they only smile in a chagrined, loving manner
and let their men do whatever they want.

Go ahead, shit on me, I don't mind.
I'm the Cool Girl.

Men actually think this girl exists.

Maybe they're fooled because so many women
are willing to pretend to be this girl."

Gillian Flynn

PROLOGUE

To those who would love me — I offer you a warning.
Do not get too close. You won't survive.
There is a dark place inside my mind and a melancholy, masochistic streak running through my heart.
I am a hedge maze of razor-sharp thorns without a map.
Unnavigable. Inexplicable.
A tangled, twisted place with more spikes than a cactus. Prickly and liable to draw blood whenever you draw near.
There is danger, here.
There are demons lurking below soft skin and sloping curves, the kind that can never be brushed off or expunged. No exorcism can root them out, no priest with holy water can wash them away.
That's all right.
We've grown quite close, my demons and I, after so many years intertwined.
But I fear you will not find their presence a comfort. You will see the shadows of my soul and falter. Even the bravest of you will quake, shaken to your core, when you realize just how broken I am. That I am not a girl at all, but a collection of shattered pieces slung together with glue made of false confidence. Taped into a shape resembling feminine grace through sheer force of will.

Get too close to me and I will infect you like the most deadly disease. My misery is contagious. I will kill whatever happiness dwells inside you, extinguish that inner light you've always carried like a gust of wind blowing out a candle.

If you meet me on the street you should hurry on without a backward glance, and later when you climb into bed beside a happy girl with simple thoughts and stroke her perfect hair with fingers that are still shaky from our near-miss, you can whisper that you had a brush with death today, darling, and somehow lived.

CHAPTER ONE

"I'M JUST NOT LOOKING FOR ANYTHING SERIOUS RIGHT NOW."
- *A guy who's about to start a long-term relationship...*
...with someone else.

I sit alone in the darkness, watching bugs fly one by one into the glowing fluorescent zapper machine my neighbors installed to keep the mosquitos away from their balcony. Every few seconds, like clockwork, the pervasive quiet that seems to wrap the world in wool at three in the morning is interspersed by the unsettling buzz of tiny winged kamikaze pilots meeting their maker.
Zap, zap, zap.
I am transfixed, entranced by the sudden flare of the bulb each time it claims a new victim. There is something morbidly fascinating about these insects, drawn against all natural instinct to their deaths by the lure of this warm, bright killer. Can't they see their brothers and sisters before them, incinerated like birds flying too close to the sun? Don't they recognize danger as they sail straight toward it?
Zap.
Apparently not.
I press the damp surface of my beer bottle against my cheek, closing my eyes at the cool sensation. It's humid tonight. Sticky heat. The kind that makes you sweat through your clothes just sitting there still as a statue, doing nothing more exerting than pulling breath into your lungs.

The sprawl of downtown is a distant glow from out here on my narrow cement balcony, which overlooks a parking lot full of crappy old cars and cracked asphalt. This neighborhood is about as far from the glitz and glamour of the Hills as you can get while still calling Los Angeles home. Cynthia, my mother, hates that I live here almost as much as I hated living under the roof she pays for with an overly-generous alimony stipend from her third husband. Moving out last year with nothing but the thin wad of cash in my wallet, my broken-down Honda, and whatever clothes I managed to stuff into a duffle bag in the hour-long interval she vacated her beach-front condo in Manhattan Beach for her yogalates class was the best decision I ever made, even if she refused to speak to me for six months after she realized I'd gone.

Cynthia — which, for the record, is what she's asked me to call her since I was in diapers— still hasn't quite forgiven me for maneuvering my way out from under her thumb, but she can't shut me out completely. After all, I'm the star on which she has pinned her every hope and dream for fame and financial security. And a trainer doesn't let their prized racehorse just *quit*. Not before they've won the damn Kentucky Derby — or at the very least been turned into glue for profit. I'll be auctioned off for parts before she willingly loses her return on investment.

I did not pay for fifteen years of dance and vocal lessons to have you flush it all down the toilet.

Bringing the bottle to my lips, I drain the dregs of my beer in one long gulp. I set it beside the six other empties lined up like fallen soldiers at my feet and tilt my head up to look at the faint stars overhead. They swim before my eyes like fireflies in the hazy LA heat.

Everything is a bit fuzzy around the edges.

Maybe I shouldn't be drinking by myself, but I live alone and right now *not* drinking is not an option. I could call Harper, but she's got work in the morning and dragging her out of bed to deal with my drama in the middle of the night would only make me feel worse. I sure as shit can't call Cynthia. She'll never let me hear the end of it.

Drinking on the night before your big audition? You'll have bags under your eyes! You're competing with perfect little seventeen-year-old sluts for this part. We can't afford mistakes like this, Katharine.

If my ancient twenty-two-year-old ass can't land this shitty part because of a few beers, I'm sure my darling mother will still manage to spin it to our advantage. She's a pro at it. I'll be enrolled in rehab for a nonexistent drinking problem before I can blink, in some elaborate scheme to rebrand me as a bad girl and "broaden my image" — something she reminds me at least twice a week is in severe need of a makeover if I want to land any kind of steady role during pilot season.

I snort at the thought and lean back on my elbows.

There's very little allure in the prospect of securing the lead as a teenage airhead on some vacuous new network television show — a last-gasp effort at appealing to a generation much more inclined to binge-watch on their laptops than tune in every Tuesday at eight for yet another vampire show. That's not my dream — hell, that stopped being my dream about six years ago, when I realized my stint on a short-lived kids' show called *Busy Bees* was not going to impress the casting directors of edgy indie films or big Hollywood blockbusters.

Frankly, I'd like nothing more than to fade quietly into my mid-twenties, working nights as a bartender at Balthazar, the trendy nightclub downtown where I regularly serve bottles of champagne that cost more than my rent, and slowly scraping together enough money for college tuition.

Unfortunately, Cynthia is not quite so eager to relinquish her dreams of stardom. Despite my apathy, she remains doggedly determined to make her only daughter into an A-list celebrity, come hell or high water. Hence the audition tomorrow.

Another role I won't get, another disappointment she'll bear with all the grace of a blunt battle axe.
If you'd just smile more enthusiastically, Katharine...
If you'd just put in a bit more effort, Katharine...
If you'd just...
If you'd just...
If you'd just...
A deep sigh rattles out between my teeth as I rise, collect the empty bottles at my feet, and head through the sliding glass door into my dingy kitchen. The glowing green numbers on the microwave panel inform me it's nearly three thirty. Going to sleep now will probably leave me groggy and exhausted when my alarm blares to life at seven, but with the beer humming in my system I can't quite work up enough energy to care much.

If I manage to make it to the audition, it's sure to be a disaster.

Cynthia is going to be livid.

I smile in the dark as I collapse onto my lumpy mattress.

***

Self-sabotage is my middle name.

A psychiatrist would have a field day with me.

My Honda makes a scary noise as I punch the gas and hurtle toward downtown LA — a death-rattle, of sorts. Fitting, since this will go down in history as the day Kat Firestone finally managed to kill her acting career. Twenty-five minutes late, with last night's mascara still caked beneath my eyes and hair that hasn't seen a brush since well before my little balcony-bender last night, I know I'll probably miss my audition slot and, even if by some miracle I get there in time, I'll look more like a crack addict than the "fresh faced All-American girl-next-door type" they're looking for, according to the call sheet.

I press the gas pedal harder, wincing when the Honda begins to shudder, and pray I don't hit traffic. Though, not hitting traffic in LA would mean something ghastly has happened.

The nuclear apocalypse, perhaps.

Or, worse... *rain*.

I am self-aware enough to admit the irony of my race to read for a part I don't want, my headlong flight to salvage a career I severed all emotional ties with long ago. Yet, here I am. Hurtling down the freeway full-speed toward the demise of something inevitable. Racing toward an ending I don't necessarily want to reach.

That's life though, isn't it?

We're all in such a damn hurry to grow up — to turn eight and strap on a big-kid backpack and declare yourself too old for naps and dolls and dress up; to turn sixteen and get angry because, *god*, Mother, I'm old enough to stay out until midnight with my friends; to turn twenty-five and squeal *yes*, honey, of course I'll marry you and settle down in a suburban house far from the city lights in a marriage I'm not sure I'm ready for because, well... what's the alternative?

We move. We rush. We run.

Sharks in the water: stop swimming and you die.

And then quite abruptly we are old and wrinkled and frail, lying on our death beds looking back at a life we didn't even pause to enjoy. We are so busy speeding toward that damn finish line, trying to keep up with everyone sprinting alongside us, we forget sometimes that the finish line is death and the trophy is a coffin six feet beneath the earth.

I press the pedal a little harder and the Honda groans precariously. A strange smell has begun to emanate from the vents in my dashboard. By the time I screech to a stop in the parking lot of the talent agency holding the casting call, it's a quarter-past eight and my head is aching from the fumes. At a run, I drag my fingertips through my dark tangled mane and scrape it up into a pony-tail at the back of my skull. The weight of it tugs at my temples, exacerbating a headache from a hangover that hasn't even properly hit me yet.

I skid to a halt just inside the doors. They slam shut at my back with a bang loud enough to make me flinch, drawing the gazes of nearly everyone in the starkly decorated waiting room.

There are a few dozen girls scattered along the aluminum seats lining the wide hallway, waiting for their turn inside the thick double doors — biding time until they get their shot to read lines they've likely memorized and rehearsed a thousand different ways, for a character with the emotional complexity of a hamster. They all look nearly identical — glossy blondes in sweater sets and heels. A few of them are wearing pearls for god's sake, which says something about the role we're reading for. Between my mussed, chocolate brown waves, thready jean cut-off shorts, and faded *Ramones* t-shirt, I don't exactly blend with the crowd.

Damn Cynthia to hell for signing me up for this.

A wave of smug condescension crashes over me as sets of eyes coated with two perfect swipes of mascara scan my disheveled appearance from top to toe. Immaculately-lined lips purse in amusement and self-affirmation. Their thoughts are thinly-veiled as they examine me like a wad of gum stuck to the bottom of a Manolo Blahnik slingback.

I may not get the part, but at least I don't look like her.

Grabbing a script off the stack on a table by the door, I sigh heavily and collapse into the closest aluminum chair.

I probably should've read the call sheet Cynthia emailed me last week, accompanied by a terse note reminding me that I am not getting any younger and haven't had a steady role since I was wearing training bras a full decade ago. As is the case more often than not, her admonitions fell on deaf ears. I haven't exactly bothered to prep — unlike the perfect, pretty, petty girls littering the room around me like mannequins in a store window. Heads buried in cue cards and hand mirrors, they run through last minute lines and check their makeup.

My eyes drop to the phone clutched between my

fingers. I scroll through a week's worth of backlogged spam emails until I find my mother's message. I pick absently at my chipping black nail polish as my gaze sweeps the casting call. It's a recurring guest role on a new pilot set during high school, featuring vampires or fallen angels or some other incomprehensible shit. Beth or Becky or some equally non-threatening name suited for a sidekick. A best friend.

Not the lead. Those were cast weeks ago.

I snort and the girl in the chair closest to mine makes a deliberate show of scooting away from me, as though my unkempt state is contagious and I'm liable to lessen her chances by sheer proximity. Twin spots of color appear on her high cheekbones when I waggle my fingers at her in a teasing wave.

"Don't worry, sweetie," I confide in a whisper. "I don't want the part. But if *you* do, I think we both know what kind of *qualities* the casting director is really looking for."

I make a crude pumping gesture with my hand and push out the inside of my cheek with the tip of my tongue.

With an indignant huff and a resolute shake of her slim shoulders, she turns her attention to the phone in her hands and attempts to ignore my existence.

That suits me fine.

The double doors at the opposite end of the room swing open and every head pivots to watch, faces etched in various expressions of critique, as a production assistant wielding a clipboard steps out, trailed closely by a girl who's just auditioned. Looking a bit green around the gills, the girl makes her slow march through the gauntlet of aluminum chairs on which her competition sits, her eyes never wavering from the exit. Judging from the way her hands are shaking and the thoroughly bored look on the PA's face, it's clear she won't be playing Becky.

A new name is called. A girl clamors to her feet and vanishes into the inner sanctum. I read through the script sheet briefly, grimacing at the cheesy lines. It's even worse than I imagined, and not just because my headache has evolved into a migraine. This is bad writing, even by network television standards.

After a few moments of painful study, I close my eyes and lean back in my seat, wishing I'd had time to grab a bagel in my mad rush to get here. The thought of composing myself enough to walk through those doors and say the words, "What do you mean, Stefano is a... a... a *vampire?*" in a tone of breathy incredulity is almost more than I can bear without any carbs in my system.

Every few minutes, I hear the sound of the doors swinging open, of girls exchanging places, of heels clicking against tile floors as those who have failed to impress the producers escape eagerly into the parking lot where they will sit in their cars and cry until their perfect mascara is smudged beyond recognition. The hopefuls — those who still cling to this impossible dream of "making it" — always take rejection the hardest.

I should know. I used to be like them. I used to give a shit.

Slumping down so my neck is braced against the curved back of my aluminum chair, I fight the waves of nausea coursing through my veins. God, I'm hungover. I haven't felt this crappy since last April, when Harper and I did mushrooms at Coachella. Fun at the time; not so fun the next morning, when I woke up naked in a stranger's tent covered in glitter, missing both my panties and my dignity.

An abrasive tapping sound intrudes on my recollections, followed shortly by an impatient cough. I open my eyes to find the stony-faced PA staring down at me, her clipboard clutched so tightly it's a wonder her acrylic fingernails don't pop off with the force of her grip. When our stares meet, her lip curls in a hint of disdain.

"Katharine Firestone?"

I blink. "Guilty."

"You're up," she says coolly, turning on a heel and marching toward the double doors without another word. I push to my feet and follow her at a leisurely pace, feeling the heat of glares from the rest of the girls in the room burning into me from all sides, an inferno of female contempt. Just before I reach the doors, I turn and blow them a goodbye kiss.

"They're waiting," the PA informs me testily, tapping her pencil again.

I push down the urge to reach out and break it in half. Denying her a snappy retort will spoil her dramatic little power trip, so I simply arch my brows and wait patiently, a small smile playing on my lips, until she shoves open the doors and ushers me inside.

There's a table set up across the room, about twenty feet from where I'm standing, its surface littered with empty iced coffee cups and stacks of notes. Sitting behind it are three people, none of whom bother to glance up when the door closes behind me with a resounding click. I hear the PA take a seat somewhere out of sight.

"Stand on the X in the middle of the floor, please," one of the women says in a tired voice.

I walk soundlessly to the spot marked with masking tape.

"Name?"

The woman at the center of the table is speaking again. She seems to be in charge. There's something insectile about the way she moves that reminds me of a large praying mantis — too thin, too jerky, highly inclined to bite your head off. Every strand of hair in her bleached blonde bob stays perfectly in place when she tilts her head to scan the sheet in front of her.

"Katharine," I say, my voice parched and cracking. Cynthia always says I have a voice made for radio, but my hangover has made me sound even huskier than usual. I clear my throat and try again. "Katharine Firestone. But I go by Kat."

The man on the right looks up when I speak, interest written plainly on his angular features. He's in his early thirties and strikingly handsome — tall with an athletic build, his blondish-brown hair pulled back in a man-bun. I usually hate that look, but he somehow pulls it off effortlessly. I suppose, if you're attractive enough, it doesn't much matter what you do with your hair.

He looks like a Viking.

Or maybe an Instagram model.

His eyes rake me from my messy pony-tail down to my battered Doc Martin boots. Surprise flickers in his dark blue irises as he takes me in.

"You're here to read for the part of Beth?"

There's an unmistakable note of incredulity in the question, fired at me from the other woman at the table — a middle-aged brunette with an air of superiority wrapped around her like an afghan. It's clear she's wondering what a girl like me, who sounds like a sex-line operator and dresses like a punk rocker, is doing here.

"Yes."

"I see." She glances down at the sheet in front of her and I see a flash of comprehension on her face. "Oh. *Firestone.* You're Cynthia's client."

"I am," I agree, forcing myself not to fidget under their unwavering stares. I'm not sure what's more humiliating — the implication that my mother had to make a call to get me this audition, or that she is so eager to be seen as my manager instead of the woman who physically pushed me from her womb twenty-two years ago.

The brunette murmurs something under her breath. It sounds suspiciously like *I should've known.*

"Why do you want this part?"

This time, the man is speaking. There is none of the brunette's arrogance or the blonde's apathy in his tone; he radiates a quiet intensity that commands attention. His voice is crisp and clear — it hits me like a splash of water and trickles down my spine in a sensation that's not altogether unpleasant.

I jerk my chin in his direction and hold his gaze. I contemplate mustering up some false enthusiasm, giving a fabricated answer about my passion for the role, but when my mouth opens I find myself answering honestly.

"My rent is due in two weeks and I currently have seventeen dollars and twenty-three cents left in my checking account."

The blonde titters, as though I've made an uncouth joke. The brunette pretends I haven't spoken. But the man shifts in his seat, the curious look in his eyes intensifying.

I try not to let it bother me. Men have been giving me that look for as long as I can remember. Like I was bred for sex and sin — a creature who exists only in the hours between midnight and dawn, when proper girls are sleeping. I'm not sure what makes them see me in that light, have never quite been able to pinpoint what part of me screams out to be degraded and deconstructed down to my basest parts.

Daddy issues?
Lack of self-esteem?
Fear of commitment?
Some other bullshit psychological diagnosis that reaffirms my deep-seated emotional damage?

Oh, who the hell knows.

Back in my elementary school days, boys used to tease me about the natural rasp in my vocal cords, about my too-large lips and masculine jawline. Funnily enough, when they hit puberty and started imagining how that rasp might sound if I were breathing out their names in the back seat of their cars, how my bee-stung lips might feel pressed against their own, the teasing came to an abrupt end.

There's a moment when they just sit there, the three of them, blinking at me. It's quite clear whoever they were expecting, it was not me. Likely another cog in the wheel of sweater-set wearers who came before. Pearls and pumps and well-practiced introductory speeches.

"Well, then... I'll prompt you with Angelica's lines," the praying-mantis woman says in a voice that sounds like air hissing from a balloon.

I nod and say nothing.

Sure, I should probably spend a bit of time trying to convince them why I'm suited for this part, but frankly... I'm not. I know it; they know it. Hell, even the bitchy PA knows it.

"Okay." The brunette woman slides her glasses down the bridge of her nose and stares at me like a pigeon who's just crapped on the hood of her freshly-waxed Mercedes. "Whenever you're ready, then."

It's clear before I ever open my mouth that there's very little point in even trying. There's a greater chance of this woman asking me to go tandem bicycle riding with her this afternoon than actually giving me the part. But I wasted a quarter tank of gas getting here, and then there's the small matter that Cynthia knows everyone in this industry; if I walk out without reading a single line, she'll hear about it — and I'll never hear the end of it.

Clearing my throat once more, I glance at the lines on my script as the blonde starts to speak.

"Oh, Beth! You'll never believe it... Stefano..." Her hand flutters to her heart and I try desperately to bury a laugh. "He's... he's..."

"What is it, Angelica?" I croak in a strangled voice. "I'm your best friend. You know you can tell me anything."

"But *this*...Oh!" The blond is quivering with passion. "This is not my secret to tell. I cannot betray the trust of the man I love..."

I gasp in an unconvincing show of surprise. "You *love* him?"

"Yes! I do!"

"But you barely know him," I choke out, gripping the script so hard my fingertips turn white. "How is that possible?"

"Beth, *anything* is possible when it's true love! Stefano is my soulmate..."

A snort of laughter slips out. I can't help it — this is cheesier than fettuccine alfredo. I try to cover it with

14

a coughing fit, to maintain a serious tone as we make our way through the rest of the lines... but, judging by the cold glare darkening the brunette's face, I don't think I convince anyone in the room that I'm taking this seriously. My suspicions are confirmed a few moments later, when she cuts the audition short.

"That'll do." The brunette's eyes slide to the PA, who leaps to her feet and appears at my side, more than eager to escort me out. "Thank you for coming in. We'll reach out if we're interested in a call-back."

"Right." I grin ruefully. "I'll wait by the phone, night and day."

The women have already tuned me out, fixing their attention back on the papers in front of them, but the man shifts in his seat as his eyes scan me again. I swear his lips are twitching as he watches me turn and stride toward the exit, a jaunty bounce in my step because, as shitty as the audition was, it's *done*. Even the prospect of walking through the gauntlet of bitchy girls outside the door is not enough to dampen my spirits.

Now I can go get tacos.

I'm halfway to my car when I hear the sound of footsteps trailing close behind me in the long shadows cast by the building. Twenty-two years of possessing ovaries in modern-day America has taught me that, no matter the time of day, there is a fifty percent chance you are about to be raped if you hear someone walking behind you in an empty parking lot, so I reflexively position my keys between my fingers like little blades before whipping around to confront my stalker.

"Listen, buddy, I don't know what you—Oh." The words dry up on my tongue as I recognize the male producer from the casting session. He's slightly out of breath, as though he's run to catch up to me. "It's you," I finish lamely.

"It's me," he echoes, his eyes crinkling up in amusement. "Were you planning to key me to death?"

15

I glance down at my hand and find the keys still clutched tightly in my grasp. "Only if you were planning to rape me."

"I'm not."

"That's comforting."

His head tilts. "Are you always like this?"

"I assume by *like this* you mean charming and delightful."

"I was going to say abrasive and caustic, but I'm not one to judge." He leans in conspiratorially. "My therapist says I'm chronically distant and damaged."

"Well, shit, mine says I use humor as a defense mechanism for deep emotional pain." I shrug. "I told him I don't have any deep emotional pain. Maybe I'm just a bitch."

He laughs. "What are you doing right now?"

I glance around. "Standing in a parking lot with a stranger, contemplating the possibility that I'm an asshole by nature. Also contemplating the likelihood that my favorite food truck is serving tacos at this time of day."

He laughs again. "What are the chances of you putting your taco quest on hold?"

"I don't know. I'm pretty serious about tacos." My eyes narrow. "Why?"

"I want you to come with me somewhere."

"I don't even know your name."

"That ever stopped you before?" he asks.

I grin in lieu of a reply.

"It's Wyatt." He reaches out a hand and I slowly shake it. "Wyatt Hastings. And yes, I do mean *that* Hastings."

I feel my mouth gape a bit. The Hastings family owns half of Hollywood, controlling majority shares in AXC — one of the largest media conglomerates in the world. Their family fortune makes most A-list celebrities look like paupers.

"My father runs the network. That's why I'm here," Wyatt explains, jerking a finger toward the building behind us. "He likes to have someone from the family

16

supervise casting calls for our newly green-lit shows, make sure everything is running smoothly before they start filming."

"Well... *shit*." I blink at him, feeling lost for words.

His grin widens. "Does that look of stunned disbelief mean you'll come with me?"

"You're not going to have me read for that role again, are you? Because, I'm sorry... Hastings or not, I don't think I'm cut out to play Biffy the best friend on your new vampire show."

"I don't think you are either," he says, stunning me. "In fact, I don't think you're meant for television at all. I've got something else in mind."

"Oh."

"Just get in the car, please." He turns and walks toward a shiny black Audi convertible parked a few spaces down from my decrepit Honda.

"Is this, like, a sexual thing?" I tilt my head curiously as I watch his retreating back. "Because, honestly, I'm confused."

"Sexually confused?" he teases, clicking a button to unlock the doors.

"No. Just the regular kind of confused."

He pulls open the driver's side, grinning at me over his shoulder. "No, this is not a *sexual* thing. I'm old enough to be your... well, not your father. But maybe, like... your cool uncle. The one who buys you a keg after prom and beats up your boyfriends when they cheat on you."

"I'm twenty-two," I point out. "And this is LA."

"Your point being?"

"Most men date women at least two decades younger than them. I'd peg you at thirty-five, tops."

He looks affronted. "And here I thought I was passing for thirty-three. My life is a lie." He pauses. "Actually, it may just be my personal trainer who's lying."

I snort. "My point still holds. Walk into any coffee shop in this city, you'll spot a loving father-daughter duo having breakfast... until he starts to feel her up beneath

17

the table and you realize he's just another sugar daddy treating his whore-of-the-week to crepes."

"That may be true. But we're getting off topic." He pulls his door fully open and pins me with a serious look. "I promise my intentions toward you concern nothing but your career. Now get in the damn car, Katharine, before I decide you aren't worth the hassle."

I arch a brow. "You're going to help my career?"

"No." His eyes gleam. "I'm going to change your life."

CHAPTER TWO

"Let's definitely still be friends, though, okay?"
- *A man you will never, ever hear from again.*

Wyatt doesn't speak as we cut a path across LA, changing lanes with an aggressiveness typically reserved for soccer moms and race-car drivers. He shifts with one hand and punches buttons on his steering wheel with another. My fingertips curl around the leather seat edge as we cut off a massive flat-bed truck going sixty miles an hour, our bumper barely clearing his license plate. The roar of his horn is audible for only a moment before we zoom out of earshot. My heart palpitations are drowned out by the sharp ring of Wyatt's call connecting over the car speakers.
"Sloan Stanhope's office, may I help you?"
"Mary — it's Wyatt."
"Sloan isn't in. He's working from home today."
"All right." He downshifts and we hurtle around a particularly sharp corner, leaving my stomach lying on the pavement fifty yards back. "Can you let him know I'm on my way over? And tell him…" He grins and slams us into a different gear, making the engine scream. "Tell him I found *her*. He'll know what I mean."
"Right away, Mr. Hastings," Mary says in a composed voice. "Anything else?"
"Yeah. Call Dunn, tell him to get over to Sloan's place. I'd like to get them in the same room for a screen test as soon as possible."
"Very well."

"Thanks, Mary." He jabs his thumb against a button to disconnect the call, then glances over at me and grins. "It's going to be a good day, Katharine. I can feel it in my bones. Can you feel it?"

I smile weakly in return. I can't feel anything in *my* bones except a faintly nauseous sensation, but I keep that to myself as we barrel along toward a destination he still hasn't bothered to share with me.

I don't have to wait long. Not twenty minutes later, we screech to a halt at a gated residence somewhere in the Hills so far out of my socioeconomic bracket, I'm pretty sure my mere presence brings down the average home value. There's a drought in California, but you'd never know it — here, the lawns gleam green and bright in the midday sunshine. We roll down a limestone driveway, passing two giant lion statues and a garish fountain where naked cherubs clutch spouting pots of water, finally coming to a halt in front of a sleek, split-level mansion in the boxy, modern design LA architects are so very fond of constructing.

"Is this your place?" I ask as he turns off the engine.

"No. Sloan Stanhope lives here." He glances at me. "My place is much bigger."

Without another word of explanation, he throws open his door and climbs from the car. I scramble out my side and hurry down the driveway after him.

"Sloan Stanhope." I reach his side, hustling to match his pace. "The director?"

"The very one."

"But..." Maybe it's the hangover, maybe it's the fact that he has shared exactly zero details as to why we're here, but I am suddenly incapable of coherent thought or speech. "But..."

"Katharine." Wyatt stops walking as we reach the massive black front doors, their ornate oriental handles glinting bronze in the sunlight. "Relax."

"I'd be more relaxed if you told me why we're at the home of a man who's directed three Academy Award winners for Best Picture. Stanhope has more Oscars than the *de la Renta* family."

"Cute."

"Tell me why we're here, Hastings."

"And spoil the surprise?" Wyatt grins. "What fun would that be?"

I sigh.

He reaches out and rings the doorbell. Abruptly, the grin fades from his lips. "Though... you're right, maybe we should've discussed your rate before we got here."

"My... my rate?"

"You know." He shrugs casually. "For the night."

I swallow hard. "*What?*"

"Don't worry, you'll be well compensated for your services."

"For my— do you think I'm— what do you—" My voice goes up an octave each time I speak. I can feel my face flaming red as I finally manage to squeak out a full sentence. "I'm not a *hooker!*"

Wyatt stares at me for a moment, expression entirely blank, then barks out a laugh that bends him double.

"God, your face," he gasps. "Firestone, I'm just fucking with you."

"You're joking?" I pull in a relieved breath as I watch him wipe tears from his eyes. "You're joking," I confirm, crossing my arms over my chest. "*Asshole.*"

He's still chuckling when the door swings inward to reveal a middle-aged bald man in wire-rimmed glasses. I recognize him from numerous award shows — not one's I've attended, of course; one's I've watched from my couch dressed in ratty pajamas, eating whipped cream straight out of the can as I critique red-carpet dress choices like I'm some kind of haute couture authority.

Sloan Stanhope is barefoot and grinning as he gestures us inside, booming out a greeting.

"Wyatt, my man!"

"Sloan, good to see you."

The two engage in a strange handshake-hug ritual.

When they break apart, I find myself the subject of Sloan's acute study.

"So," he murmurs, examining me like an inscrutable piece of artwork in a modern museum — the kind you squint at as though that might somehow help discern its meaning. "This is *her*."

Wyatt nods. "Perfect, isn't she? Knew it the moment I saw her."

Sloan continues to stare at me.

Wyatt continues to congratulate himself.

I continue to pretend it's not strange that they're discussing me like an inanimate object, or that I still haven't the faintest idea what's happening here.

"It'll all depend on the chemistry between them, of course," Sloan murmurs, then claps his hands. "Let's get to it, shall we? No point waiting. Come on, come in."

"Is Dunn already here?" Wyatt asks, following Sloan deeper into the house.

"Oh, yes, he's around somewhere. Probably out by the pool." Sloan leads us into a gorgeous kitchen full of white marble and stainless appliances. He pulls a bottle of green juice from the transparent sub-zero refrigerator and holds it out to me. "Kombucha?"

I shake my head and try to hide my revulsion. Wyatt's snort when he catches sight of my expression indicates my efforts were wasted.

"Wyatt, you want one?" Sloan calls, his head inside the fridge.

"No, thanks."

"Something else? Purified water? Cold-brew? Oh, I have this excellent new pressed chia-seed juice you should try, it's chock full of antioxidants—"

"Actually, I'd like something," I interject.

Sloan whips around at the sound of my voice and blinks as though he's just noticed me for the first time. "Name it."

"An explanation would be great."

"An explanation?"

"Yeah." I lean a hip against the white marble island. "You know... as to what the hell I'm doing here."

A bemused expression twists Sloan's face as he glances at Wyatt. "You didn't tell her?"

"And spoil the surprise?" Wyatt laughs. "Of course not."

I take a deep breath and remind myself it would likely be a bad career move to crack glass kombucha bottles over the heads of two of the most powerful men in Hollywood.

"Can someone please just tell me?" I ask between clenched teeth.

"All right, all right. No need to torture her anymore." Sloan sips his vile green juice as he walks across the kitchen toward a set of sliding glass doors that lead onto his patio. As I step out after Wyatt, I bite my lip so I won't gasp at the incredible view of the valley below. I've never seen LA from quite this angle before.

"Nice, huh?" Wyatt mutters.

I don't say anything; I'm too busy gawking.

"Dunn!" Sloan is standing by the side of a large infinity pool at the edge of the patio, intermittently sipping his juice and bellowing at the tanned, male figure swimming laps. "DUNN! Get out of the damn pool!"

The swimmer finally seems to realize he's in demand because his arms stop windmilling through the water and a second later, he's braced his hands against the side of the pool and heaved himself out. Dripping wet, he grabs a towel off the nearest chaise lounge and walks to Sloan's side. I linger in Wyatt's shadow as we approach, staring at the water droplets making slow trails down the swimmer's washboard abs and reminding myself to breathe.

"No need to yell, Sloan," the water god says, his voice muffled by the towel as he dries his face and dark head of hair. "I'm here. I have plans at six, though, so can we get this over with as soon as possible?"

Sloan's expression turns thunderous. "Since it's *your* fault we have to recast this role in the first place, you will stay and read lines until we are satisfied, plans be

23

damned. It takes as long as it takes. But now that we have—" He glances at me a bit desperately.

"Kat," I prompt.

"Right, now that we have *Kat* here to read with you, I hope we can put all this nasty casting drama behind us and make a goddamned movie." He takes an aggressive sip of his juice and looks skyward. "Actors. If I could somehow make movies without them, I wouldn't need to meditate…"

He murmurs something else under his breath, but I'm too busy staring at Wyatt to pay much attention. Wyatt looks entirely relaxed, grinning back at me.

"I'm here to read for a part?" I hiss at him.

"Of course," he says cheerfully. "Way better than spending the night as a call girl, am I right?"

I shake my head, exasperated.

"Kat," Sloan says, calling my focus back to him. He gestures to the man at his side, who's finally stopped toweling off, and my entire body goes rigid when I catch sight of his face. "This is Grayson Dunn," Sloan is saying, but his voice sounds far away. "If your screen test goes well, you'll be co-stars in my new project. Assuming you're free to start filming next week. We're on a rather tight timeframe…"

I'm frozen, starting at the chiseled features of *People* magazine's "Sexiest Man Alive" four years running. His gorgeous face puts his perfect abdominal muscles to shame, but that's not why I'm suddenly finding it so hard to breathe.

I *know* Grayson Dunn.

We met ten years ago, long before he was the biggest action hero in Hollywood, on a daytime kids' show called *Busy Bees*. He was older than me by a handful of years, and his time on the show didn't last long — at fourteen, he landed his first big movie contract and disappeared from the ranks of our cast like a phantom, leaving half the girls nursing broken hearts they never fully recovered from. In the years since, his rise to fame has been meteoric… and his heartbreak record has only grown more impressive. His eyes meet mine, green and bottomless, and suddenly my tongue feels swollen to three times its normal size. I open my mouth to say something witty and memorable — like *hi* or *long time no see, asshole* — but before I can vocalize a single word, he's shoved his hand into the space between us.

"Grayson Dunn. It's nice to meet you."

I flinch, stunned, and feel my back hit the solid warmth of Wyatt's chest. His big hands close over my shoulders to steady me.

Of all the things I thought Grayson Douche-Nozzle Dunn might say or do if we ever crossed paths again, pretending not to remember me wasn't one of them. After what he did when we were kids... after the hell he put me through...

A split second later, it occurs to me that perhaps he truly *doesn't* remember me — that I was such an insignificant thread in the woven patchwork of his past I've simply been deleted from recollection, like a foreign language you don't use daily or the ability to read any sheet music more advanced than *Chopsticks*.

I've still made no move to take his hand, and the air grows stale and awkward the longer it remains suspended between us. If he's not going to acknowledge that we know each other, I'm certainly not going to.

"Does she speak?" Grayson mutters out the corner of his mouth at Wyatt.

"Usually," Wyatt replies, giving my shoulders a small shake. "You still with us, baby?"

I sigh and pull out of his grip. "Kat Firestone," I murmur slowly, reaching out and sliding my palm against Grayson's.

There's a flash of something in the depths of his stare as his large hand engulfs mine, but it's gone before I can decide if it's attraction, recognition, or the simple interest that comes along with meeting someone new. He releases his grip almost instantly, then turns to Sloan.

"So, are we doing this now? I really do have plans at six..."

"Yes, yes, we all know how important your social agenda is." Sloan drains the rest of his juice and walks back toward the house. "Then again, if you'd been a little *less* focused on the women in your life, we wouldn't be in this predicament."

Wyatt scoffs. "He has a point."

"Am I missing something?" I ask.

"No," Grayson mutters.

"Yes," Wyatt counters. "Our golden boy here couldn't keep it in his pants with the last actress we'd lined up to play this part — they hooked up, he pulled his usual vanishing act, and that was it. They couldn't work together. Set us back months." Wyatt shoots Grayson a sour look. "Only silver lining of the whole damn mess is that we hadn't started filming. That would've been an even bigger nightmare."

"You talk like I'm the first actor in history to date a co-star." Grayson's tone borders on petulant.

"That's the thing though. You didn't *date* her." Wyatt shakes his head. "You added her to your fuck-buddy roster."

I roll my eyes.

"Don't listen to him," Grayson insists. "You'll get the wrong idea about me."

"The thing is, I already have a pretty good idea about who you are," I inform him, tilting my head and contorting my features into something of a grimace. "And, to be candid... I doubt anything you say at this point is going to alter my perception."

Grayson's eyes narrow and he opens his mouth to speak, but I cut him off.

"What is this mystery project, anyway?" I ask Wyatt. "I can't picture Stanhope taking on an action blockbuster, but... based on current casting choices..." My eyes dart to Grayson, who looks suddenly insulted.

"I don't only do action movies," he growls. "I have range."

"Range," I echo dryly. "Like... sometimes you play a shirtless military general, and other times you play a shirtless superhero?"

Wyatt snorts.

Grayson's eyes narrow. "Did I do something to offend you that I'm unaware of? Because you seem to have a problem with me."

"Nothing at all," I say sweetly. "No problem here."

Our eyes clash like swords on a battlefield. Wyatt coughs gently to break the tension.

"Katharine, the movie is called *Uncharted*. In a nutshell: it's a love story about two people who are the sole survivors of a plane crash on an uncharted island in the South Pacific, who fall in love while they're stranded, despite the fact that he's married to someone else back in the real world and she's several years younger than him. Sloan and I have been working to adapt the screenplay from the original novel for a few years now, and we've finally gotten it to the point where it actually reads like a movie. I'm funding this independently, without AXC Studios, so we've got a limited budget... and Sloan has three projects lined up starting next month, so we've got a much shorter shooting schedule than any of us are accustomed to... but that's half the fun of it."

"Wait... did you say *Uncharted*?" My eyes fly to his face and my heart starts beating faster. "Based on the book?"

"You've read it?"

"Only about six times." Excitement is churning through my veins. "It's brilliant."

Wyatt's face contorts in surprise and he stares at me in stunned silence.

"You know," I say dryly, "If I were a lesser girl, I'd be insulted that you're *this* shocked I know how to read."

"No, no." He shakes himself out of his stupor. "It's not that you've read it, it's that you've even *heard* of it." His lips twist. "It wasn't exactly a New York Times bestseller."

"Who gives a shit?" I ask, shrugging. "Some of the best books I've ever read are the least critically acclaimed. In fact, the more praise something gets from the masses, the less I seem to like it."

Grayson mutters something that sounds like "hipster" under his breath, and I shoot him a dark look before turning back to Wyatt.

"*Anyway*," I say pointedly. "It's a great book. Poignant. Packed with gorgeous prose. It has a kickass heroine. A badass hero. A slow-building, self-destructive love story... What's not to like about that?"

Grayson snorts.

I ignore him, sighing dreamily as I recall the first time I flipped from cover to cover, clutching the paperback with white-tipped fingers until the wee hours of the night, desperate to know what would happen to the couple in the story — two people who'd learned to survive, to even *thrive*, on their isolated island, and ultimately been ripped from it... and each other... when the rescue they'd once prayed for finally arrived.

The story of Violet and Beck touched me deeply, in a way only the best books can. It was the most delicious kind of novel. Sumptuous, sensual. I wanted to race to the end but also savor every word, to let the author's thoughts roll around in my mouth for a while before I swallowed them down and made them a part of me. Alone in the darkness, I'd traced my fingertip across the embossed letters of the name on the front cover, feeling sad and strangely lonely at the thought that I'd never meet Tywin G. Hassat, the man responsible for inspiring such emotion inside me.

The first time I read *Uncharted*, I actually Google-searched for any scrap of information I could find about him — desperate to know who this stranger was, out there in the world, who could create a piece of art so profoundly personal to me. To my lasting disappointment, scouring the internet uncovered almost nothing about the author or his life.

"Besides the original crash scene, most of the movie is just the two of you," Wyatt says, bringing my focus back to the moment.

"So... I'd be playing Violet?"

Wyatt nods. "Yes."

"Shit." I'm barely breathing as the prospect of bringing one of my favorite literary heroines to life on screen tumbles around inside my head. *Violet*. The offbeat protagonist who sucked me into the pages of a paperback and held me captive for days; the girl who falls for a man she spends half the novel hating; the woman who falls for her own damn *self* as the story unfolds. One of the best parts of *Uncharted* is watching her discover how badass she is over the course of three hundred pages.

"Shit. Shit. *Shit*," I repeat under my breath, barely able to believe this is happening.

"I take it this means she's excited?" Grayson asks.

"I assume so," Wyatt agrees. "She hasn't even heard the best part yet. I'm worried it might break her."

"What could possibly top this?" I demand, dumbfounded.

"We'll be shooting the plane crash scenes here on an AXC soundstage, taking advantage of the green screens and sets we've already constructed, using some extras to play the other passengers and flight attendants... but the rest will be filmed with a small crew on location." He pauses, grin widening. "A beach in Oahu."

"Hawaii?" I suck in a breath. "I've always wanted to go to there."

"Well, *aloha*, baby. We'll be there next week." He sobers slightly. "Tricky part is, we have less than three weeks to get everything done if we want it ready in time to debut at the film festivals this spring. Editing and postproduction take at least three months."

I blink. "You want to film the entire movie in three weeks."

Wyatt nods. "Starting Monday."

"Starting Monday," I echo faintly.

"You've read the book, which should help you get in character relatively quickly — that'll definitely help." Wyatt's eyes scan my expression. "Breathe, Katharine."

I suck in a breath as I glance over at Grayson. His exquisite green eyes are watching me carefully, waiting for me to put the pieces together.

"So, you..." I swallow hard. "I assume you're playing—"

"Beck," he supplies, winking. "Your onscreen love."

I glance at Wyatt. "You sure he's cut out for it? Beck isn't your average action movie hero. He's got some heavy emotional shit to contend with."

Wyatt frowns at me, but his eyes are laughing. "Part of the reason we cast Grayson is that no one will expect him to star in a film like this — especially an indie film. Not at this point in his career. The shock value of an action star in a quiet, character-driven project about loss and love and learning to survive when you've lost everything you've ever known... It's going to rock Sundance and the rest of the festivals."

"I can see that, I suppose," I concede.

"Generous of you," Grayson says, scowling.

"You know..." Wyatt is looking slowly back and forth from me to Grayson. "Normally, I don't encourage such open hostility between co-stars... but I think it'll actually be perfect for Violet and Beck. If you remember, they pretty much loathe each other at the beginning of the book."

"So, you think there's a chance I might actually get the part?" I ask, barely daring to hope.

Wyatt nods. "I'd say more than a chance."

"If I were a hugger, I'd hug the fuck out of you right now, Wyatt Hastings."

"Not a hugger?" Grayson asks quietly. "What does that even mean? Who doesn't like hugs?"

"Me."

Wyatt laughs. "Well, thank god for that. Really trying to maintain an air of professionalism. You know, since I'll basically be your boss, if you get this gig. Hugs tend fuck with my street cred as a producer."

I roll my eyes. "You have street cred?"

"You can try to act aloof and indifferent, but I know you're excited about this part." Wyatt leans in, eyes twinkling. "Admit it."

"I'll admit no such thing." I shrug, trying to act nonchalant and not like every dream I've ever had is suddenly within reach. "If I got the part, it'd be cool. I guess. Whatever."

Wyatt and Grayson both grin — they know I'm full of shit.

"You two stay out here grinning at each other. I'm heading inside." Too excited to wait another moment, I turn on one heel and head for the house. I make sure to put a little extra sway in my step as I go, and when I reach the glass doors, I glance back to find both men's eyes are locked on my ass.

"Thought you were in a hurry, Grayson? You don't want to keep your date waiting," I call over my shoulder. "Then again... if she knows you at all, she's probably used to it."

A dark look flashes across his gorgeous features.

I smirk as I step into the chilly air-conditioned kitchen. Perhaps I shouldn't be so snarky, but Grayson Dunn deserves every bit of my attitude.

It's alarming to realize that if I get this part, I'll see him *every day* for almost a month. Co-starring with a man I've loathed from afar for a decade won't be a walk in the park. We'll never be friends. We'll probably never be able to stand in the same room without trading barbs and insults back and forth.

But, for the chance to play Violet, I'd do just about anything.

Even make out with my mortal enemy.

***

"Stand a little closer."

Sloan absently strokes his scruff as he directs Grayson and me from across the room. He's got a small studio set up in his basement where we've been cooped up for the past two hours, reading lines from the script, discussing our characters, and going over the plot. Now, he's positioned us in front of the camera to test our *on-screen chemistry*, which is just a fancy way of checking to see if we're attractive enough to get people to pay $13.75 for a ticket to the theater so they can gawk at us on a thirty-foot screen.

And they will pay, if what I saw in the script is any indication. This film is going to be a hit. Epic. A love story for the ages. A modern Romeo and Juliet.

Why the hell they want *me* for the role, I'll never understand. I'm not complaining, though — playing Violet would be career-defining. It would skyrocket me from nobody to A-lister. Wyatt wasn't messing when he said he was going to change my life.

I sneak a glance at the corner, where he's sprawled on a plush armchair, staring at his phone. A long tendril of blond hair has escaped his man-bun and fallen across his face. He somehow senses my gaze, because he looks up and winks at me.

I roll my eyes in return.

"Okay, I think I'm finally ready to shoot some test film." Sloan's voice draws my eyes back to him. He's leaning over the camera, training the lens on the middle of the room where Grayson and I are waiting, making minor adjustments to the aperture and angle. "Let's take it from the top of page seventeen... The scene where you finally make it to the beach. You have your scripts?"

We nod like twin bobble-head dolls. I glance at Grayson out of the corner of my eye and see he's standing a careful distance from me in an almost identical pose — arms crossed over his chest, face set in a blank expression.

Sloan pushes his glasses up the bridge of his nose. "Violet, after the crash you're in better shape than Beck. He took a pretty sharp knock to the head when one of the overhead compartments came open during the descent — he's bleeding from the temple, he's got a concussion. You barely got him into the life raft. You're exhausted, thirsty, you've been drifting for days... and you finally see it. The island."

I nod, trying to breathe normally.

"Beck, you're barely conscious at first — you just know someone's tugging at you, trying to get you to move, pulling you from the raft and across a sandy beach you've never seen before. You're disoriented. You don't know how this tiny slip of a girl is even carrying you. You're twice her size and soaking wet... but you trust her. There's no other choice. There's no one else."

Grayson nods solemnly and I notice, for the first time, the perpetual glint of amusement has faded from his eyes. He's totally focused, listening intently to Sloan's directions.

"This is just a rough take, to see how you two look together. To test your vibe. Don't get too hung up on the speaking lines." Sloan steps back behind the camera. "I just want to see if things *flow*."

Abruptly, my heart is pounding and my mouth goes dry. I'm nervous. I don't want to fuck this up. It's an odd sensation — actually giving a shit, for a change.

"Grayson, sling your arm around her shoulders. You're weak, exhausted. You can't quite stand on your own." Sloan is frowning mightily. Probably because Grayson and I are standing so far apart, you could fit three of his bimbos in the space between us. "And for god's sake, *look* at each other."

"Don't worry, Kat," Grayson whispers as my eyes drift up to find his. They're startlingly green, in the flood of bright light from the track over our heads. I can see my own face reflected on their glassy surface, distorted and distant. It's a bit like looking into a carnival fun-house mirror. His lips twitch. "I don't bite."

"Too bad," I mutter back, voice dropping to an octave only he can hear. "I do."

He laughs, white teeth flashing and eyes crinkling at the corners. It's disarming.

33

I feel my heart thudding like a battle drum as he reaches out and slides an arm around my back, leaning his considerable weight against me. Each pitter-patter beat against my ribs reminds me of those same gorgeous features, ten years younger and twisted into a condescending mask in what was, till that point, the worst moment of my inconsequential little life.

Thump-thump.
Hate-him.
Thump-thump.
Hate-him.

"Okay, do a practice run — move across the room, I want to see your natural body language." Sloan crouches behind the camera. "On my count... *Five!*"

"You okay down there?" Grayson whispers from somewhere over my head. "I can ease off a bit, if it's too much weight..."

"I'm fine," I snap. "I can handle anything you throw at me, Dunn."

"*Four!*" Sloan calls.

"Fine," he grumbles back, doubling his weight on my shoulders. My knees nearly buckle under the strain of holding us both upright. *Shit*, he's heavy. My arm winds around his waist as I struggle to stay vertical.

"*Three!*"

"Still good?" Grayson sounds downright cheerful.

"Peachy," I grit between clenched teeth.

He laughs and I feel it vibrate through his chest. "Stubborn little thing, aren't you?"

"You don't know anything about me," I volley under my breath.

"*Two!*"

Grayson's mouth is so close to my ear, I feel the warmth of his breath against my skin when he whispers a single word that sends lightning shooting through my system.

"Yet."

I suck in a gulp of air. My retort is lost as Sloan shouts. "And, *ACTION!*"

I begin to move, each step an acute struggle as I hold Grayson upright. He's not making this easy for me. I drag his dead-weight across the space, pretending not to notice the firm ridges of his six-pack beneath the thin fabric of his t-shirt, or the faint scent of chlorine lingering on his warm skin, or the way his large frame drapes over mine, somehow making me feel petite and strong all at the same time.

I cling to the image of my nine-year-old self, tears tracking down my cheeks into the corners of my mouth, my tight-pressed lips struggling to contain a sob of humiliation in front of a dozen other kids as fourteen-year-old Grayson laughed down at me.

He broke my pre-pubescent heart. And the bastard doesn't even have the decency to remember doing it.

I set my teeth and hobble a little faster.

"Oh, that's good." Sloan's voice seems a million miles away as Grayson and I move across the room like a three-legged race gone awry. "Kat, I like the conflicted expression you've got on," Sloan murmurs, half-concealed behind the camera. "You want to help him, you're determined not to leave him, but you're also traumatized from the crash, from the realization that you're so far from civilization you might never make it home again... You're running on pure adrenaline, but you haven't quite shaken the shock that the family who hired you as an au pair is dead, along with everyone else on that small plane... Yes, yes, that looks good."

Grayson leans on me a little more heavily.

I grind my heel down on his toe in retaliation and hear him gasp in sudden pain.

"Good, Grayson. I like that you're grimacing. Your head injury would be throbbing, the slice in your leg is deep enough to need stitches..." Sloan sounds approving as he walks away from the camera, picks up a Nikon and shoots some stationary shots.

35

"You two look great on film together." He clicks the shutter again. "That should do, for now."

Grayson and I push away from each other as fast as physically possible; two magnets repelling with equal force. Sloan is so lost in his thoughts, he doesn't seem to notice the negative tension between his two potential co-stars. He's already sitting at his desk, scrolling through the test shots on a nearby computer.

"Didn't I tell you?" Wyatt calls from the corner, rising to his feet and walking to look over Sloan's shoulder. "She's the one."

"I'm still supposed to have several others read for this part..." Sloan sounds hesitant. "I'll have to think it over..."

Wyatt leans in, grabs the mouse from Sloan, and zooms on a still photograph until the screen is full of two faces. Grayson and me, in the highest possible resolution, filling every pixel of the display. Snapped the moment before we pushed away from each other, our eyes are locked, our arms wrapped around each other's waists... The tension is palpable, even from here. We look more like two gladiators engaged in a death-match than we do future lovers. But maybe that's what Sloan wants, because he reclines back in his chair with a content sigh, staring at the image in front of him like it's the answer to a prayer.

"Look at the fire in her eyes. The way she carries herself." Wyatt's eyes drift over to mine as he speaks, blue and bottomless. "She may not have the experience. But she was made for this role. I'd stake my career on it."

There's a sliver of frozen silence where nobody moves or breathes too loudly, and I know this is *it* — the moment where everything changes. The exact point when this spark of possibility, lit by a blond, hipster-Viking with too much time on his hands, is either fanned into flames of stardom and success... or flickers out like a candle left too close to the wind, never to reignite.

Sloan holds Wyatt's eyes for thirty seconds, engaging him in an inscrutable silent conversation, then gives a sudden nod. Spinning around in his leather computer chair, he pins me with a look. I gulp loudly, and hope Grayson isn't standing close enough to hear my throat convulsing in panic.

"So. Kat." Sloan leans back, arms folded behind his head. Light glances off the shining surface of his wire-rimmed glasses. "Do you happen to have plans this Monday?"

CHAPTER THREE

"You're so paranoid, babe. It's just my roommate."
- *A guy who is definitely texting girls he met on the internet during your dinner date.*

    The sky is dark when Wyatt drives me back to my car. The wind rushes through the convertible's open roof, whipping my hair into a vortex of waves and frizz, but I make no move to tame it. I'm lost inside my head, trying to wrap my mind around everything that's changed in the past ten hours.
    I'm the lead actress in Uncharted.
    The new Sloan Stanhope movie.
    Co-starring with Grayson Dunn.
    I've repeated those thoughts so many times to myself, they barely sound real anymore; like staring at the same word over and over on a page until it's a jumble of nonsense, and you become convinced you've been spelling it wrong your entire life.
    After informing me that I'd landed the part, Sloan drifted upstairs for his nightly yoga session, promising to see me in a few days. Grayson jetted off to rendezvous with his flavor-of-the-week without bothering to say so much as goodbye. Wyatt simply laughed at the dazed look on my face, grabbed me gently by the hand, and tugged me to his car. With the exception of asking for my home address, he hasn't attempted to strike up conversation, assuming — rightfully — that the powers of speech are currently lost on me.

*Violet. Me.
Beck. Grayson.*

My reverie is interrupted when I see we've sped past the turn for the talent agency where my beat-up Honda is hopefully still parked.

"Hey, you missed the turn."

Wyatt glances over at me, brows raised. "I bought a two-seater for a reason — no place for backseat drivers."

"I'm not giving you directions," I say, rolling my eyes as I sit upright. "My car is back there, remember? At the talent agency."

He waves my words away. "I'll take your keys and have someone drop it off at your place later."

"Oh."

Wyatt grins at my expression. "Why do you look like you've received a life sentence in Alcatraz? You just landed a role most people would kill for. You made it. You should be celebrating."

"It doesn't feel real. It feels like…"

He glances over at me as he shifts the car into a different gear and merges onto the highway. "Like…?"

"Dumb luck," I say faintly. "Like… at any moment you're going to realize you've made a colossal error in judgment, that I'm not actually the girl you seem convinced I am, and change your mind."

"Oh." Wyatt sounds exceptionally bland. "Is that all?"

"What do you mean, is that *all*? Is my existential crisis not enough?"

"Baby, everyone feels that way." He sighs. "The most successful people on this earth always feel like the biggest frauds."

"Says the man whose first words were probably *I'd like to thank the Academy*."

He shoots me an indulgent look. "Do you actually believe the majority of successful people have an ounce more talent than the average unemployed Tom, Dick, or Harry still struggling to make it?"

"Um…yes?"

He snorts. "Success is a quarter timing, a quarter talent, a bit of fate, and a hell of a lot of dumb luck."

"So, essentially, you're saying everyone at the top of the food chain is a total moron who got there by pure chance."

"No, not exactly."

I raise my brows at his swift reversal.

"I forgot nepotism," he adds, looking thoughtful. "And a blatant disregard for moral scruples. Plus, it certainly doesn't hurt to be really, really good-looking. Those things definitely factor in at least a bit, if you're intent on making it to the top."

A laugh slips out of my mouth before I can stop it and he grins at the sound, his eyes on the road as we zoom through the night. A few minutes pass in silence. We're almost to my exit when he speaks again, and his voice is uncharacteristically serious.

"This movie... working with Sloan... it could be huge for you. Sure, he's a bit wishy-washy, what with the yoga and the meditation and the quirky bonding exercises he likes to torture the cast with every morning before shooting. And, dear god, stay away from him when he does one of his juice cleanses because the man is a terror." He winces as though remembering the horror. "But at the end of the day, he's a damn fine director. The script is solid. And Dunn, who I admittedly think is a total twat, is perfectly cast for this role, even if he did fuck things up royally with the Helena situation."

I take it by *the Helena situation* he's referring to Helena Putnam, the former front-runner whose role I've just fortuitously walked into. The one Grayson got a bit too friendly with, before first-takes. Poor girl should've kept her panties on and her priorities straight.

"Trust me, Katharine, I wouldn't attach my name as the executive producer if I didn't believe in this movie. But, I have to tell you, until today, I wasn't entirely sure it was going to come together. Casting the right people is the most important part of any project, besides maybe the

writing. And Helena would've been great."
Something unpleasant stirs to life in my stomach.
I will always be second best.
The replacement. The understudy. The alternate.
Selected out of obligation, rather than desire.
The insecurities roar so loud inside my head, it's hard to focus on Wyatt's next words.
"She would've been fantastic, I do believe that. But... I think you'll be better."
I blink. "What?"
"You heard me." His lips twitch. "Don't make me say it again, or I'll think you're one of those girls who needs the validation of strangers and Instagram-likes to prop herself up."
I roll my eyes and brush back the hair whipping across my face as we exit the highway at full speed, the convertible hugging so low to the ground I could probably reach out and touch the pavement. Neither of us breaks the silence until we've pulled up outside my building. Wyatt's sleek Audi looks laughably out of place beside the dozen or so rust-buckets scattered around the cracked asphalt lot. I point to the unit at the end of the blocky, cement row of condos and we glide to a soundless stop in front of it.
"You live here," Wyatt says, his tone a mixture of concern and condescension as he takes in the sight of my townhouse. To call it *shabby-chic* would be a stretch — infinitely less chic, considerably more shabby.
"Home sweet home." I grin and swing open the convertible door. "Thanks for the ride, Wyatt. And for..." I trail off as our eyes meet, and I know we're both remembering the same moment: this morning, standing in almost this exact position around his car, and the words he'd spoken with such conviction.
I'm going to change your life.
"Don't mention it. I'll see you Monday."
"Monday," I echo dully.
"My assistant will be in touch with all the details."

41

I nod, feeling distinctly removed from my own body. Wyatt seems to realize I'm barely holding myself together.

"Breathe, baby." His eyes crinkle at the corners. "And promise you won't forget me when you're famous, okay? After all... I'm the one who discovered you."

A bark of laughter flies from my lips. "I don't think I could ever forget you, even if I tried."

Something flickers in his eyes and when he speaks again, his voice is softer than I've ever heard it.

"Goodnight, Katharine Firestone," he whispers, tucking a flyaway strand of hair back behind her ear. It makes him look a bit devil-may-care in the dim, flickering light of the streetlamp overhead. Almost anachronistic — a modern-day Norse god behind the wheel of a two-seater.

"It's Kat," I correct automatically. "Not Katharine."

"Why?"

I shrug.

"Waste of a lovely name, in my opinion."

"No one calls me that except my mother." I glance at my feet. "She named me after her favorite movie star, Katharine Hepburn. Thought it would inspire greatness, I guess."

"Maybe it did."

I look up. "Or maybe it just pre-destined me to chase after an unattainable standard of success. To live forever in shadows cast by someone I've never even met, and cannot possibly live up to."

"Who do you think you're talking to, exactly?" His grip on the leather steering wheel tightens ever so slightly. "I'm a *Hastings*. I know a bit about living in shadows."

I feel my cheeks flame. "I didn't mean—"

"Thing about shadows is—" He cuts me off. "—They can't exist without light around them. So, the way I see it, you've got a choice about what you focus on. You want to see the world as gloom and doom, that's your prerogative. Me?" He grins. "I stay in the sunshine, baby."

"Don't call me baby."

"Can't call you your full name, can't call you a nickname…"

"Baby is not a nickname." My nose scrunches. "It's a pet name. And it's condescending. Who wants to be an infant? What self-respecting woman wants a man to equate her to a mewling, defenseless creature, unable to walk or talk or do anything with an iota of expertise except fill a diaper to capacity every two hours? Thanks, but no thanks."

He stares at me for a long beat, then shakes his head as if mystified by my very existence. "You never let up, do you?"

"I don't know what you mean."

"I know you don't, baby." His eyes hold mine. "That's what I like best about you. No bullshit."

"Don't call me baby!"

"Then grow up," he says in a voice that's not cruel, but not exactly kind.

I sigh. "I'm not going to win this fight, am I?"

He shakes his head. "Probably not."

"Figured as much." I stare at him and my voice goes so gentle I barely recognize it. "Goodnight, Wyatt Hastings."

He winks, waits for me to shut the door, and speeds back toward the land of glitz and glamour where he belongs, leaving me standing on the trash-strewn sidewalk, listening to the sounds of my neighbors' TV sets blaring through too-thin walls and questioning my own sanity because, surely, this entire day has been a dream. A delusion. A detour into an alternate reality.

Good things don't happen to girls like me.

And yet, as Wyatt's taillights disappear around the corner, I can't quite suppress the small flare of hope deep down inside my chest where no one else can see that maybe, now, they do.

※※※

"You're joking."

I shake my head.

"Then you've signed us up for one of those hidden camera shows and you're pranking me."

I shake my head again.

Harper stares across the high-top and takes a large gulp of her cucumber-wasabi cocktail. We're at one of the trendier sushi spots in the valley, a tiny place with amazing dragon rolls that hasn't yet been discovered by anyone except locals and hipsters. Once it's on Yelp, it'll be flooded with tourists wielding smartphones, more interested in photographing their food than actually consuming it, and we'll have to find somewhere else to slug down drinks in relative quiet.

"Harper. I'm serious."

She takes another sip. "You're serious."

"As a heart attack."

"Serious like the time you decided you wanted a pixie cut, forced a pair of scissors into my hand, and then changed your mind after I'd chopped off half your hair?" she asks. "Or serious like the time you dragged me to a tattoo parlor in a majorly sketchy part of downtown because you wanted something—" She makes air quotes with her index fingers. "—*authentically Los Angeles* before realizing you were going to get Hep-C, so we got frozen yogurt on the boardwalk instead?"

"No, Harper. I'm actually serious."

"You. Grayson Dunn. *Uncharted*. In Hawaii." She shakes her head. "I'm sorry, it's just a little hard to believe."

I take a sip of my own drink, a sake-infused mojito with sesame seeds floating on the surface. "Trust me, I know. I've been in a state of confused disbelief since Wyatt dropped me off last night."

"Wyatt?"

"Wyatt Hastings, the executive producer. He's the one who got me the part."

Harper chokes on a piece of sashimi and her chopsticks go flying. I hunt for them beneath the table as she composes herself.

"You gonna make it?" I ask wryly, nodding in thanks to the waitress who's delivered a fresh set of utensils. "Or should I see if there's a doctor in the building?"

"I'm... It's just..." Harper looks wan, her pale skin practically luminescent next to the startling magenta hair framing her face. As a makeup and beauty stylist, her looks are ever-changing; I never know whether my best friend will be a brunette, redhead, blonde, or some other ambiguous hue plucked from the rainbow at random. Annoyingly, she can pull off pretty much any color.

"Words, Harper. Use them."

She shakes herself. "I just never thought my best friend would ever, in a million years, land a role like this."

"Your confidence in my acting abilities is such a comfort," I drawl. "Really, thank you for the vote of support. I'll remember you in my memoirs."

"Oh, shut up. You know what I mean." She glares at me, looking more like her typical fiery self. "I think you're an amazing actress, but the odds of landing this part are..."

"Astronomical?" I supply.

She nods. "Exactly."

"Well, call me Buzz Aldrin."

Harper pops another piece of sushi in her mouth. "The Hastings are Hollywood royalty. They founded the friggen AXC Network, for god's sake," she says around a mouthful of rice. "And Wyatt is absolutely gorgeous. I was doing makeup for that teen show *The Werewolf Chronicles* last year, and he dropped by the studio one day. Jesus Christ, I thought Thor had wandered off the *Avengers* set next door."

I laugh. "He may look like a Viking, but he's actually a big softie."

"Have you seen his muscles? Nothing soft about that."

My nose wrinkles. "I don't know. He's not really my type."

"Since when is *hot* not your type?" She stares at me like I've got a few screws loose. "Or are you holding out for Grayson? Not that I'd blame you. If I had a chance to bang the Sexiest Man Alive, you bet your ass I'd take it."

"Ha!" I snort. "I hate him, remember?"

"Don't tell me you're still holding a grudge from your *Busy Bees* days."

My tone is defensive. "What if I am?"

"Katharine Firestone!" she chastises. "You were kids. Let it go, already."

"He embarrassed me!"

"What did he do, again? Something about a love letter? I forget the specifics."

"I don't want to talk about it," I grumble, a blush creeping up my cheeks. "I already lived through it once; that was enough for a lifetime."

She shrugs. "Well, teenage boys are idiots. Maybe he's grown up."

"Doubtful, considering he pretended not to remember me when we were introduced yesterday. Or, hell, maybe he really doesn't remember me, now that he's a big movie star with a Malibu mansion and thirty Victoria's Secret models on speed dial."

Her face contorts in sympathy. "Shit, that's rough. I'm sorry, honey."

"It's fine. It didn't bother me," I lie. "In fact, it's probably better he's forgotten the nine-year-old version of me. Braces, frizzy hair, and chubby cheeks — not my best years, to be honest."

"True." Her expression says she's not buying my indifferent act, but she doesn't push the issue. "And think of it this way: it'll certainly be easier to act the part of enemies-to-lovers while the cameras are rolling if you're still pissed at him when they're not."

"Honestly, I think that's the only reason I got the role," I say, swallowing a bite of spicy tuna. "They confused my very real hatred of the man for genuine acting ability."

Harper laughs and raises her glass. "Cheers to that. And cheers to you, my friend. You deserve all the success in the world and I am so unbelievably excited for you."

"I was already planning to bring you to the cast party, Harper. You don't have to lay it on so thick," I say, scowling as my eyes start to prick with emotion and clinking my drink against hers.

"You're a cow," she says fondly.

"Right back at you, jackass," I reply, grinning.

We drain our glasses.

"What did Cynthia say?" Harper's eyes are wide with anticipation. She's met my mother on several occasions. "Was she over the moon? Did she start writing your Oscar acceptance speech? Coordinating your red-carpet outfits? Or did she just keel over and die on the spot because all her wildest dreams for exploiting her only spawn have finally come true?"

I grimace. "I haven't told her yet."

Harper shakes her head. "You can't put it off forever. She's going to find out eventually. In fact, I'm surprised she doesn't already know. Once the paparazzi catch wind of this, you're going to be officially on the radar."

My brows raise. "Meaning?"

"Meaning people are going to take an interest in you. Where you go, what you wear, who you date. You'll be a real celebrity — by which I mean *stalked-within-an-inch-of-your-life-until-you-have-a-nervous-breakdown-and-wind-up-in-rehab-with-the-Olsen-twins.*"

"I'm too boring to stalk." I roll my eyes. "SPOTTED! Kat Firestone eating tacos. Again."

"A good tabloid can spin a simple picture of you eating a burrito into a story about food cravings from an unplanned pregnancy in less than forty-five minutes. That's all I'm saying."

"Well, I'd better enjoy shamelessly stuffing my face in anonymity while it lasts then." I pick up another piece of sushi with my chopsticks and pop it into my mouth. "And as for an unplanned love child, I'd have to actually

47

be dating someone for that to be possible. Unless they're going to try to sell the whole immaculate conception byline."

"Still in your dry spell?"

I groan. "This is more than a dry spell. This is a drought. This is the fucking Serengeti of sexual frustration."

"Haven't you been using the *Tingle* app I told you about?" she asks sternly. "That's how I met Greg, and I've never been happier. If you'd just try... I'll even help you set up your profile."

"You know how I feel about dating apps," I hedge. "I tried it a few times. Went on a few dates. But it just felt so... superficial."

"Kat." She throws up her hands. "You can't complain about celibacy if you refuse to put yourself out there. Everyone uses dating apps these days. How else do you expect to meet someone?"

In real life, with actual conversation and chemistry, at the whims of fate instead of a forced iPhone matchmaker.

That's what I want to say, but can't. Not when Harper thinks the dreaded dating apps are what delivered true romance straight to her smartphone.

True romance.

Ha.

The only thing true about romance these days is that it is *dead*.

It died the day a gangly technology whiz with coke-bottle glasses who'd never been on a date in his twenty-three years of life sat down at a laptop, punched out a string of code, and created an application he'd later sell to a Silicon Valley tycoon for billions.

The concept is simple enough — hundreds of singles at the tips of your fingers. A virtual, veritable matchmaker, taking the guesswork out of crossing a crowded bar to talk to a stranger or — *heaven forbid!* — actually making eye contact with someone at a coffee shop as you sip your six-dollar caramel frappuccino.

Now, you don't have to put yourself out there. You can "date" from the comfort of your couch.
See photo. Swipe right if sexy. Swipe left if snaggle-toothed.
Easy.
Convenient.
And, thus, the complete, total antithesis of everything that makes falling in love so terrifyingly, gut-churningly wonderful. Harper may call me old-fashioned and cynical, but... since when was love ever supposed to be convenient? Simple? Something to be squeezed in between your forty-minute elliptical session and half-hour nightly news program?
Swipe, swipe, swipe.
We've never had so many options... And we've never been so miserable.
We are waiting longer and longer to settle down into relationships that begin with the flick of a fingertip. Courtship has been usurped, eradicated. Fuck flowers and old-fashioned wooing; we declare our interest by staring at pixelated profile photographs and exchanging stilted text messages. We go out on awkward first dates and have nothing to talk about because we've already engaged in thorough virtual stalking, gleaning information from web pages and Internet searches like detectives digging up clues.
Oh, look! He likes dogs. And he's got a photo with his niece! He'll make a great father for our kids one day.
We have no idea what to do with our hands or where to look or how to behave when confronted with someone without the safety of a screen between us. Because we are never quite as polished in person as we appear in our photographs, never quite as witty or charming as we pretend to be when we have four hours to craft the perfect written response to a text message.
There was no spark, we tell ourselves as we walk home alone. *Something was missing.*
He was different than I thought he'd be, we tell our

49

girlfriends over margaritas, shaking our heads as though mystified that a total stranger failed to live up to expectations we conjured out of thin air. *I don't think I'll see him again. Plus, I have three dates lined up next week with new matches that seem promising.*

And on we swipe, until we are so fucking exhausted by the prospect of another awful first date, we settle down with a guy we aren't even all that sure we like, but stay with because the idea of faking an orgasm every now and then isn't quite as daunting as swiping on into oblivion.

I watch friends like Harper settling down into lackluster relationships that will morph into loveless marriages and eventually disintegrate into bitter divorces, and wonder if we are all just playing an endless game of musical chairs, wandering round and round in different social circles until, abruptly, you turn twenty-eight and the music stops and whoever you happen to be sitting next to winds up being your spouse.

Call it timing, call it dumb luck... Call it anything except romantic.

It bears repeating: *romance is dead.*

I know for a fact it's not just me who feels this way.

I know because I have a dozen twenty-something single friends who bartend with me at Balthazar and spend most every night lamenting their lack of eligible male partners over shitty, eight-dollar bottles of Merlot they bought at a pharmacy on their way home from day jobs they hate. I know this because the divorce rate still hovers around fifty percent, yet we rush headlong into marriage as if it's ever a good idea to throw yourself into anything with a higher failure rate than the pull-out method. I know this because there are a million millennials still living at home with their parents, who are full-grown adults and haven't been out on a date since they moved back into their childhood bedrooms post-college.

And even if you do defy the odds and meet someone who makes you feel giddy and sort of nauseous, like you've just stepped off a roller coaster on a ninety-degree day after consuming too much cotton candy, it's almost certain you'll fuck it up by doing what we all do — asking those pesky, persistent two words: *what if.*

What if there's someone better out there?

What if there's another match I'm more compatible with?

What if I go on just one more date, just to see what it would be like...

Swipe, swipe, swipe.

We have never been so connected.

We have never been so alone.

"Hello?" Harper snaps her fingers in front of my face. "Earth to Kat."

"Sorry," I murmur. "Zoned out. This drink must be stronger than I thought."

She shoots me a look. "Just think about using the app, okay?"

"Sure," I tell her. "I'll think about it."

There's a beat of awkward silence; we both know I'm lying.

"Cynthia is going to flip her lid about you getting the part," Harper says, tactfully changing the subject. "You realize that, right?"

I nod. "Why do you think I'm avoiding that conversation? She's been calling me nonstop since yesterday, probably hoping to yell at me for blowing that damn vampire show audition. I had to put my phone in airplane mode, just to stop the incessant buzzing."

"The sooner you get it over with, the sooner she'll leave you alone."

"This is my mother we're talking about," I remind her. "She doesn't have an off-switch. There is no *leaving me alone*. She lives to micromanage me."

Harper laughs. "She's not that bad."

"Easy for you to say. *Your* mother is safely back in the cornfields of Iowa, separated by thousands of miles and a very expensive plane ticket."

She doesn't contradict my words. "Well, let me know how it goes. When does filming start?"

"Monday."

"As in… three days from now? That's fast."

"Everything has been fast-tracked. They were supposed to be filming weeks ago, but apparently things were stalled because Grayson banged his co-star and she stormed off set rather than continue working with him."

"Helena Putnam, right?" Harper's eyes narrow. "She's beautiful, but I've heard she's a bit…" She trails off and twirls her finger in the air by her temple, the international symbol for *bat-shit crazy*.

I snort. "She'd have to be, if she thought Grayson was going to commit to her. The man is about as loyal as a junkyard dog."

"Maybe he hasn't met the right girl yet."

"Or maybe he's just a douche."

"Presenting Kat Firestone, ladies and gentlemen." Harper claps her hands slowly. "Yes, she's single — *shocking*, I know, with charm like that. Line forms behind me."

"I dislike you."

"That's all right, I don't mind. As long as you're still picking up the bill — now that you're making the big bucks, I'm pretty sure I never have to buy drinks again."

"I don't even know how much they're giving me. The contracts haven't been signed yet."

She sighs. "I'm guessing whatever the figure, there will be lots of zeroes on the end of it."

I open my wallet and pull out my only credit card without a maxed-out balance. "I just want enough to keep me stocked in tacos for the rest of my life."

Her head tilts. "Grayson Dunn pulled in six million for his last movie."

All the breath leaves my lungs in a gust at the concept of that much money.

"That's a lot of tacos," I murmur, when I've recovered.

"Tell me about it."

CHAPTER FOUR

"I really need to work on myself."
- *A man who thinks you should probably work on yourself.*

The emerald green Cadillac parked in front of my condo is unmistakable; the woman leaning against it is downright terrifying. Her honey blonde hair has been teased into a beehive so tall, it would bow a lesser woman in half. Arms crossed over her chest, acrylic nails tapping impatiently against her power-blazer, she fixes me with an unflinching gaze that never wavers as I park my car, sigh heavily, and approach.

"Hi, Cynthia."

Her eyebrow ticks. "Why haven't you been answering your phone?"

"Oh, did you call me? I didn't realize." My innocent act is thin at best. "Maybe I left it in airplane mode by accident."

"Funny," she says in a tone that conveys her total lack of amusement. "I don't recall you flying anywhere recently."

I swallow. "Did you need something?"

"I wanted to know how the audition went. When I couldn't get ahold of you, I called the talent agency." Her blue eyes, the only feature I inherited from her, narrow lethally. "Tyra was very… informative."

I assume Tyra was the brunette who conducted the vampire show audition — it seems a million years ago, with everything that's happened since.

53

"Ah," I say lightly. "I take it she had nothing but lovely things to say about me?"

"Katharine!" Cynthia's voice cracks like a whip. "This is not a joke. Do you know how many strings I had to pull to even get you in that room? The favors I had to cash in? The number of phone calls and hours spent networking on your behalf, just to get you in front of those women?"

"From your tone, I'm guessing a lot," I murmur under my breath. Thankfully, she's too busy ranting to hear me.

"They didn't want you! They want a rosy-cheeked seventeen-year-old with a perfect ass and breasts that still defy gravity! But you don't seem to care about that. You don't seem to realize that your prime years are slipping away." Her arms uncross and suddenly there's a razor-sharp acrylic nail pointed straight at my nose. "You won't be young forever. In this industry, you've only got another decade, at best, before you're relegated to the scrap heap."

She makes it sound like I'm closer to my mid-eighties than my mid-twenties. I fight the desire to roll my eyes, knowing it will only further incense her.

"This part would've been a source of steady work for at least a season, maybe opened some doors to other roles on the AXC Network. And you just strolled in there unprepared, looking like an unwashed streetwalker, from the sound of it, and couldn't even be bothered to take the audition seriously." Cynthia pushes off the car and takes a step closer to me; in her sky-high stilettos, she towers over my five-foot-three frame. "Tyra says you *laughed*."

"If you'd read that dialogue, you'd have laughed too. It was ridiculous."

"I don't care how ridiculous it was," she hisses, advancing on me. "Where you got this prideful, high-and-mighty streak of yours, I'll never know. It wasn't from me, I'll tell you that."

"But I got your cheekbones and in the long run I think that matters more, am I right?"

Before the joke is even out of my mouth, she's reached out and slapped me full across the face. I reel back, eyes watering as pain radiates through my cheek. My hands clench into fists at my sides, but otherwise I show no reaction to her strike.

"You are going to call Tyra and apologize." Cynthia's breaths are shallow with rage. "You are going to make this right. And if by some miracle she gives you another chance and finds you some small role on one of their shows, you will take it. No matter how ridiculous or beneath you it may seem."

"That's not going to happen."

"You stubborn, selfish girl!" Her hand twitches and I know she's aching to hit me again. "You are just like your father."

"I'll have to take your word on that," I grit out. "Seeing as we've never been introduced."

"I don't know why I bother with you anymore. After all I've sacrificed... The years I've spent getting you to this point... And you're just going to flush it down the toilet. All my hard work, wasted on a girl who's determined to amount to nothing but a disappointment."

"Wonderful words from a mother to her only daughter." No amount of sarcasm can cover the sharp zing of pain in my chest.

"If you want respect, you have to earn it," Cynthia says coldly. "You know that."

Of course I know; she's been pounding that into my head since I was old enough to comprehend such things. The point she's never seemed to grasp is that I never wanted her respect in the first place. I wanted her love. And even two decades of disappointment on that score haven't been enough to alter that aspiration.

"Call Tyra." She holds out her cellphone in the space between us. "Apologize. Beg her to give you some small part."

My jaw clenches. "Like I said before, that's not going to happen."

"Katharine, if you don't take the phone this instant—"

"Because," I say, talking over her. "I start filming *Uncharted* in Hawaii next week and I already have enough scheduling conflicts with my work at Balthazar, since I haven't even given Vince my notice yet."

The air goes completely still. Cynthia's head swivels slowly until our eyes meet.

"*Uncharted*," she whispers. "The new Stanhope movie."

I nod.

"You got a part?"

I nod again. "The lead. Co-starring with Grayson Dunn. I should have my contract tomorrow." I cross my arms over my chest and stare down at the phone in her hand, which is now trembling in the air between us. "Unless, of course, you'd like me to turn it down, call Tyra, and beg for an inconsequential part in her next teenage-angst after school special. You know... *If she'll still have me*, that is."

For a full thirty seconds, my mother stares at me with a look I've never seen before, and I think maybe she's about to say something crazy like *I'm so proud of you* but instead her mouth twists into a smirk and she says, "I can't wait to tell that cow Tyra to shove it. Too good to give *my* client a part? Ha! Well, the joke is on her now, isn't it!"

I should be used to her treating me as her client instead of her child, but it still makes my stomach twist. No matter how awful she is, no matter how cruel or unkind, I don't think I'll ever be immune to her words.

"I wonder if Sergio has any appointments before production starts..." She's eyeing my dark, messy waves with a scary look. "Maybe he can do something with you..."

"I'm not cutting my hair. I got this part because they like my look as it is," I point out, but she's not listening. She's snatched her phone back and is pecking at the screen with her talons like a large predatory bird.

"I have to call Stanhope's people. See if they'll be

putting out a statement or whether I can draft a press release. Oh, and we should see if we can get an exclusive interview with *Entertainment Weekly* or one of the late night talk shows..."

I shake my head in disbelief. "Good talk, mommy dearest. If you'll excuse me..."

She doesn't look up from her phone as I step around her on the sidewalk and beeline for my front door, fishing the keys from my slouchy purse as I walk. I've got one hand on the knob when she finally realizes I've left the conversation.

"Katharine!"

I turn, holding my breath, and stare at the woman who gave birth to me with arched brows.

"Don't do anything to screw this up. Stanhope is the hottest director around, these days — one film with him, and you'll be on the map for good."

"I wasn't planning to," I call back, my voice only the tiniest bit bitter. "But thanks for the tip."

I turn back to the door and bump my hip against it — the damn thing always jams in its frame. It swings inward with a sudden lurch.

"Grayson Dunn is single and he's worth millions!" Cynthia shouts, before I can shut her out. "If you can get your hooks in him now, even with a prenup you'll never have to work again—"

I slam the door so hard it rattles the wall, cutting off the rest of her poisonous words. Leaning my back against the wood, I slide down to rest against the peeling laminate floor and attempt to regulate my breathing. My skin is crawling as her words swarm over me like ants on a picnic blanket.

Don't do anything to screw this up...
Get your hooks in him now...

My mother has the unique talent of making you feel like you need a shower after being in her presence for longer than five minutes. Probably her only talent, if I'm being honest, which is why she's so goddamned set on

57

exploiting mine to the fullest degree.

I sit on the floor until I hear her Cadillac roar to life and peel out of the parking lot. When I know it's safe, I head upstairs to my bedroom and begin to gather my things. My shift at Balthazar starts in a little over two hours, and in Friday night rush-hour traffic it'll take almost that long to get downtown on the 405.

The glamorous life of a movie star, I think, smirking as I step into the shower. *Sitting in traffic and tending bar.*

Watch out, Hollywood. Here I come.

***

"You're late!" Vince barks as I rush through the back door. "Again."

"Sorry, Vin, traffic was a bitch."

"This is LA. Traffic is always a bitch." He shakes his bald head sternly. "Don't make me fire you, Kat. I like you, but you're gonna give me a heart attack if you keep showing up late."

"A heart attack? In your peak physical shape? Impossible." I grin and tug at my leather mini-skirt, which rode up alarmingly high during my dash inside. "You're the picture of health, Vince."

"Flattery will get you nowhere," he says, crossing massive arms over his chest, but his lips are twitching. Vince may look like a badass bodybuilder, but he's about as tough as a marshmallow. He gave me this job when I moved out of Cynthia's house last year, despite the fact that I had basically no experience and spilled a full tray of Dom Perignon champagne flutes during my first shift. Still, as I eye the vein popping in his temple, I somehow doubt this is the ideal moment to tell him I need several weeks off work to shoot a movie.

"Listen, it's only eight and we're already slammed." He takes the purse and jacket from my hands and gives me a small push toward the double doors that lead onto the floor. "I have a feeling tonight is going to be one for the books. Go help Holly in the downstairs lounge bar, and later I'll move you upstairs if we get any big VIPs."

"Sure thing, boss."
"Don't call me boss."
"You got it, jefe."
"Kat."
"Sorry." I laugh.
"Get moving."

"I'm going, I'm going," I mutter, pushing open the doors. A bouncer nods to me as I step into the club, his black-on-black suit rendering him almost invisible against the ebony wall. The pulsing base hits me like a wall of sound, vibrating up through the soles of my stilettos into my bones. My eyes strain to adjust as I cut through the throng toward the bar. It's dark inside the club, the large multi-level space illuminated only by the occasional flashing strobes overhead. Dozens of people gyrate on the dance floor, groping and grinding in time to the beat. In another two hours, this place will be so packed you won't be able to see the ground beneath their feet.

I glance up at the second level and see the velvet-roped balcony is empty — for now, at least. Balthazar is a hot spot for celebrity sightings, with its chic table-service, exclusive VIP area, and lush decor. Plus, the fact that Vince makes all his girls dress in what basically amounts to lingerie doesn't hurt. My black lace corset is so tight, it's hard to breathe. I console myself with the thought that by the end of tonight, I'll have enough in tips to take my Honda to the mechanic for a much-needed checkup. The engine was wheezing like a geriatric patient when I peeled into the staff parking lot ten minutes ago. There is a zero-percent chance it will make it through another bumper-to-bumper drive on the 405 without overheating, and, somehow, I need to get to the studio on Monday morning.

Holly is manning the lower-level bar alone, moving at warp-speed to accommodate the crush of patrons. Her hands are a blur of motion — pouring shots, shaking cocktails, sliding glasses across the LED-lit bar without ever spilling a drop. She's wearing a strappy leather getup that makes my outfit look positively demure and her jet-black hair flashes blue-green in the pulsing overhead strobes of the club.

"Thank god you're here," she calls as I hop up over the bar-top and swivel my legs around. "Haven't been able to take a damn breath for the past half hour."

"Where do you need me?"

"On your left!" she calls, tossing a vodka bottle high in the air. "Bachelor party. Give 'em one more round, then cut them off."

I move toward a group of ten men waiting on the opposite side of the bar. White, preppy, and practically indiscernible from each other in their identical jeans and v-necks, they're so drunk they can barely string together enough words to order another round, let alone calculate a decent tip.

Every bartender's dream.

"Shots!" One of the men pounds a beefy fist on the bar. "Though no amount of tequila's gonna make my man here forget he's getting shackled in two days!" He grabs a very inebriated man in a headlock and hauls him close. "Isn't that right, Trevor?"

Trevor blinks glassy, rid-rimmed eyes.

"BALL AND CHAIN!" A redhead howls at the top of his lungs. "TILL DEATH DO YOU PART!"

"OR UNTIL SHE GETS FAT!" another chimes in, laughing uproariously. The two of them clink glasses and chug down the rest of their beers.

"Charming." I clench my teeth. "What do you want to drink?"

"Trevor's getting married," the beefy-fisted man informs me, swaying on his feet. He's slightly more coherent than his friends. "We're the bachelor party."

"So I gathered."

"TEQUILA!" the redhead roars.

I pull a bottle of tequila from the bottom shelf, the kind that tastes a bit like lighter fluid, and start lining up empty shot glasses. These fools are so loaded, I could charge them for cat piss and they wouldn't even taste it going down.

"Trev, tell us," the redhead slurs as I flourish the bottle and begin pouring. "Does Andrea even let you fuck her anymore?"

"Not in the ass, that's for sure," a blond guffaws. "No room, what with the stick she's got shoved up there all the time."

"Piss off." The groom-to-be halfheartedly bats his friends away. "That's my wife!"

"Not yet!" A large tattooed arm reaches out and starts passing around the shots to his friends as I chop a lime into wedges for them. "Two more days of freedom, bro. Let's find someone for you to fuck. Lots of prime slam-pieces here, tonight."

It takes an abnormal amount of effort to keep the knife steady in my hands. I finish chopping their limes and slide a small bowl of salt toward Trevor. He doesn't notice — his vacant eyes are fixed on the dance floor, where half-clothed girls writhe in time to the music. I watch two men in the group slide wedding bands into their wallets before throwing back their shots, each yelling a toast to their friend before slugging down the shitty tequila.

"To Trevor!"

"To the end of freedom!"

"To wife number one!"

"To prenups!"

I snatch the credit card from the redhead and turn to run their bill, gritting my teeth as I listen to them congratulate each other on their utter lack of decency. I'm still seething five minutes later when I take a break between mixing cocktails for a few girls — or "slam-pieces" as the men so affectionately referred to them — and return to pick up the receipt.

They didn't even leave a tip.

There's nothing I can do about it besides cast a fervent

wish up to the powers-that-be that every member of the bachelor party catches crabs tonight. Cosmic justice in the form of an itchy crotch — the thought makes me smirk.

We're so busy I don't stop moving, mixing, and pouring for the next two hours. I'm so intent on making drinks, it takes me a while to register the sound of someone saying my name and tapping my shoulder.

"Kat!"

I turn to find a willowy blonde in fishnet stockings and sky-high stilettos staring at me. I don't recognize her — she must be new.

"Vince told me to replace you down here. He wants you to go up and work the VIP section." She scans the crowd around the bar with wary eyes. The throng is three-deep, many waiting impatiently with credit cards extended into the air, hoping the promise of shiny limitless plastic will entice a bartender to serve them next.

"You'll be fine," I tell her, making eye contact with one of the bouncers who's come to clear a path for me upstairs. When the club gets this jammed, men on the dance floor tend to get aggressive if a lingerie-clad girl walks past. It helps to have a six-foot-five shadow. I shove a vodka bottle into the girl's hands as I move toward him.

"First night?"

"Yes," she squeaks.

"Just keep your head up, your eyes down, and your hands steady."

I see her nod nervously.

"That guy needs a gin and ginger, his girlfriend is waiting on a rum and diet, and there's a bachelorette party in the corner who want six blow-job shots. You know where we keep the whipped cream?"

"Th-the fridge?"

I sigh and give her a slight push toward the crowd. "Breathe. It helps with the nausea. Ask Holly for help if you get confused."

Holly shoots me a death glare as the new girl turns toward her, eyes full of hope, like she's just spotted a rescue helicopter after a month on a deserted island.

"Thanks a lot," Holly hisses. "Now she'll be stalking me like my landlord on the first of the month."

I laugh as I hop over the bar, grabbing the bouncer's hand for balance as I slide down on the other side.

"Lead on, Hercules."

"My name is Mark," he says, grinning as his eyes sweep me head to toe. "You should remember that for later, when you're calling it out in my bed, babe."

"The only thing I'll be calling you is *unemployed* if you keep hitting on me." I smile sweetly. "The longer you stand here flirting, the longer the VIP section is understaffed, the more pissed off Vince is gonna be." My voice drops lower. "You ever seen Vince pissed off? Not a pretty sight."

The bouncer's grin drops away and without another word, he turns and starts pushing a path through the crowd. When we reach the velvet-roped spiral staircase that leads upstairs, I step around him. Two guys in suits are blocking the club's exclusive upper level, but they move aside to let me pass. The line of attractive girls waiting nearby look up hopefully, but the velvet rope clicks closed behind me without letting any of them enter. Either there's someone important in the VIP section, who doesn't want to mix with the plebeians, or we're already at capacity.

There's a dull ache in the balls of my feet as I ascend, the high heels pinching my toes like some kind of torture device. It's somewhat quieter up here, away from the massive speakers that flood the dance floor, but the air still seems to vibrate all around me as I step onto the balcony. Low-slung black couches litter the floor. Red sconces light the walls, where gold-gilded wallpaper gleams dully in the dim light. Massive candles drip wax into piles on every free surface, like some kind of strange pagan alter. The entire space has a gothic vibe —

something you'd sooner expect to find in New Orleans than posh, whitewashed downtown LA.

Perhaps that's why Balthazar is so popular. There's nowhere else quite like it in the city.

I eye the crowd as I make my way to the bar. It's much less dense than the one downstairs, to my everlasting relief. Lacey and Cher, the identical twin blondes Vince hired for sheer novelty, are busy serving drinks and appetizers to the patrons on barstools. Their massive breasts are barely contained in matching bustiers — every male eye in the room is fixed on them as they shake cocktails with enthusiasm. I can't fathom the amount they rake in from tips each night.

Stepping back behind the bar, I nod to Kylie in greeting. With the twins covering the front, the two of us are left to serve the lounge, where the true VIPs tend to congregate. Kylie is lining up frosted champagne flutes on a tray and looks even more badass than usual with a section of hair shaved short by her temple, a long black pony-tail teased high on her head, and a pissed-off expression contorting her delicate features.

"Who's here?" I ask, not spotting anyone particularly famous among the dozen or so people scattered on the couches and clustered around high-top tables.

"Some washed-up rockstar and his posse. Woody something or other."

"Where?"

"Back corner. On the right."

I crane my neck and catch sight of them — a few men are on the couches, surrounded by a flock of beautiful women. I can't make out most of their faces, but I recognize the man in the center from the tabloids I see in line at the grocery store around the corner from my condo.

"Ryder Woods," I murmur, staring at the former frontman for the band Wildwood. He's been on a year-long bender since his career fell apart and, from the looks of the lines of cocaine on the table in front of him, tonight won't be the night he turns sober.

Kylie sighs disgustedly. "There's someone else with him, too — some hotshot actor, apparently. I have no fucking clue. All I know is, the girls with them ordered about ten bottles of Dom, then complained that their glasses weren't frosted. Swear to god, if I have to make one more trip over there I'm going to pop a champagne cork right up their perfectly-toned asses."

I snort. "Vince will love that."

"Fuck Vince. And fuck all these damn poser celebrities, with their bottle service and their bimbos."

"You stay here. I'll take them over for you," I say, grabbing the tray of frosted glasses from her. "But you owe me."

"You're a saint."

"I'd rather be a sinner than a saint."

She swats me on the butt as I pass. "Then go get 'em, Lucifer"

As quickly as I can manage without tripping over my own feet, I cut across the room toward the corner where our resident rockstars have made camp for the night. Tray poised in front of me like a shield, I come to a stop beside the group and gently clear my throat to get their attention. No one so much as blinks at my arrival — the group of women clustered around the couch are fully focused on the men occupying its cushions.

"Excuse me," I say, somewhat impatiently. "Someone requested frosted flutes."

"Make some room," a slurred male voice commands. "Let the girl through."

With small huffs of inconvenience, the women clear a path for me so I can set the tray down on the low coffee table in front of the couch. I step forward and feel them instantly close ranks at my back, unwilling to lose their spots when they've finally gotten up close and personal with a real, honest-to-god A-lister.

I bend to deposit the tray and my eyes meet the bleak, bleary stare of Ryder Woods. He's got mismatched irises —

65

one blue, one brown — and they're so empty of anything resembling life, I feel like I've been socked in the stomach. There's no truth in the carefree grin plastered on his lips. One glance tells me this man harbors a deep, unsettling sense of misery.

"Thank you, darling," he says, smiling that empty smile as I straighten back to full height. "What's your name?"

"Kat." I reach for the bottle of champagne in the closest ice bucket and begin working the cork. Months of practice enable me to pop it with only the slightest shower of foam. My hands are steady as I begin filling glasses, eager to escape back behind the bar with Kylie.

"Pleasure to meet you, Kat," Ryder drawls, that faint southern twang that made his first record go platinum still alluring despite his obvious inebriation.

I pop another bottle and fill more glasses as the girls lean closer to grab them off my tray. Ryder drains the remnants of his whiskey in a single gulp and pushes up from the cushion, dislodging the two girls tucked on either side, before hunching close over the table top, and snorting a line of cocaine off the mirrored surface.

"Fuck, that's good." His head shakes like a dog emerging from a bath. The girls pull him back between them, giggling like he's said something exceptionally witty.

"Do you need anything else? Another whiskey?" I ask, stacking the empty champagne bottles on my tray and lifting it into the air. Ryder's eyes are even less focused when they land back on me.

"I'm good, for the moment." His stare wanders to the far end of the couch, where another man sits silently in shadows, his features entirely hidden from view. "How 'bout you, Dunn? You need a refill? What are you drinking?"

I feel my heart drop into my stomach like a cannonball as my gaze flies to the corner, just in time to see Grayson Dunn lean forward, his chiseled features startlingly attractive in low light. There's a sardonic, almost seductive twist to his mouth as he takes in the sight of me in my corset and mini-skirt. My fingers clench so hard around the tray in my hands, I damn near lose circulation.

"Oh," he says lowly, eyes locking on mine. "I think Kat knows exactly what I'd like."

CHAPTER FIVE

"I'm, like, totally cool with the casual thing."
- A girl who's been planning her wedding day since she was six years old.

I turn on a heel and try to leave, but my path is blocked by the line of eager bimbos. Before I can shove my way through them, Grayson's up off the couch and looming at my side, his large hand closing around my forearm like a warm set of shackles. I grit my teeth but don't struggle as he pulls the tray from my hands, sets it down on the table, and begins to steer me away from the group. Vince will be infinitely pissed if I cause a scene with his biggest VIP.

Ryder's groupies make small sounds of disappointment as we walk out of earshot toward a secluded corner of the balcony where a drunken couple is making out against a circular, matte-black column. Grayson shoots them a severe look and they scurry away without a word, leaving us alone.

He leads me into an alcove behind the column, where the candles burn low and the music is muted by velvet wall-hangings. The crowded club suddenly feels a world away as I stare up into his eyes, daring him to speak first. He doesn't; he just stands there, lips twisting in that infuriating half-grin of his.

"Can I get you a beverage?" I finally ask through clenched teeth, yanking my arm from his grip. "Or perhaps a car-service, so you can get the hell out of this club and away from my immediate proximity?"

His lips twitch. "You really don't like me, huh?"

"What gave me away?" I gasp. "Was it my open hostility? My clear contempt? My unbridled anger at your very presence?"

"Hard to pick just one," he says cheerfully. "What were the choices, again? Hostility, contempt, and attraction?"

"I said anger, not attraction."

"Maybe." His eyes gleam. "But you definitely *meant* attraction."

I cross my arms over my chest and ignore the way my heart is thudding inside my chest. "You're drunk."

"I'm only a little drunk," he informs me, swaying on his feet. It makes him look blurry and boyish — his dark hair somewhat mussed, his eyes glittering with humor. Like this, he's not a mega movie star trailing a posse of half-naked girls and paparazzi; he's the boy I remember from his early teen years. Carefree and unguarded.

And dangerous.

"Did you come here just to piss me off?" I force myself to say in a cold tone.

"I didn't even know you worked here. Ryder dragged me out tonight." He smirks. "Guess it's just fate throwing us into each other's paths again."

"I really need to get back to work."

"Why are you even working? You just landed a movie deal. You should be here doing shots, not serving them."

"That's none of your business."

He stares at me for a long moment and I see thoughts working in his eyes. "You don't believe it yet."

"Excuse me?"

"You still think this whole thing is going to fall through," he murmurs, watching me carefully.

I do my best to keep my expression blank.

His eyes narrow. "You're scared."

"That's not true."

He takes a step closer; I immediately move backward. My bare shoulders brush the velvet tapestry, sending a shiver of sensation down my spine.

His voice is quiet but intense.

"You're so used to having the rug ripped out from under you, you haven't let yourself believe this is for real."

"You don't know me." I feel a flush of red stain my cheeks. "Don't pretend to understand anything that goes on inside my head."

His mouth opens then abruptly closes, as if he's changed his mind about whatever he was about to say.

"Fine." He holds his hands up. "Maybe I'm totally off base."

"You are."

"Uh huh." His eyes drop to scan my body and my corset suddenly feels even tighter than normal, compressing my lungs until it's a struggle to draw proper breath. "I like the outfit, by the way. You've got a real Catwoman vibe going." He chuckles. "*Kat*-woman. Is that leather?"

He reaches out a finger toward my corset; I smack his hand down before it makes contact.

"Don't touch me."

"Oh, kitty has claws." His grin broadens, but he makes no move to touch me again. "I wonder… do you use them in the bedroom, kitten?"

"Don't call me that."

"I bet you'd scratch my back to all hell."

"The only part of your anatomy I'll be scratching are your eyes, when I tear them out of their sockets if you put a hand on me without permission ever again."

"You've got fire, Firestone, I'll give you that." His eyes drop to my lips. "And I must say, the fact that you'd like to break every bone in my body just makes me want to do unspeakable things to yours."

I scoff. "God, are you always like this?"

"Stunningly handsome in a roguish yet cavalier fashion?" he asks.

"An outrageous flirt who acts like women were put on this earth for the sole reason of falling at his feet, just because he happens to be good looking."

"You think I'm good looking?"

"No."

"Liar." His eyes are still locked on my lips.

"Stop looking at me like that."

"I hate to break this to you, but you'll have to get used to me looking at you, Kat." He moves a bit closer and I feel my mouth go dry. "Touching you." His head tilts down and his voice drops to a whisper. "Kissing you."

"Back off," I hiss, pushing his chest with both hands. He barely budges. "I'm serious, Dunn. Did you learn nothing from the Helena situation?"

My words hit him like a bucket of ice water. His eyes clear of the lustful haze and he takes an abrupt step out of my space, so I can breathe again.

"I was just messing around." His gaze scans my face, suddenly serious. "I just wanted…"

"What? What exactly did you want that required you to drag me away from work into a dark corner like some kind of fraternity boy at a keg party?"

He pauses. "I wanted to try to clear the air between us before Monday. Believe it or not, this role is important to me. I already fucked it up once with Helena — I realize that. But you don't know the full story. Maybe you should learn the facts before you go making snap judgments about shit you don't understand."

"Fine. Whatever." I toss my hands up. "Air is clear, as far as I'm concerned."

"Great," he growls. "Glad to hear it."

"We about done here, then?"

"Yeah. We're done." His expression darkens. "Screw me for trying to be a nice guy and fix things."

"That's the thing though, isn't it? You aren't a nice guy, Grayson. You never were."

"There she goes again, making snap judgments."

"It's not a snap judgment. It's the truth."

"You don't know what my life is like."

"Yeah, it seems like a real struggle." My eyes drift over

to the table where his posse waits. "The drugs, the booze, the women, the fame... Gosh, I'd rather be cooked slowly over hot coals than contend with those horrors!"

He smiles, but it's joyless and bitter. "You'd think that. But you have no idea what it's like — not yet, anyway. Soon you will."

"Enlighten me, then."

There's a brief pause before he speaks, as if he's weighing his words carefully. "I'm constantly surrounded — fans, friends, agents, directors, paparazzi... There's never a moment of peace. Never a moment where I'm really able to be myself, because the cameras never stop rolling, even when I'm off set. I can't buy a damn latte without making headlines in the tabloids." He runs a hand through his hair. "I can't do anything, can't even breathe, without it being documented and photographed and catalogued for all eternity."

"Oh, the *injustice*." I roll my eyes. "People adore you *so* much, you can't buy a four-dollar coffee without making them swoon. How hard your life must be!" I cross my arms over my chest. "Do you even hear yourself? How entitled you sound?"

"I'm not trying to be a prick. I'm not trying to be cocky. I'm trying to be honest with you." I see a flare of anger in his gaze. "I thought maybe if I explained a little bit about my life, you might stop looking at me the way you're constantly looking at me."

"And how exactly do I look at you?"

"Like I'm nothing but a spoiled rich boy who's been handed the world on a sterling silver plate and is squandering it."

"Well, if the Prada shoe fits..." I stare pointedly at his feet.

"The clothes, the girls, the booze... that's not who I am." A note of frustration creeps into his tone, along with something else. Something almost desperate. "I don't want you to see me that way."

"Actually, that's not how I see you at all."

"Oh?" He sounds doubtful. "How do you see me, then?"

"Why do you even care what I think? I'm nobody. My opinion shouldn't matter to you."

"And yet... it does."

I hesitate. "If you really want to know..."

"I do."

"I think you're a faker."

He blinks. "What?"

"You're a faker. A bullshit-artist. You complain about not being able to buy a latte without the cameras on you, but I don't think you even know who you are without them. The truth is, I think you're terrified of dropping that shiny celebrity front you put up, even for a moment, because you'd have to stop being *Grayson Dunn the action-movie hero* and actually be yourself."

I bite my tongue to keep the rest of my words in, worried I've gone too far.

"Don't stop now, Kat," he growls, stepping closer. "Get it all out. You're the expert on me, apparently."

"I'm not an expert."

"Could've fooled me."

"You asked for my opinion," I snap. "I gave it."

"Yeah." He snorts. "And you think I'm some kind of massive con artist. That's great to hear. Thanks."

"You're a chameleon. You adjust your personality to fit whoever you're sharing space with — for the fans, you're a sweetheart; for the ladies, you're a charmer; for your friends, you're a drugged out partier; for Sloan, you're a serious actor. Regardless of the situation, you're always careful to be the best, most likable version of yourself."

"And that's *so* terrible in the eyes of high and mighty Katharine Firestone, I suppose — wanting to be liked."

"There's a difference between being liked for who you are, and being liked for who you pretend to be." I narrow my eyes at him. "You want me to stop looking at you like a faker? Stop *being* one. Drop that front you're constantly putting up, to please the crowds and the cameras. You want me to like you? I can't do that unless I know you. The *real* you. Not some act you're putting on because you think it'll impress me, or Sloan, or the damn paparazzi. Be yourself. Be genuine. Let me see that guy you claim to be, beneath all the bullshit. Otherwise there's not a chance in hell of us ever getting through this movie without killing each other."

My passionate words finally die out. I blink, startled to find I've moved alarmingly close to him during my tirade. My chest is heaving, my breaths are coming too fast, and one slight push up onto the balls of my feet would crush my mouth against his. Anyone walking past would sooner think we were lovers sharing a stolen moment behind this pillar than a pair of feuding co-stars spitting harsh truths at each other.

He's glaring down at me through slitted eyes, his own breaths labored. I see the moment our proximity registers, see the exact second he realizes my chest is practically pressed against his, that merely an inch of space separates our bodies from aligning perfectly in the mimicry of an embrace.

"Anything else to add?" he whispers, his voice full of grit. "Any more offenses to lay against me tonight, Kat?"

"No." I lick parched lips; his eyes follow the sweep of my tongue. "That about covers it."

"Great. Let me know if you think of anything else I've done to personally offend you."

"I will."

With that, I push past him and stalk away before he can say something else. Before his honeyed words, his little jokes, his sidelong glances, his gorgeous looks all start to sink under my skin and invade my senses like the most intoxicating perfume, poisoning me before I've even realized what's happening.

Men like Grayson Dunn are game-players. They're experts at manipulation. They've spent so many cumulative hours of life messing with the minds of the women unfortunate enough to cross their paths, it's no wonder they're able to disarm even the bitchiest of us with a few calculated words, a strategic graze of calloused fingers against the sensitive flesh inside your elbow, a husky whisper against the lobe of your ear.

I've played this game before, too many times to count, and I've lost every time.

I'm not playing this round. Not again. Not with him. Even if it means being a colossal bitch.

I'd rather be hard as nails than a heartbroken mess.

***

By the time the bouncers clear the last stragglers off the dance floor downstairs, it's nearly three in the morning and my feet feel like anvils. I wipe down the high-top tables as Kylie clears empty glasses and the twins restock the bar. We work in exhausted silence, all eager to finish up so we can get the hell home.

If only the VIPs in the corner would leave.

Every few moments, a chorus of drunken giggles erupts from the couches where Grayson and Ryder are still camped out, entertaining the women draped around them like tinsel — decorative and insubstantial. After our confrontation, Grayson proceeded to escalate his status from "a little drunk" to absolutely wasted. Cutting across the floor to deliver drinks to other patrons, I've watched him pour shot after shot of whiskey with hands growing shakier by the second.

There's no quelling the tide of guilt rising inside me. I'm not blind to the notion that perhaps this newfound dedication to destroying his liver has something to do with the harsh words I spoke.

I didn't force the bottle of Jack into his hands, I tell myself over and over. *He's not my problem.*

Still, I can't stop myself from peeking at him from the corner of my eye as I clear off the final table. Most of their group has dissolved, but two statuesque beauties still cling to Ryder's sides, pressing kisses into his neck and whispering things that make him smirk. Grayson, on the other hand, is either asleep or passed out on the other end of the couch — eyes closed, head tipped back to the cushions, arms crossed over his chest. He's going to wind up with a killer neck-ache in the morning, if he stays like that much longer.

When the house lights start to flicker on and the lower-level DJ lets his table spin into silence, I know it's time to prod them along.

"Kylie?" I say hopefully, turning desperate eyes on my co-worker.

"Nope, sorry." She shoves a stack of tips at me, pockets the rest of the cash for herself, and starts heading for the door. "All you, babe. My boyfriend is waiting outside and he's already pissed we're getting out this late. *Again*."

I sigh as she disappears, fingers curling around the thick wad of bills. Even the cash in hand can't cure my disappointment when I turn and see the blonde bartender twins have also vanished. I could walk downstairs and find a bouncer to eject Ryder and Grayson, but that'll just delay me getting home until even later.

Shoving the cash deep inside my handbag, I slide on my thin jacket so I'm slightly less scantily-clad, steady my shoulders, and force myself to cross toward the couches, trying my damnedest to think of something to say and coming up short every time.

"Kat!"

Halfway there, I stop at the sound of my name and glance back to see Vince walking toward me. His large strides eat up the space between us in a flash.

"What's up, boss?"

"You clearing them out?" He gestures toward Grayson, Ryder, and their bimbos.

I nod. "Planning on it."

"Thanks." He winks at me. "You girls tend to use a lighter touch than the boys who work the door."

"Maybe you should hire nicer door guys."

He laughs. "Having scary bouncers is kind of the whole point. If they aren't intimidating, no one listens to 'em."

"True," I concede. "Hey, Vince?"

"Whatever it is, the answer's no, sweetheart."

"What? I haven't even asked anything yet!"

"Yeah, but you're doing that same cutesy head-tilt thing you did last year, when you told me you couldn't work on Halloween." His eyes narrow as I hastily straighten my head to a normal angle. "Don't tell me you're busy on New Year's Eve. That's a non-negotiable night, you know that."

"No, it's not about New Year's. The thing is...I got this part in a movie..."

"Shit!" His loud curse startles me. I've never heard him swear before, let alone at that volume. "This is why I don't fuckin' hire wannabe actresses."

I swallow and move back a step. "Vince—"

"...always a damn mess. Inconsistent, drama-filled, vapid little girls with no sense of responsibility..."

I'm starting to think Vince isn't the marshmallow I judged before, watching as his expression grows stormy and he mutters nasty things under his breath. I try a final appeal to his sense of logic.

"Listen, it's only a short span of work. Three weeks — four tops. I can come back after we're done filming, if you still have space for me on staff."

"Oh, yeah? You'll come back? How sweet." He shakes his head. "And when exactly does your big turn playing Dead Hooker Two on *Law and Order* start filming, huh?"

I grit my teeth. "It's a movie. And it starts Monday."

"Two fucking days from now?" he explodes. "You've gotta be shitting me!"

"Look, Vince, I'm sorry—"

He takes a rather aggressive step into my space and before I know what's happening, he's grabbed hold of my arm and is squeezing so hard I'm sure I'll have a bruised bicep in the morning. "You're sorry?" he scoffs. "Leaving me understaffed, no fuckin' notice—"

"Get off me, asshole!" I hiss, trying to pull out of his grip. My eyes are watering in pain. "I mean it, let me go!"

"So sick of girls like you thinkin' they can walk in and out of this job, no accountability, and I'll be the nice guy. Guess what? I'm tired of being the nice guy." He leans so close I can feel spittle fly from between his lips as he speaks. "Didn't anyone ever teach you manners?"

A cold voice interjects. "Didn't anyone ever teach you not to put your hands on a woman?"

My head whips around just in time to see a fist fly out and clip Vince across the jaw. The man's a giant, but he still stumbles backward against the bar. I search for the source of the swift blow and am stunned to see Grayson standing there, knuckles bright red, swaying slightly on his feet. His eyes are hazy, but they're locked on my arm.

"You okay?"

My flesh is still smarting. I ignore it. "I'm fine."

He nods and aims his attention back at Vince, who's regained his balance and looks about as happy as a vegan at a steakhouse as he advances on us. Recognizing the scary light in my boss's eyes, I don't hesitate another moment. I grab Grayson by the hand and try to tug him toward the exit.

The oaf is so drunk he doesn't move an inch, despite my efforts.

"Grayson, he will *kill you*," I hiss, yanking his arm with all my might. "We have to go. Now."

He still doesn't move, except to jerk his arm from my grip.

Shit.

Vince is six-feet-five-inches of pure rage. He makes Grayson, who is by no means a featherweight, look like a scrappy freshman going up against the senior quarterback in every soapy, stereotypical high school movie of all time.

I hear Ryder coming up behind us and hope he might intervene, but it's too late — Vince reaches out, grabs Grayson by the lapels of his jacket, and shoves him up against the closest wall with so much force, the light fixture rattles overhead.

"You're dead." Vince sounds absolutely lethal. "You hear me?"

"Sorry, I don't speak imbecile," Grayson growls.

That's the final straw — Vince's hands tighten as he lifts Grayson clean off his feet and hurls him across the room like a discarded rag doll. In his drunken state, Grayson doesn't stand a chance at keeping his footing. I wince as he hits the floor like dead weight, skidding to a stop against a row of upside-down barstools with a clatter.

"Stop!" I yell at Vince, who brushes me aside like a fly. "Stop this right now!"

Grayson's staggering to his feet, barely conscious but still trying to fight. It's painful to watch.

"You fucking asshole," Ryder growls, moving to help Grayson up. In their first intelligent move of the night, his bimbos have made a break for the exits, but I don't think he cares. The musician's bloodshot eyes are fixed on Vince with vengeance.

I hear the sound of heavy, booted feet coming up the stairs as the bouncers hurry toward us, and have a feeling things are about to turn seriously violent unless someone intervenes.

I just wish that *someone* was someone other than *me*.

Hoping like hell I don't catch a rogue fist across the cheek, I push myself into my boss's path and block his way to Grayson and Ryder.

"Vince," I say desperately. "Think about who these guys are. Think about what'll happen if you hit Grayson Dunn, or give Ryder Woods a black eye. It's not worth it. Just let us *go*."

Vince seethes in silence for a moment, his massive hands curled into fists at his sides. "You're lucky you're famous," he mutters finally, never looking away from Grayson. "Now get the fuck out of my club and don't ever come back." His eyes slide to me. "Same goes for you."

I nod. "Consider us gone."

Scooping my purse off the table, I sling it over one

shoulder, then turn and grab Ryder by one hand and Grayson by the other. I thank my lucky stars that this time they don't resist. With stumbling steps, we begin to move toward the stairs. We pass three bewildered bouncers, never pausing.

"Come *on*," I hiss, pulling them down the steps as fast as they can manage with this much alcohol in their systems. When we reach the exit, I drop their hands and spin around, mind racing. "Do you have a car here? A chauffeur? Security team? Anything?"

"Ditched 'em," Grayson mutters, eyes drooping closed. He looks like he's about to keel over, so I grab his arm and sling it over my shoulders. He leans on me just like the other day, when we rehearsed our first scene together, and I can't help but think of Violet and Beck.

"I'll have to call you a car... I'd drive you home in mine, but I don't think it'll make the trip..." Straining under Grayson's weight, I glance at Ryder. "My phone is in my purse, can you get it out for me?"

Ryder ignores my instructions, reaches into his pocket, and fishes out a red valet tag. "Car's out back."

"You're wasted," I say flatly.

"Very," he agrees.

"You can't drive."

He grins crookedly at me. "You know how to drive a stick, Kit-Kat?"

I sigh and snatch the valet tag from his grip. "Let's just get him to the car. We'll take it one step at a time from there. Okay?"

Ryder salutes me.

Grayson shoots me a smile so dopey, it's almost enough to make me forget that it's three in the morning, I've just lost my job, my feet are on fire, and, oh yeah, I loathe him.

"Come on, drunky," I chide, securing his arm more firmly around my shoulders. "Let's get you home."

Ryder pulls open the doors with a chivalrous sweep and bows. "After you."

I step out onto the sidewalk, expecting fresh air and the dimly lit streets of early-morning LA... and instead find myself blinded as camera flashes explode from all sides. I curse and try to cover my eyes, but I can't do much without dropping Grayson on his ass. Paparazzi are screaming as they shoot picture after picture, relentless in their pursuit for any morsel of gossip they can sell to the tabloids.

"RYDER!"
"Look this way!"
"GRAYSON!"
"Sweetheart, what's your name?"
"Is it over with Helena?"
"Does this mean you're single again, Grayson?"
"Who's the new girl?"

I keep moving, squinting my eyes to keep Ryder in sight as we push our way to the curb. When I catch a glimpse of the valet's red polo shirt, I shove the ticket in his direction and bark, "Hurry!"

He takes off like a shot.

Ryder is flipping off the paps with both hands to ruin their pictures — much to their annoyance.

"Yeah! You like that?" He makes another obscene gesture that, under any other circumstance, would make me laugh. "Put this on your front page, asswipe!"

Even with Ryder running interference, their bombardment of questions and camera flashes never ceases. I don't give them my name or make eye contact, but I have a distinct feeling that by this time tomorrow they'll know exactly who I am. My heart starts to pound and my throat constricts so tight, it feels like I've swallowed a golf ball.

There's a brief moment where I consider dropping Grayson to the pavement, making a beeline for my car in the staff lot, and vanishing into the night... but I can't quite bring myself to abandon him. After all, the man did practically get pommeled into ground beef by a former WWE star while defending my honor.

For what seems like an eternity, I stand on that curbside, Grayson draped over my shoulder like a heavy, half-sleeping blanket, wishing adamantly that on the first occasion of my life the members of the press have ever wanted to know my name, I was wearing something besides a bustier corset, pleather micro-mini skirt, and four-inch hooker heels.

Welcome to fame, Kat Firestone. You look like a goddamn mess.

My eyes, still watering from the ceaseless flashes, widen when a massive black SUV screeches to a stop beside us on the curb, platinum rims still spinning. It's been propped up on shocks so tall, I'll need a crane to lift me into the driver's seat. I turn to Ryder, mouth agape.

"You've got to be kidding me."

"Isn't she a beauty?" He beams and runs his hand down the flank of the car. "Brand new. Custom everything. Only twenty miles on her. Be gentle, you hear me?"

Before I can answer, he pulls Grayson off my shoulders, opens the back door, and pushes his friend face-first onto the backseat with a rough shove. There's a faint moan from Grayson as his face skids across the leather.

Rounding the hood, I hear the sound of a door slamming as Ryder climbs into the passenger seat. The paparazzi trail me, their giant lenses so close I feel like an exotic zoo animal, and I try to breathe through the sudden claustrophobia enveloping me.

"Give us a smile, sweetheart!"

"What's your name?"

"Are you dating Ryder?"

"When did you meet Grayson?"

The valet hops down from the driver's side and holds the door open for me. Reaching blindly into my purse, I grab the first bill my fingers land on from my stack of tips and shove it in his direction. He pockets it and disappears, leaving me alone with the paps.

What a gentleman.

I grit my teeth and contemplate the odds that I'm about to flash my private bits on the national news circuit while attempting to climb into this car in a barely-there miniskirt.

More than likely.

Before I can truly start to panic, Ryder's face appears above me. Grinning like a mad-man, he extends both hands down and waggles his fingers.

"Coming, Kit-Kat?"

I'm so relieved, I let the awful nickname slide. As soon as I grab his hands, he locks his wrists with mine and hauls me up into the cab with surprising strength, considering his lean build. I manage to keep exposure to a minimum as I settle into the seat and slam the door shut behind me, extremely grateful for the heavily-tinted windows and muffled silence.

Camera shutters are still clicking as I adjust the steering wheel, strap myself in, and force the mammoth vehicle into gear. I imagine it feels similar to driving a tank across a battlefield.

"Are you strapped in?" I ask the drunkards.

There's no answer.

I glance at Ryder and see his eyes are half-shut as he doses against his window like a child on a long car ride. In the rearview I see Grayson sprawled across the backseat, now fully unconscious.

My fingers curl tighter around the steering wheel as we leave Balthazar and the crowd of paparazzi behind.

It's three in the morning. I'm driving a three-hundred-thousand-dollar SUV with two of the most sought-after celebrities in Hollywood, both of whom are drunk out of their skulls, one of whom I don't even like. There are thousands of unflattering pictures of me being uploaded to the internet at this precise moment in time. I have absolutely no idea where I'm going. And, to top it all off, I'm absolutely starving.

How in the *hell* did my night end up like this?

CHAPTER SIX

"I'M ABSOLUTELY NOT A FUCKBOY."
- *A fuckboy.*

"I think I love you."
"You told me that already." I stuff another handful of French fries into my mouth. "Twice."
"Well, I'm serious." Ryder takes a truly massive bite of his quarter-pounder and moans. "Hitting the drive-thru was the best idea ever."
"I'm not sure the girl working the window would agree," I say dryly. "The shock of seeing Ryder Woods in the passenger seat damn near killed her."
He smirks. "I tend to have that effect on women."
"I can't fathom why."
"So good." He moans around another bite. "We should make you come out with us every weekend."
I snort. "Yeah… I wouldn't count on that."
"Ah, right. You'll be too busy to eat burgers with me at four in the morning — Grayson mentioned you guys start filming on Monday." Ryder glances in the backseat, where his friend is still passed out cold. "He also mentioned there's some kind of weird beef between you."
My eyebrows go up. I'm surprised he mentioned me at all. "It's a long story."
"Uh huh." Ryder shoves another mammoth bite into his mouth. "There's a security gate up ahead — don't worry, I know the code."
After getting some food into Ryder, he sobered up enough to program the GPS to take us to Grayson's place

in Malibu. Sure enough, the next turn I take brings us down a narrow lane to a set of stately black security gates surrounded by a towering row of hedges, concealing the house beyond. I have to unbuckle and climb halfway out my window to reach the buttons on the security panel. Ryder whistles and waggles his eyebrows at me as I settle back in my seat and tug my mini-skirt into place.

"You weren't supposed to look," I grumble as the gates swing open.

"Piece of advice: you don't want men to look, don't wear leather."

"Are you as chauvinistic as you seem?" I ask, darting a glance at him.

"Are you as cynical as *you* seem?" he counters.

I roll my eyes and steer us down the long, sloping driveway until the shape of a house appears in the darkness. Ryder's out of the car before I've cut the engine, darting for the front door like a bullet.

"Where are you going?"

"I think there's leftover pizza in Grayson's fridge!" he calls, sliding a key into the lock.

"You just ate a cheeseburger!"

Echoing laughter is his only answer.

"Wait! Ryder! You have to help me with him!" I yell, but he's already disappeared inside. I leap down from the driver's side and slam the door harder than necessary.

Goddamn rockstars.

Yanking open the back door, I turn tired eyes to Grayson. An irrepressible giggle bubbles up from my stomach at the sight of him — face slackened in a drunken stupor, a puddle of drool forming on the leather seat beneath his cheek, dark hair even messier than usual.

"Dunn. *Hey!* Dunn. Time to wake up." I prod him gently on the arm. When that yields no results, I shake him lightly. "Grayson!"

Still nothing.

With no other option, I flick him in the middle of the forehead.

Green eyes crack open and focus on my face. "Kat."

His voice is slurred with sleep and liquor as he mutters my name, but it still sends a shiver down my spine.

"Come on, drunky." I poke him again. "Let's get you inside."

"Where are we?" he asks, struggling to sit up. His hair is completely flat on one side, sticking straight up on the other.

"Your place." I offer him a hand. "Come on."

He stares at me for a moment, then nods and slides his giant palm into mine and climbs slowly from the car, stumbling a bit on the dismount. I reflexively wrap my arms around his waist, steadying him as best I can.

"Whoa, careful."

I'm suddenly very conscious of the lack of space between us. My hands are at his waist, fingertips digging into his sides to keep him upright; his arms are draped over my shoulders, and he's looking down into my eyes while smiling that dopey, drunken smile.

"Kat," he whispers again.

My heart starts skipping beats.

"Let's get you inside." I force myself to release him and move back to the driver's seat, where I retrieve my purse and the greasy white fast food bag. "Here, I bought you a cheeseburger. Eat it. You'll feel better with some food in your system."

He blunders along behind me, unwrapping the burger with clumsy fingers. Ryder's left the door ajar. When I step through it into the house, I try not to gawk at the obvious show of wealth. The ceiling soars twenty feet overhead; marble floors gleam underfoot. A wall of windows looks out at an incredible view of cliffs that drop straight down to the Pacific. I can see the first hints of dawn staining the sky — soon, the sun will illuminate the whole house with early morning light.

The gorgeous atmosphere is marred somewhat by the sight of Ryder passed out on the couch: face on the cushions, feet on the floor, snoring so loud it could wake the dead. There's a half-eaten piece of pizza still clutched in his hand.

I hear the door click closed as Grayson shuffles in behind me, chewing the last bite of his cheeseburger. He doesn't bat an eye at Ryder's prone form, he simply stands there swaying in place, blinking his glazed green eyes like he's never been here before.

"Come on, you," I say, sighing deeply and grabbing his hand. "Let's get you into bed, before you fall over."

He doesn't say anything, but his fingers twine tightly with mine and he begins to shuffle forward through the house, flicking on lights as we walk down a hall, around a corner, through an amazing living room with about ten skylights, and past what looks like a library full of floor-to-ceiling bookshelves which, under any other circumstance, I would insist upon stopping to investigate. Eventually, we reach his bedroom.

It's lacking what they'd refer to in a vaguely sexist manner as "a woman's touch." The walls are blank except for a single abstract canvas I'd bet my life was picked out by an interior designer. With the exception of a laptop and various other electronics scattered around his desk, there are very few traces of life. A leftover coffee cup sits on his bedside table, a few sweaters are tossed haphazardly across the back of the arm chair in the corner, a motorcycle helmet sits askew on his desk. The king bed is half made, as if he rose in a hurry.

Grayson stumbles toward it on unsteady feet. I try to release his hand, but he holds me fast and before I can stop it, I'm pulled down next to him on the edge of the mattress. He collapses instantly back against the blankets with a heavy sigh, his eyes slipping closed, his hand still holding me firmly in place.

"Dunn."
"Mmmm."
"Dunn, let go of my hand."
"Mmm."
"DUNN!"

Green eyes sliver open and focus on my face. "Kat."

"Hand," I say, lifting our interlocked fingers and shaking them. "Let go."

His drunken smile returns. "You're here."

"Yes, I brought you home, remember?"

It's clear he doesn't remember. He's still totally wasted.

"So pretty," he says, staring up at me. "You were always so pretty."

I laugh, still trying to tug my hand from his. "Who'd have guessed, the asshole gets sweet when he's plastered out of his mind—*Hey*!"

An unexpected yank on my arm sends me reeling off balance — I sprawl forward onto Grayson's chest with a squeak. Before I can roll off him, his other arm snakes around my waist and he buries his head in my hair. I feel his warm breath at the nape of my neck as he inhales rhythmically.

"Are you *cuddling* with me?" I ask, when I've regained the ability to speak. "Seriously?"

"Shhh."

"I'm not a cuddler. I don't *do* cuddling." I pause, but he doesn't respond. "Are you hearing me right now?"

"Mmmm." His voice is fainter; like he's hovering on the edge of consciousness.

"Grayson Dunn! Don't you dare fall asleep!"

He doesn't even murmur in acknowledgment this time, which I take as a bad sign. I try to slide out of his hold, but he doesn't budge. I attempt to shift him sideways to reach my purse, which he conveniently collapsed on top of when he timbered like a felled tree in the forest, but he's far too heavy.

Great. I'm snuggling with a goddamned giant.

All I can do is lie there with him, listening to the faint thud of his heartbeat through the fabric of his jacket, watching the steady rise and fall of his chest as he slips further into sleep. I know there's a part of me that should be filled with rage at this man, for ruining my night...

and getting me fired...and making me take care of him...and forcing me to spend half my tip money on drive-thru food...and reading the love letter I wrote him out loud to an entire cast of pre-teen boys all those years ago... but lying in the circle of his arms, I can't seem to muster even the smallest bit of anger.

Head on his chest, I stare at the small clock on his bedside table and watch the minutes tick by, feeling the warm puffs of his breath like a metronome against my skin and trying not to succumb to the strong lure of sleep.

After a few moments, the arms around me go completely slack and I know he's fully asleep. Moving gingerly so I don't accidentally shake him awake, I slide from his hold and scramble off the bed on light feet, stopping only when there's a safe distance between us, lest he wake suddenly and try to grab me again. Hands planted on my hips, I shake my head in exasperation as I stare down at his prone form. He looks totally uncomfortable in his jacket and jeans. His shoes are still on, for god's sake.

Sighing, I bend and start to undo the laces. I can't let him sleep in his shoes.

I may be a bitch, but I'm not a monster.

They're knotted tightly — it's a struggle to yank the expensive leather loafers from his feet. When I finally get them off, I toss them into the corner of the room, wincing when they thud against the hardwood so loudly, Grayson stirs in his sleep. I should probably be worried I've woken him, but I'm too busy staring at the feet dangling off the edge of the bed to care. A shocked giggle bursts from my mouth.

His socks aren't the standard, solid black you'd expect of Hollywood's leading action hero. Instead, they're navy blue and covered in shooting stars and moons, suns and planets — something you'd sooner find in the closet of a seven-year-old than a twenty-seven-year-old.

I don't know why, but the sight of those damn socks makes something inside me snap. The hilarity of this whole circumstance hits me all at once: I'm wearing a corset, in Grayson Dunn's bedroom... marking perhaps the first time in history he's had a half-naked girl in here and done nothing more than amuse her with his little-boy socks while drooling onto his pillow.

Once I start to laugh, I can't stop. I sit there for a long while, laughing so hard I start to wheeze; so hard my eyes start to stream; so hard I don't notice those socked feet shifting down onto the floor, or their owner sitting up on the edge of his bed like a zombie rising from the dead.

"What's funny?" a slurred voice asks.

My laughter dies instantly and I scramble to my feet, wiping tears from the corners of my eyes. When our gazes meet, I can't quite suppress a grin.

"Nice solar system socks, Dunn."

His head cocks to the left and he stares down at his feet like they belong to a stranger. "Thanks," he murmurs, wiggling his toes so the shooting stars dance. "They're my favorite."

My grin widens. "Who'd have thought the Sexiest Man Alive was a closet science nerd?"

"Don't mock my socks," he says, rising to his feet. He's a little steadier than earlier, but not much. I take the opportunity to swipe my purse off the bed, before he falls on top of it again, and raise my hands defensively.

"Would I ever mock you?"

"...Absolutely."

I snort. "Well, that's probably true."

"I'll have you know," he informs me drunkenly. "These socks are out of this world."

"Did you just make a space pun?"

He's too busy laughing at his own terrible joke to answer.

I sigh. "Dunn, take off your jacket and get in bed. It's late and I want to go home."

"Home?" he asks, laughter abruptly stopping. His eyes are wide and glassy. "*Kat*. Stay. You should stay. We can make pancakes. It'll be great."

"I can't stay, drunky," I say, rolling my eyes as I take hold of his jacket cuff. I pull until his arm slides out. He doesn't struggle as I move to the other sleeve — he lets me pivot his body like a sleepy, overgrown child, arms falling back to his sides like dead weight as soon as they're free.

"Okay..." I stare at his jeans and t-shirt. "I've done my duty. You can handle the rest yourself."

He grins and starts to swing his hips as his hands move to the hem of his shirt.

"What are you doing?" I ask flatly, backing away. "Is that supposed to be a dance?"

He doesn't answer — he just moves around the room like a drunken fool attempting a strip tease, practically tripping over his own feet multiple times. I'd run away, but I'm afraid he's going to fall and crack his head open on the edge of his desk.

"I should be filming this," I mutter to myself, watching as he lifts his t-shirt up over his head. It gets snagged on his chin and he blunders around blindly for a moment before freeing himself. "Dunn's drunken strip tease — I could sell it to TMZ for a zillion dollars."

Now shirtless, Grayson starts to dance in earnest — he booty-drops like a slutty seventh-grade girl, and it's so ridiculous I can't help laughing.

"Dance with me," he says, reaching for the button of his jeans.

"I'm plenty entertained just watching. Trust me."

He shimmies out of his pants, trips over the fabric, and nearly wipes out. "Your loss, Kat," he mutters, recovering his balance just in time.

I snort at the sight of him, now in only boxer-briefs and his damn solar system socks, drunk off his ass and dancing around his room like a crazy person. Under normal circumstances, I might feel guilty about blatantly ogling his chiseled abs but, considering he won't remember any of this when he wakes up, I don't scold myself for checking him out.

"Get under the covers," I order, pointing at his bed. "I'm serious."

"*So* serious," he mocks, making a face at me. His arms swing and his hips sway as he moves, undeterred by the lack of music. He leans back and shakes his shoulders toward the sky, doing a terrible impression of "The Bernie" dance, followed by a number of other god-awful gyrations.

"Grayson," I say, desperately trying to cover my laughter with a stern voice.

"Kat," he says, moving closer, dopey smile firmly affixed to his face.

"Bed. Now."

He grins and reaches for the elastic band of his boxers. "Fine."

"AH!" I yell, reaching up to shield my eyes. I hear the sound of fabric hitting the wood floor. "What are you doing?"

"You said get ready for bed." His voice is slurred, seductive, and far too close; I back blindly toward the door. "I'm ready, now," he says, following me step for step.

"I didn't mean get naked! I meant... *sleep*."

"But I sleep naked."

I try to breathe normally at the thought of Grayson Dunn standing three inches away, nude except for his little boy socks. It's not easy.

"Grayson," I squeak. "Please go get under the covers."

He chuckles lowly, but I hear the uneven shuffle of his feet as he moves across the room. The tension in my body eases the farther he gets from me, and I feel myself starting to breathe again as the sound of him sliding beneath the covers reaches my ears.

"Are you decent?" I ask after a moment of silence, peeking through my fingers when he doesn't answer.

He's lying on the bed, sheet pulled up barely to his hips. My eyes lock on the trail of hair leading down from his belly button beneath the thin fabric, transfixed by the slight rise and fall of his muscled chest as he breathes in and out. Feeling a bit weak in the knees, I lean back against the door to keep myself standing.

Dear lord, he may lack common sense and all semblance of rhythm, but there's no denying he's the most attractive man I've ever laid eyes on. Even black-out drunk.

There are deep shadows under his closed eyes. An errant lock of hair falls across his forehead. From the looks of it, he's already dead to the world.

"Okay, then." I pull in a steadying breath. "I'll just be going then."

Grabbing my purse from the floor, I turn and force myself to walk out the door before I can do something utterly stupid... like cross the room and brush the hair off his face, or strip down to my skin and climb into bed beside his warm frame, wrapping myself around him until heat sinks into my bones and that feeling I got earlier, when he was dancing in his space socks and the whole world seemed made of stardust, settles back over me like a blanket.

That would be more than stupid — it would be downright crazy.

Because he's your co-star, a snarky internal voice reminds me. *Because you hate him.*

You do hate him...

Don't you?

"Goodnight, Grayson," I whisper, pulling his bedroom door closed with a soft click and shaking my head at my own ridiculous thoughts. "I'll see you Monday."

***

Someone is pounding on my door.

I groan and bury my head deeper beneath my pillows, praying whoever it is will either be struck dead by lightning or simply give up and go away. After a few beats of silence, the pounding continues.

"KAT! I know you're in there!" A fist pounds again. "Open up!"

93

I recognize Harper's voice. Imagining a myriad of ways to kill her, I force myself out of bed, still barefoot and dressed in the baggy t-shirt I slept in, and stalk down the stairs with vengeance on my mind.

"Come on, Kat!"

She bangs again. Her fist is still poised in the air, ready to strike, when I slide off the security chain and yank open the front door, a dark scowl contorting my features.

She's standing there smiling at me, her hair a dizzying shade of turquoise, dressed in spandex workout clothes and clutching what appears to be a stack of magazines.

"Morning, sunshine!"

I blink rapidly, struggling for coherent words. "Why... you... and the pounding... I was asleep..." I trail off with a squeak of distress, which she ignores, pushing past me into the apartment and heading straight for the kitchen. Her voice drifts back to me as she disappears from sight.

"I'll make coffee!"

I slam the door closed and follow her, grinding my teeth. "I don't want coffee. I want to go back to bed."

"It's noon!" She snorts, as though the idea is ludicrous. "And you promised you'd go running with me this morning."

"When do we ever run?"

"We run," she says defensively, pouring a scoop of ground beans into a filter and shoving it into my crappy coffee maker. "Sometimes."

"No," I say, collapsing onto a wobbly kitchen chair, its wooden legs uneven on the peeling laminate. "We get dressed up in yoga pants and cute sports bras, stroll the boardwalk, and drink vile green smoothies. I'm sorry, but that doesn't constitute working out. Even in LA."

"Whatever. You still promised."

"When did I promise?"

"Yesterday. After sushi."

"Yes, but I was younger then, and full of hope."

"And, of course, you didn't know you'd be out all night, hooking up with Grayson Dunn."

My mouth falls open. "What? I didn't! How did you even know—"

"It's all over the tabloids." She gestures at the stack of magazines on the table in front of me. My eyes move to the one on top. My hands shake a bit as I reach out and turn it over, revealing a blurry photo of myself — all bare legs and big hair and high heels, standing on a dark sidewalk with my arm wrapped tight around Grayson's waist. He looks half-asleep in the photo, leaning heavily on my shoulder. The bold yellow title spans nearly the entire front page.

GRAYSON'S NEW GIRL! Their secret romance caught on camera... Details on Page 13!

My teeth sink into my lip as I flip through the stack of remaining tabloids, all bearing similar pictures and captions. Harper doesn't interrupt my silent freak-out session — she just sets a steaming cup of black coffee on the table in front of me and waits until I've gotten myself under control enough to speak.

"I knew it would be bad," I murmur, taking a sip that scorches my tongue. "But not *this* bad."

She shrugs. "Grayson's big news, babe. Looks like now you are, too."

I grimace at the thought.

"So?" Her dark brows lift. "You gonna spill, or do I have to tip you over and pour it out of you?"

"It's not what you think." I take another sip before giving her a brief run-down of what happened last night at Balthazar, followed by the drive back to Grayson's. I skim over the naked-dancing bits and, thankfully, she doesn't press for too many details.

"Damn." She lets out a low whistle when I finish my recap. "Ryder Woods *and* Grayson Dunn, in one night? You lucky little bitch."

"Lucky? *Lucky?* My ass is plastered on every magazine stand from here to Toledo, my car is stranded at Balthazar, and I had to take an Uber back here at five in the morning, driven by a creepy dude named Pedro who kept checking me out in the rearview."

"That's at least an hour away — what'd that cost you?"

"Everything I made in tips last night, and then some. Which means I might as well leave my car sitting in the Balthazar lot, because I can't afford to fix it."

She winces.

I push the stack of tabloids away with a huff. "Cynthia's going to flip out when she sees these. God forbid I show my face in public without her express permission! You know, if she worried half as much about her own life as she does about my *image*, she might actually be happy."

"Doubtful." Harper tucks a strand of blue hair behind one ear. "Your mother thrives on misery. She'd have no purpose, without someone to yell at."

"Well, I just wish I wasn't the one taking the brunt of her yelling so often. Her last three assistants have quit about ten minutes into the job."

"Can you blame them?"

"Not at all." I catch sight of a thick white envelop sticking out from the bottom of the stack of tabloids. "Hey, what's that?"

"Oh, right! That was on your doorstep when I got here. I forgot."

I reach for the package, tear it open, and pull out a thick, spiral-bound stack of papers with a sticky note on the front.

"It's from Wyatt," I murmur, skimming the note.

Katharine–

Here's your script and filming schedule. A car will pick you up from your apartment and drive you to the AXC Pictures soundstage at 9AM on Monday morning. We'll be here in LA for the first few days, shooting the CGI crash sequences with green screens. After that, we'll head to Hawaii and film the rest on location.

Rest up, read through your lines, and, for god's sake, stay away from Dunn. I thought you were smarter than that, Firestone.

–WH

"He's such an ass," I say affectionately, both amused and annoyed by his implications. Not to mention his use of my full name, knowing it would piss me off.
"I can't believe you're on a first name basis with Wyatt Hastings," Harper mutters bitterly. "The man is a god."
"He's mortal, trust me."
"Listen, I was wondering…" She trails off and her cheeks go red. My interest is immediately piqued — Harper doesn't embarrass easily.
"What?"
"It's nothing. Never mind."
"Harper. Tell me."
She sighs. "It's stupid. But, well… I was wondering if maybe you could talk to Wyatt about getting me a spot on the costume crew doing makeup and hair? I'm between jobs right now, so I have free time." Her words come out in a rush. "If that would be weird, or put you in a bizarre situation, absolutely forget about it. I know it's an indie film, so they have a limited crew and budget, but I was just thinking—"

"—that it would be awesome to have you on set with me all the damn time to keep me sane and prevent me from murdering Dunn between takes?" I finish, beaming. "Because I fully agree."

"Really?" she asks, grinning back at me.

"I don't know why I didn't think of it myself. Sorry — I'm a shitty friend."

"No, you aren't! You've had a lot going on. I understand."

"I'll talk to Wyatt first thing Monday."

"You're the best."

"You realize you'd have to come to Hawaii with us, right? We're filming on the beach, since the majority of the movie is just me and Grayson on the island. There'll be a small production crew, of course, plus Wyatt and Sloan… But we'll be there for more than two weeks."

She nods. "Yeah, you told me. I think it would be good to get away. Things with Greg are…"

"What? Did something happen?"

"Nothing major." Her eyes are on the scratched tabletop. "He's just been distant, lately. And whenever I ask about it, he accuses me of *smothering him*. Which, honestly, I'm not trying to do. At all. I'm just concerned about him." Her voice goes up an octave. "Why does asking if someone is okay, or calling to check in on them when they're two hours late for the special dinner you spent all afternoon slaving over in front of a hot stove, mean you're somehow *clingy* or *desperate*? I mean… do you know how expensive filet mignon is? I had no idea! And I don't even like steak that much! But I went out and bought it specially for him, and then he doesn't even bother to show up."

"Rude."

"Tell me about it." She sighs heavily. "He's just… not himself."

"Just that one night? Could've been an off day at work, or—"

"No, it's more than that." She hesitates. "Lately, I've noticed… He doesn't come home at his normal time… and when he does finally get home, he hops straight into the shower as soon as he walks in the door. And… he doesn't even kiss me goodnight, anymore." Her fingertip traces absent patterns on my crappy tabletop. "It's probably all in my head. He wouldn't cheat on me. Would he?"

Yes! Yes, of course he would! I want to scream. *This is Greg we're talking about.*

I take a purposeful sip of coffee to avoid responding right away, trying to buy some time to compose my thoughts into something that sounds vaguely supportive. In truth, I'm practically giddy to hear she and Greg are having problems. I realize on the surface, this may seem selfish and sadistic; in my defense, Greg is a total loser. The day Harper swiped right on his shirtless mirror-selfie was the dawn of a horrid new era of her life. My deep love for her is the only reason I even attempt to keep a lid on my extreme hatred of him.

Greg.

His name alone pisses me off; the fact that he's driven a wedge between me and the girl I once considered my best friend in the world infuriates me beyond belief.

Because how can we be best friends anymore, if we can't discuss the most important part of her life with anything approaching honesty or candor? How can we eat sushi and drink smoothies and talk about our lives without ever mentioning the elephant in the room that is her jackass of a boyfriend?

I didn't start dating the jerk, but he's affected my life all the same.

Harper no longer invites me over for dinner parties at their new apartment by the beach. We have been reduced to bi-monthly lunch dates at a neutral location halfway between our apartments, during which we sip expensive cocktails and pretend not to notice how strained our conversations have become.

Perhaps it is because I have never had a great love, a true love, a soulmate, and thus never had my heart broken thoroughly enough to feel the true sting of a break up, but the slow disintegration of my friendship with Harper has been more painful than losing any of my idiot ex-boyfriends. I have lost my closest confidant, my truest ally, my most stalwart drinking buddy... and to a thirty-year-old pot dealer who "doesn't want to be tied down" with a career, no less.

There's very little I can do to rectify the situation. Greg, lame and immature as he may be, has latched onto my friend with all the tenacity of a barnacle on the bottom of a ship, and I have a feeling it'll take more than my murmured sarcastic comments and snarky side-eyed glances to force him out. It pains me to see that Harper, like so many before her, has fallen victim to the lure of a man whose immaturity she mistakes for playfulness and whose lack of ambition she confuses for free-spiritedness.

There is an epidemic in our country, affecting men in their twenties. I'm not talking about the man-bun — that's another issue entirely. No, I'm referring to the sweeping diagnosis known as Peter Pan Syndrome, which has birthed a terrifying new specimen: the man-child. The Gregs of the world. You know the type. The one who never grew up and, frankly, has no intentions of ever doing so because, well, why the hell would he want to do that when instead, he can scrape by exploiting the resources of his parents just long enough to land himself a successful woman who'll take care of him for the rest of his life?

The man-child is the guy who never wants to work or dream or do anything except *Netflix and chill*. He has no interest in your ambitions because he hasn't got any of his own. His plans extend no farther than where he will be getting drunk next weekend. The two-hundred-thousand-dollar college degree his parents paid for out of pocket sits in a cardboard roll beneath his childhood four-poster bed where he still sleeps because he doesn't have a job, let alone an apartment.

I've dated this guy in several different variations, over the years — the hipster barista version, the sky diving adrenaline-junkie version, the wannabe tech-startup version, the Instagram travel blogger version. At the end of the day, it has never amounted to anything more than a paralyzing sense of self-doubt accompanied by several months' worth of obsessing over someone who was never emotionally equipped to be in a relationship in the first place.

Don't get me wrong — it's not that I don't understand the general appeal of the man-child.

Yes, he is *fun*. He will make you laugh and tell you jokes and make you feel like that small, broken part deep down inside you doesn't matter. But eventually you will realize that's only because he never bothers to look that deep. He doesn't care enough to.

There's a certain kind of safety in the superficiality of your interactions. A feeling of anonymity in the circumference of his arms. He knows you in the most intimate way — the curves of your body, the shape of your hips, the way your hair looks when it's mussed and frizzy at two in the morning after a few rounds between the sheets.

And yet, he knows absolutely nothing about you. Not your dreams or your hopes or your fears. Not the way you take your coffee or the story of how you got that jagged scar on your left forearm at summer camp when you were eight.

The man-child lives always in the moment and, for a time, he might manage to convince you that you can live that way, too. Shucking off your Type-A tendencies. Never looking forward or backward. Perpetually pleased by your surroundings.

Babe, you're so tense, he'll say, rubbing your shoulders. *Relax.*

I hate to break this to you, but the man-child is an illusion. He does not exist. He is zero-calorie ice cream. He is a day at the beach without sunburn. He is a weight-loss diet consisting of fresh-baked baguettes and bottomless glasses of red wine.

Too good to be true.

We all realize this, eventually. It's only a matter of when.

In Harper's case, I hope it's sooner than later. Because if I have to stand up on an altar and hold her damn bridal bouquet as she pledges eternal devotion to Greg, there is a zero percent chance I will not speak now or forever hold my peace.

For now, however, I will bite back the words I'm dying to say and attempt to be a decent friend.

"Honey, if he's cheating on you, he's the stupidest man who ever lived." I reach out and place my hand on top of hers. "Don't worry. I'll talk to Wyatt. You'll come to Hawaii with me, get away from here for a bit, clear your head… It'll be great."

"Yeah?" She glances up hopefully. "You really think so?"

"Yeah. Just you and me, like the good old days. No boys to mess with our minds."

"…Except for the movie star you'll be making out with," Harper points out, laughing.

Grayson's handsome features flash through my mind.

"That's just acting," I say, heart thudding too fast. "Trust me, there's nothing between us off screen."

"Uh huh."

"Don't *uh huh* me. It's true."

"Sure it is," she agrees, glancing at the magazine stack. The top page shows a close-up — Grayson's arm tight around my shoulders, my side pressed up against his like we've been superglued together. I'm glancing up into his face, looking concerned and maybe, if I'm being honest with myself, a little dazed by his presence.

"Would you look at that?" Harper smirks knowingly. "Totally platonic, the two of you. Practically related! I, for one, *always* hold my brothers just like that."

"Do shut up."

"I'll shut up if you agree to come running."

I pause, contemplate continuing this conversation, and push back my chair.

"I'll go get my sneakers."

CHAPTER SEVEN

"Don't you think monogamy is such an antiquated concept?"
- *A man who will cheat on you as soon as the honeymoon stage ends.*

Monday morning arrives far too quickly for my liking. A beep outside my condo announces my ride — a sleek black town car, driven by a smartly-dressed man in a suit pulls up to my front curb at nine on the dot. I try to act unruffled as he holds open the door for me, scrambling into the back seat like I've done this kind of thing a million times, but I'm pretty sure he knows I'm a rube when I trip over my own feet and upend my purse all over the floor mat, sending lipsticks rolling in several directions. I spend the majority of the ride downtown subtly retrieving items from under the floor mat and, by the time I've reorganized the contents of my bag, we've reached the gilded security gates of AXC Pictures.

Before I know it, the town car is pulling away and I'm standing on a narrow asphalt lot, staring up at the imposing warehouse-style building marked STAGE 13, trying to breathe around the sudden knot of nerves that have lodged in the back of my throat like a dollop of peanut butter.

It's infinitely bigger than the studio across town where I filmed *Busy Bees* a decade ago, and infinitely more intimidating. People are milling around, clutching clipboards, barking orders, murmuring into headsets, running packages back and forth from one soundstage to another before active filming starts for the day. I see two well-known actors from a popular sitcom walking inside the warehouse next door, and try not to gawk like a starstruck pre-teen. A flatbed truck carrying a beat-up car riddled with fake bullet holes rolls past, en route to the backlots.

I am a single, steady drop in a swirling ocean of activity. Feet fused to the ground like cement, I stand and watch the chaos unfold, trying to take calming breaths.

I've been here once before, when I was six years old. Cynthia took me on a behind-the-scenes tour in one of those god-awful tourist trolleys, hoping it would inspire me to try harder at my auditions, arabesque higher in my dance lessons, sing louder in my vocal classes, win bigger at the pageants she signed me up for starting when I was an infant. I remember staring at the labyrinth of buildings — the elaborate replica of a full New York City block, the Old West style street facades complete with tumbleweeds and wagon wheels, the special effects lab where they turn blank green screens into expanding universes and tropical rainforests and stormy oceans — feeling like I'd never, in a million years, be lucky enough to peek behind the roped-off areas where only the stars and authorized set workers step foot.

It's the strangest feeling, finding yourself awake in a reality you were sure would only ever remain a dream. I thought I was prepared for this moment, but now that I'm here I feel utterly out of place.

After our run on Saturday, Harper drove me back downtown to retrieve my car from the Balthazar lot. Blessedly, the Honda rumbled to a start without giving me too much trouble, making it home to my condo before it rattled into silence. Sunday was a blur of signing contracts and reading through scripts, fending off Cynthia's calls and avoiding the internet, not wanting to witness the bombardment of tabloid stories about my supposed "secret love affair" with Grayson.

I know from the increasingly-snippy series of text

messages Cynthia fired my way that she released a statement to the press about my role in *Uncharted* sometime yesterday afternoon. Since then, the paparazzi have been in full-on stalker mode, desperate to dig up anything they can about my history. The persistent buzz of my cellphone beneath my pillow woke me from a sound sleep long before my alarm had a chance this morning — a flood of text messages, emails, and news alerts about my newfound celebrity status.

I'd barely wiped the caked, day-old mascara from beneath my eyes when I made the mistake of logging online. It was more than a little disconcerting to see my name trending with Grayson's as the number one news article, just above a story about nuclear warheads in some remote, war-torn region half a world away. It's strange enough to live in a universe where celebrity gossip ranks above nuclear weaponry in terms of newsworthiness; stranger still when that gossip concerns you.

I hesitated only for the briefest of moments, finger hovering in uncertainty, before jabbing my thumb against the screen and sweeping my eyes over the story.

SCANDAL ON SET: Hollywood's Hottest New Couple!

Quotes from "insiders" sat alongside the photo of Grayson and me outside the club the other night. I don't know who these "insiders" are, but apparently, they're positive Grayson and I are doing it like bunnies behind the scenes. I read about myself getting caught *in flagrante* in a trailer, in the back of a limousine, and even on the director's chair after hours — which, honestly, doesn't seem like it would be all that comfortable but, hell, at least my fictional sex life is full of spice.

Then again, according to TMZ, since Grayson and I don't follow each other on Twitter or Instagram, there's likely already trouble in paradise and I may be headed for a broken heart, just like poor, jilted Helena before me.

Damn. My fabricated relationship, doomed before it even began.

Please, someone pass the tissues.

Judging by the scathing tone of the comment section at the bottom of the article I read, the public seems divided about whether Grayson and I are truly star-crossed lovers or simply another publicity stunt, executed for the sole purpose of selling movie tickets. My eyes didn't linger long — one internet troll's opinion that I'm a "fugly, fame-chasing whore" was enough for a lifetime.

There's nothing like the anonymity of a keyboard and the prospect of tearing down a celebrity to get people revved up at six in the morning.

Disgusted and wide awake, I'd tossed my phone back onto the bed, yanked off my pajama shorts, and headed for my tiny, fluorescent-lit bathroom with its ugly 1950s pink subway tile and paint-chipped, claw-foot bathtub my landlord never bothered to update. Standing beneath the scalding shower-head, I tried to empty my mind of everything except lines from the script and action sequences from the scenes we're running through today, but my brain kept circling back to my new role as half a celebrity couple.

I should be upset that the news is full of lies about me, that the press adheres to the truth about as stringently as a dieting socialite confronted with a frozen yogurt stand, but I found myself more bothered by the idea that, should I suffer some kind of delusional episode and actually fall for that cocky co-star of mine, our relationship would never be *ours*. It would belong to the masses, to the reporters, to the paparazzi. We would never have a private instant to just be *us*, outside the scope of our onscreen characters, or the world's perceptions.

Love can't flourish beneath a microscope. Maybe that's why so many celebrity marriages fall apart.

Brad and Angelina...
Ben and Jen...
Blake and Miranda...

Honestly, if two people with millions of dollars and faces straight out of a catalogue can't make it work, is it really any wonder the rest of us are wandering around like neanderthals, grunting at each other in the monosyllabic, melancholy hope that someone will like us enough to procreate?

With odds like that, the whole human race is totally fucked.

In the old days, people used to go through their closets and throw out reminders of their ex's — gather all the clothes and CDs that reminded them of that person and box them away in cardboard, where they couldn't be seen. Now, post-breakup, it's more important to clean out your social media accounts than it ever was your closet. Untagging shared photos and deleting cute posts about what, at the time, seemed a love that would extend into perpetuity has become the new norm.

Everyone does it, from celebrities to the couple that once lived around the corner from you, back before he screwed his secretary and forfeited half his annual income in exchange for his wife quietly fading into an existence of Botox treatments and banging the cabana boy to quell her deep misery at aging out of her own marriage bracket.

This culling of all digital traces is somewhat irrelevant — no matter how many photos you untag or posts you hide from your timeline, there will always remain a vestige of that relationship, a technological footprint that anyone can find, should they choose to delve deep enough into your internet history. At all times, you are just one screen-shot away from reliving a past love over again.

And again and again and again and again.

That's probably why it's more intimate for someone of my generation to follow you on Instagram than fondle your boobs in the backseat of their car after a semi-awkward second date. Our utter lack of permanence — for how can anything achieve longevity in such a fast-moving world — is coupled with the startling sense that everything — and I do mean everything, even that unflattering photo of you at your friend Sarah's bat mitzvah in seventh grade — is permanent. Etched into the archives. Un-deletable.

I don't remember a time in which it was impossible to follow someone's existence from present day back into the frizzy-haired, braces-wearing past with the simple scroll of a finger. I can't recall a time when I could not examine someone from origin to actuality with the click of a button — though I know from the nostalgic, poetic waxings of older generations that such a time did once exist and, according to them, was wondrous in all its shaken-polaroid, watercolored, impermanent glory.

There is no such thing as privacy, anymore. Especially now that I'm a *quote-unquote* celebrity.

Just one more worry to add to my list, as if I wasn't already anxious enough that I'm about to royally fuck up my first day on set.

Yesterday, I felt confident, composed, completely sure that this wouldn't be a total disaster. And yet, standing here now, every line I memorized has fled from my head. I'm suddenly back in high school, sitting at a metal-legged desk, staring at the blank answer section on the physics test in front of me and wondering why, for the life of me, I can't remember anything about acceleration or inertia or wind resistance.

"Miss Firestone."

The sound of my name brings me crashing back down to reality. A petite man with flawless caramel-colored skin, blocky, black-framed glasses, and skinny jeans that have more rips than any of the pairs in my closet is staring at me with thinly-veiled impatience. I get the sense, from his expression, that it's not the first time he's said my name. A single glance tells me it's a struggle for this man to stand in one place for very long; he's practically vibrating as seconds tick by and he's forced to wait, immobile, for me to respond.

"Sorry." I force my arms to uncross and hang casually by my sides. "Just... taking it all in."

"*Right.*" He blinks. "I'm Trey, one of the production assistants. I was told to bring you straight to the costume department as soon as you arrived. They need to get you outfitted before the rest of the cast gets here and we start shooting. The costumes were designed with Helena in mind and they'll need to make some..." He tilts his head and peers at me over the rims of his glasses. "...adjustments."

I bite the inside of my cheek and remind myself that there's probably no *tactful* way to tell someone their size-two body won't squeeze into Helena's double-zero outfits, no matter how much sucking-in they do.

"Lead the way," I murmur.

Trey jolts into motion like a sprinter off the blocks, making a beeline to a side door inside the warehouse, then leading me down a narrow hallway toward a series of dressing rooms. We stop in front of a door that says HELENA PUTNAM on the name plate. I feel my eyebrows go up.

"Sorry about that," Trey says, looking a little embarrassed as he slides the plate from its metal frame. "I'll have someone replace it for you."

"It's not a problem."

Trey reaches out and holds open the door for me. "This is your dressing room. Someone should be by in a few minutes to take your measurements. If you need anything at all, just let me know, okay?"

He doesn't wait for me to respond; he's already walking away, speaking rapidly into his headset. I watch him disappear down the hallway and belatedly realize if I actually *did* need something, I have no idea how I'd even contact him to ask for it.

Sighing, I step into the brightly lit dressing room, briefly taking in the sight of the plush couch against the left wall, the mini-fridge in the corner, and the illuminated vanity table on my right, before my eyes fall on the full-length mirror directly across from me. I feel them widen in shock — not at my reflection, but at the word that's been scrawled across the glass surface in bright, hooker-red lipstick.

SKANK

My first thought is that if you're going to go to all the trouble to vandalize company property and risk the wrath of Wyatt, you might as well commit to the damn act with something as permanent as paint. Hell, even Sharpie would last longer. My shock is quickly overtaken by flattered disbelief that I've managed to piss someone off *this much* without shooting so much as a single second of film.

Sometimes, I impress even myself.

I'm at a loss about who would've left such a lovely message for me... until I see the imprint of lips, where my admirer kissed the glass with that same, hateful shade of red, and abruptly realize there's only one person on earth who had access to this dressing room and also has cause to loathe me with such passion.

"Hey, I heard you were here— oh, shit."

I turn to look at Wyatt, who's come to a full stop just inside the doorway, his expression twisting in anger. His blue eyes drift over to mine, full of anger and apologetic concern. "Helena left a parting message for you, I see."

"Yep. Nice of her."

"I'll have someone come clean it up." He takes a few steps into the room, so he's standing close by my side. He rubs the back of his neck, clearly tense. "I should've known she'd done something like this. She showed up here earlier, wasted out of her mind, making a huge scene about how she wanted the part back, that we couldn't replace her... I had to have her escorted off the property."

"Jesus." I stare at the deep shadows beneath Wyatt's eyes. "You look tired, Hastings."

His lips twitch. "Do you have any idea how much work goes into producing a movie?"

"Not really, no."

"Well, you're about to find out." He grins at me. "Come on, let's go find Sloan. I'm sure he wants to talk to the whole cast as a group before we start shooting. You can leave your bag here, you won't need it."

"I'm supposed to stay put, though — someone's coming to take my measurements."

"That can wait."

"But I don't want to get in trouble on my first day—"

"Baby." His grin widens as he heads for the door, shaking his head in amusement. "This is my movie. I make the rules around here. If I say you're good, *you're good*."

"Oh. Right." My cheeks flame as I drop my bag on the couch and trail after him, eyes fixed on his broad shoulders. Wyatt's laid-back nature makes it easy to underestimate just how important he is around here. He's so boyish, I often forget he's closer to Sloan's age than mine.

"Hey, Wyatt? Can I ask you something?"

"You're cute when you're nervous," he calls back to me.

I scowl as I follow him. "I'm not nervous."

"Just spit it out."

"I was just wondering... I have this friend who does makeup. She's actually worked for AXC in the past, on that weird werewolf show you guys put out. And I was thinking... or I guess I was *hoping* you might be able to pull some strings and..."

He stops walking, brows lifting. "And... give her a gig on this movie?"

I nod, feeling foolish. "Yeah."

He stares at me for a beat. "First of all, the werewolf show isn't that weird."

"It's pretty weird." My voice drops to mimic the narrator of a horror movie trailer. "Boy wolves, more haunted by the acne craters on their faces than the craters of the moon that controls them... Girl wolves, contending with two monthly curses, both of them bloody..."

Wyatt laughs. "You're terrible."

"I know."

"This friend... is she any good?"

I nod.

"And having her there with you on set will make you happy and complacent and listen to all my directions without question?"

I smile. "Sure. If that's what you need to tell yourself, *sure*."

"Uh huh." He sighs, reaches into his back pocket, and pulls out a business card. "Give her this. It's got a direct line to my assistant on it. Have your friend send over her information and we'll see if we can get her paperwork filed before we ship out to Hawaii on Thursday."

"Really?"

He shrugs. "It's no big deal. Told you before, that's how this industry works — it's all about who you know."

"Still... Thanks, Wyatt. I really appreciate it."

"Don't get all mushy on me, Firestone." He starts walking again, making his way down the hallway until we've left the dressing rooms behind.

"I'm not mushy," I growl.

"Uh huh." He slows until I fall into step beside him. "Hate to break it to you, but I see straight through that prickly exterior you put up."

"Oh, like you're some tough guy?" I snort. "You're a big softie, we both know it."

"Have I ever pretended to be anything else?"

I think about that for a moment. "No, I guess not. It's just rare to meet someone in this town who doesn't have an ego so large they can't fit through standard door frames without ducking. Especially someone with your... pedigree."

"Pedigree? What am I, a prized schnauzer?"

"You know what I mean. Your family. Your career. The films you've worked on... It's a little intimidating, you have to admit."

"*You* don't seem all that intimidated by me," he says dryly, turning down another corridor. "In fact, you seem quite happy to give me a hard time every step of the way."

"Well, *I'm* an asshole," I volley back, only half joking.

"True enough."

I shove him on the arm. "You're not supposed to agree with me."

"One thing you can count on with me, baby — I'll always tell you the truth, even if it's a truth you don't want to hear."

"Okay. Then tell me this one." I suck in a breath as we come to a stop before a door marked STAGE 13 in blocky, bold white letters. "How intense is today going to be?"

"Most of the intense stuff comes later, when we do the island scenes on the beach. That's where the real drama and tension of the film happens. The next few days are all fun special effects stuff, don't worry." He pauses. "I just hope you don't have any objections to getting wet."

"Why?"

He reaches out and grabs the doorknob, eyebrows arching in amusement at the look on my face as he throws it open and ushers me inside.

"That's why," he says cheerfully

My eyes widen.

Stepping through the doorway, I expect an empty soundstage; instead I find myself at the scene of a plane crash. I'm staring at a mid-sized jetliner, its metal body twisted horribly out of shape as though it's actually plummeted thirty thousand feet out of the sky and landed in the shallow waters of a coral reef somewhere in Indonesia's infinite chain of islands. The plane is resting inside a massive water pit, two times the size of an Olympic swimming pool. The cockpit is divided from the cabin and the tail is skewed at a strange angle, as if in the first stages of sinking. Debris floats on the surface of the pool — seat cushions, suitcases, all manner of personal items. A bright red life raft, likely the one I'm supposed to pull Grayson's waterlogged body into during one of our first scenes together, drifts gently across the water.

Sloan is standing next to a control panel, accompanied by three men I've never seen before. From their black-on-black outfits and the way they keep gesticulating at the plane, I assume they're special effects designers, testing out their handiwork for Sloan's approval before filming. This is confirmed a few seconds later when they trigger a button on the panel — fake smoke streams into the air and trick flames shoot out the sides of the twin propulsion engines, which spin like massive deadly blades. Another push of a button makes the body of the plane shudder violently in the pool and begin to sink, manipulated by underwater metal cranes I can't quite make out from here.

"Water scenes tomorrow," Wyatt says, sounding like a little kid at a theme park as he walks toward Sloan. "Don't worry, you won't be inside the fuselage while it's on fire. Apparently it's against the Screen Actors Guild rules to burn actresses alive. Shame, really."

"You're hilarious." I roll my eyes and follow him, gulping at the impressive show of flames. They hiss and crackle as the jet is fully submerged, coming to rest on the bottom of the pool with a crash of waves. "Seriously, are we sure that's safe?"

"Safe? Of course it's safe!" Sloan interjects as we reach the group. "These boys here are the best in the business. They've done the sets for my last three films — stuff way more complex than a simple plane crash scene. You're in great hands, Kat, I promise."

I smile weakly, watching as one of the black-clad men hits a series of buttons on the panel to raise the plane back up to the surface, plumes of water streaming off the metal fuselage as it slowly emerges and straightens into a less-twisted shape, the tail and cockpit aligning back with the cabin like giant puzzle pieces. It's eerie — like watching a crash happen in reverse.

"Is the rest of the cast here yet?" Sloan asks, turning to face Wyatt, his eyes gleaming behind his spectacles. He's sipping another god-awful green juice, but at least he's not barefoot today.

"They should all be here within the hour."

"Excellent. I'd like to start running through the choreography for the airport scenes as soon as everyone's here. I've mapped it all out, but it's going to take more than a few practice runs before we can actually start filming. Anyone heard from Dunn? Is he on his way in?"

Wyatt shakes his head. "Chances are, he's still in bed with a bimbo. I'll have my assistant call him, get him moving—"

"I'm here, actually." The warm, male voice cuts through the air like a whip, accompanied by footsteps as Grayson makes his way over to us. Sloan and Wyatt both turn toward the sound of his voice, but I stand there paralyzed, feeling tension saturate the room. Climbing into the mangled wreckage in the water pit before me suddenly seems far less terrifying than turning to face the man at my back.

I force my feet into motion, pivoting around when it becomes impossible to avoid his arrival any longer. Looking gorgeous as ever in a plain black t-shirt and jeans, he's standing with Sloan and Wyatt, listening to something Sloan is saying, but his eyes are locked on me. I'm instantly caught up in his intent green stare. I want to evade it, to look away, but I can't; I'm trapped like a fragile-winged creature in tree sap, reduced to an artifact in iridescent amber the longer his eyes hold me captive. In those long, dragging seconds, I see a thousand thoughts swimming in the space between us.

We need to talk about the other night, his eyes communicate wordlessly.

No, we really don't, I fire back with a jerk of my chin.

Sloan's words die out; I think he realizes he's lost the attention of his actors. In my peripheral, Wyatt crosses his arms over his chest and looks slowly back and forth between Grayson and me, his expression wary.

"Kat," Grayson says lowly. "Can I talk to you alone for a second?"

"Actually, I have to go get fitted for my costumes now." The excuse is out of my mouth before he's even finished his question. "Right, Wyatt?" I look at him, desperation in my eyes. "Right?"

"Right," he agrees slowly.

With a relieved sigh, I start heading for the side door.

"That's fine, Kat," I hear Grayson call after me, sounding amused and frustrated at the same time. "We'll be spending all day together. I'm sure I'll find time to talk to you between takes."

My breaths are ragged as I slip out the door and head for the sanctuary of my dressing room, where Helena's mocking lipstick message greets me like an old friend.

CHAPTER EIGHT

"Eight rock-hard inches."
- *An exaggerator.*

To my everlasting relief, Grayson is wrong about us finding time to talk between takes. After getting fitted for my costume — a gauzy blue sundress and impractical platform espadrille sandals, just the thing you'd want to be wearing during a plane crash — I'm sent to hair and makeup, where they apply approximately forty-eight products to my face in an attempt to give me a "natural, no-makeup look." Successfully transformed into Violet, I head back on set and find the rest of the cast and crew gathered for Sloan's twenty-minute pre-shooting pep talk.

I meet the actors playing Susan and Frankie, the ill-fated husband and wife who've hired me as their au pair during a summer holiday in the islands, as well as an adorable seven-year-old actress named Amy with bright blonde pigtails, who's taken on the role of their onscreen daughter. Several other extras playing plane crash victims, pilots, and flight attendants are milling about, already in costume. Sloan wraps up his speech with a moment of communal silent mediation to "channel the cast's energy into one form" and from that moment on, we're so busy I barely have time to think, let alone talk with Grayson about things better left unacknowledged.

Sloan is a cerebral director, who sees the movie play out inside his head long before he starts rolling film, so we spend the entire morning walking through the crash scenes step-by-step on a set built to look like the inside of an airport terminal. The designers have also created an impressive, full-scale plane interior for in-flight scenes, complete with rows of reclining seats, round thick-paned windows, plastic tray tables, and overhead storage bins.

Time ticks by slowly as Sloan moves around the space, adjusting our props and repositioning our bodies as though we've never done anything so complex as take a seat inside an aircraft before. Grayson seems less than enthused — I hear him grumble something about it "not being the first time he's ever boarded a plane, for Christ's sake" under his breath, making the two extras standing closest to him giggle.

I try to act attentive as we are told where to walk and how to stand and when to move, but by midday, I feel an edgy sort of intensity settling under my skin. I'm eager to prove myself. To show them all that, second-choice or not, I'll play this part better than Helena ever could've. To actually start *making* this damn movie instead of walking through it and talking it to death.

I sense a similar impatience from my dark-haired co-star; Grayson looks downright grumpy. Even Wyatt, standing in the wings, seems frustrated. I can tell we're all starting to wonder whether our director might have a few screws loose, when suddenly Sloan smiles like he's discovered the cure for cancer and claps his hands together in unbridled excitement.

"There it is!" He stares around the group of disgruntled actors. "You all look positively miserable. No — you look like a group of people about to board an airplane. Ill-tempered, impatient, and irritated things are taking too long. That shiny, first-day-of-filming enthusiasm has finally disintegrated!" He pushes his glasses higher up the bridge of his nose and heads for the massive camera on the tripod. "That means we're ready to film."

I've heard of method actors — I've never heard of method directors.

I roll my eyes at Sloan's tactics and hear a snort from Grayson's direction. Wyatt is shaking his head, but there's a small smile on his lips as the cameras finally boot up, the overhead lights flip on, and the black-clad members of the tech crew take their positions. I feel a bubble of excitement rise up inside me like helium as we all get into our places around the fake airport terminal like passengers waiting at their gate. My heart thunders against my ribs when a film assistant with a clapperboard yells, "Scene One, Take One!"

This is really happening.

Sloan's dedication to getting us into the right mindset may've been manipulative, but it's also pretty damn effective. It's easy to slip into character as the cameras finally start rolling. I let Katharine Firestone fall away and become the young, hopeful girl who's landed the job of a lifetime — a summer nannying position in the tropics, with a cute kid to look after and a family that seems too good to be true. A switch flips inside me and I stop seeing the set, the cameras, the PAs and prop managers waiting in the wings. I'm just a girl walking through an airport, suitcase wheeling along behind me, about to jet off on an adventure. Impatient to start my life.

I'm Violet.

The rest of the day flies by so fast, it's a blur in my mind. Over the course of the day, we do at least fifteen takes of the airport scene — who knew walking through a terminal could be so damn complicated? — before Sloan is satisfied. I lose count of the times we film the crash flight scenes. Even the man with the clapperboard is looking weary as he holds up the black slate for the last time and announces the double-digit take number.

I feel buzzed, almost drunk, when Sloan calls "Cut!" for the last time and orders us to head home for the night. For a moment, I just sit there breathing in and out, trying to regulate my heartbeat. The emotional turmoil of surviving a plane crash — not once but dozens of times in a single day — has left me shaky and drained, as though I really lived through a trauma.

It wasn't difficult to conjure real terror while sitting in my fake plane seat, which shook and rattled to simulate turbulence, with only a thin fabric belt across my lap separating me from free-fall. There's something disturbing about seeing flight attendants ruffled, their faces etched in lines of panic instead of that typical cool composure... something unsettling about watching air masks fall from the overhead compartment as the lights flash and the air around the plane seems to somersault forward... something terrifying about clutching the hand of the little actress playing my summer charge, shoving a yellow inflatable life vest over her bright blonde pigtails, all the while knowing she'll never make it out of the water...

It may be fiction, but the emotions it has stirred within me are quite real.

Ignoring the catered spread of sandwiches, soups, and salads they put out for the actors, I make my way back to my dressing room in a daze, absently noting that someone's finally cleaned Helena's lipstick from my mirror as I get undressed and return my costume to its zippered garment bag.

Only when I've wiped the makeup from my face and changed back into my own clothes does the adrenaline rush thrumming through my veins start to wear off. Grabbing my purse off the vanity table, I feel utter weariness start to sink into my bones. My bodily needs, suppressed for hours as I pretended to be someone else, return with a vengeance. I'm not sure what I require first — a bed, a bathroom, or a hot meal. Frankly, I'd be fully prepared to accept any of them.

I'm *not* prepared for what I encounter when I step outside my dressing room.

Grayson is leaning against the wall directly across from my door, arms crossed over his chest, hair even messier than usual, eyes half-lidded as he waits for me.

"Shit, Dunn, you scared me!" I say, heart pounding against my ribs. "What the hell are you doing out here?"

"Waiting for you."

"Listen, I don't know what you're expecting, but—"

"Kat," he says in a quiet voice that makes my heart clench. "Let me drive you home."

"What?"

He pushes off the wall and steps into my space. My mouth feels parched as he stares down into my eyes.

"Let me drive you home."

"Why?"

He shrugs. "Because I'd like to. And because I think, bullshit aside, you'd like that, too."

"I live, like, forty minutes from you," I point out. "We aren't exactly neighbors."

He doesn't say a word. He just stands there, waiting for me to make up my mind.

I sigh.

He's determined to talk to me about the other night — I suppose we might as well clear the air sooner than later. After all, I'll be spending every day with him for the next few weeks. I got lucky today, but it's going to be pretty impossible to keep dodging him. Especially once we're in Hawaii, and the cast dwindles down to just the two of us.

"Fine," I agree, too weary to fight him. "Let's go. But you'd better not kill me in the Porsche you bought to impress models."

"I don't drive a Porsche."

"Whatever," I mutter. "Just lead the way."

He smirks and starts walking. I glare at his back as we make our way toward the side door to the parking lot, stopping to say goodbye to Wyatt as we pass him in the narrow hallway.

"Need a ride?" Wyatt asks me. "I was just headed to your dressing room to offer to drive you back to your place. Or I can have one of the AXC drivers take you home — we have a service on retainer here."

"I'm taking her home," Grayson interjects. There's a

note of challenge in his tone, as though he's daring me to contradict him.

Wyatt's eyes slide to me. "Katharine?"

I nod.

Something indecipherable flickers in his blue eyes. "All right. I'll see you tomorrow, then. Sloan's going through the takes from today right now, but it looks like the airport scenes and interior flight shots are pretty solid. We should be able to get you two in the water tomorrow to start filming on the raft, so make sure you get some sleep tonight."

"Yes, Dad," I drawl sarcastically.

He smirks, but the humor fades out of his eyes when they move to Grayson. "Night, Dunn."

"Night, Hastings."

Neither of the men moves — they just stand there, eyes locked in some weird battle of wills I'm not entirely sure I understand. I'm not privy to whatever silent words they exchange, so I turn and start walking for the side door.

"I'll be outside, whenever you two finish eye-fucking," I call back over my shoulder.

Men.

I'm standing in the parking lot soaking up what little remains of the sunshine when Grayson finally catches up with me. It's gorgeous outside, especially after being on set all day — warm and windy, more like summer than an October evening. I've always found it hilarious that in Los Angeles we don't really experience fall — at least not the way they do in New England or up the coast — and yet one day every year, as if alerted by some unspoken signal, everyone in the city starts wearing layers and scarves and boots. Who gives a damn that there's been no significant alternation in weather patterns? Here, seasonal shift is dictated by fashion choice, not actual climate change.

"You ready?" Grayson asks, stopping to look down at me. He gestures at a sleek black sports car on our left. If it were an animal, it would be a lynx or a jaguar or another

123

deadly cat — low and lethal. "This is mine."

"I thought you didn't have a Porsche."

"I don't." He grins and walks around to the passenger door, pulling it open so I can climb in. "It's a Bugatti."

"It's a *deathtrap*."

"Just get in, will you?"

I scowl as I climb inside and allow him to close the door after me, strapping myself in and eyeing the complex navigational system. I'd sooner be able to launch a rocket into space than figure out how to start it.

"Thank god you had Ryder's car the other night," I murmur as he settles into the driver's seat. "I never would've gotten you home in this thing."

He glances over at me. "Oh, we're allowed to talk about that now?"

"Isn't that the whole reason you asked to drive me home? To discuss the other night?"

"Maybe I just enjoy your company."

I snort. "You spent all day with me."

"And yet, I'm not ready to say goodbye." He waggles his eyebrows. "What does that tell you?"

"That you make crap life choices."

He laughs, flashing a set of mega-white teeth. "It's a keyless ignition. You use this button over here." He punches his thumb into a shiny silver lever and the car purrs to life. "See? Not so space-aged."

"Speaking of space aged..." My lips twist as he pulls out into traffic, his darkly tinted windows concealing us from the paparazzi lurking outside the AXC gates. "Tell the truth, do your socks currently have stars and planets on them? Or are you changing it up, going for something a little more unique today — unicorns and rainbows, perhaps?"

His smile turns almost sheepish. "Hate to break it to you, but they're nothing exciting. Just plain black. I try to save the good patterns for the weekends — I only have a few pairs, so I have to pick and choose my days."

"You have a million-dollar car, yet a limited quantity

of patterned socks." I shake my head, baffled. "You're an enigma, Dunn."

"Glad I'm such a mystery. Now, tell me where I'm going."

I hesitate. Do I want Grayson to know where I spend my nights? Even the paparazzi haven't discovered my condo yet. It may be a shit-hole, but it's the only stronghold against this bizarre Hollywood world that I have left...

"Oh, come on. You know where I live," he points out. "Fair trade. I even promise not to stalk you."

Grudgingly, I give him my address. He pulls into the right lane and exits onto the highway.

"You know, you really didn't have to drive me," I say after a moment of stilted silence.

"I wanted the chance to talk to you. Figured, this way, you can't dodge me unless you actually hurl yourself into traffic." He glances over at me. "Don't do that. I refuse to stop on The 405, even if you change your mind. This car is not about to be slammed by some soccer mom in a minivan who's too busy yelling at her kids to pay attention to a car on the shoulder."

"Yes, that would be the true tragedy of me hurling myself into oncoming traffic. The *car* getting slammed."

He strokes the steering wheel lovingly.

I snort.

"Anyway." He clears his throat. "I felt like I needed to apologize. You know for..."

"The drunken dancing?"

He blinks slowly. "I *danced* for you?"

"Drunk," I confirm. "And naked."

"Jesus." The car swerves a little as he loses momentary focus, staring at me.

"Hey!" I bark. "Eyes on the road!"

Twin spots of red appear on his high cheekbones. It's endearing to see someone as cocky as Grayson embarrassed.

"Now I definitely need to apologize." His hands

125

tighten on the wheel. "I'm sorry about the drunken naked dancing. I don't even remember that part. Mostly, though, I'm sorry for making you take care of me and Ryder. I realize we were..."

"Shitfaced?" I supply. "Wasted? Blasted out of your minds? About as easy to herd through the streets of LA as two feral cats?"

"Exactly." He laughs. "Also, I vaguely recall getting into a brawl with your boss. Pretty sure I only remember that portion of the evening because there's a large bruise on my lower back... as though I got into a fight. A fight I *lost*."

"Yeah... that wasn't so great. Vince threw you into a pile of bar stools." I wince, remembering.

"Ah. That would explain the bruise. But why did I pick a fight in the first place?" His brows pull together. "I'm usually so affectionate and affable when I'm plastered out of my mind."

"You were, uh..." My voice drops low and the words come out so fast they slur together. "Defending my honor."

"What?"

I force myself to annunciate. "You were defending my honor. My boss didn't react well when I told him about the movie. He started yelling, grabbing my arm, shaking me... You stopped him."

He looks over at me, eyebrows raised, and grins at my scowling expression.

"And you're clearly pissed off about it," he says happily.

"No, I'm not."

"You are." His grin widens as my scowl deepens. "It's killing you that I did something nice, because it's harder to hate me now."

"It's not harder to hate you," I lie. "You got me fired! And it's a good thing I have this movie gig, because I doubt I'll be getting a job recommendation from Vince after the stunt you pulled."

"Kat, I seriously doubt you'll have to work in a bar ever again."

"Maybe I like working in a bar," I say just to be mulish.

He shoots me a look.

"Okay," I admit. "I don't like it. I won't miss it at all."

"So contrary."

"So cocky."

His eyes gleam. "Ryder won't shut up about you, by the way. He thinks you're pretty much the greatest person he's ever met."

"That's only because I bought him fast food at three in the morning. He's an easy mark."

"No, it was more than that. He thinks you're funny and badass."

"Badass?"

"His words, not mine." He laughs, but it fades quickly. "It was good to see him happy, though. He's been having a tough year, since his band fell apart. His fiancé Felicity was his songwriting partner, and he's pretty much been on a bender since she disappeared."

"That sounds rough. He seems like a nice guy."

"He is."

We're quiet for a moment.

"Listen..." I see his Adam's apple bob as his throat works. "I also want to pay you for driving us back to my place and buying us food and everything else you did—"

"No," I say flatly. "I'm not taking your money, Grayson."

"Why?"

"It was a favor amongst—"

"Friends?" he finishes wryly. "I thought we weren't friends."

"We aren't."

"Face it, Firestone. You've seen me naked. You've seen my dance moves. You've seen my solar system socks. There's no going back, now."

I laugh, despite myself.

We drive for a few moments, Grayson expertly

weaving through the light traffic, going well above the legal limit. We're making good time — we missed the worst of rush hour, getting out so late, but we're still at least five minutes from my place.

I figure it's now or never.

"Can I ask you something?"

He glances over at me. "No, I will not give you my autograph. Honestly, stop asking, it's getting embarrassing. "

"Hardy har har."

His grin is distractingly handsome. "You can ask me anything, Kat."

I glance out the window at the highway flying by. "Do you think this movie will be a success?"

"What do you mean?"

"I mean... you and me. Mostly just me, actually. Do you seriously think audiences will pay money to see me on the big screen?" I bite my lip. "I just have a hard time imagining it."

"Are you serious?"

"Yes."

"Kat, I think you're going to be amazing. I watched you today — the way you embody the character on screen, the amount of attention you give to Sloan, the dedication you offer to your craft... I have no doubt you'll be incredible."

I bite the inside of my cheek so I won't do something stupid, like burst into tears. I've never felt this way before — emotionally frayed. Jagged at the edges. As though at any given moment, someone will tug on a loose thread and this whole dream will unravel into nothing but another disappointing spool in the tapestry of letdowns that make up my past.

I've never been the girl who needs validation.

The world wants to be an asshole to me? That's just fine. I'll be a bigger asshole.

Fuck you, world.

Except this time, things are different. This time, I

actually give a shit what happens to this movie. To this character. To my future. And, abruptly, I'm clinging to my cavalier, cool-girl composure with nothing but my fingertips, praying no one looks too deep beneath my surface for fear they'll notice I'm barely keeping it together.

Grayson and I don't speak as we exit the highway and drive through the crappy neighborhood surrounding my condo, the Bugatti fitting in about as easily as a porn star at the Oscars.

"Up here," I say softly, pointing at the turn for my building.

We pull into my parking lot and my eyes lock on a truly horrifying sight.

"Oh, shit!"

"What?" Grayson asks, alarmed. "Paparazzi?"

"Worse!" I hiss, ducking low in my seat as we roll past the familiar bright green Cadillac parked outside my apartment. "It's my mother!"

"Shit," Grayson repeats.

"Don't *stop*, you idiot!" I smack him on the arm. "She'll see us!"

"Ow! Okay, okay, I'm going!"

I stay crouched down in my seat as he turns the wheel, feeling the slight bump of the tires over the curb as we pull back out of the lot onto the main road. My heart is thundering, my palms are sweaty, and there's a queasy, nauseous feeling in my stomach, the kind you get when you slam on your breaks and miss smashing into the car in front of you by barely a millimeter. A near-miss with death.

"You can sit up, now," Grayson says, smirking at me. "She's gone. Though I'm pretty sure she noticed the Bugatti peeling out of your parking lot."

I push into an upright position.

"I take it your relationship with your mother is..." He searches for the right word. "Complicated?"

"You could say that." I push a lock of hair behind

my ear. "Or, you could also say that she's a controlling, manipulative, former pageant mom gone mad with power, who now attempts to manage not only every facet of my acting career, but my entire life."

"Don't hold back." He laughs. "Tell me how you really feel."

"Hungry, if we're being honest. But I'd rather starve than go back there and face her." I sigh. "Just drop me off somewhere on the block up ahead, I'll kill time until she leaves and it's safe to walk back."

"I'm not abandoning you on some random street corner, Kat."

"The chivalrous card doesn't suit you, Dunn."

"I'm not being chivalrous. I just think it'll be a real pain in the ass if we have to re-cast your role *again* because you get mugged and murdered by drug dealers."

"This neighborhood isn't that bad," I protest. "It's *up and coming*. Apparently."

He looks at me skeptically.

"I'll prove it. Take your next left, at the light."

His expression is wary, but he follows my directions. After a few moments, we reach our destination — my favorite park in the area, complete with running trails, a thick copse of trees, and a small, muddy-banked pond, built a few years back in an attempt to break up the grid of condominiums and convenience stores with some much-needed green space.

"Wait here," I say, pushing open my door and hopping out before he can object. I jog across the parking lot to the food truck idling by the sidewalk and order two burritos, loaded with rice, beef, beans, and cheese. I fork over a few bills and seconds later they're in my hands, radiating warmth through their aluminum foil wrappings like mini nuclear reactors. When I slide back into the passenger seat, I find Grayson staring at me with both brows raised.

"What?"

"You cannot eat those in here. I just had the leather interior detailed."

"First of all, I'm not planning to eat both of them. One of them is for you — or, it *was* for you, until you decided to be a prick." I roll my eyes. "Secondly, why would I want to eat in your stupid car? Drive."

He's still muttering under his breath as I direct him out of the parking lot, around a bend, and deeper into the park. We pull to a stop beneath a stand of giant eucalyptus trees and walk to a picnic bench looking over the pond. It's getting dark — the park is empty of its usual daytime strollers. In another hour the sun will set entirely, but for now there's nothing but dusky twilight shining across the calm water's surface.

I pass Grayson his foil-wrapped burrito and we settle in on the bench. He takes a massive bite and groans.

"Oh my god," he says around a mouthful of rice.

"Told you." I smirk and unwrap mine eagerly. I'm starving.

We both devour our dinners in record time, leaning back in satisfaction when the last bites are gone. Grayson burps loudly.

"*Cute*," I drawl.

"Damn, that was good."

"You're welcome."

"I can't remember the last time I had a burrito. My trainer has me on this damn high-protein, gluten free, dairy free diet. It makes me want to die."

"That's the cross you bear for baring your six-pack on the front of every magazine in the country."

"Not *every* magazine." He grins. "Only the fitness and health ones."

"So, what you're saying is, if I'd snapped a picture of you eating that burrito, I could've sold it to TMZ for thousands while simultaneously ruining your image as a fitness freak?"

131

He nods. "Thank god you're not smart enough to think ahead."

"Ah, well. There's always next time."

"Next time?" He waggles his brows. "There's gonna be a next time?"

"Don't ruin it, Dunn."

He sighs and looks around at the park, as though seeing it for the first time.

"It's pretty here. Peaceful. Do you come here often?"

"Sometimes." I shrug. "I run the trails around the pond when I'm feeling masochistic. I used to feed the ducks but last time I brought them my stale bread, a lady yelled at me. Apparently Los Angeles citizens have become so intense about their condemnation of gluten, even mallards aren't allowed to enjoy the occasional carb."

"Doesn't surprise me at all." His eyes are on the weathered old chess board by the edge of the pond. Usually, there's a duo of old-timers occupying the stools, maneuvering the pieces from dawn until dusk, but the seats are empty at the moment. "You ever play?"

"Not since I was little."

The last time I played chess was against my mother's second husband, the investment banker. For the two years he lived with us, he insisted we play a few times every week. I used to think it was his way of attempting to bond with a child he shared neither common interests nor biological correlates with. Looking back, I'm pretty sure it was just his way of seeking sanctuary from Cynthia's company, if only for a few hours.

"Come on," Grayson says, pushing to his feet. "Let's play."

"I'm no good at it."

"Neither am I." He holds out a hand. "Come on, Firestone. What are you afraid of? That I'll kick your ass?"

I stand, ignoring his outstretched fingers. "No. I'm afraid I'll drown in the river of your tears that pour forth when I whoop your ass."

"Those are fighting words. This means war."
"Oh, I'm *so* scared." My words drip sarcasm. "I mean... famous actors are *known* for their stunning intellect and savage logic."
"...Said the famous actress."
"I'm not famous."
"Soon-to-be famous, then."
"I don't know about that."
He pauses and his eyes grow serious. "I do, though."
I swallow and turn away, to break the tension. "Are we playing, or what?"
"Bring it on."
We settle on the stools, staring at each other over the cracked, chipping chessboard. The small side-drawer barely wrenches open, warped from too many days left in the elements, but we manage to get the pieces out and make quick work of setting up the board. When the pawns and rooks and kings and castles are all lined up in sequence on the black and white squares, our stares lock.
And hold.
The board seems to shrink down to nothing. He's far too close. I can smell his aftershave, see the tiny scar on the edge of his jawline, make out the flecks in his irises like gold glinting at the bottom of a stream. Quite suddenly, I realize that perhaps this game was a bad idea. In fact, perhaps agreeing to do anything with Grayson Dunn outside the parameters of work was a bad idea.
His voice is so soft, it makes me shiver — but not with cold.
"Your move."
I drop my gaze to the board in front of me, so I'll stop looking into those eyes that make my head spin, and push a pawn out two spaces at random. He moves his knight, in a far more strategic move, and I force my mind to empty of everything except the board in front of me. There's no way I'm going to let him win.
He wins anyway.

I put up a valiant fight — our game stretches on for nearly an hour, before he manages to checkmate my king with his rook — but in the end he defeats me.

"I like playing games with you, Kat," he murmurs as we make our way back to the car later that night, when the sun has faded into full darkness and the moon has peeked out from behind the hills.

I wish I'd realized then — he wasn't just talking about chess.

CHAPTER NINE

"Maybe someday, when the timing is better."
*- A guy who could not be less interested
in ever seeing you again.*

    Grayson drives with none of his earlier haste on the way back to my condo. In fact, it's almost as if he's pushing the pedal as lightly as possible to preserve this moment. For once, we aren't fighting or snapping or trying to outwit each other with banter and insults. A rare peace has settled over us, since we played chess in the growing darkness at the edge of that muddy pond, and I must admit, it feels rather nice.
    Cynthia's green Cadillac is blessedly missing from the lot as we roll to a slow stop in front of my blocky condo complex. Unbuckling my seatbelt, I grab my purse off the floor and reach for the passenger handle without looking over at him.
    "So, I guess I'll see you tomorrow."
    "Kat." He says my name in a terrifyingly soft voice that demands my attention more absolutely than any shout or scream or curse ever could. "I know you probably don't want to hear this, that I probably shouldn't say it... but I had a great time with you. In fact, I had one of the best nights I can remember in I don't know how long."
    "You should get out more."
    "I get out plenty." When our stares meet, there's something dangerous stirring in the depths of his. He's looking at me with those startling green eyes — eyes in which I once saw nothing but shallow self-obsession, yet now seem to contain a whole, unfathomable universe.

I can't breathe, when he's looking at me like that. I bite down on the inside of my cheek and my hands fist so tightly around the strap of my bag, I feel my nails cut small crescent moons into my palms.

"Well, maybe you're not getting out with the right people," I say, trying to lighten the mood. "I'm a delight. In case you haven't noticed."

"Trust me, I noticed." He's still far too serious for my liking. "You'll probably think this is a line, or a gimmick, or yet another chameleonic attempt at altering myself to suit the situation, but the truth is, I like being with you, Kat. I like that you're not starstruck, or clingy, or trying to change me into someone I'm not. You already think the worst of me, so there's no pressure to impress you."

I snort.

"I'm serious," he says in a tone that confirms it. "I can just be myself with you. I can eat a damn burrito and pay chess and spend all evening staring at a distractingly pretty girl, and not one moment of it feels fake or forced."

My heart is pounding. My composure is spread so thin, it's nearly evaporated.

"Don't get all girly on me, Dunn," I retort. "It was a burrito, not a declaration of marriage."

"That's twice, you've bought me dinner."

I shrug. "Who's counting?"

"I am." His eyes narrow. "Next time, it's on me. No exceptions."

I open my mouth to say something snarky, but he cuts me off.

"And yes, there will be a next time, Firestone. Get over yourself."

"Fine. But this doesn't mean we're friends or anything."

"Oh, of course not." His lips twitch. "That would be terrible, actually getting along with the co-star you'll be spending every waking hour with for the next three weeks."

"God-awful," I agree, laughing to cover my nerves.

"Atrocious."
"Reprehensible."
We both grin. He strokes the slight scruff along his chin in a thoughtful gesture.
"Though, I feel obligated to point out, I make an excellent friend."
My nose wrinkles in doubt. "Really?"
"Really." His head tilts. "Admittedly, all my friends are of the male variety. You would be my first ever female friend. But that would make you a trailblazer. A trendsetter, even."
"You really think a lot of yourself."
"You know me so well. It's like we're already friends." He leans forward into my space a bit, and I feel my heart lurch in response. "Come on, Firestone. I dare you. Be my friend. No more bullshit."
"Why are you so determined to make this happen?"
"Why are you so dead-set against it?" He leans farther across the center armrest, words intent. "You hated me from the first day we met, long before I ever gave you a good reason to. You feel like finally telling me why?"
Do I feel like telling him that I spent nearly a year in love with him as a pre-teen, penned him a mortifying love-letter describing my deep affection, and ultimately got my heart smashed to bits in front of our entire cast when he and his friends decided to read every flowery, fawning piece of prose out loud? Or that, ten years later, I was still so pissed off at him, I couldn't see straight when he had the nerve not to remember doing it?
Hmm, let me think...
"Not really, no."
His arm lifts to brace against the headrest of my seat. He's frighteningly close, leaning into me until his face is all I can see.
"Unless..." His eyes flicker down to my mouth for a fraction of a second. My heartbeat kicks into overdrive. "You're worried you can't handle being *just* my friend."
"Don't kid yourself."

"Then tell me why we can't at least try to get along."

"Fine!" I throw my hands up in defeat, willing to agree to anything if it'll stop his invasion of my space. I don't think my heart can handle any more arrhythmias without giving out. "Fine, we can be friends."

"Great!" He pulls back. "I'll see you tomorrow, then."

I'm out of the car before he can say another word, pulling in deep gulps of night air as I practically run up my limestone walkway. I slide my key into the lock and bump my hip against the door, trying to focus on the sound of my neighbors screaming at each other through the thin-walled condo next door. That way, I don't hear the sound of his car idling by the curb, waiting for me to make it safely inside, or the echo of his words, still ringing in my mind.

There's nothing I can do to escape the weight of his eyes on me though. Even after I've slammed my door shut between us, closing myself inside the haven of my shitty apartment, I can still feel them burning holes into my back, as though they've scored into my flesh and laid waste to some secret part of me, deep down where no one can see.

I lean back against the door and slide down to the ground, staring unblinkingly at the white wall of my living room as my mind turns over memories of a cracked chess board and twilight gleaming on the surface of a pond and messy black hair and, more than anything, the tangled constellation of stars inside a set of endless green eyes.

Unless you're worried you can't handle being just *my friend*, his voice mocks.

I press my eyes closed and rub my temples. It's nearly nine; less than twelve hours until I see him again. Less than half a day to compose myself into something resembling professional and aloof and unaffected.

I am so fucking screwed.

***

The town car appears like magic the next morning. I manage not to face-plant as I climb inside this time, but I'm no less jittery or nervous as Ignacio, the AXC chauffeur, cuts through the morning traffic and turns into the studio gates for the second day in a row. The butterflies in my stomach are relentless beasts, swarming as I enter the soundstage and head for my dressing room. I half expect Grayson to jump out at me every time I round a corner or pass a particularly shadowy doorway.

After he dropped me off I tossed and turned for hours, attempting to tune him out of my thoughts, but there was no suppressing him. Well past midnight, exhausted from rolling fruitlessly around beneath my blankets, I shoved out of bed, stalked into my bathroom, and chugged down a double dose of NyQuil to send myself into a drug-induced drowse. It probably wasn't the best choice to self-medicate, but I was desperate for some shut-eye — desperate to escape him, even if only for a few unconscious hours.

In the bold light of day, under-caffeinated and still foggy-headed from the aftereffects of the medicine, I'm wishing I'd just pulled an all-nighter.

I open the door to my dressing room and stop short when I see it's already occupied.

"God, what happened? Did you run out of coffee? Get hit by a bus? Switch to a cheap drugstore concealer brand?" Harper grimaces at me from her spot on the plush couch along the wall. "Seriously, you look half-dead."

"Just the pep-talk I needed. Thanks, Harper." I collapse beside her on the cushions and glance in her direction. "What are you doing here?"

"Didn't Wyatt tell you?"

"Clearly not, or I wouldn't be asking."

She's practically quivering with excitement. "I got the gig! I'm doing makeup for *Uncharted*, starting today. I'll be helping the full studio team they already have in place here, but when we're in Hawaii it'll just be me and one other woman named Cassie who, to be honest, seems a bit uppity about me scooping the job out from under her... but all's fair in love and contouring, am I right?"

Her giddy expression falls a bit when she catches sight of my flat one. "Why aren't you excited? Don't you want me to be here with you, on set? I thought you were thrilled about me coming to Hawaii. Girls' trip, remember?"

"Wooooo. I'm excited. See?" I make a half-hearted attempt at jazz-hands. "I'm sorry, Harper. It's not you. I'm just exhausted. Barely slept last night."

"It shows," she says dryly. "What kept you up? Not the tabloids, I hope. Honey, you can't let yourself get upset over anything they print in those awful magazines. Everyone knows it's total bullshit."

"I haven't seen them, actually. And I wasn't at all worried about what they were printing until you said *that*." I sit up a bit straighter. "What's in them?"

She flushes red. "Oh. Nothing you should concern yourself with."

"Harper."

"Seriously, it's not a big deal."

"Just tell me. I'm going to see it sooner or later — might as well be sooner."

Resignedly, she pulls out her smartphone and clicks the internet icon to open her web browser. A few quick keystrokes later, I'm staring at a celebrity gossip website capped with a bold red headline.

DUNN IS DONE! THE MEGA-STAR DITCHES EX, FINDS LOVE WITH NEW CO-STAR

The headlines only seem to worsen, the father down the page I scroll.

ON FIRE FOR FIRESTONE: WHO IS HOLLYWOOD'S NEW IT-GIRL? WE'VE GOT THE SCOOP!

And worse...

KAT HAS CLAWS! GRAYSON'S NEW GIRL LASHES OUT AT HELENA. INSIDERS TELL ALL!

And worse still...

PUTNAM PREGNANCY SCARE — HELENA ALONE, ABANDONED...AND EXPECTING? DETAILS INSIDE!

Harper snatches the phone back before I can read any more. "Seriously, don't worry about it. Who reads that shit anyway?"

"You do, for one." I lean back against the cushions with a groan. "Plus just about everyone with a computer in every developed nation in the world. Other than *that*..."

"Since when do you care what people think?"

"I don't." I crack open one eye and glance at my best friend. "You don't think Helena is really pregnant, do you?"

"God, I hope not. That girl drinks like a fish. If there's a fetus in there, let's hope it has a fully developed liver."

"Not funny."

"It was a little funny." She stands up, grabs my hand, and drags me to my feet. "Now, come on. Let's make you beautiful for the cameras. We only have an hour to get you ready to film and to be truthful..." Her nose wrinkles. "We're going to need absolutely every second."

"And the hits just keep coming..."

I drag my feet as she leads me over to the vanity table, but I can't deny I'm happy to have a friendly face with me. Once I get two cups of coffee in my system, I'll be back to normal.

Or, as normal as my crabby, curmudgeonly, cynical self ever manages to be.

***

"I'm so wet."

"Under almost any other circumstance, I might think you were coming on to me, Firestone."

"Gross. Let's keep it PG-13, shall we? This isn't a porno."

"What can I say?" Grayson grins through chattering teeth. "I'm a walking X-rated film."

"You *do* look like something out of a wet t-shirt contest."

"Oh stop — if I had any warm blood left in my body, I'd be blushing."

141

"Ah, yes, you're the king of modesty." I snort at the absurdity of my own statement, then look pointedly at his abs, which are on full display through the thin white t-shirt plastered to his body like a second skin beneath the water. "You know, I can almost see the outline of that burrito you ate last night. Maybe you should hop out, do some sit-ups..."

"Oh! Now you're asking for it!" He swims over to me, drags me into a headlock and dunks me fully beneath the water.

I surface, gasping for air, and squirm out of his grasp. Ducking back under, I take in a full mouthful of water and spit it straight into his face. He splutters. I see the flash of retaliation in his eyes as he reaches for me again, and quickly paddle out of reach with a squeal.

"Children," Wyatt calls from dry land in a faux-stern voice. "Please, control yourselves."

Grayson and I both snicker like scolded kids at a pool party. The brief moment of levity helps distract from the fact that I'm slowly becoming hypothermic, the longer we tread water between takes.

We've been shooting ocean scenes all morning — struggling underwater after the crash, swimming as the flaming plane wreckage slowly sinks in the background, scrambling into the inflatable red life raft as the engines explode into a ball of flame. After breaking for a quick lunch and makeup reapplication — even Harper's industrial waterproof mascara was no match for three hours in the pool — Sloan ordered us back in the water.

The rest of the day is even more physically demanding — Violet spots Beck's lifeless body floating on the surface and does her best to rescue him. We've done about six takes of me pulling Grayson into the raft using all the strength left in my limbs, pounding on his chest until he coughs up water, scanning helplessly for other survivors as the light fades and the current carries us away...

They'll make good use of the bright green screens around the pool in post-production, working their special effects magic to make it seem like we're adrift in the middle of the South Pacific, instead of a ten-thousand square foot warehouse in downtown Los Angeles. The shallow end of the pool where we've been treading isn't particularly deep — if I stretch my legs fully, the tips of my sandals just manage to scrape the solid bottom. The water temperature, however, is a click above freezing.

It laps at my skin, which is nearly as blue as the gauzy sundress floating around me like a fabric cloud. My fingertips turned to prunes several hours ago, my hair reeks of chlorine and I'm well past the point of exhaustion, despite the brief reprieve we've been given while Sloan repositions the cameras to capture a different angle.

My arm muscles ache from pulling Grayson's body inside the inflatable raft. I've made several pointed comments about his weight under my breath, but he seems to think I'm complimenting rather than insulting him. He laughs like a child whenever I scowl in his direction.

He's taking our newfound friendship quite seriously. There's been not one smoldering glance or inappropriate comment out of him all day, for which I am eternally grateful. He wasn't lying when he told me he cares about this role. As soon as they call "Action!" the playful man I know fades away and he's fully focused on embodying Beck... Which means I've actually been able to focus on playing Violet, instead of ogling his muscles.

"All right, we're ready for another go!" Sloan calls from behind the camera. "Let's run the rescue scene once more, then we'll call it a day. I don't want you to catch pneumonia, or you'll be of no use to me tomorrow."

Grayson catches my eye. "You up for one more?"

"Yes, but I think I need something a little more nutritional than a burrito for dinner, if we're going to be doing this all over again tomorrow."

"Sorry, you're on your own for fuel tonight, Firestone." His grin is wicked as his eyes slide to the edge of the pool.

"I've got other plans."

I follow his gaze to the buxom brunette PA, lingering on the outskirts of the film crew. Her ample chest is visible behind the clipboard she's clutching. She giggles and waves when she notices Grayson's eyes on her.

Something unpleasant churns in the pit of my stomach, but I swallow it down as I swim over to the raft. Why should I care that Grayson is boinking some slutty PA on the side?

He's nothing to me.

Less than nothing.

I repeat those words to myself over and over as Grayson assumes his face-down, floating position — limbs spread-eagled on the surface, one shoe missing. My silent mantra continues as they announce the take number, as the slate slams down, as the cameras start rolling.

He's nothing to me.

He's nothing.

Nothing.

My insides feel as numb as my fingertips as I heave him up into the raft, nails digging into his sides like spears. I'm not sure what expression is on my face as we film the rest of the scene, but Sloan seems pleased when we finally wrap for the day.

"Kat, you were perfect, that last take," our director calls. "Perfect balance of fear and fatigue."

Is that this uncomfortable feeling swirling around inside my stomach?

Fear?

I don't let myself look too closely at my own emotions as I hop out of the raft without a word to Grayson and make my way to the edge of the pool. When I reach the side, a large, calloused hand appears in front of my face.

I glance up and find Wyatt there, his eyes guarded as they hold mine.

"Violet, you're turning violet."

"Are you quoting *Willy Wonka and the Chocolate Factory*?" I laugh up at him. "Really?"

"It's one of my all-time favorite movies."

"Which version?"

"The original, of course." He scoffs. "As with all things, remakes rarely measure up. Imitation can't compete with authentic. I don't care about special effects and CGI. There's something to be said for the magic of something completely original. Not the same old watered-down, recycled, regurgitated ideas thrown together and branded as *unique*."

"You're an old soul, Hastings. Anyone ever tell you that?"

"Maybe I'm just old."

"Thirty-five isn't *that* old."

"Said the twenty-two-year-old." His lips twitch. "How reassuring."

I brace my elbows on the edge of the pool. "Almost twenty-three."

"An old maid." His fingers wag. "Come on, baby. I mean it, you're turning blue."

My pruned-up fingers lock with his and he heaves me out of the pool so easily, you'd think I weighed no more than a feather. My feet have barely settled on solid ground when his arms go around me, wrapping a fluffy black towel over my shoulders until I'm fully cocooned. I sigh gratefully as warmth starts to sink back into my chilled skin, as the safe feeling of Wyatt's strong arms wrapped around me cancels out that strange, uneasy sensation Grayson's after-hour antics stirred up inside my stomach.

"Thanks," I whisper against Wyatt's chest as his hands run over my back through the towel, big and steady, smoothing the fabric until most of the water is absorbed. Swamped by a sudden wave of tiredness, I sway toward him like a plant reaching for the sun, seeking heat and light. He doesn't push me away; his hold only tightens, perhaps recognizing that I've reached my physical and emotional limits.

"I've got you, baby."

My eyes slide closed as he holds me. Wyatt's arms feel solid and safe, after all day in the pool. Like stepping through your front door after a week away, seeing all your belongings, breathing in that indescribable, intangible aroma that announces to all your senses, *you're here, you made it, you're home.*

"So! That's a wrap on Day Two." Sloan's voice shatters the moment. I step hastily out of Wyatt's arms and turn to face our director. Grayson, wrapped in a black towel of his own, lingers a few feet away, his eyes moving slowly from me to Wyatt. I can't read a damn thing in his expression — and I'm not sure I want to. I force myself to look at Sloan instead.

He takes a sip of his kombucha and smiles faintly. "I'm off to review footage. Tomorrow is our last day here in the studio, so we all have to be fully focused. Once we're on location, it'll be much harder to superimpose green screens, so I really want all the main CGI stuff wrapped before we leave. Get some sleep; I'll see you bright and early."

Grayson doesn't hesitate. As soon as we're dismissed, he turns on a heel and heads for the brunette in the corner. I watch them walk off set and bite the inside of my cheek so I can focus on a physical ache, the only kind of pain I know how to handle with any success.

I force myself to look away from the sight of his retreating back, directing my focus up at Wyatt. He's already watching me, a knowing look in the depths of his eyes.

His voice is soft. "You need a lift?"

I shake my head. "I'll catch a ride with Harper. She doesn't live too far from me."

"All right. I'll see you tomorrow, Katharine."

"You're never going to give up calling me that, are you?"

"I told you — the original is always better than a derivative." His lips twitch up into a smile. "You won't convince me otherwise. And, anyway, I'm older and therefore much wiser, so I think that means you have to listen to me."

"If you think *that's* true, you're so old you're getting senile."

He grabs his chest. "Shot to the heart!"

"You'll live." I roll my eyes. "Night, Hastings."

Turning away, I hug the towel closer around my body as I head for my dressing room. I'm weary down to my bones. And yet, even after I strip off my wet costume and change into a pair of warm, dry jeans and a sweater, I can't quite shake the chill running through my veins every time my mind wanders to thoughts of dark hair and a sardonic smile and infinite green eyes…

Eyes currently fixed on a set other than mine.

Harper's waiting for me in the parking lot, her car idling quietly by the curb. Earlier, when she informed me we'd be hanging out after filming wrapped for the day, I didn't argue. If she's avoiding going home, there's probably a good reason. Best guess is, she's fighting with Greg again. I figure she'll tell me when she's ready to talk about it — likely after two or three glasses of Riesling have loosened her tongue.

I slide into the passenger seat with a sigh.

"Tired?" she asks.

"Exhausted."

"I was going to suggest we go out for dinner somewhere, but why don't we just grab Thai takeout instead? We can rent a movie and gossip about all the shit that happened on set today. You wouldn't believe what you hear when you're working behind the scenes — I got the full scoop on the next season of *Vampire High*, which they're filming on the stage next door, and let me tell you, it's going to be bloody fantastic." She grins. "Get it? *Bloody.* Because… vampires."

"Life rule: if you have to explain why a joke is funny, it's not a good joke."

"Bitch."

"Cow."
"Are you in, or not?"
"You had me at Thai takeout."
"I knew we were friends for a reason."

***

We're almost to my door when we're ambushed.

Someone steps out from behind a withered hedge, scaring me half to death. Harper reels back, nearly dropping our bag of takeout to the sidewalk as the figure stomps closer, her high heels rapping against the pavement like gunfire.

"Finally. I've been waiting over an hour."

My fear that it's a stalker or paparazzo is replaced by horror as I realize the intruder is someone far, far worse: my mother.

"Funny, I didn't see your car in the lot." My voice drops lower. "And we checked before getting out. *Twice.*"

"Yes, I parked around the corner."

"How very covert-ops of you, Cynthia." I narrow my eyes. "Though, generally speaking, if you have to lie in wait for someone like a Bond-movie villain, it's probably a sign they don't want to speak to you."

"I'll just wait inside," Harper says smoothly, plucking the keys from my hand and making a quick exit. "Nice seeing you, Mrs. Firestone."

The front door closes soundly behind her.

"I had no choice but to *lie in wait*, as you so charmingly phrased it." Cynthia's eyes narrow on me. "For some reason, every time I've come by in the past week, you seem to be out of the house."

"What a strange coincidence!"

"I'm sure. And the reason your phone goes straight to voicemail whenever I call you?" Her pause is frosty. "Also a coincidence?"

"You know, I've been meaning to check with my wireless provider about that. LA is just notorious for dead zones. They should really look into it."

"Katharine. I'm growing tired of this game. I shouldn't have to track you down like bail bondsman hunting a skip."

An eye-roll is the only response I offer.

"I'm your agent — what if I had something important to discuss with you?"

I'm your daughter — what if I want to discuss something other than business?

I push the ridiculous thought away and ask the pertinent question. "What are you doing here, Cynthia? What could be so vastly important that you'd resort to subterfuge just to tell me about it?"

"I've been completely stonewalled by the people in the AXC office. Apparently, the executive producer on the project told them not to give me any information unless it was specifically approved by you first." She sounds thoroughly pissed. I can imagine why — there's nothing that bothers her more than thinking she's out of the loop, or that I'm slipping out of her control. "Do you know anything about that? Why would Wyatt Hastings make such a request?"

Because he knows you're a witch. I smile to myself as I think of my hulking blond Viking. *Because he wants to protect me from everyone, but especially from you.*

"I don't know, Cynthia. I'll have to ask him." I cross my arms over my chest. "Anything else?"

"Anything else? What do you mean, anything *else*?" she hisses. "This situation is out of hand. I can't manage your career if I'm not kept appraised of everything happening with the *Uncharted* project."

"Let's see… We have one more day of filming at the studio tomorrow. We leave for Hawaii the following morning. I'll be gone for two weeks, three at the most." I tilt my head. "There — consider yourself appraised."

"You were just going to take off to Hawaii without speaking to me?"

"Well, I *was* going to ask if maybe you could water my plants while I'm gone but, based on the tone of this conversation, I'm guessing you'd probably be more likely to slaughter my succulents than nurture them according to a slow, regimented watering schedule."

"Was that supposed to be a joke?"

"I never joke about succulents."

Her glare intensifies. "I am at my wit's end with you, Katharine."

"I wasn't aware you had any wits to begin with."

"More jokes." Her long-nailed hands curl into fists. "Don't you have any appreciation for everything I've done to get you this role?"

"*Excuse* me?" My heart picks up speed and I feel the first sparks of anger flare to life inside me. "You didn't get me this role. Wyatt got me this role. You had nothing to do with it."

"I got you in that audition room. Without me, you'd never have met your precious *Wyatt*," she spits. "Without me, you'd be nowhere. You'd be *no one*."

"Everything I am, I am in spite of you," I say very quietly. "Not because of you. *Never* because of you."

"I gave you everything!"

"All you gave me was a near-lethal teenage eating disorder, thanks to your constant comments about my weight, along with a flawless ability to dodge older men's wandering eyes — and hands — thanks to your third husband. Or was it your fourth? There've been so many, they all start to blur."

I see the hit coming, but I don't duck or flinch back or even move to block her. I let her clip me full across the cheekbone, and as the eye-watering ache of pain radiates through me, some small, stubborn part of my soul cries out in triumph at my flawed show of defiance.

The therapist I used to see, before I told him to fuck off, would call this "textbook passive resistance." He'd also call it unhealthy — but that's probably why I fired him. Hearing his double-talk about my "backwards struggle to free myself without actually making any strides to break from my mother's hold" week after week grew tiresome.

And expensive.

I pull in a steadying breath and, when I speak, my voice reveals none of my anger.

"If that's all, I'll be going now," I say calmly, gaining twisted satisfaction from the blotchy redness of her face as she struggles for control. "My Thai food is getting cold."

"Get back here!" she calls as I head up the walkway. "Katharine!"

I don't look back.

"Goodbye, mother. Always a pleasure."

CHAPTER TEN

> "No, nice guys don't always finish last!"
> - A girl who has never dated a nice guy in her entire adult life.

I slam the door behind me, hauling deep breaths in through my nose and out through my mouth. When my heart rate has returned to normal, I turn and find Harper staring at me, a bowl of takeout extended in my direction.
"Drunken noodles?"
"Hold the noodles," I mutter, heading into the kitchen and pulling a bottle of vodka from my freezer. "The *drunken* part, on the other hand, I'm perfectly okay with."
"You should eat something."
"She ruined my appetite."
Harper sounds stern. "You barely touched your lunch. And you did a lot of physical activity today. All those water scenes..."
"Harper. You're harping."
"Fine. More for me." She lifts a set of chopsticks to her mouth, but her chewing doesn't quite mask the sound of disapproval that escapes as she watches me slug back two shots of vodka in quick succession. Ice cold and unflavored, they go down almost too easily.
"So." Harper casually sidesteps, positioning herself between me and the counter to block my access to the bottle. "Let's talk."
"Subtle." I snort.
She ignores me. "Can you believe you actually spent all day filming with Grayson Dunn? The man is

distractingly good looking. I caught myself drooling more than once."

"He's much less attractive up close."

"Really?" she gasps.

"No. Not really." I hop up on the counter, so my legs dangle, and lean back against the cabinets. "He's even more beautiful. It's annoying."

"Annoying because now you're supposed to be his *friend* and nothing more?" She smirks. "If I didn't know better, I'd say you were happier when you hated him."

"You're not wrong."

"Do you think it's because you... you know..."

I raise my brows.

"Because you have feelings for him?" she finishes weakly, tucking a strand of blue hair back behind her ear.

I scoff. "Don't be ridiculous."

"Why is that ridiculous? You're spending lots of time with him. You're playing lovers onscreen, for goodness sake. You'll be filming sex scenes with him in less than a week's time. I don't think it's such a stretch of the imagination to consider you might develop real feelings for the man."

"It's ridiculous because he's not any man — he's Grayson Dunn." I reach deftly behind her and grab the vodka bottle. Before she can stop me, I've poured myself another shot and thrown it back. "He's incapable of loyalty, of love, of anything resembling an adult relationship."

"How do you know?"

"I just know."

"I think you're being pretty hard on him without any real cause for it."

"Trust me, he'd be the first one to agree with me." I screw the cap back on the bottle and hop down from the counter, stumbling a bit on the dismount. The shots have started to kick in. "Grayson has no interest in dating. In fact, at this very moment, he's probably balls-deep in that busty brunette PA."

153

"I've seen the way he looks at you, though," Harper protests. "I think, if it was you, maybe he'd be different."

"And by *different* I assume you mean monogamous."

"Yes."

"That, my dear, is exactly the kind of delusional thinking that leads to getting your heart broken. You think you can *change* a guy, that he'll be *different* with you, that you'll finally be the one to *tame* him… and before you know it, you're alone in your underwear at nine o'clock on a Saturday night, crying to Adele songs, eating ice cream straight from the gallon, and wondering what the hell is the matter with you that you fell for such a goddamned man-child, after he explicitly warned you not to."

Harper blinks. "I think you really need to get laid."

"Yeah, well, I've been a bit busy, what with getting cast in this movie, and the constant filming, and dodging the paparazzi, and trying not to fall for my goddamned idiot of a co-star."

"So you admit it — you could fall for him."

"Harper, honey, half of America has fallen for him. He's hot. He's cocky. He's charming." I roll my eyes. "Point is, I'm not getting involved with him. All a guy like Grayson is good for is meaningless, mind-blowing sex."

"And that's a bad thing because…?"

"Because casual sex only works under certain conditions. It's one thing to shamelessly exploit a random stranger for the occasional screaming orgasm. It's another thing entirely to sleep with someone you interact with in close proximity." I sigh. "If I started sleeping with Grayson… and working with him every day… and playing his star-crossed lover in front of the cameras…" I shake my head. "No good would come of that."

"You're probably right," she concedes. "But what about your other man?"

"I wasn't aware I had another man."

"Wyatt."

My eyes widen. "Wyatt is *not* my man. He's not even my type. We've been over this."

"Yes, we've been over it... and yet, I still don't understand it."

"What's not to understand? He's my friend. He's my employer. He's thirteen years older than me. I don't see him like that."

"Have you tried?"

"What do you mean?"

"I *mean* have you actually allowed yourself to think about Wyatt in that way."

"You talk about attraction like it's a choice. You can't always control who you're attracted to, Harper."

"I think that's a cop out."

"Well, *I* think it's bullshit to listen to some computer program that tells you who to love instead of actual things like pheromones and chemistry and a real goddamned connection, but you don't see *me* shoving *my* opinions down *your* throat, do you?"

My words come out far sharper than I intended. I want to snatch them back as soon as they're out of my mouth, but it's too late. A horrible stillness settles over the room as I watch my best friend's face go completely white, her turquoise hair a stark contrast against her skin.

"Harper... I'm sorry. I didn't mean that."

"You did, though." Her eyes are welling with tears.

I've never felt lower in my life. "I'm just hungry and overtired and pissed off about Cynthia and annoyed about Grayson and his new girl..." I shake my head. "I'm an asshole. I realize that."

She nods and brushes at the corner of her eye.

"I need you not to hate me." I pause. "I need you, period. You're my person. You get that, right?"

"I don't hate you."

"What can I do to fix it?"

"For starters, eat something." She pushes a takeout carton in my direction. "You being drunk tonight and hungover tomorrow isn't going to help matters."

I open one of the Thai cartons and use my chopsticks to grab a small dumpling. Under her scrutiny, I pop it into

155

my mouth and chew, tasting nothing.

She nods in approval. "Now, you're going to listen to me."

"Fine."

Her gaze drops to my chopsticks. "And you're going to eat at least one more dumpling."

I roll my eyes, but don't argue as I wield my chopsticks once more to fish another dumpling from the carton.

"I know my relationship with Greg isn't perfect. I know it probably won't end in marriage and babies and a ride off into the sunset like I'm the heroine of some ridiculous romance novel. I *know* that." She sighs. "But at least I try. At least I haven't given up. Honey, you don't even put yourself out there anymore. I worry about you. It's not normal to close yourself off so completely."

"I'm not closed off," I lie. "I date. Sometimes."

"Who do you date?"

"I dated that guy I met at the gym. Pablo? Paolo? Who cares what his name was, the sex was good and he made a mean chicken piccata."

"Your gym membership expired two years ago."

"Okay, but I also dated Michael."

"Michael?"

"You remember, the guy who used to live in the unit next door before the screaming couple moved in."

"You mean the neighbor with the good weed who'd occasionally get you high and fuck your brains out?"

"That's the one."

"*That's* not dating," she counters. "Dating involves a meal. Perhaps some conversation."

"We'd get the munchies and order pizza after, sometimes."

"Romantic." She rolls her eyes. "You never date. And it's not because you don't have the option. There are guys who would kill to take you out for a nice dinner, hold your car door open, notice that you're cold when you're strolling along the boardwalk and offer you their jacket…"

I make retching sounds until she punches me in the arm.

"Laugh all you want, but you're missing out on an opportunity for love. You've gotten so good at being alone, you don't know how to let anyone in, Kat."

"I like being alone."

"I know you do. But do you really want to be alone *forever*? When you see your life ten, twenty, thirty years down the road... are you single? Or is there someone by your side? Someone to hold you when you're sad and the world feels too fucked up to comprehend? Someone to stroke your hair and tell you it'll all be okay, even when it won't? Someone to father your children, and peel the potatoes while you slice the carrots, and take pictures of you looking cute for your Instagram account so you can make all those dumb bitches you went to high school with jealous?"

I scoff. "Yes, because *that's* the sign of true romance."

"Whatever. You know what I mean." She sets her bowl in the sink and runs the tap. "You're terrified to like someone who might actually be good for you. You talk yourself out of people before you ever give them a chance. You have all these bullshit rules about *types*... but I think we both know you're just fabricating excuses not to date guys you could actually have feelings for."

"Maybe my *type* is just *asshole*."

"Or maybe you're protecting your heart at any cost."

"Maybe I'm not protecting myself from them. Maybe I'm protecting *them* from *me*. You ever think of that?"

"You talk about yourself like you're toxic," she says softly. "Like you're poison, and you'll kill them if they get too close to you."

My voice is so quiet, I'm not sure whether I'm talking to Harper or myself. "Maybe I am."

"Honey, that's just not true."

"Oh, but it *is*." I look at her and see sadness and stark worry in her eyes. "I'm fucked up. Damaged goods. What the hell kind of man would want someone like me? Some guy with a savior complex, whose heart I would break in the long run? Or, the alternative, someone with a penchant for emotional messes, who would leave me even more of a train wreck when he walked away?"

"There's a third kind of man you're not considering."

"All ears, Harper."

"You say you're poison. I disagree — but, for argument's sake, if you're right..." Her eyes narrow. "Even the most venomous poisons on earth have antidotes. Even the deadliest strains are useless against someone with a natural immunity. Maybe you just need to find a guy who can withstand your specific brand of toxicity. Maybe you need someone strong enough to cure you without killing you both in the process."

"And what kind of man is that?" I snort "A *fictional* one."

"No." She shakes her head. "A soulmate."

"I'm sorry, I didn't realize you'd taken on the role of my shrink as well as my best friend."

"I'm not trying to shrink you. I'm trying to help you."

"You know what would help? Not talking about this anymore."

"Fine." She follows me into the living room. I try to ignore her as I turn on the TV and start flipping through channels, but apparently she's not quite done lecturing. "Kat?"

"Mmm?"

"Just remember — even if you're a little bit broken, it's okay. Without those cracks in that impenetrable outer wall of yours, I'd never see the beautiful person you are inside."

I keep my stare trained on the stupid nature documentary flashing across the screen so she doesn't see the tears filling my eyes. But a moment later, when her head lands on my shoulder and her hand twines with mine, squeezing so tight my fingers start to ache, I don't scoff or move away.

I just squeeze back.

***

"This is amazing."

"Uh huh."

"Kat! We are on a private jet." Harper barrels past me, eager to explore the AXC plane's luxurious interior. "Look! There's a full bar. And it's freaking catered, for god's sake."

"Uh huh."

"There are canapés, Kat! *Canapés.*" She sighs. "Please, muster up a little enthusiasm."

"I don't even know what a canapé is."

"Oh! They're—"

"I don't want to know. I like a little mystery in my life."

She huffs. "You're impossible."

"Apologies for not being totally psyched to get on a tiny-ass aircraft and fly over open water for six hours, after spending the past three days rehearsing a plane crash." I glance around — the cabin looks more like a lounge than a plane, with couch-like seats built facing each other along either side, a fully-stocked bar, a massive flatscreen television mounted on the wall, and a sleek coffee table, where trays of appetizers are waiting to be consumed. I sit down on one of the cream leather couches, buckle my seatbelt as tight as possible, and lean back with my eyes closed.

The previous day flew by in a blur, with Sloan pushing everyone to their breaking point as we finished in-studio filming. Grayson and I traded no more than a few words all day. I wasn't ignoring him, necessarily, but I also didn't go out of my way to converse. Then again, he was so busy trading sultry glances with the slutty PA, he didn't seem to notice my taciturnity while the cameras were off.

When they were on, we didn't have much chance to speak — most of the scenes we shot featured Beck unconscious, and Violet doing her damnedest to prevent him from bleeding to death due to the deep gash in his leg, all while keeping the raft upright as simulated waves crashed over the sides.

I found the hurricane scenes even more draining than the swimming ones — by the time we wrapped filming for the day, I was so cold and grumpy, I took Wyatt up on his offer for a ride home and promptly fell asleep on the way there. I woke in his arms as he carried me through my front door and tucked me into bed, barely stirring enough to murmur a thank you as he left.

Harper, bless her soul, helped me pack my travel clothes the previous night, so my only worry was setting my phone alarm to ping at six this morning — just enough time to scramble out of bed and make myself presentable for the ride to the airport. Ignacio seemed just as flustered by Harper's enthusiasm as I was, when we collected her from her apartment along the way, Greg waving sourly from the window as we pulled from the curb.

Now, I hear her pouring herself a drink at the bar, murmuring under her breath about mimosas in a giddy tone.

"Who the hell thought filming on location in Hawaii was a good idea?" I grumble to myself, pulling my belt tighter and jostling to get more comfortable on the leather couch.

"That would be me."

I crack an eye open to glare at Wyatt. He's grinning down at me without a care in the world.

"I hate you," I inform him darkly.

"Noted. Feel free to file a grievance with the union." He glances down at the seatbelt across my lap, so tight it's cutting off circulation to my legs. "You know, we aren't actually taking off for another twenty minutes. You probably don't have to strap in just yet."

"I'm fine, thank you very much."

He holds his hands up in a defensive gesture, drops his laptop bag on the couch across from me, and walks to the back of the plane to fix himself a drink. I hear him chatting with Harper, but I'm too anxious to focus on their words.

I hate flying.

Even before I was cast in this damn movie and forced to live out one of my lifelong fears, I've never been fond of hurtling through the air in a tin can with wings. I barely felt safe on the 787 jumbo jet Harper and I took down to Mexico for a girl's weekend a few years back; it's safe to say I feel even more uncomfortable on this tiny jet.

To my surprise, I feel someone settle in on the couch beside me and hear the telltale click of their belt snapping into place. I open my eyes to find Grayson has adopted an identical pose of anxiety — head leaned back, eyes pressed closed, hands clasped tight against his knees as though we're already coasting at thirty thousand feet.

"Nervous flyer?" I ask.

He looks over at me. "Just waiting for my brownie to kick in."

"Your brownie? As in…"

He grins. "It's medicinal. I have a note from my doctor and everything."

"Seriously? Pot brownies? What are you, a fourteen-year-old boy left unsupervised for the first time with his parents out of town for the weekend?"

"My parents live in San Diego, so no."

"Not really my point, Dunn."

"I don't even bake them myself — I buy them from a dispensary."

"I'm not sure if that makes it better or worse."

"Don't knock it till you've tried it. I swear, it's the only way to get through a long flight."

"I'll have to take your word on that."

"Or…" His eyes gleam. "You want one? I have an extra."

"Seriously? You have a surplus of pot brownies on hand?"

"I always come prepared." He reaches into the leather messenger bag at his feet and pulls out a small package, wrapped in parchment paper. "Here."

I unfold the wrappings and find myself staring down

at what appears to be a totally innocuous fudge brownie. It's not particularly large and, actually, it looks delicious. All I've eaten this morning is a stale microwavable waffle I scarfed down thirty seconds before the chauffeur pulled up outside my condo to bring me to the airport.

"They're pretty strong," Grayson says as I lift it to my lips. "Maybe you should only have half of one to start— Oh."

His suggestion comes too late. I've already popped the entire chocolatey square in my mouth and swallowed it down.

"Huh. Well, I'm sure you'll be fine." He grins. "High off your ass, but fine."

"Grayson!" I stare at him in horror. "Why didn't you warn me?"

"I tried!"

"Not hard enough." I groan. "Why do I ever listen to you? You're a terrible influence."

"Possibly. But, hey, think of it this way — you're not even worried about the plane crashing now, are you?"

"No, I'm far too focused on the extremely high probability that I'm about to make a total ass of myself in front of everyone onboard."

He chuckles.

"Don't worry, honey," Harper says, settling on the couch across from us. "We all already know you're an ass. Nothing to worry about."

"Thanks," I mutter dryly, accepting the mimosa she hands my way. Grayson winks at her as she passes another to him, and I try not to roll my eyes too hard when she flushes red in response.

Wyatt lifts his glass, a stout tumbler of amber liquid with a large round ball of ice submerged in it. "Cheers."

"What are we toasting?" I ask.

"To *Uncharted*!" Harper holds up her glass. "And a free trip to Hawaii."

"To clear skies, warm seas, and favorable filming conditions," Wyatt adds.

"To free time spent exploring the island," Grayson says, smirking. "And its many beautiful inhabitants."

"To not plummeting into the ocean on the way there," I grumble.

The three of them laugh. They think I'm joking.

I sip my mimosa and lean back against the cushions to wait for takeoff as the others chat about the hotel where we'll be staying for the next two weeks, a lavish resort on the north side of the island, flanked by white sand beaches and lush, green coastline. Wyatt used his AXC connections — and a large chunk of our production budget — to rent out the entire property, so we won't be bothered by fanny-packed tourists while filming on the coastal stretch surrounding the resort.

A few minutes before takeoff, Sloan finally arrives with two of his assistants following short on his heels — Trey, the PA I met my first day on set, and Grayson's busty brunette, whose name I've since learned is Annabelle.

Annabelle.

What kind of bullshit name is that?

After a brief hello, Sloan leads his posse to the back of the plane to go over the footage from the past few days. I try to hold back my scowl when Annabelle walks past, waving coyly at Grayson with three perfectly-manicured fingers, but I don't think I succeed because I catch Harper staring at me with a bemused expression seconds later.

"What?" I hiss at her.

"Nothing." She blinks innocently and sips her drink. "Nothing at all."

Perhaps I'm being paranoid — a side effect of my unfortunate brownie snack — but I doubt it. It's clear Harper hasn't abandoned her belief that my heart is somehow caught up in the man sitting beside me, his arm radiating heat as it presses against mine, his shoe nudging the side of my sandaled foot on the carpeted plane floor, his aftershave lingering lightly in the small slice of air between us.

And, *obviously*, that's not the case.

At all.

I shift out of his space, so we're no longer touching, and turn to look out the window as the flight crew arrives. The captain makes an announcement over the speakers, but I barely hear it. The world has gone a bit dull around the edges, like I'm watching events unfold from underwater, and as the plane begins to taxi down the runway, I find I'm experiencing none of my typical take-off anxiety.

"Told you," Grayson whispers, somehow reading my thoughts. He's so close I feel his warm mouth against my earlobe. "High is the only way to fly, kitten."

My throat convulses violently, swallowing down words I'd rather choke on than ever say out loud to him. It's a struggle to keep my eyes on the window, to stop myself from turning to look at him when he's this close to me and all my normal safeguards have been swept away more easily than pawns on a chessboard.

The plane picks up speed until the world goes blurry. With a lurch, we pull up into the air and, like magic, we're flying. Water droplets stream over the windowpane, which vibrates with the force of our ascent. The mechanical buzz of the plane wheels shifting back into place in the underbelly of the aircraft reaches my ears, but it seems somehow distant. All my focus is used up by the man at my side and the tilt-a-whirl world out my window.

I suck in a breath as we shift directions and the earth goes askew beneath us. Grayson's hand finds mine, his warm fingers stroking my palm in a soothing gesture, like I'm a skittish horse in need of a sugar cube.

"There," he says as we level out, the topsy-turvy ground replaced by clouds and clear blue sky. "The worst is over, now."

I nod in agreement, but as his fingers twine even more thoroughly with mine… as my heart starts beating inside my chest at twice its normal speed… as that giddy, nauseous feeling fills my stomach cavity… I can't help thinking he's wrong.

The worst isn't over.
The worst hasn't even started, yet.

***

"Shhh. You'll wake her."
"We're going to have to wake her soon, anyway." Wyatt's voice is wry. "We'll be landing soon."
"Well, I'm not finished yet," Harper murmurs, sounding distracted. "And once she wakes up, I'll never get another chance."
I blink my eyes open and take in the sight of my best friend, crouched over my cellphone like a convict with a pack of contraband cigarettes. Her fingers move at warp-speed across the screen, typing god knows what.
I sit up abruptly and groan as the world spins. The after-effects of the brownie I consumed are still not entirely gone from my system.
"Too late, it seems." Wyatt smiles at me. "How you feeling, Sleeping Beauty? Still stoned?"
"Ugh." I glare at him. "No, I don't think so."
I look around bleakly and see Grayson sprawled across the other end of the couch, head pillowed on his arms like a child, hair mussed, mouth agape as he snores lightly. The sight makes me smirk.
"Please, tell me someone got that on camera."
"Oh, don't worry — it's been thoroughly documented." Wyatt's grin widens. "Got some gems of you, as well. Did you know you talk in your sleep?"
"I do not!" I protest.
"You *so* do," Harper murmurs, still typing furiously. "You once recited the entire Gettysburg Address, I swear on my entire supply of MAC cosmetics."
"What are you doing with my phone?" I press a hand to my aching temple. "God, my head is splitting."
"Pot tends to have that effect." Harper doesn't take her eyes off the screen as she speaks. "Especially when you top it off with three mimosas, two finger sandwiches,

and an entire tray of chocolate chip cookies. You and Grayson gave a whole new meaning to the word *munchies* about an hour into the flight."

"Sugar coma," I mutter, deeply regretting my life choices. "Yep. That explains the headache."

"Hang on a second." Wyatt rummages around in his bag for a moment, then passes me two Advil tablets and a bottle of water. "Here. Take these, you'll feel better."

I smile weakly at him before I swallow down the pills and drain the entire bottle. The water instantly eases the pounding inside my head. "Thanks."

He winks at me.

"Can I please have my phone back?" I ask Harper.

"Just one more second..." She types another string of letters, then looks up with a smile. "Did you know you have a guy in your contact list named *Horny Harry*?"

"He's one of the Balthazar bouncers. And, that was me being nice. Trust me, if you'd ever met him you'd find that descriptor pales in comparison to his actual behavior."

"Okay, but there's also a guy listed as *Gym Steve*." She scrolls, looking vastly amused. "Plus, there's *Hot Phillip* and *Regular Phillip*. Oh, and *Lifeguard Boy*. Care to explain those?"

"Nope."

Her eyebrows arch. "There's also one number listed as *Coachella Sex* — pretty sure that's self-explanatory."

"Don't forget *Taco Bell Pete*," Wyatt chimes in. "That's my personal favorite."

"You guys are assholes."

"Well, not to be outdone, I changed my name to *Sex Pants*," Harper informs me merrily.

"Great. That won't be weird or anything, when you call me and strangers see *SEX PANTS* pop up on my screen." I glance at Wyatt. "I suppose you're in there, too?"

His lips twitch. "*Wyatt Albus Percival Wulfric Brian Dumbledore Hastings*, at your service."

"Nerd." I shake my head, laughing. "You guys suck."

"We also programmed in Grayson's number as *Jake From State Farm*."

"Great." I sigh. "Is the reorganization of my contact list all you did?"

I know Harper well. I doubt, given free reign with my phone, she restricted herself to harmless name changes.

"Maybe." She shrugs. "Maybe not."

"Hand it over."

She sighs and extends it toward me. "Fine. But just... keep an open mind."

I take my phone back with hesitant fingers and narrowed eyes. "Do I want to know what you've done?"

"Probably not." She laughs.

Filled with trepidation, I glance at my screen. It doesn't take much sleuthing to discover what she's been up to — there's a freshly installed application in the middle of my home screen.

"What the hell is *SingleMingle* and why do I have a profile?" I ask ominously. Toggling open the app, I see several pictures of me alongside a bio I would never write in a million years.

Fun-loving, upbeat girl seeking lifelong snuggle buddy who loves to laugh!

Sense of humor is a must. Bonus points for cooking skills and six pack abs.

There's an eggplant emoji at the end, for god's sake.

I'm not sure whether I'm more outraged by her description of me as *upbeat* or the insinuation the I'm looking for a *snuggle buddy*, whatever the hell that might be.

"Harper," I growl. "What am I looking at?"

"Your new profile! Did you know, this plane is equipped with high speed internet? During your little nap, I caught up on the past two episodes of *Vampire High* and then had a little free time, so I decided to use my powers for good and make you a profile." She sounds completely unapologetic. "You already have twenty-three matches! In an hour! I think that's a record."

"This isn't happening," I mutter darkly. "There's no way you did this."

"Oh, but I did. And you should be thanking me! Think of how many men you'll have lined up to date you by the time we get home."

"*Thank* you? For what — putting me up for auction on the Los Angeles meat market?"

I hear a muffled laugh from Wyatt — when my glare slides in his direction, he tries to disguise his amusement with a fit of coughing, swiftly looking down to hide his smile.

"So, Hastings, you think this is funny, do you?"

"Don't blame me." His blue eyes are twinkling with humor when they lift to meet mine. "I had nothing to do with it."

"You could've stopped her."

"In his defense," Harper interjects. "I was pretty determined."

I toss my phone on the cushion beside me. "Well, I'll never use the damn thing."

"That's all right." Harper shrugs. "I know your username and password. I'll just set up dates on your behalf and ambush you when you least expect it." A crazy glint creeps into her eyes. "You think you're meeting me for sushi? *SURPRISE*! It's actually Stanley. You think you're having drinks with me at the new cocktail bar downtown? *NOPE*! It's Ned waiting there instead."

I look at her in horror. "And you call yourself my friend."

"It's for your own good!" she insists. "You need to put yourself out there. Meet people. Make conversation. Make *love*."

Grayson sits up from a sound sleep, abruptly awake. "Who's making love?"

"Figures, *that* wakes him up," I mutter, shaking my head. "No one is making love. No one is doing *anything*." I glare at Harper. "I'm not going to meet my soulmate on a swiping app."

She glares back at me. "You never know."

"Soulmate?" Grayson scoffs sleepily. "Who the hell wants a soulmate?"

"Everyone!" Harper says, shocked.

There's a condescending edge to Grayson's smile. "Frankly, the idea of monogamy and marriage is so outdated. Loving someone *forever* was all well and good when the average life expectancy was thirty. Now, people live to well over a hundred. That means, hypothetically, if you meet the so-called love of your life tomorrow, you'll spend over *eighty years* with them. That is a long time to spend fucking the same person. I don't care how inventive you get between the sheets — eventually, things get stale. The spark fades. The shine wears off. And you're left with an iron-clad commitment to someone you feel virtually nothing for anymore, besides resignation and resentment for constraining your erections to a twice-a-month schedule, with the occasional birthday blowjob thrown in for good behavior." He shakes his head. "No thank you."

Harper sniffs indignantly, staring at Grayson like he's just informed her Santa Claus doesn't actually deliver presents to every child on Christmas Eve. "That's the least romantic thing I've ever heard."

"It may not be romantic, sweetheart, but it's true." Grayson rubs his bloodshot eyes. "People aren't meant to be together forever. And marriage just guarantees you're stuck with one woman for the rest of your damn life, trying to make her happy while convincing yourself that you wouldn't rather be banging other, younger, probably hotter women."

"That's awful!" Harper looks like she's about to burst into tears.

"Maybe it is." Grayson shrugs. "But it's also honest."

"And you're telling me all men think this way?" she asks, bottom lip trembling.

"Yep, pretty much," he says, stretching and pushing to his feet. "Damn, I'm starving. Are there any cookies left?"

He walks to the back of the plane in search of

sustenance, leaving the three of us in frozen silence. I wish I could say something to comfort Harper but, the sad truth is, I think Grayson is probably right, despite his indelicate phrasing.

Maybe humans simply aren't meant to love each other forever.

People don't like to talk about that possibility, because it makes them feel lost. Restless. Reckless. After all, if we cannot make marriage work, if we cannot find someone to create meaning in the chaos, to laugh with us as the rest of the world burns, to shelter us from the existential terror of adulthood and responsibility... what is the point of living at all?

If there is no one there to hold our hands as we grow old and wrinkled and useless in the eyes of youthful society... if there is no one to ward off the encroaching darkness as we near our expiration dates... if there is no one to hold vigil, brittle-boned and weary, as we meet our makers... What exactly is the purpose of this harrowing, horrible, heart-wrenching existence?

Are we no more than animals, driven by the basest biological impulses to procreate and populate this pale blue planet, in a universe so large our lives are no more than motes of dust in the unfathomable expanse of time?

I suppose Grayson could've been more tactful with his words, but I'd take truth over tact any day. In my experience, tiptoeing around something unpleasant doesn't make it any more palatable when the time comes to swallow it down. Better a man who is upfront about his desires from the start than one who reveals his true nature after vows are exchanged and contracts signed.

I have met these men — these closeted misogynists, bolstered by tradition and entitlement. I have watched my mother marry three of them, unhappily and unsuccessfully. I have watched my friends swoon for them, and say yes to their proposals, and start lives with them, only to find themselves divorced and disenchanted at the ripe age of twenty-six.

These are the men who talk about couples engaged in equitable relationships with unease lurking in their voices, just below that surface of bravado they brandish around like a sword to stave off their own insecurities.

These are the men who say things like "he's so whipped" and "she wears the pants" to cover their deep discomfort at the prospect of a partnership where both people are mature adults who make decisions together, who engage in co-dependence rather than feminine submission.

These are the men who expect the casserole on the table by six o'clock when they walk in the door, the quick peck on the cheek from an apron-wearing wife and a prompt, "How was your day, honey?" before falling into an arm chair in front of a television set.

These are the men who think making love is exactly three and a half minutes of pumping away in missionary position before rolling over, farting, and falling asleep as their wives crack open romance novels and dream of dashing pirates and lustful lairds.

This version of marriage — a throwback to the Donna Reed days of domestic subservience and strict gender roles — has long served as a justification for my commitment issues. I could never bend myself to fit such a marriage or such a man, no matter my love for him. I have no such flexibility of character, no ability to compromise my convictions for the sake of someone else, even if I loved him more than my next breath. I would break at the first attempt to shape myself into something more palatable for my husband's peace of mind.

And yet... it seems, some days, that I am alone in this thinking. That as I grow older, I watch more and more women diluting themselves from reckless wild-child to responsible wife-material. Even Harper, who believes in true love and soulmates and long-lasting passion, has settled for a man like Greg, who she knows will never make her happy, because she would rather be with him than be alone.

I swing wildly between blind conviction that I am right to rage against the utter banality to which those around me seem to resign themselves, and the unsettling fear that it is not them, those who have *settled*, who are so banal and boring.

Perhaps, instead, it is me who is broken.

Maybe that small, invisible slice of my DNA programmed for marital bliss and total, wholesome satisfaction at all life has to offer is simply absent from my biochemical matter.

I sit in crowded coffee shops and watch couples on first dates holding hands and staring lovingly into each other's eyes and feel utterly empty. Untouched by their cooing coexistence.

Harper says that I need to date, to *put myself out there*, because being alone is unhealthy… It would be easy to follow her advice — to swipe on *SingleMingle* until I find a nice boy with a white smile and a strong head of hair and settle down with him so the weight of the world is only slightly less crushing.

But I refuse to immerse myself in a relationship that is not right for me, simply so I have someone to go to the movies with on a lonely Wednesday night. Given the choice, I'd rather be a lonely wolf than a mindless sheep, stuck in a mediocre partnership.

So, as Harper huffs and sniffs at Grayson's stark honesty, I find a sordid sort of solace in his remarks. It's almost validating, to hear my worst fears about commitment voiced by someone else for a change.

"I can't believe he's so cynical." She shakes her head. "You'd never know it, watching his movies. He plays the romantic lead so sincerely…"

"He's an actor," I say dryly. "It's his job to convince you he's sincere."

"Still. I can't believe he really feels that way — that marriage is outdated, that all men are resentful of being tied down to one woman forever. It's terrible."

I shrug. "No more terrible than being trapped in a loveless marriage, I'd imagine."

Wyatt, who's been totally quiet up till this point, shifts restlessly in his seat. There's an amused twist to his mouth, but his eyes are serious when they meet mine.

"You're suspiciously silent, Hastings."

He laughs, flashing white teeth. "I was taught if you don't have anything nice to say, you shouldn't say anything at all."

"Oh, now I'm intrigued." I narrow my eyes. "Come on. Out with it."

He leans forward, eyes on mine, elbows on his knees. A strand of bronze hair falls into his face — I have the abrupt, alarming urge to cross over to him and push it back into place.

"Dunn made a valid point," he concedes. "We are living longer than ever. I'm in my mid-thirties; if I get married now and manage to keep kicking till I'm a hundred, that's still nearly three-quarters of a century to spend with a single partner."

"And you don't think you'd get tired of being with one woman, for all that time?" I ask, goading him. "You don't think, after all those years, you'd fall out of love or lust or whatever it is that makes people commit to each other forever?"

"It *is* a long time, I'll grant you that." His blue eyes hold mine steadily. "But even if I marry one woman, I won't be spending my life with just one woman."

Harper gasps.

"So you're saying you'd cheat?" My voice goes up an octave. "You condone cheating, but you're giving Grayson crap for *his* opinions?"

"I didn't say I'd cheat. You didn't let me finish." Wyatt's lips flatten into a serious line. His voice goes low, laced with passion. "Marrying one woman doesn't mean spending your life with one woman, because the funny girl you fall in love with on a first date at twenty-eight eventually becomes the fascinating creature you

173

propose to at thirty, then evolves into the stunning bride you wait for at the end of an aisle at thirty-two, and finally grows into the astounding mother to your children at thirty-four. By forty, she has blossomed into the businesswoman, the force to be reckoned with. By the time you're fifty or sixty or seventy or a hundred, she's been everything — your wife, your lover, your friend, your companion, your sous-chef, your travel partner, your life coach, your confidant, your cheerleader, your critic, your most stalwart advisor. She grows with you. She changes with you. She is always stable, but never stagnant. *She is not one woman.* She is a thousand versions of herself, a multitude of layers, an infinite ocean whose depths you plumb over a lifetime, whose many treasures and intricacies, quirks and idiosyncrasies you need an entire marriage to explore." His voice softens. "A man should be so lucky to spend his life *stuck with one woman* such as that."

He sits back, letting his words fade into silence, leaving me lost for words. Reeling. Inexplicably, on the verge of tears.

I blink rapidly, trying to compose my splintered thoughts into something resembling indifference, something pithy and witty and unaffected, but I can't think of a single damn thing to say. I can't breathe, can't move, can't do anything but stare into Wyatt's eyes and wonder, vaguely, if all my carefully constructed beliefs about marriage and commitment are total fucking bullshit.

"Oh my *god*," Harper wails, hiccupping as tears stream from her eyes uncontrollably. "That's the m-m-most romantic t-t-th-thing I've ever h-h-heard."

Wyatt's eyebrows lift.

"I just k-k-knew it!" She's so emotional, she's barely able to get the words out. "I k-k-knew there were s-s-st-still some good men l-l-left out there."

Wyatt silently passes her a tissue.

"T-t-thank you, Wyatt."

He stares at her in alarm. "I didn't mean to make you upset—"

"Oh, I'm not. Ignore me." She blows her nose loudly and excuses herself to use the bathroom. Or weep in private.

When it's just the two of us, I let my eyes drift to find Wyatt's.

"I think you broke her."

"I'm sure she'll recover."

"You really believe all that stuff?" I ask, heart thumping. "That love can last forever? That marriage isn't always doomed to fail, despite all the statistics?"

He doesn't hesitate even a beat. "Hell yeah, I believe it."

"So why aren't you married?"

"I'm waiting for the right girl."

"What if she never comes along?"

"She will."

"You seem awfully certain of that."

"I am."

"You could be waiting a long time."

He shrugs. "It doesn't matter how long I have to wait. Because I'm waiting for my wife. And, however long it takes her to find me, I know she'll be worth every second."

My eyes are prickling suspiciously again, so I turn and look out the window to distract myself from his too-blue eyes and too-sincere words. Wyatt is so genuine, so pure, so *good*, it makes me feel dirty and broken just being in his presence. Like I'll somehow poison his light with my darkness, taint his unfailing optimism with my deep cynicism.

"I think we're descending," I murmur, watching the jet's wings slice through the clouds. A few seconds later, the captain's voice comes over the speakers, asking everyone to strap into their seats for landing. I'm relieved when Harper returns red-eyed from the bathroom and Grayson settles back on the couch beside me, a cookie still clutched in one hand, because being alone with Wyatt was setting off strange, scary feelings inside me.

    I'm careful not to look at him again until we touch down on solid ground.

CHAPTER ELEVEN

"I NEED SOME SPACE."
- *A guy who's too nice to tell you
he hates the way you chew.*

 After landing, we disembark down narrow stairs straight onto a private runway where a pair of green, roofless Jeep Wranglers are waiting to take us to the hotel. Sloan and his PAs head for one — Trey and Annabelle are scribbling down notes on their clipboards as quickly as our beloved director can voice them. The rest of the crew, flying commercial, won't arrive until tomorrow morning — till then, we're free to explore the island and enjoy a brief respite, so long as we don't get ourselves killed or so injured we have to delay filming. Harper and I have plans to soak up as many rays as possible, in our spare hours.
 The humidity hits me like a wall as soon as I step out of the plane, squinting at the harsh glare of the sun against the tarmac. It's so hot, the blacktop steams. Water mirages float like illusory puddles at the other end of the runway.
 "Shit, it's hot," Harper says, stripping off her light cardigan and stuffing it into her small duffle as we make our way down the stairs single file. I stare at the space between Grayson's broad shoulders, at the strap of my duffle bag slung alongside his own. He insisted on carrying it for me, probably in an attempt to appear gentlemanly after his speech, earlier.
 "It *is* Hawaii," I point out, looking around at the lush green mountains rising up into the misty clouds. I feel like we've been transported to some craggy, prehistoric

era. Crystalline blue skies stretch for miles in every direction. It's like nothing I've ever seen before. "God, it's beautiful."

"It *is* Hawaii," Harper mocks.

I shove her lightly. "It looks like something out of Jurassic Park."

"Probably because they filmed it here." Wyatt grins over his shoulder at me as we hit the runway. "Though, if we stumble across any velociraptors, I'd suggest you run. Fast."

I roll my eyes. "Ever the film buff."

"Who's driving?" Harper asks, looking at the second Jeep.

There's a fraction of a second where Grayson and Wyatt stare at each other. Simultaneously, they burst into motion, racing for the Jeep like two teenagers given car privileges for the first time.

"Boys," I mutter, snorting as I watch them jostling for the driver's seat. Harper and I walk leisurely in their wake. By the time we get there, Wyatt's settled his hulking frame behind the wheel, relegating a somewhat put-out Grayson to riding shotgun. We scramble into the back, grinning like mad as the engine rumbles to a start.

The other Jeep is already en route, pulling through the gated exit onto the main road. Sloan is wasting no time getting to the hotel, eager to start micromanaging the staff so we have a green light for filming bright and early tomorrow morning.

"It's about thirty minutes to the hotel if you take the main roads," Wyatt says, watching as their taillights fade from sight. "But I say we take the scenic route. Any objections?"

At our lack of protest, he shifts into gear and we head through the gated tarmac exit. Foregoing the turn for the main highway, we head onto a winding, narrow road that snakes along the coast, at some points dropping down to a single lane as we pass endless stretches of white sand beach, rocky outcroppings, and more palm trees than I could ever count. Stray chickens wander the dusty shoulder like squirrels, but human sightings are few and far between. The stretch is undeveloped and largely unpopulated. Every now and then, we pass food stands offering shaved ice, giant seasoned shrimp, fresh coconuts and tropical produce.

"I could get used to this!" I shout over the rushing wind, hair whipping into my face. Harper throws her hands straight up into the air, like we're on a roller coaster, as Wyatt shifts into a higher gear and the Jeep flies down the road, kicking up dust behind us in a cloud.

Grayson flips on the radio and messes with the buttons until the familiar strains of a Wildwood song drift out the speakers. It's strange, hearing Ryder sing, now that I've met him in person. Just one more oddity of my new life as a so-called A-lister, I suppose.

We drive for about twenty minutes, singing to the radio and staring around at the island in awe. When we pass another food stand, nestled by an empty stretch of beach, Harper and I whine until Wyatt concedes to pull off onto the side of the road. As the boys take turns learning how to hack open a coconut with a machete from a local expert, Harper and I strip off our shoes and wander onto the beach, plunking down in the sand to eat our ice. I let the sugary sweetness dissolve on my tongue as I stare out at the azure blue ocean, my heart thumping in time with the steady waves of the Pacific that crash against the coast, and feel a deep peace settle into my bones.

"I can't believe we're here." I hear the awe in my own voice. "I can't believe this is my life."

"In case I didn't say it before — thanks for bringing me along for the ride. Some people in this business... they make it big and they forget where they came from. They get fancy new friends to match their fancy new life." Harper swallows a bite of ice. "Thanks for not being one of them."

"Well," I say quietly. "You know how I feel about fancy people."

She bumps her foot against mine in the sand. "Fancy is just another word for fake?"

"Exactly."

We both smile.

After a while, the boys join us at the beach, each bearing half a coconut with a straw poking out the top. Spoils of war.

We sit together, taking in the view, until my spoon scrapes the bottom of my empty bowl.

"Where are you going?" Wyatt asks as I rise and head for the water.

"I'm going to stick my feet in."

"Watch out for sharks!" Harper advises.

"I'm not going deep," I call back, rolling my eyes. "I'm not even wearing a bathing suit."

I'm almost to the water when someone sprints past me at top speed, shirtless and kicking up sand with each powerful stride. A laugh bursts from between my lips as I recognize Grayson's messy black hair a second before he hits the water, diving straight into the waves and disappearing from sight. Harper, stripped down to her lace blue bra and boy shorts, bolts in after him, giggling like a lunatic. I see a flash of purple hair against blue water and then she, too, dives out of sight.

I'm so busy watching for them to reemerge, I don't hear Wyatt coming until it's too late. He hits me like a freight train, strong arms scooping me up against his warm chest and cradling me close as he charges headlong into the waves. I shriek and struggle in his hold, recognizing his intentions, but it's no use.

"Hey! What are you doing? What—Wyatt!" I squawk in protest, but he pays me no mind. "Put me down! Don't you dare— WYATT!"

I feel the laughter rumbling through his chest, hear the sound of the crashing waves getting closer, and then, before I can even pull in a full breath, he's propelled us into the air with a great flying leap. We hit the surface still intertwined. I brace for a rush of cold, but it never comes

— the ocean is warm as bathwater as it closes around us.

He pulls me back to the surface and I'm laughing even as I gasp for air. I hear Harper giggling at me from a few feet away; Grayson is oddly silent as he watches Wyatt and me, but I don't pay him much attention. I'm too busy glaring at the grinning man before me. Wyatt's arms are still looped loosely around my waist, his long hair unbound from the leather tie he always uses to keep it back. A Viking at sea.

"You're so dead!" I hiss. My hands find his shoulders and I push down with all my strength in an attempt to dunk him under. He's so sturdy, my efforts are completely wasted. In fact, he just laughs harder as I try — and fail — to retaliate.

With a huff, I pull back. "I'll get you back when you least expect it, Hastings. Just you wait. You'll think you're safe and *WHAM!* Revenge will be mine."

"*Wham*?" he asks, light blue eyes brighter than the sea and sky all around us.

"Yep. *Wham*." I swallow hard.

"I've never been so terrified," he drawls lazily. "I don't know how I'll get through the day. I'll never sleep soundly again."

"First the plane ride, now this... You're really on my shit list. For the record."

"Oh, come on. I thought you wanted a swim."

"I said I wanted to *dip my feet in*."

His eyes drop down to my toes, visible through the crystal clear water, and he smirks. "And so you did."

I push away from him, laughing in spite of myself, and start trudging back toward the beach, wringing out my hair as I walk. I'm thoroughly soaked, my tank top and jean shorts plastered to me like second skin. When I reach the beach, I collapse back against the hot sand and close my eyes. The sun overhead beats down so strongly, I know I'll be dry in no time. And as I lay there, listening to the sound of the others laughing and splashing in the waves, I think this, right there — stretched lazily in the sunshine,

181

surrounded by friends, the whole horrid world reduced to wind and waves and warm sultry breezes, with sugar on my tongue and joy in my heart — is the closest to heaven anyone who's ever lived has managed to get.

***

We arrive at the hotel waterlogged and trailing more sand than an hourglass. The lobby resort is empty but gorgeous — floor to ceiling windows offer a spectacular view of the Pacific. There's a cafe equipped with an espresso machine and a full array of baked goods, a sleek bar area complete with a cute bartender and several rows of top-shelf liquor, and a concierge desk where a woman named Kelea is waiting to greet us with a tray of tropical drinks.

After brief introductions, she informs us we won't be staying in the hotel with the rest of the film crew and production staff. We sip our mai-tai cocktails as she leads us out a side door, down a landscaped path toward the beach.

"This way — it's not much farther."

We follow her down the sloping lawn in silence. The rum hits my empty stomach like a bullet. Harper and I trade excited glances as we step through a small row of palm trees and find ourselves staring at four private bungalows, practically on the beach itself, each with a thatched roof. Brightly colored hammocks are strung between nearby palms trees. A fire pit surrounded by massive driftwood logs sits at the edge of the sand, waiting to be lit.

"We reserve the villas for our most exclusive guests, to ensure you have the utmost privacy during your stay with us," Kelea says, smiling as she leads us to the closest hut. "The grounds are fully monitored at all times with video surveillance and armed security personnel — you're completely safe from outsiders, so long as you stay on the property."

I blink slowly, digesting that statement.

I've come to know Grayson so well, I sometimes forget

that he's one of the most sought-after celebrities on the planet. It wouldn't surprise me in the least to learn he has stalkers or overly-obsessive fans following him to filming locations, not to mention all manner of paparazzi seeking a money shot whenever he strips down to a swimsuit.

"The beach where you'll be filming is a five-minute walk down that way," Kelea notes, pointing past the bungalows to where the path disappears around a bend. "Now, let's get you settled in."

She uses a keycard to swipe open the door and holds the entry ajar so we can step inside. I can't contain my gasp as I stare around the villa. I hear a similar sound from Harper as she takes it in.

It may look like no more than a shack from the outside, but stepping through the doors you'd think you were in the finest of French mansions. Decorated in lush tones of cream and pale blue, the entire space boasts a provincial elegance, from the massive king bed to the elegant writing desk to the round, copper bathtub basin sitting in the middle of the ensuite bathroom. There's a box of chocolate-dipped strawberries on the duvet and a bottle of expensive champagne on ice in a bucket on the table.

Kelea picks up a remote control and pushes a button — two bamboo panels along the far wall slide apart to reveal a large flatscreen. I can't help but wonder, looking out at the beach twenty feet away, who comes on vacation to a place like this and wastes a single moment watching television.

"This remote controls everything in the villa," Kelea says, calling my attention back to her. "Absolutely everything is customizable to your exact preferences, from the temperature to the lighting to the window shades." She hits a sequence of buttons on the space-age looking remote to demonstrate. "You can order room service day or night, and book spa appointments, if you find yourself in need of any relaxation services. There is also an instant assistance button, which will connect you to our exclusive villa support staff, should you require anything from us."

My knees seem a bit weak as my eyes drift around. I must be dreaming. This, surely, is not my life.

Grayson and Wyatt hover in the doorway looking entirely bored, as if they've heard this same song and dance a thousand times before. Then again, they probably *have,* at every hotel they've ever stayed in. I'm relieved that Harper, at least, appears as stunned and starstruck by our lavish accommodations as I feel.

"Miss Firestone, you'll be in here." Kelea glances down at her phone to check something, then passes me the room-control remote with a smile. "If the rest of you will follow me, I'll show you to your own bungalows. Mr. Dunn, I have you in the villa to the left, Mr. Hastings on the right. Miss Kline, you're down at the end of the row."

"I get my own hut?" Harper says, sounding thrilled. "I figured I'd crash with Kat."

Kelea tucks a strand of glossy black hair behind her ear. "Originally, Mr. Stanhope was supposed to stay in our fourth villa, but he said he'd prefer to be in a suite at the main resort, with the rest of the film crew. The crashing waves keep him awake, sleeping this close to the beach."

"If I know Sloan, he's more worried about Grayson's late-night partying keeping him awake than he is the waves," Wyatt mutters as the three of them follow Kelea out. "Probably interferes with his yoga meditation sessions."

Grayson laughs, not denying it.

Harper waves dazedly at me as she disappears after them.

"Bye!" I call as the door swings shut with a soft click.

Alone for the first time since I left my apartment this morning — which seems an eternity ago — I revel in the quiet. A warm breeze stirs the floor-length white curtains covering the French doors — I pull them aside and a slow smile spreads across my face as I see the sky streaked every shade of orange, as the sun dips low over the water.

I have no idea what to do first.

Chug champagne? Devour dessert? Order room service? Take a bath in that glorious copper tub? Have an emergency dance party to celebrate how fucking awesome my life is, at the moment?

The only thing I do know, without a semblance of doubt is...

I could get used to this.

***

The four of us spend our first night out by the fire pit, passing around a bottle of rum in the ever-growing dark, laughing and talking until our voices run hoarse and the stars are shining overhead like stark, stagnant fireflies. There are no awkward silences, no stilted moments — Harper tells horror stories from her time doing makeup on different TV show sets, Wyatt lets slip several juicy secrets about industry insiders, Grayson has us all near tears when he describes his first time filming a sex scene, which evidently resulted in a case of blue-balls so severe a doctor was called in to consult.

It's past midnight and the fire's burned low — we're all too liquored-up and lazy to go find more driftwood logs to feed it. Harper is the first to turn in. Her eyes are drooping shut when she plants a sloppy kiss on my cheek and stumbles toward her villa, swaying like a hula girl and singing off-key. I watch to make sure she gets inside, giggling under my breath when she nearly hulas her way straight into a palm tree.

Wyatt doesn't outlast her by much. He pushes to his feet, looking stone-cold sober despite the fact that he's had more than a few swigs of rum. Probably because he's solid muscle.

I, on the other hand, am solid *drunk*.

I blink up at him, fascinated by the way his hair gleams gold in the light of the dying flames.

"Hastings!" I lament, clutching a hand over my heart. "Not you too!"

"Sorry, kids, this old man is off to bed. I'm beat." He stretches his arms over his head with a groan, his shirt lifting to reveal a taught slice of tan skin above the hem of his jeans. "See you bright and early. Don't get too drunk, Dunn, or you'll forget all your lines."

Grayson flips him off halfheartedly as he disappears into the dark. When we hear the distant thud of Wyatt's villa door shutting, he looks over at me with hazy eyes and grins crookedly.

"Thankfully, Beck is the strong silent type."

"True. There aren't many speaking lines tomorrow," I say sleepily, leaning back on my elbows in the sand and craning my neck to look up at the stars. "I think we're filming the scenes where we arrive at the beach and I stitch up your leg with fishing line."

"That'll be fun." Grayson grimaces. "I bet you're looking forward to sticking me with a needle."

"I doubt Sloan will let me use a real needle."

"Thank god for small favors."

I smile at the stars and listen to the sound of him taking another swig of rum. He extends the bottle in my direction again, but I shake my head. I've had more than enough.

He screws the cap back on and a second later, I feel him settle in the sand beside me. Our shoulders, hips, and ankles are pressed together, three indisputable points of contact that seem to echo through every atom in my body as we lie there, side by side, looking up at the infinite constellations overhead. They seem to be swimming, drifting in and out of focus like a camera lens shooting straight into the sun.

"Grayson?" I ask after a few minutes of silence.

"Kat?"

"Can I tell you something?"

I hear the slur in my words. A small, distant voice in the back of my mind is screaming at me — *shut up, shut up, shut up* — but I'm too far gone to listen. In my peripherals, I see his head turn to look at me. I keep my eyes on the stars.

"You can tell me anything," he whispers, so close his breath stirs the fine hairs at the nape of my neck.

"I'm sorry," I blurt. "I'm sorry I was such a judgmental bitch to you, when we first met. Sometimes I have a hard time letting people in, giving them a chance. It wasn't fair to you."

He's silent for a long time. I start to think he's not going to reply, but then he shifts a bit closer and his mouth moves, forming words I feel against my skin before they ever reach my ears.

"When we first met? You weren't a bitch at all. You were wearing purple overalls and braided pigtails."

My heart stops beating.

He remembers.

"You had the prettiest eyes I'd ever seen. So blue. So full of fire. Even back then, you had more passion in your pinky finger than most people ever muster up in their entire lives." He chuckles lowly. "Nine years old, and you could've conquered the whole damn world, given half a chance."

I've stopped breathing entirely.

"I remember looking at you and thinking, *shit*, if she's like this now, what's she going to be like when she's grown up?" He shifts closer still, voice going gentle. "I'm so damn happy I got to find out, Kat."

My eyes are burning, my throat is closing, and I'm having trouble formulating thoughts, let alone words. So I do the only thing I can — I shift onto my side, cheek pillowed on my arms, fingers digging into the sand. He's right there, a millimeter away, his gorgeous face backlit by the fire, which is slowly collapsing into ashes as we lie here, staring at each other. His eyes are warmer than the flame.

"You remember," I say in a choked voice.

"Or course I remember," he says softly. "How could I ever forget you?"

"Then why?" I demand.

"Why what?"

"Why did you pretend not to know me, that first day at Sloan's? Why didn't you say anything, all this time?"

His eyes move over my features like a caress. "I thought, after all the shit that went down with Helena, if I said we had a history — even one as innocent as child co-stars for a short-run season on a crap daytime TV show — Sloan would never give you the part." He pauses. "And I wanted you in this movie with me, Kat. As soon as I saw you that day... I knew I couldn't fuck it up, no matter what. So, I kept my mouth shut."

"Oh." My voice cracks.

All this time, I've been so angry he pretended not to recognize me... I never stopped to consider he might've had a good reason.

His mouth twitches. "It wasn't entirely selfless. I didn't necessarily want to admit I remembered what I did to you, back when we were kids."

I groan. "I was hoping you'd forgotten *that* part."

"Kat." He puts a hand over his heart and leans closer, voice intent. "A boy never forgets his first love letter."

I roll onto my back, creating some much needed space between us. "That's really unfortunate for me."

"*Dear Grayson, I think U R 2 cool*," he recites in falsetto. "*If U think I'm cool 2—*"

"Stop!" I look away from him, so he won't see the way my cheeks are flaming.

"Did I embarrass you?"

"Back then, or right now?"

"Then. Now. Both."

"No," I lie. "Not embarrassed at all."

"I never thought I'd see the day!" He sounds even more smug than usual. "Kat Firestone is actually blushing!"

"I am not. It's warm by the fire, that's all."

"Uh huh." He sighs happily. "You know, we're scheduled to film sex scenes next week. If you can't even relive an innocent childhood declaration of love without blushing, how are you ever going to get through several hours of pressing your naked body against mine, while an entire crew of filmmakers looks on?"

My heart pounds a bit faster at the visual created by his words. I scramble up onto my feet, so I'm no longer breathing his air or sharing his space or staring into those distracting eyes, and stumble around to the other side of the fire pit. I feel infinitely safer with a red-hot pit of embers separating us.

"What are you doing?" he calls, sitting up. I feel his eyes tracking my every move through the night, a nocturnal predator stalking clumsy prey.

"I'm getting more firewood," I lie, wandering down the beach toward the water on unsteady feet. The closer I get, the damper the sand beneath my toes. I don't stop until I'm ankle deep in the dark waves. Pulling in a deep breath, I wrap my arms around my body as if it'll somehow keep all the dangerous feelings stirring inside me contained. An emotional straight jacket.

It doesn't help.

Despite my stupid self-protective rules, despite the fact that I know he's all wrong for me, despite the knowledge that he's even more of a cynical mess than I am… Grayson Dunn is in my head. He's under my skin. He's invaded me like a deadly disease and hijacked my immune system until I don't even bother fighting it anymore. I look at him, and I'm twisted into knots. Tangled into a messy spool of desire and desperation.

I want his lips on mine, not because of some script.

I want his hands touching me, not on the orders of some director.

I want his eyes burning me alive, not for the cameras or the crowds.

I don't want a co-star.

I don't want a character.

I don't want *Beck*.

I want him.

I feel him behind me before he announces his

presence. The hair on my neck rises and I simply know he's there, standing five feet away, as though I've somehow summoned him with my thoughts. He doesn't make a sound, doesn't speak a word. But somehow, I know.

My shoulders stiffen, the arms crossed around my chest tighten as I struggle to keep myself staring out at the dark water instead of turning to him and saying all the things I'm dying to express. My battle for control intensifies when he steps into the water. Into my space.

His front comes up against my back, a warm wall of heat. His hands slide around my waist so gently it's almost like he's afraid to touch me. As though he thinks, if he moves too fast, I'll slip beneath the surface like a mermaid and disappear forever.

The thin fabric of my long-sleeved t-shirt is little protection against his touch. One graze of his palms and I'm already shaking.

"Kat," he whispers, his mouth descending to land on my neck. The feel of his lips against my skin sets off an explosion inside me, frazzling my nerve endings like I've been electrocuted. Powerless to stop myself, I arch back into him, neck craning to give him more room as he trails kisses down the column of my throat. He presses closer, hands gripping the fabric of my shirt to anchor me against him. I hear the thundering of my pulse roaring inside my head, somewhere beneath the deep tide of alcohol and attraction drowning my senses.

Stop, stop, stop!

My remaining bits of self-preservation are screaming at me, but I don't heed them. I'm lost — swimming in sensation. He plants a kiss in the hollow just below my ear and a needy, breathless sound escapes me before I can stop it. Grayson hears it and goes still, his grip tightening almost violently against my hips.

"Tell me to stop," he growls, mouth moving against my shoulder. I feel a graze of teeth and I shudder. "Tell me to walk away."

I clear my throat, close my eyes, and gather all my self-control.

"Stop," I whisper into the dark, so faintly it sounds like a prayer. "Walk away."

I'm not sure what's worse — the thought that he'll ignore my words, or the idea that he might actually heed them. His grip tightens again, until pleasure is teetering on the edge of pain, and I think, *goddammit*, he's going to listen to me, going to turn and walk away before this forbidden spark ignites into an inferno we can't take back...

"Fuck that," he mutters, spinning me around with rough hands. "I've been dying to do this for too long. I'm not going anywhere."

I don't have a chance to respond. His mouth hits mine with such force it steals my breath, and then he's kissing me.

Grayson Dunn is kissing me.

His kiss is hard. Unfamiliar. Almost angry.

His big hands come up to cup my cheeks, holding me captive — as if I'd ever be tempted to pull away. His mouth dominates mine. I'm not his to own, but he conquers me anyway.

Domineering. Demanding.

I can't breathe, can't even properly kiss him back. I just cling to his shoulders and let him wreck me, one tongue stroke at a time, until my head is spinning and my heart is pounding against my ribs like a mallet on a drum. The world falls away — the splash of the ocean at my feet, the warmth of the breeze against my skin, the sight of the stars over my head. All that's left is him. His lips. My lips. This moment.

This kiss.

This kiss ruins me for all other kisses. In the space of a second, he obliterates every other man who's ever put his mouth on mine. All the boys who came before are a pale imitation of this passion.

My mouth opens under his, our tongues brush, and I feel the ferocity of his response in the grip of his hands against my cheeks, the way his fingers dig into my jawline and his body presses up against mine. For a dazed, deluded instant, I think he's going to throw me down in the sand and fuck me into oblivion with the waves crashing over us, like some shadowy imitation of *From Here To Eternity*.

Thankfully, he's still clinging to his sanity, even if mine has fled on the wind. With a groan of self-restraint, he tears his mouth away. I'm shaking in his arms. Trembling with heat and need and insane, insatiable hunger. His forehead comes down to rest against mine and I realize, for the first time, how much taller he is than me. If I were to step forward, I could tuck my face comfortably in the crook of his neck and his chin could rest against the crown of my head.

A perfect fit.

We're both breathing too hard. My pulse is pounding too fast. It takes a long moment for my thoughts to stop spinning, for reason to return, as we stare at each other, eyes locked.

Who is this man, who owns me so completely, so effortlessly, so unreasonably?

Friend, enemy, co-star, stranger, lover.

I cannot sort him out any more than I can decipher my feelings for him.

"We shouldn't have done that," I whisper eventually, when I can speak again.

I watch his lips curl into a grin. "I had to do it at least once, for real. Before it's staged for the cameras, scripted for Sloan... I had to know what it would be like."

There's an unfamiliar tightness in my chest. I can't quite catch my breath.

"Just once," he murmurs again. I'm not sure if he's trying to convince me or himself.

"Just once," I echo, a thread of disappointment weaving its way through me.

"Come on. It's late. We should get some sleep." His lips brush mine softly, a ghost of his earlier passion. "I'll walk you to your door."

I feel my brows lift in surprise. "Such a gentleman."

"Don't look at me like that," he warns.

I blink innocently. "Like what?"

"Like you'd like me to be *less* of a gentleman."

I grin. "I'm just surprised. Grayson Dunn — an unlikely source of chivalry."

"Trust me," he murmurs, stepping back carefully. "It's taking all my self-control to walk you to your door and say goodnight without laying another finger on you. I'd like nothing more than to carry you into my bed and hold you captive for the next few days. But…" He runs his free hand through his hair. "We have to be on set in about three hours. And the things I'd like to do with you would take a fuck of a lot more time than that, Kat."

My thighs clench together as a bolt of desire shoots through me.

"Oh," I whisper breathlessly.

His hand laces with mine and he leads me slowly up the beach toward the dark row of bungalows. "I meant what I said, before. I don't want to fuck up this movie. This project means a lot to me."

"I know," I murmur. "It means a lot to me, too."

He nods. "It has to come first. Before anything else. Before you and me."

We reach the door to my villa. I see the tension brewing inside him like an electrical storm, just below the surface — desire, restraint, worry, longing, need, fear. His deep eyes are, for once, totally unguarded. Or, maybe I'm just getting better at reading him.

I unlace my hand from his and take a cautious step back.

"Don't worry, Dunn. I'm not going to get all clingy and needy and start doodling your name in the margins of my script."

His crooked grin returns. "I already have one love note from you that suggests otherwise."

"Hey! Don't use my embarrassing childhood memories against me." I smack him on the arm. "That was low."

He laughs. "But true."

"Well, it won't be happening again."

"We'll see."

"It was one kiss," I say rolling my eyes. "Get over yourself."

His gaze captures mine. "It was a pretty fucking great kiss."

I clear my throat and break eye contact. Staring at his forehead instead, I try to smile as I reach out and brush a flyaway strand of dark hair off his face.

"Night, Grayson. I'll see you in the morning."

I turn and slip inside my villa, closing the door just after his soft whisper slips through the crack.

"Goodnight, Kat."

CHAPTER TWELVE

"Hᴇ's ʀᴇᴀʟʟʏ... ғᴜɴɴʏ."
- *A girl who thinks you're cute,
but not cute enough to date.*

"Don't you walk away from me!" I shout, stalking after him. My feet kick up sand and my arms shove against his back with as much force as I can muster. "This conversation isn't over."
"It is."
"How can you say that?" I cry, palms striking the broad planes of his back again. "How can you pretend you aren't feeling this too?"
He spins around and catches my fists in his grasp, before I can do any more damage. His green eyes burn like fire.
"I feel it. Of course I feel it. But there are things you don't know. Things that could change everything."
"Nothing could change how I feel about you," I whisper brokenly. "I want you. I need you. I love—"
"Don't!" He yells, shaking me. "Don't say it."
My eyes narrow and my volume only increases, until my words ring out on the abandoned stretch of beach like a battle cry.
"I love you, damn it! And I refuse to stop!"
He clutches at my shoulders with a brutal grip, as if not sure whether to tear me to pieces or pull me into his arms. "You *have* to stop," he growls. "You have no choice."
"Why? How?" I blink back tears. "I could sooner stop breathing! I could more easily pull the clouds down from the sky!"

His yell is heart-rending. I hear the sorrow in his voice, the conflict, the pain and passion as his words slice through the air between us like a knife strike.

"Because I'm already married!" he roars, shaking me again. "Don't you understand? I said *vows*, I made *promises*... just because I'm here with you... it doesn't change that. Doesn't erase it."

I feel my heart splinter inside my chest, breaking into irreparable pieces as his words wash through me in a tidal wave of despair. His hands hold my shoulders tighter, his face comes so close I think he's surely going to kiss me, even though it's forbidden, even though we shouldn't...

"And *CUT!*"

Sloan's voice fractures the moment.

I suck in a startled gasp of air and take a hasty step back from Grayson as soon as his hands drop away. My heart is hammering at twice its normal speed. It takes longer than it should to shake off the emotional turmoil of the scene, still swirling around inside me like a tornado.

"All right, folks, that was a definite improvement from last time." Sloan plants his hands on his hips, rocks back on his heels, and surveys the beach with speculative eyes. "We'll go again in a few minutes — I want to change cameras, get some wide-angle shots from up by the tree line." He mutters something under his breath, then looks up again. "Oh, and Dunn, for the record, that line is *because I have a wife at home* not *because I'm already married*. That's the second time you've fudged it."

"Got it, boss," Grayson calls in a carefree voice, walking to the break tent and grabbing a piece of pineapple from the spread of refreshments and snacks on the table. The hotel staff have assembled a small, shady refuge for the cast and crew to get out of the sun between takes; it's stocked with so much food you'd think there were fifty people working on this film instead of fifteen.

Grayson throws his body into a chair by one of the large rotating fans and tosses the fruit into his mouth. He's the picture of relaxation as he strikes up a conversation with Trey, laughing about something I can't hear from here.

I don't know how he can be so unaffected. My presence-of-mind is hanging by rapidly-thinning thread, after running that intense scene between Violet and Beck three times in a row.

A water bottle appears in front of my face. I follow the tanned brown fingers up a muscular arm and find myself staring into Wyatt's chiseled features.

"Here." His eyes narrow on mine as he presses the bottle into my hands. "Hydrate. It's about a hundred degrees out here."

With a grateful nod, I take the water and chug it down. "Thanks."

"Let's get you in the shade," Wyatt says, heading toward the tent area. "You're looking a little crispy around the edges."

I roll my eyes as I fall into step beside him.

When we reach the tent, I spot Harper sitting on the far side with the other makeup artist, Cassie, looking dour as the girl drones on about something — blending brush brands or shading techniques or the proper way to apply fake abrasions so they look like a genuine wound. According to Harper, Cassie is incapable of making conversation about anything except work, which has left my best friend grumpy and starved for human interaction since we arrived in Hawaii last week.

When she sees me collapse into the chair next to Wyatt's, she excuses herself and bolts in our direction. She starts blotting my face with some kind of sponge as soon as she reaches me.

"Is this how we're greeting each other now?" I ask dryly. "Should I be sponging you back?"

"Shut up. I told her you looked blotchy, okay? It was the first excuse I could think of to get away from her."

I close my eyes as she starts patting my forehead. "That actually feels kind of nice," I murmur. "Please, feel free to brush out my hair after you finish blotting me."

"Your hair is fine. Do you know how long those perfect-but-not-too-perfect beachy waves took to create?"

"Yes, I was sitting in the chair as you created them," I point out.

"True enough." She starts touching up my matte lip stain. "Can you believe we've been here over a week already?"

I shake my head. "No, it's a bit unreal."

"Things are going smoothly," Wyatt interjects, looking up from the script in his lap. "We're on track to wrap early, assuming the weather holds."

"Early?" I scrunch my nose. "How early?"

He shrugs. "Maybe five more days? Six, at most, if we stay on track."

Harper pouts. "I don't want to leave Hawaii. I still haven't learned to hula properly."

"I think you should let that dream die," I say gently. "Your lack of rhythm is truly remarkable."

She jabs me a little harder than necessary with a contouring brush.

"Ow!"

Her eyes narrow. "You were saying?"

"That you're a delightful dancer, should quit your day job, and become a professional hula-girl."

"Thought so."

Wyatt snorts. "If it's any consolation, the hotel is putting on a luau for us before we head home. I'm sure there will be plenty of hula opportunities."

"Really?" Harper squeaks.

He nods and tilts his head. "You do know they roast a full pig, right? Some of you vegan girls take issue with—"

"Vegan?" I snort.

"Dude." Harper's eyes are wide. "Bacon is the base of my food pyramid."

"How are you from Los Angeles?" he asks her incredulously.

"I'm not." She grins. "I'm from Iowa."

"Ah." He nods, like that explains everything.

Annabelle walks into the tent, hips swaying a little more than necessary, in my opinion. Her eyes are locked on Grayson as she announces that Sloan needs us back on set in five, since they're ready to start shooting again.

In an act of extreme maturity, I stick my tongue out at her as she sashays from the tent with her clipboard clutched pertly in front of her perky breasts. When Harper spots me, I try to play it off as a yawn, but it's useless. Her smirk is all too knowing.

I close my eyes, in part so she can finish touching up my makeup but mainly so she can't read the emotions in them.

It's hard to believe we've been filming for more than a week already — the first few days on the island flew by so fast it makes my head spin just thinking about it. Our set, a stretch of gorgeous white-sand beach a few minutes' walk from the villas, where designers have constructed Beck and Violet's "home" of thatched palms and driftwood logs, may look like the site of a dream vacation, but our time in front of the cameras has been anything but relaxing. Sloan is more like a slave driver than a director, getting us out of bed to shoot before dawn and keeping us there until the fiery red sun is sinking into the waves. Whether we're running lines, blocking out new scenes, or shooting takes of Beck and Violet struggling to find food, water, and shelter, there's hardly been a moment of downtime.

I barely appreciate the accoutrements of my gorgeous bungalow, with the exception of the king size bed which I collapse into face-first every night, exhausted from all day out in the elements. We may not really be castaways, but after twelve straight hours of hacking at palm trees, sparking fire from flint and twigs, stitching fake injuries, and dragging huge logs to spell out H-E-L-P on the beach, in the off-chance a rogue fictional plane flies by to rescue us, I feel as though I've actually survived on an uninhabitable island with no company except a taciturn ex-photographer who, until about halfway through the script, says all of three words to me.

Beck.

Truth be told, the actor portraying him isn't much more talkative.

Since our heated kiss that first night on the island, things have cooled significantly between Grayson and me. We never discussed our drunken indiscretion, the passionate moments we shared standing ankle-deep in the waves, mouths devouring each other without reserve. In fact, he's been so unfathomably normal toward me, so wholly unchanged, I could almost convince myself I made the whole thing up. That it was nothing but a dream — some far-flung fantasy conjured by an overactive imagination and too much rum.

Almost.

I know it was real. That it actually happened.

The sad reality is, my imagination never felt half as good as his lips claiming mine, his hands gripping my hips, his eyes roaming my features as though he could stare at them for days without ever tiring of the sight. No dream, no figment of my subconscious, could ever live up to that moment with him.

I'm not sure whether he's consciously creating some distance or simply too focused on the project to pay me much attention, but we've spent no more than a few minutes alone together in the past week. Then again, Harper is never far from my side, nor is Wyatt, so even if Grayson wanted to speak to me about our drunken slip-up, he'd have a tough time catching me unaccompanied.

I tell myself it doesn't matter.

That it was one kiss.

That I'm being ridiculous.

And yet, I can't deny how often I find my eyes following him between takes, or the inexplicable fury that simmers inside my chest like a dormant volcano when I see him making small-talk with Annabelle in the morning as she delivers coffee to everyone on set, tossing her glossy hair like she's auditioning for a damn Herbal Essences commercial. Accepting my cappuccino from her — with smile, without comment — is the first in a long line of daily demonstrations in self-control.

This should be the most invigorating week in my life. The culmination of everything I've been working toward since I was three months old and Cynthia enrolled me in my first baby beauty pageant. And yet, I feel no joy at the accomplishment of my dreams, no fulfillment at the prospect of attaining all the fame I've ever strived for.

Instead, I feel distracted and distant, as though I'm watching the events of my world unfold through a wall of glass. All day I smile and bite my tongue and say my lines perfectly, and all night I toss and turn beneath the sheets, trying to forget the way Grayson's mouth burned into my skin like a hot brand.

I have morphed into a needy, unrecognizable creature. And I know exactly who's to blame for it.

***

Later that night, after I've changed out of my costume and Harper's wiped the makeup from my face, instead of walking back to my villa I linger at the edge of the set. Grayson is filming a solo scene at the other end of the beach as the sun slowly dips below the edge of the horizon, turning the waves into a kaleidoscope of color.

"Hey!" Harper appears by my side, snapping her fingers in front of my face. "Are you all right?"

"Of course," I say brightly, blinking at her. "Why wouldn't I be?"

"You just seem a little... *off*. At first, I thought it was just the stress of you being here, working so hard to get all your lines right, to live up to Sloan's expectations... But now..." Her eyes dart down the stretch of beach to

Grayson. The cameras are tight in on his shirtless, sweaty frame as he uses a makeshift axe of sharpened rock to chop firewood.

I swallow audibly.

"Now, I'm pretty sure there's something you aren't telling me," she finishes dryly.

I look back at my best friend. "I have no idea what you're referring to."

"Uh huh." She looks doubtful. "You can tell me, you know. I'm always here for you. No matter what it is, I'll listen and promise not to judge."

My eyebrows lift.

"Okay, I'll judge," she concedes. "But the point is, I'll listen. I'm here. You can talk to me about anything, don't you know that by now?"

"I know." I sigh. "Thanks, Harper."

She nods. "Worried about you, babe. You seem distracted. I don't want you to spiral."

"Who's spiraling?" Wyatt appears beside us, munching on a crisp apple.

"No one, eavesdropper," I say, standing up, snatching the apple from his hand, and taking a colossal bite from the side.

"That was mine," he says forlornly, watching me devour the rest of his snack. "And I wasn't eavesdropping. I happened to walk by while you were saying intriguing things."

"Do we ever not say intriguing things?" Harper asks. "I, for one, think we are fascinating creatures."

I snort. "You also thought Taylor Swift's last single was the most important contribution to music since The Beatles' *White* album."

"I stand by that."

"I agree," Wyatt mutters. "T-Swift is a mastermind."

I stare at him for a beat. "For the record, this is me judging you."

"For the record, I don't give a shit." He shrugs. "There's a certain kind of beauty in the ability to create art from the aftermath of someone fucking you over. Not to mention making millions of dollars in the process."

"Fair enough," I concede. "But do you think it's healthy to dwell on someone after they've walked away? I mean, she spends months writing albums about guys who've long since moved on."

Wyatt glances at Harper. "Clearly, Katharine has never been in love."

"True," Harper agrees, putting away her makeup kit for the day.

"What makes you say that?" I protest.

"Because," Wyatt says, eyes narrowing. "When you get your heart shattered by someone, you're going to spend months dwelling on them regardless. Most of us just suffer in silence… but artists have the rare chance to turn their pain into passion. And money, if they're half-decent at it."

I blink at him, surprised by his serious tone.

"Someday, you'll get your heart broken," he continues softly. "And you'll understand."

"Gee, thanks."

"I'm not wishing it on you. I wouldn't wish it on anyone. I just know it'll happen at some point." His eyebrows pull together and a dark look flashes across his features. "It happens to us all, eventually."

"Even you?" I ask.

"Even me."

"Who broke your heart, Hastings?"

"That's not your business, baby. Not yet. Maybe not ever," he says, smiling before turning on a heel and walking down to join Sloan.

When he's gone, I glance at Harper and shrug. "He's a mystery, that one."

"He's just… intense. When he looks at you, it's always like he's searching for something deeper. Something *more*."

"Like a rogue planet seeking a sun," I murmur, eyes drifting from Wyatt, standing on the sidelines behind the cameras, to Grayson's tanned form, posing in front of them. "Like you might be the center of his universe, instead of a passing meteor."

"What?" Harper asks, brow furrowing as she snaps the last clasp on her case. "I didn't hear you."

"Nothing. Never mind. It doesn't matter anyway." I press my eyes closed. "Let's head up to the resort and grab something to eat. I'm starving."

***

Days continue to pass with alarming alacrity.

After a week and a half of nonstop work, while breaking for lunch one day, Sloan announces we've filmed three quarters of the script and should be fully wrapped within four days' time. The news should make me buoyant with joy — things are going so well, we're actually ahead of schedule.

Instead, the announcement instills an unshakable sadness inside me. For the rest of the day, I fudge lines and misstep well-rehearsed scenes. Sloan, frustrated by my mediocre performance, cuts our filming short and gives us the rest of the day off to "recoup and rebalance."

Whatever that means.

We're not scheduled to shoot again until the next afternoon — we're filming night scenes from dusk till dawn — so we have a mini break for the next twenty-four hours.

Seeing Harper is still tied up with Cassie, I walk back to the villas alone, lost in my thoughts. I let my mind drift to the character I've embodied for the past two weeks and feel a restless sort of kinship with her.

Violet.

She has become so much more to me than a fictional character torn from the pages of a dog-eared novel, evolved so far past an imagined girl in a stranger's screenplay. The longer I play her, the more I relate to her words, her feelings, her inner contradictions.

In front of the cameras, Violet and Beck have morphed slowly from unwitting allies to co-dependent survivors to reluctant friends. The more time they spend together, the more they depend on each other to make it through their stranded nightmare, the deeper the tension between them grows. I can't help but feel, as I act out Violet's stolen glances and underhanded comments for the cameras, as I play a girl in love with a man who cannot ever love her back in the way she craves, that we have far more in common than I ever assumed.

Sometimes, when the cameras are rolling, it's hard to tell where she ends and I begin. And, when I look at Grayson, it's becoming harder and harder to differentiate him from Beck, the reluctant hero whose gruff exterior harbors a pure heart, the steadfast man whose unbridled passion for a girl on the island wars with unfailing loyalty to a wife back at home.

I know *Uncharted* was written to tug at viewers' heartstrings — I just didn't think it would tug so deftly at mine. Every time I think of Violet and Beck, my chest aches.

I can't help but worry this will only intensify, after tomorrow.

The night shoot. The cave scenes.

In the script, Violet and Beck are forced to retreat from the home they've carved out for themselves on the beach when a hurricane hits the island. Taking refuge in a cave, they're trapped for days as rain and strong winds pummel the world outside. Huddled together for warmth to stave off the cold, for the first time since the crash they give in to the magnetic pull between them... and take comfort in each other's arms.

A flutter of butterflies erupts to life inside my stomach.

Having sex with Grayson — even fictional sex, in front of a camera crew — will be the ultimate test of my self-control. I don't let my thoughts linger too much on it. If

I did, I'd drive myself to distraction. Plus, after a week of pretending not to be bothered every time Annabelle flips her hair in his direction, I'm getting better at shutting him out of my mind altogether.

I'm nearly back to my villa when the sound of his voice halts me in my tracks.

"Kat! Kat, wait!"

He sounds out of breath, as if he's run to catch up with me. I turn slowly to face him and see his green eyes are uncharacteristically serious, his mouth is set in an uncompromising line.

My eyebrows go up. My voice is cool, casual. "What's up, Dunn?"

"I wanted to see if you were okay."

"Why wouldn't I be okay?"

"You weren't focused. You messed up your lines." His eyes narrow. "You never mess up your lines. In fact, you're always so prepared, it's a little annoying. You usually make me look bad. But not today."

"Maybe I'm just having an off day."

"Because of me?"

I blink. "Are you kidding? Why would it possibly be because of you?"

He hedges, shifting from foot to foot. "I don't know. You just seem pissed at me or something."

"Shockingly, not everything is about you, Dunn."

"This is what I'm talking about." He takes a step closer. "You're always snappy. You're always sarcastic. You're not *scathing*, though. There's usually a softness under all that bitchiness, and it's missing today. I want to know where it went, why it's gone, and how I get it back."

My mouth is parched. My palms are clammy. "Like I said before, I'm not pissed at you. I'm just having an off day. It'll pass."

His eyes hold mine and I get the distinct idea he doesn't believe me. "If you say so."

"I do," I snap.

I realize I'm being a bitch, lashing out at him for breaking promises he never made to me, but I can't seem to contain myself. I have absolutely no right to be angry... and that only seems to make me angrier.

I know it isn't fair, but I don't know how to stop. I'm trapped in a paradoxical circle of suppressed emotions.

"What are you doing right now?" he asks abruptly.

"I was planning to take a nap, climb into my hammock, and enjoy a few hours of peace and quiet with my nose buried in a novel. You know, so my *bitchiness* doesn't affect any innocent bystanders." I narrow my eyes. "Why do you ask?"

"Screw that," he says, reaching out and grabbing my hand. "You're coming with me."

"What? Grayson, let me go! I'm not in the mood for this!"

"Nope."

"Are you serious?"

He drags me along, holding me fast despite all attempts to struggle away. "I want to show you something."

"If it's the thing you like to *show* girls when they come back to your place after a night of inappropriate binge drinking, I'll pass."

"Cute." He pulls me faster. "You'll actually like this surprise, I promise. And, if you don't, you can go back to being a bitch in a few hours."

"A few *hours*?" I hiss. "Where are you taking me, Montana?"

"Just shut up and go with the flow, for once."

"I'm not a *go with the flow* kind of girl."

"Ride or die, Firestone."

"I don't *ride or die* either. I have questions. Where are we riding? Why do we have to die? Can we stop and get tacos on the way?"

"See, you're already cheering up. A few more hours in my presence, you'll be back to your normal, caustic self."

207

"I spend almost every waking moment with you. Have you ever considered that's why I'm in such a foul mood to begin with?"

"Nope," he says cheerfully.

"*Grayson.*" I groan. "Seriously, I was looking forward to my nap."

"Just trust me, okay? This is way better than a nap."

I scoff. "Not possible. Naps are the greatest thing of all time."

"This is better."

I stop trying to tug my hand from his, but my eyes are still narrowed in doubt as we cross a road onto a narrow trail, officially leaving hotel property behind.

"I thought we weren't supposed to leave the grounds."

"We're celebrities, not prisoners." He grins at me. "And what the security detail doesn't know won't hurt them."

"Shouldn't we at least tell someone where we're going?"

"Live a little, Firestone. I thought you were a badass."

"I am a badass," I grumble.

"Then buck up and stop resisting." His eyes twinkle. "I'm taking you on an adventure. And I'm not taking no for an answer."

"Fine," I relent with a heavy sigh, as if he's torturing me.

In reality, there's a heady excitement building inside me like a fault line overdue to quake. I keep my eyes on the spot between his shoulder blades as he leads me through the thick brush deeper into the forest, the trail incline getting steeper and the plant life growing denser the farther along we travel.

"If you wanted to murder me, we could've gone snorkeling," I note wryly, wiping sweat from my brow. It's late afternoon, but the Hawaiian sun still beats down like an oven broiler. "The sharks would've taken care of the evidence. Much cleaner, as murders go."

"I'll keep that in mind for next time." He smirks.

"You're really not going to tell me where you're taking me?"

"Nope."

I sigh again.

We walk for about twenty minutes. He's still holding my hand. I repeatedly tell myself to pull away, but I can't seem to actually do it.

"Just a little farther," he mutters, helping me over a particularly rough part of terrain. I'm not exactly dressed for a hike — since we arrived on the island, I've either been in costume on set or wearing the requisite vacationer uniform: a white string bikini, a sheer lace cover-up, and cheap flip-flops.

We push on, up a final stretch of incline. I hear the telltale sound of rushing water a few moments before it comes into view, and suddenly know exactly where Grayson is leading us. Even knowing what I'm about to see doesn't prepare me for its beauty. Rounding a bend, we step into a clearing and come up short at the sight before us.

The hidden pool is totally secluded. Mist fills the air around the base of the waterfall, a damp cloud kicked up by the steady stream of water free-falling forty feet over a cliff into the turquoise green grotto. Massive, prehistoric ferns and lush green lichens flank the sides of the clearing, growing vertical along the rocky cliffside. The shallows closest to the shore are so tranquil, you can see straight down to the bottom.

There's something sacred about this place — something old and untouched. Neither Grayson or I speak as we step over mossy stones to an overhang of rock a few feet above the pool's surface. I'm hesitant to fracture the silence.

He looks over at me when we reach the edge, a slow smile dawning on his face.

"Better than a nap?"

"Definitely better than a nap."

"Come on, Firestone." With a final squeeze, he drops

my hand. Reaching for the bottom hem of his t-shirt, he whips it over his head and tosses it to the ground. "We're going swimming."

He doesn't have to twist my arm. I'm warm from the hike, a faint sheen of sweat coating my limbs, and the water looks almost as heavenly as the man jumping into it.

I force myself not to watch too closely as he lets out a shout of delight and makes a running leap into the grotto. He dives in, arms extended, and emerges a moment later, grinning broadly. Shaking his head, he sends water droplets flying in all directions. The sight of his hair standing on end makes me smile.

"Get your ass in here, Kat!"

I reach down and pull my cover-up over my head, feeling his eyes on me the entire time. He's seen me in a bikini a thousand times over the past week. This shouldn't be a big deal. My heart shouldn't be racing like I'm doing a private strip-tease for him. And yet, it feels different. Everything about this day feels different. The very air between us seems to buzz with unspoken words and all manner of things I'd much rather keep pushing under the rug than ever address out loud.

No good can come of these things I've been feeling.

Kicking off my flip flops, I race for the water. Propelling myself as high as possible from the edge of the outcropping, I curl my limbs in toward my body as I plummet toward the surface, landing close to him in a perfect cannon-ball that sends an arc of water splashing straight into his face. I surface, laughing, and immediately get dunked under again as he retaliates.

What follows can only be described as a splash fight. We swim around the pool like children, dunking and circling, sending waves into each other's directions, play-wrestling. I catch him full across the face with a particularly good splash and he grabs me in a head lock, growling. I squirm against him, trying to get free, and his hands slip beneath the water to get a better hold on me.

I laugh in his face. He pulls me in closer.

He's holding the small of my back; my hands are resting on his broad, bare shoulders. The water around us is so warm it feels like a massive bathtub. The sky overhead is streaked with pink as the sun begins its descent into twilight, but I can't look at it.

His eyes and mouth are so close, they're all I see.

Quite suddenly, nothing is funny at all. The laughter shrivels up and dies in my mouth like a flower left out in the frost. I'm staring at Grayson and he's staring back. I see the moment our closeness registers in his eyes, see the second they drop down to laser-in on my lips, and I breathe out something that sounds like, "*we can't*," but he's well past the point of listening.

He kisses me — ardently, wholeheartedly.

And I kiss him back, with all the pent-up passion I've been harboring for the past week, since he walked me to my door like a gentleman and left me balanced on the razor's edge of wanting. My hands slide into his hair as my legs wrap around his waist beneath the surface of the water. I pour everything I have into the kiss.

My frustration, my fear, my anger, my adoration.

Worry, desire, need, longing.

With a kiss, I speak the thousand words I'll never, ever let myself say to him. With my hands, I whisper secrets that will never pass my lips. With my body, I unequivocally declare all the things I want from him that he can't ever give me.

His lips work over mine with expert precision even as his hands clutch me closer. Our bodies, slippery from the water, move together like a dance — skin on skin, barely anything to separate us. And it makes no sense, this feeling that I'm about to combust, because water can't catch fire. I know that, logically. Yet, somehow, here in his arms, I've never felt more flammable.

There comes a moment when we could stop — a point when, maybe, we could laugh it off as another drunken slip-up and vow to forget it ever happened.

But we aren't drunk.

And I don't want to stop.

He pulls back to rest his forehead against mine, breathing hard, and opens his mouth to speak — perhaps to ask me something mundane and considerate like *are you sure?* Perhaps to suggest we slow down, swim to the edge of the grotto, step back into our clothes, and return to the resort before things go too far. Perhaps to tell me something I'm scared to hear, like *I care about you* or *this means something to me.*

I don't let him get a word out. I kiss him into silence.

The moment of turning back passes like an afternoon rain shower.

He moves against me and I feel the firm length of his cock through his thin bathing suit. I grind down against it, feeling my bones dissolve into pure, blissful need. I think I make a noise, maybe a moan, but his mouth is still claiming mine in a brutal kiss that I have little doubt will leave my lips bruised and swollen.

I feel his fingers leave my back and begin working at the strings of my bikini top. My legs cling tighter around his waist as he strips the wet tangle of fabric from my body and tosses it blindly in the direction of the shore. When his palms cup my breasts beneath the water, the sensation is so acute, so mind-numbingly intense, I nearly come apart in his hands. My whole body arches back, bent like a sapling in a storm. Eyes to the sky, legs at his waist, I feel his mouth trailing over my collarbones, down between the valley of my breasts, closing over my nipples.

"God, Grayson," I whisper like a prayer — a benediction from the sinner I've become in his arms, praying at his altar as he worships my body into a sublime state of need.

My hands lace into his hair as my heels push at the hem of his bathing suit. He understands what I want without words.

In the space of a second, he's rid me of my string bottoms and kicked out of his own. I force myself to focus on his eyes as I reach down between us, searching for his length. Wanting to see the way the constellations rearrange themselves inside his irises when my fingers close around him.

My hand moves over rock-hard ridges, stroking rhythmically, and satisfaction sluices through me as I watch his pupils dilate in pure desire.

"Grayson," I whisper, my hand moving faster.

"Kat," he echoes, sounding half tortured, half triumphant.

"Fuck me," I beg.

He doesn't need to be told twice.

His hands find my hips as he lifts me slightly in the water, then pulls me down hard, impaling me on his shaft. I clench around him, feeling full in the best possible way — as though my body was missing a vital piece and I didn't even realize it. As though I was walking around without the ability to see color and didn't even know how sad my grayscale world was until he pushed inside me and unlocked something I didn't know existed.

I cling to him soundlessly as he fucks me beneath the waterfall, my soft cries swallowed by his kisses, my fingertips digging into his shoulders so hard I worry I'll break the skin. He moves faster and faster, sending me reeling like a meteor across the sky, and with each powerful thrust I lose another piece of myself in him.

When I can take no more, when the orgasm crashes through my system with so much force it makes my head fall back to the sky and my legs convulse around him, I cry out loud enough to send a flock of birds bursting from their roost in a nearby tree. Dazed and half-drunk on sensation as pleasure spirals through me, I watch them disappear over the horizon, into the pink-streaked sky. I hear Grayson shout as he finds his own release, his head falling into the crook of my neck as my arms wind tighter around him and aftershocks pump through me.

The birds disappear from sight as we stand there wrapped around each other, waist-deep in the warm water, neither wanting to move just yet. And I think, more than almost anything in the world, I'd like to be one of those birds — to fly away with this man in my arms, out over the water, into infinity, where no one can catch us.

Grayson and me.

Free from real life, from obligation, from reality.

Just two wild creatures chasing wind currents under the stars, pushing each other faster, further, until we're so far from land there's no turning back.

If I could only build us wings.

CHAPTER THIRTEEN

"You never said we were exclusive."
- *A guy with multiple side-chicks.*

We sneak back onto hotel property like kids caught out after curfew, hands held fast in the darkness. He doesn't try to be a gentleman this time — he pulls me straight into his villa, shuts the door firmly behind us, and backs me up against it.

"Shower?" he murmurs.

I nod, my half-hooded eyes locked on his mouth. We're soaked to the skin. After a day of filming, a hike to the waterfall and back, plus our off-script activities in the grotto, I'm covered in salt and sand and god knows what else. In silence, he strips me naked and carries me into the massive walk-in shower.

There's a satisfied ache between my legs, the kind you get after a thorough fucking, and it only intensifies when Grayson bends me over and takes me from behind with the water running over us from the massive shower head. Not quite a Hawaiian waterfall, but close enough.

"We're supposed to be getting clean," I gasp, hand thrown out to the tile wall so I don't fall over.

"First..." His voice sounds rough with need as he pounds into me, words forced out in time with his thrusts. "I need... to make you... a little... dirtier."

I'm too far gone to protest.

Later, when the hot water has run cold and we're finally clean, we don the fluffy white robes hanging in the bathroom closet and order room service. We're both starving, so we raid the mini-fridge while we're waiting for our cheeseburgers to arrive. I lie on the bed, eating maraschino cherries from a tiny glass jar, while he mixes us both a Manhattan.

"You're doing it wrong," I call, smirking.

"You can't make a Manhattan wrong," he counters, turning to glare at me. "It's impossible."

"I'm a bartender. I know these things." I roll off the bed, cross to him, and pull the bottle of whiskey from his hands. "Let me do it."

He relents, spanking me lightly on the butt as he walks over to the fridge and pulls out a bag of trail mix. Tossing a handful in his mouth, he cocks his head at me.

"You *were* a bartender."

"What?"

"You said you are a bartender. Present tense."

"Oh. Yeah, I guess," I murmur, eyes on the chilled glasses in front of me. I stir in the sweet vermouth, add a dash of bitters, and garnish the glasses with a cherry. It would be better with an orange peel, of course, but it'll do. "Here you go."

His eyes are still narrowed on my face as he takes the glass from my hand. "You know this movie is going to be a success, right?"

I sip my drink, skirt around him, and settle on the edge of the bed. "Of course."

"Kat."

"What?"

"Look at me," he says softly.

When I meet his eyes and see the knowing look in their depths, I feel the sudden urge to gulp down my drink. He approaches hesitantly, crouches down between my legs, and drapes his arms over my thighs. I can't avoid his stare — not when he's this close. Those green irises are like a tractor beam, pulling me in.

"You've got to start believing things are going to be okay." His voice is steady, unshakable. "You've got to let yourself enjoy this."

"I am enjoying it."

"Then why do you act like, at any given moment, things are a hairsbreadth from falling apart on you?"

"Because they usually do," I say quietly. "We didn't all land our first six-figure deal at age fourteen, Grayson. We didn't all have the world handed to us before we'd ever known struggle. You don't know what it's like to worry about money, about making rent payments, about spending every day going to a job you hate in a car that's more likely to catch fire than deliver you safely in time for your shift, just so you have enough dollars in your paycheck to keep your bank account out of the negatives."

"That may be true. But, Kat, you must realize... those things you just said? You'll never have to worry about them again. You've made it. You just have to let yourself believe it."

I close my eyes, shutting out the view of his face. I try to focus on his words, but all I hear is Cynthia's cold condescension, ringing in the back of my mind like an incurable cancer.

If you'd just lose ten pounds, you'd be much more likely to land some younger roles...

If you'd just cut your hair in that pixie style that's so popular right now...

If you'd just practice your pirouettes a few more hours every day...

If you'd just work harder...

Just push...

Just...

"Kat." Grayson's voice grounds me.

I open my eyes and look at him, trying not to tear up. "You don't understand."

"Then explain it to me."

"When you've spent your whole life not being good enough, it takes time to let yourself believe that you finally are. Self-worth isn't a switch that flips inside you. It's a daily struggle not to sabotage your own success. Not to cave into the voices inside your head that whisper you're not good enough, or you'll fuck things up, or that someone else could do things better than you." I can't believe I'm saying these things out loud. I hear my voice crack precariously and I know, if I keep this up much longer, I'm going to cry. "I'm working on it. That's all I can tell you. Every day, every moment... I'm trying to make myself believe. But it's hard. It's so fucking hard to replace insecurity and inferiority with confidence and composure."

"Kat." His voice is as warm as his hands when he removes the drink from my grip, sets it on the bedside table, and pulls me up into his arms. Lacing our fingers together, he looks down into my eyes. "You think you're the only one who feels that way? I've made a lot of movies in the past few years. I've got more money than I know what to do with. I live a life that is, by any standards, full of privilege. And I still feel those things you're talking about. In the past, you've called me cocky and condescending... Maybe I am, but I still feel doubt and worry. We all do. It's *human* to second-guess yourself. That doesn't go away just because you win a film award or make your first million." His hands squeeze mine tighter. "You're amazing. Everyone sees it — Wyatt saw it, when he spotted you at that audition. Sloan saw it, that day you came to his house and read lines. Harper saw it, long before you'd ever *made it*. And I see it. I've seen it since you were nine years old. I still see it." He leans closer. "The only one who can't seem to see it is you."

I bite my lip and take that final step forward, closing the sliver of distance between us. And, for just a moment, with my head on his chest and his arms tight around me, I let myself be weak.

"I thought you weren't a hugger," he murmurs against my hair. "I think this definitely constitutes hugging."

"This isn't a hug," I insist, near tears.

"Oh? What is it then?"

I sway back and forth a bit, so our bodies rock. "We're dancing."

"This isn't dancing."

Laughing through my tears, I pull back to peer up into his face. "Yes, you're right — I've seen you dance. There's a lot more booty-dropping involved. Some shimmying. Shoulder shaking. Definitely less rhythm. And far fewer clothes, if my memory serves me right."

"You should be honored I felt comfortable enough to dance naked in front of you."

"Honor was not my primary emotion, that night."

"Ohhh." His voice is suggestive. "You thought I was sexy."

"I thought you were ridiculous." I grin. "Though, I did really enjoy the sight of you gyrating like a wheezy geriatric without his walker, wearing absolutely nothing but your solar system socks."

"Leave my socks out of this."

I narrow my eyes at him. "You totally packed them, didn't you?"

"No." His denial comes a little too quickly.

"They're totally in your suitcase right now."

"No!"

"You're lying."

"No, I'm not! Wait—Kat!"

I pull out of his arms before he can catch me and dart toward his closet. He gives chase, but I'm too quick. I reach the suitcase first, stick my hand inside, and triumphantly pull out the first round ball of fabric my fingers land on. To my delight, it's a pair of patterned socks, the stars and planets clearly visible.

"I knew it!" I crow in victory.

Grayson narrows his eyes at me from a few feet away. "Cruel, Firestone. Just cruel."

Leaning down, I pull them on my feet. They're way too big — stretching halfway up my calves, they fall down whenever I take a step — but damn if the sight of those stars and moons doesn't bring a huge grin to my face. His mouth is set in a glare, but his eyes are full of humor. When I start moving in an imitation of his drunken dance moves — wiggling my booty, shimmying my shoulders, twirling like a lunatic — he completely loses it.

Laugher rumbles through him, making his shoulders shake. Turning, he walks away from me. For a second, I think he's leaving, but instead he crosses to the room-control remote and presses a handful of buttons. A few seconds later, music pours through the speakers — a trashy pop-song from about a decade ago. I know every single word, and sing them shamelessly as I pelvic-thrust in his direction like an '80s workout instructor.

"Now who's ridiculous?" he asks, grabbing my hips and pulling me close.

"Still you."

He hesitates no more than a beat before releasing his hold on me, turning his back, and dropping lower than one of Beyoncé's backup dancers, his hip bumping mine with enough force to send me stumbling off balance. I dissolve into giggles at the sight of him.

He really *is* ridiculous — in the best kind of way. My heart feels infinitely lighter than it did five minutes ago, and I know I have Grayson to thank for it.

A few moments later, he retrieves a second pair of pattered socks from the depths of his duffle bag and pulls them onto his feet. They're covered in lobsters and other sea creatures — a truly atrocious article of clothing.

We strip off our bathrobes so we're naked except for our little-kid socks, and for what feels like an eternity we dance around in the dim light of his bedroom, laughing like fools and holding each other close until our touches change from playful to passionate and our gasps of mirth turn to gasps of an entirely different nature.

And I think, as he makes slow love to me against the hardwood floor, there have never been two people like us in the entire existence of the world, who fill the gaps between each other's heartbeats with such perfect timing.

Afterward, we lie together intertwined, neither in any rush to untangle. He doesn't tease me — *Isn't this cuddling, Kat?* — and I don't stand up in a huff and say, *Fine, then let's get dressed.* We stay close, until our breaths even out and our hearts stop pounding like we've just run a marathon, only breaking apart when the polite rapping of knuckles against the door to his villa announces the arrival of our dinner.

Grayson gets up and puts on his robe to deal with room service, tossing mine over me like a blanket as he walks by with a devilish grin. Smiling so wide my cheeks ache, I slide my limbs into the plush cotton fabric and watch him move, feeling lazy and lustful and luckier than I've ever been in my entire life.

Hello, happiness.
It's nice to finally meet you.

***

A knock sounds at the door of my villa the next morning.

I race for it, giddy and breathless, a grin already stretching my features wide as I pull it open. My expression falls instantly when I see it's not Grayson standing there in the entryway. He made no promises to come by, after I left him around midnight... but I'm disappointed regardless.

Apparently, it shows.

"Gee, what a greeting," Harper drawls, pushing past me. "I think Jehovah's Witnesses have been received with more excitement."

"Sorry," I say, closing the door and attempting to school my features into something resembling happiness. "What's up?"

"Oh, nothing." She pins me with a look that says it's definitely *not* nothing. "Just wanted to see what you were up to."

"Up to? Me?" I squeak. "I'm not up to anything."

Oh, good, that didn't sound suspiciously guilt-ridden at all.

"Uh huh."

"Yep." I swallow. "Just hanging. Me, myself, and I. You know. Doing... me... stuff."

"Hmmm."

I bite my lip to keep from spewing any more nonsense and wait for her to speak.

"Funny," she murmurs, examining her cuticles with bored glance. "I came by last night, when I wrapped up on set. You weren't here."

"That *is* funny! I must've been out for a walk."

I make my way to the sitting area, avoiding her eyes. I try to act casual, instead of like I'm ready to explode from the strain of keeping the events of the past few hours to myself. She settles on the couch and stares at me. And stares. And *stares*, until I feel myself break as though she's been water-boarding me instead of sitting there blinking.

"I'm lying," I admit in a rush. "You know I'm lying."

She nods. "Easier to spot than a bad spray tan."

"I don't even know why," I wail. "I just… I don't know where to start."

"I'm guessing this has something to do with whatever's been making you so squirrelly and weird the past few days." She pauses. "And I'd also wager that *something* has green eyes and dark hair and deliciously chiseled abdominal muscles, if I had to put money on it."

"Not a bad bet." I press my eyes closed and force the words out of my mouth before I can change my mind. "I slept with Grayson. Last night. We went for a hike to this hidden waterfall, and it just… happened."

The admission is greeted with absolute silence.

No explosion, no surprise, no chastisement. Just total quiet. It bothers me infinitely more than her smacking me upside the head and screaming about the idiotic choice I've made, getting involved with him.

I crack open an eye and look at her cautiously. Her face is blank.

"Did you have a stroke?" I ask after thirty seconds, when she still hasn't spoken.

"I'm just searching for something to say that sounds intelligent and supportive but also questions whether you've thought this through, and simultaneously expresses my concern that you're going to get hurt."

I blink. "And?"

"And I haven't come up with anything yet."

We fall back into silence. I feel her words stirring inside me, a tornado tossing emotional debris in every direction.

I have no words either. No answers.

The truth is, I *don't* know whether I've thought this through. For all I know, things with Grayson could be a colossal mistake. The sex was great. Fantastic, even. But when it came time to sleep and I voiced my concerns about people noticing if I made a walk-of-shame back to my villa the next morning, Grayson didn't tell me to stay. He didn't insist I go get a change of clothes and come straight back. He didn't say, *I don't give a fuck what anyone else thinks. You're my girl, and I don't care who knows it* which, for the record, is what he would say if this were a movie, instead of real life.

Nope. He walked me to the door, kissed me goodnight, and said he'd see me soon.

See you soon.

Isn't that something you say to a co-worker when you awkwardly bump into them at the supermarket?

Hey, Bill, great to catch up. Enjoy those avocados. I'll see you soon.

I shake my shoulders, wishing I could as easily shake off the spiral of dark thoughts inside my head. I'm losing my grip on the happy glow I felt in Grayson's arms, mere hours ago. Harper can probably tell I'm beating myself up already — perhaps that's why she feels no need to lecture me. She just scoots closer and lays her head on my shoulder and, when she finally speaks, her voice is laced with worry.

"Just promise me you'll be careful. I know he's gorgeous. I know he's fun. I know he makes your insides flip like you're riding a rollercoaster. But falling for a guy like Grayson Dunn is like trying to wait out a hurricane by taking shelter in the eye of the storm. You might manage to survive for a little while, but eventually that hurricane is bound to roll over you... and when it does, the wreckage can be catastrophic."

***

Harper and I avoid talking about Grayson for the rest of the day. We spend all afternoon parked in beach chairs at the edge of the surf, soaking in the sunshine and enjoying our rare bout of free time. We sip delicious rum drinks, make asses of ourselves on paddle-boards, take selfies with a massive green sea turtle that's beached itself on the white sand, and wave to Wyatt as he catches waves on a sleek, waxed surfboard a few yards down the beach.

I laugh and splash and sip my drinks and reapply sunscreen with a smile, but deep down, there's an unsettling twang of worry in my stomach. The text I sent to Grayson about meeting us for lunch went unanswered. There's been no word from him all day.

If Harper notices me looking over my shoulder in the direction of the villas for a dark-headed form that never appears, or checking my phone every now and then, waiting for a text message that never arrives, she chooses not to comment on it.

I try to stay in the moment and out of my head... but all the while an irrepressible storm is brewing inside me.

I'm no blushing virgin, no inexperienced schoolgirl who's never had a one-night-stand before. I know the rules. I understand the typical three-day-post-sex-waiting-period some men ascribe to before calling, so they don't seem over-eager. People say dating is a game, but I've always thought of it more as a power struggle. A battle of indifference. A contest of who can care less.

Perhaps it's cynical and cold, but it's also the truth — the less you care, the more control you have over the other person.

And... indisputably... I care.
I care too much.

My head recognizes that I should not be this affected by the fact that, twelve hours post-coital, he hasn't yet reached out, hasn't asked to see me or shared how he's spending his free day in paradise.

My heart is another story entirely.

With a normal guy, I wouldn't be bothered. I'd accept his silence for the standard morning-after need for distance — the well-documented dance of unattached ambivalence two partners engage in when they haven't quite established what any of it *means* yet, or aren't ready to slap a label onto their relationship with all the sentimentality of a quality-grade stamp on a plastic-wrapped package of ground meat in a grocery store.

Grayson is anything but normal, though. Nothing about him follows any of my rules. I feel like a junkie, strung out after one hit of heroin. Craving more, now that the buzz has worn off, even if it might kill me.

It's strange — when I left his villa in the early hours of the morning, I'd never felt more certain of his affection for me. But the longer we've spent apart... the more time that passes without hearing from him... the more my mind has turned over our strange situation. And the more I've realized that nothing is certain at all.

My nerves are frayed, frazzled. I am raw with worry and self-doubt. Stripped of the surety I felt within the circle of his arms. The prospect of seeing him again in a few hours to work on the overnight shoot looms ominously on the horizon, a storm cloud hovering just offshore, about to make landfall.

The unavoidable sex scenes.

It would likely be strange enough, filming something of that nature, even without what happened between Grayson and me last night. Now, there's an even deeper level of emotional investment in our scripted passion.

Because it won't all be scripted; not for me, anyway.

I'm not sure where he stands.

My mind is full of mocking self-doubts that sound suspiciously like my mother, and they only seem to grow

louder as the seconds of our separation tick by into minutes and then into hours without hearing from him. I know it's silly to be so unsettled by his silence.
Just because he hasn't sought you out doesn't mean he's avoiding you.
Just because he hasn't texted you doesn't mean he's ignoring you.
Since when have you needed a string of emoji-laden sentiments on a smartphone screen to reassure you of a man's intentions?
Relax, crazy-pants.
Like he said... you'll see him soon.
Soon — somehow, it feels like an eternity.

We head to the filming location early, so Harper has ample time to do my makeup and help me get into costume. By this point in the film, my pretty blue sundress has been transformed into a more practical crop-top and shorts, stitched unevenly with fishing line. The costume designers worked their magic, making the fabric look convincingly bleached and battered, as if the garment has actually been out in the elements for six months on an island in the South Pacific without the convenience of a washing machine or supply of detergent.

I move away from the makeup tent into the mouth of the cave, nodding in greeting to the set workers who are testing overhead lighting and making sure the film equipment is ready to roll by the time Sloan arrives. There's a bed of palm fronds and a fire-pit — Violet and Beck's small attempt at making the rock dwelling into a home, while the storm rages outside. My eyes scan the rest of the space, looking for Grayson.

When I spot him, it feels like someone's plunged a dagger straight into the space between my third and fourth ribs. I stop short, heart in my throat. My nervous anticipation at seeing him again dissipates.

Told you so, that ugly, awful voice sneers at me from my deepest subconscious.

He's sprawled on a chair over by the far wall and

Annabelle is hovering close by his side, tossing her perfect hair as she laughs at one of his witty lines. He hasn't spotted me, yet — he's too busy looking at her.

Smiling at her.

Touching her arm in a casual gesture that makes me feel a little nauseous.

And even recognizing the absurd, unreasonable nature of my own jealousy does little to dilute its presence in my veins like some kind of deathly narcotic. It laces my bloodstream, poisoning me from the inside out.

I stand there, bleeding inwardly, facing the horrifying fact that I, Katharine Firestone, have foolishly fallen for my cocky, condescending co-star. One day swimming in grottos and the depths of his eyes, one night wrapped up in his arms and his sheets, and I am hopelessly lost. More *uncharted* than Beck and Violet ever were, in a hundred-page script.

I turn to flee one instant too late — Grayson looks up and catches my eyes, lifting his hand in a wave of welcome. There's no choice but to cross over to them. His mouth curls in a half-smile that still manages to twist my stomach into knots, but he makes no move to stand, to hug me, to greet me like I'm anything except his co-star and this is any other day.

"Hey," he says when I reach them, green eyes on mine.

"Hey," I echo, trying to breathe normally.

"Oh! Hi there!" Annabelle interjects, bouncing on the balls of her feet. "What's up, Kat? Did you need something?"

I shake my head, not looking at her. My focus is locked on Grayson.

"How was your day?" I ask him, striving for a casual tone. "I texted you, this morning, to see what you were up to…"

"It was good," he murmurs. "Didn't quite live up to yesterday, though."

My lips twitch. I feel some of the tension ebb inside me.

"It was *so* great," Annabelle gushes. "We went on a helicopter tour!"

We?

I blink, stunned, the tension swiftly returning until my limbs feel pulled tighter than a bowstring.

Grayson is watching me carefully. I feel his eyes on my face, scanning for some kind of reaction, so I'm careful to keep my expression bland. I don't respond to Annabelle's announcement, but she's so excited to spill all the details about her day with Grayson, she doesn't notice my silence.

"You just *have* to take a tour before you leave the island, Kat. It was seriously amazing!" Her voice is downright giddy. It makes me feel physically ill. "Did you know you can see the volcanos from the air? Some of them are active! We saw lava and everything! They flew us so fast around some of the mountains I was worried we were going to crash. I don't know what I would've done without Grayson there to calm me down! I must've broken every finger in his hand, I squeezed so hard!"

Breathe in.
Exhale out.
Don't spiral.

"Sounds like a thrill." My voice is hollow of feeling. "You know, I actually forgot to tell Harper something — would you excuse me?"

I don't even spare a look at Grayson as I pivot on one heel and walk away. My world has suddenly flipped on its head. I can't fathom a universe in which he has spent all day with another girl — not when I can still feel the after-ache of him between my legs, still taste the memory of him on my tongue, still recall the warmth of his arms around me mere hours ago.

I cannot wrap my mind around the possibility that he awoke this morning and chose to seek out her company instead of mine, after the night we shared together. And yet, as I walk unseeing toward the break tent, I am forced to confront the possibility that the moments we shared laughing and loving beneath a twilight sky meant so little to him, he could carry on with his life without a thought.

I've nearly made it to the beverage table when his hand closes tightly around my forearm. I don't even have a chance to struggle before I'm dragged by the bicep out of the cave, down the narrow trail a few yards, and into a dense grove of palm trees.

"Grayson! What the hell!" I hiss, pulling out of his hold as soon as he stops moving. "What do you think you're doing?"

"Talking to my co-star."

"We have a scene to shoot. They'll be starting any minute."

"Well, they can't exactly start without us, can they?"

Scoffing, I push past him to head back to the set, but find my progress halted again by his grip on my arm.

"It's rude to keep people waiting," I say coldly.

"Well, it's rude to storm away from a conversation without a good reason, but that didn't seem to stop you."

"Oh, I have plenty of reasons."

His eyes flash — in their depths, I see anger and annoyance and something else, something that calls to mind memories of waterfalls and walk-in showers. I'd call it attraction, but that's too tame a word. This look is… *animalistic*.

"And what would those be?" he asks in a dangerously soft voice. "What, exactly, did I do to make you pissed off at me again? Because, the last time I saw you, from where I stood things seemed pretty fucking great between us. But somehow, in the span of a day, you've turned crazy on me."

"Don't call me crazy."

"Then tell me what this is about."

"*Her*!" I gesture toward the set. "It's about her."

"Her? Who? Wait… you don't mean *Annabelle*?" He says her name in a tone of such incredulity, you'd think I'd suggested he spent the day on a date with a baboon.

"That's what this is about? You're jealous over some other girl?"

Of course I'm jealous! I want to scream. *You made love to me in the shadows, and gave her your daylight hours. You're mine, not Annabelle's. I don't want her holding your hand, or touching your arm, or brushing the messy hair back from your infinite eyes.*

Except… he's not mine.

That's the problem.

He runs both hands through his hair, a dark expression twisting his features. "Shit, Kat, this is exactly what I was worried about…Christ, this is Helena all over again…"

I cannot stand the way he's looking me. Like I'm a clingy, crazy girl in love with him, the kind that pokes holes in the condoms in her boyfriend's nightstand with a needle while he sleeps soundly in bed beside her, the kind who thinks about things like baby names and biological clocks and reception venues and whether or not a full string quartet is too tacky for the wedding march. He's staring at me like I'm just one more obsessed bimbo, trailing after him with stars in her eyes.

It's not fair, or right, or remotely accurate… but it hurts me all the same that he could so thoroughly misjudge my character.

You are not this girl, I tell myself. *You are not this weak, this needy, this pathetically dependent on a guy you've slept with once. He wants to pretend last night was just a casual lay? He wants to play it cool until the movie is wrapped? Fine by me. I'll play it so cool, he'll catch hypothermia and freeze to death, before I'm done with him.*

A brittle little laugh slips from my lips.

"Don't be ridiculous, Dunn. Of course I'm not jealous." My heart tears as I lie in a blithe tone. "It just would've been nice to know you had plans for the day. I texted you to see if you wanted to get lunch with me, Harper, and Wyatt. We waited for a while. It's inconsiderate to do that to your friends. Even a heathen like you should realize that."

He blinks, startled by my words. "Oh. Damn. Now I feel like an ass." His grin is sheepish. "I didn't have my phone with me. I'm sorry."

"It's all right. It was just lunch. Not the end of the world."

"Good. God, you really had me worried there for a moment. After everything that went down with Helena, the drama she caused for the project after we got involved... let's just say I'm not eager to repeat that."

"Don't worry. I'm not Helena." I smile weakly.

"Man, I think Sloan might've actually killed me if I fucked up his movie *twice*, especially when we're this close to wrapping up."

My heart hurts. Physical pain radiates from each of its chambers. I'm well-practiced at keeping it buried far below the surface, but it still kills me to know his main concern is about fucking with the movie, not fucking with my head.

"I'm so glad you're not like her," he murmurs, moving in a bit closer. "You're not like anyone I've ever met, Kat. Just being around you makes me feel..." He trails off with a sigh.

My eyebrows lift. "Feel... what?"

His lips twitch. "There's a reason I'm an actor, not a writer. I'm no good with flowery words."

I tilt my head. "Okay..."

"I guess I just want to say, I'm glad you *get it*. Our situation... it's not normal. And some girls probably couldn't handle it. But you're not just any girl."

"Well—"

He steps closer, cutting me off. "You realize how important this movie is to me, because it's just as important to you. And you're not willing to let petty personal shit mess everything up."

I swallow down my own words as his wash over me.

I don't know how, but in the space of a few sentences he's twisted it all around, so I'm left thinking *I'm* the one who's made a mistake here. So I'm left feeling like I really am crazy or irrational or blowing things out of proportion. His smooth talk makes me second guess myself until all the righteous anger and jealousy simmering within me are so tangled up with insecurity and embarrassment, there's no way to tell what's real from what's fake. Before I can begin to sort it out, he steps closer and puts his hands on my hips. When he leans down into my space so our lips are a fraction of an inch apart, my whole mind goes alarmingly blank.

"You and me..." he whispers, his mouth practically on mine. "We're good, right?"

I nod. "Yes, we're good, but—"

"Good," he mutters, cutting me off with a kiss.

I float away on a cloud of lust, letting him soothe away my worries with each stroke of his tongue, telling myself that maybe I was overreacting about the Annabelle situation, reminding myself that Grayson doesn't know how to have a relationship that's anything other than casual.

Of course he's throwing up walls, after the intimacy of last night. He's just as freaked out as I am about this *thing* between us, whatever it is.

Petty personal shit.

As I walk back toward set, lips swollen from his kisses and eyes watching the spot between his broad shoulder blades, I'm barely able to recall why I was so upset with him five minutes prior.

I suppose that's the thing about being the fly in a web. You don't know you're caught until it's far, far too late.

***

The cave scenes take all night to film.

By dawn, I've been pushed to the breaking point of both exhaustion and embarrassment. I've never been much of a sexual exhibitionist — I've never had the urge to get it on in an airplane bathroom, haven't once been tempted to do it in a dingy bar stall. Hell, I hate to even pee in front of other people. So, I can't say I particularly *enjoy* stripping down to the skin and simulating sex in front of an entire film crew.

The only silver lining is Sloan's announcement that he got everything he needed, so Grayson and I won't have to spend a second night running our hands over each other's bodies for take after take after take, until I'm so turned on it's damn near painful to even look at him or breathe his air without exploding into pieces.

As soon as the final "Cut!" is called, Wyatt appears in front of me, wrapping a large fluffy robe around my body to conceal my nudity from the eyes of the crew. I pull it close and look up at him, noting the slight flush on his chiseled cheekbones.

"Why, Wyatt Hastings, are you blushing?"

"Don't be ridiculous. I'm a thirty-five-year-old man. I've seen my fair share of boobs before, baby."

I narrow my eyes. "But you've never seen *my* boobs before. Is it going to affect our friendship?"

He grins devilishly. "I think it can only enhance our friendship, if we're being honest. Boobs are the foundation of any solid partnership. More boobs, I say."

I smack him on the arm. "I'm pretty sure that's a load of—"

"Kat."

The intensity of Grayson's voice makes my words dry up mid-sentence. I turn away from Wyatt to look at him. He's got a black towel slung low around his waist, but he's still essentially naked. His eyes are full of so much heat they practically melt me on the spot. I can tell, from one look at him, that he's just as sexually charged after the past few hours as I am. That, given a single word of encouragement from me, he'd throw me down on the floor right here, in front of the whole damn crew, and fuck me for real. He's that far gone.

I gulp, but it does nothing to dislodge the lump of passion in my throat.

"Dunn," Wyatt says in a cool tone that sounds nothing like the one he was just using with me. "Did you need something?"

"I need Kat." Grayson's eyes never waver from mine. "To talk to her, that is."

"She's talking to me, at the moment." Wyatt sounds pissed. I want to ask him why, but I find myself incapable of speech, drowning in the ocean of desire inside a set of steady green eyes.

"I can see that," Grayson growls back.

I am standing between two distinct storm fronts. The air rolling off Grayson is so heated, it makes me shiver; from Wyatt, there's nothing but frosty, freezing silence.

"Kat," Grayson says lowly. "Can I walk you home?"

"Um." I swallow. My eyes dart to Wyatt, watching as he crosses his muscular arms over his chest, biceps bulging as his hands curl into fists. "Do you need anything else from me, or can I go?"

His light blue eyes flash with an emotion I can't read, before it's shuttered away. His expression goes blank. "Of course. I'll see you later."

"Are you sure—" I start, but he's already walking toward Sloan. Before I can move to go after him, I find my hand wrapped tight in Grayson's grip.

"Come on," he murmurs against my ear, pulling me away from the set so fast we're practically sprinting. "I've spent the past seven hours fucking you for the cameras. I think it's past time I did it for real."

My grin is brighter than the sunrise peeking up over the horizon as we dash inside my bungalow and slam the door behind us.

CHAPTER FOURTEEN

> "WHAT BIOLOGICAL CLOCK? I DON'T WANT BABIES UNTIL I'M THIRTY-FIVE."
> - *A twenty-nine-year-old single woman trying desperately not to freak out her date.*

Our last stretch of time on the island is bittersweet.

I spend my days falling in love with Grayson on screen, and my nights trying not to fall in love with him in his bed. He doesn't spend any more free days with Annabelle, and I don't ask him what happened between them, though I see her staring coldly at me from across the set on several occasions. We never talk about feelings or labels, never discuss what will happen when the final scenes have been filmed and our time in Hawaii runs out. There is a part of me that realizes things will not be the same once we get back to Los Angeles. That we are living in a state of suspended animation, acting like the world is made of nothing more than orgasms and room service and awkward dance moves. Morning walks as the sun rises over the water, afternoon hikes up to our hidden waterfall, lost hours making love under the stars.

I ignore the rational side of my brain that insists my seconds here are numbered. I forget the past, shut out the future, and focus only on the moments with him.

Harper tells me this isn't healthy. That I'm asking to get my heart broken, by refusing to demand a spoken commitment from him. That fabulous sex is all well and good... but it's not going to make him stick around when the sets break down and our suitcases are packed.

I tell her maybe if more people focused on actually falling in love instead of defining it to death, the divorce rate would be a hell of a lot lower in our country.

Even her eye-roll cannot mask the worry in her gaze.

I'm not sure whether it's human nature or simply female inclination to put labels on things. All I know is, as a species, we like things neat.

Orderly.

Categorized into classes and easily defined.

Even our art — we break it down into periods, classify it by mood and theme and color scheme.

The blue period. The red period. Impressionist, watercolor, oil, abstract.

We can't let our art be messy, let alone our relationships.

We do it with literature, too. Segregate our books into genres and sub-sections. Start every horror story with "it was a dark and stormy night" and every fairy tale with "once upon a time" just to make it clear that things are going a certain way. We crave the safety of archetypes and stereotypes because it takes the guesswork out of things.

Beginning, middle, end.
Rising action, climax, resolution.
Meet-cute, conflict, happily-ever-after.

This is all well and good, except for one thing: real life rarely follows any discernible pattern. There is no rhyme or reason for most of what happens to us, no explanation as to why we must endure half the shit we go through before we finally stroke out and die.

People like to look back with 20-20 hindsight and say things like "all's well that ends well" and "the ends always justify the means." But what if they don't? What if the ending you get isn't some grand, sweeping victory? What if your tale concludes in a whimper instead of the high note you were promised? What if you live your life expecting a romance novel, and get a tragedy instead?

Preparing, labeling, classifying... it rarely changes the outcome. If I'm the heroine of a horror story, if my endgame is nothing but heartache and harrowing loss... well, the way I see it, there's not much I can do to prevent that.

Fate may be determined to fuck me over, but I'm going to have some fun before she does.

So, I make love. I skinny dip. I learn to surf. I eat poke and kalua pig under tiki torches with Wyatt on one side and Harper on the other, laughing until I snort rum out my nose. I hula-dance in a skirt made of grass with locals who teach me how to swivel my hips and shake my coconut-bra like a native Hawaiian. I spend more instants than I can count staring into green eyes that seem to contain the entire universe.

And, for a while, I'm *happy*.
Obnoxiously happy.
Disgustingly happy.
Fall-asleep-with-a-grin-on-my-face happy.
And then, quite abruptly... I'm not.

***

"Look! I think it's a ship!"

His shout once would've been a blessing. Now, I wrap my arms around my stomach and wonder what I did to deserve such a curse.

"Come on, Vi. Quick, grab a torch — we have to light the fire to signal them or they'll pass without seeing us." He snatches a torch from its stake in the sand and starts running down the beach, toward the massive pile of driftwood we built up on the rocky cliff's edge ages ago, back before we'd given up hope of ever being rescued. If a ship ever passed, we weren't going to be left scrambling for timber. We wanted to be prepared.

Wanted to be *saved*.

I watch him run. The farther away he gets, the more acute my pain becomes. When he realizes I'm not beside him, he whirls around and screams in my direction.

"What the hell are you doing, Violet? Let's go!"

I don't move an inch.

Shaking his head like he can't believe what he's doing,

he runs back, closing the distance between us. Up close, I see his eyes are half-crazed with hope and passion as he grabs me in his arms.

"What's wrong with you? Are you okay? Are you hurt?"

Hurt.

What an inconsequential word to describe such a feeling.

"No, I'm not hurt," I murmur.

"Then what are you waiting for? We have to go!" He sounds desperate. "Don't you see? This is what we've been waiting for! Praying for!"

"I can't," I whisper brokenly.

"What?" He looks at me like I'm a stranger. "What do you mean you can't? You're not thinking clearly. They're going to pass by— this is our only chance, Vi."

"I don't want to go."

His voice drops in disbelief. "What did you say?"

"I said I don't want to go!" I reach up and dash the tears from my eyes. "I don't want to leave. This is my home now. *You're* my home. And as soon as we go back..." My voice breaks. "As soon as we leave, it'll all be over. You'll go back to her. And I'll be alone."

"You're not thinking clearly," he says, taking me by the shoulders and giving me a shake. "You're being crazy! Nothing will change."

"Don't lie to me, Beck!" I yell. "Don't you dare! Not after everything!"

He grabs my face between his hands. "Listen to me. I will never leave you. I love you, you madwoman. You crazy, stubborn, complicated, awful, wonderful, beautiful girl. You lovely, charming, horrid, funny, sweet, strong woman. *I love you.* And I will keep loving you until I take my last breath, whether that's here on a deserted island with only sea turtles to witness it, or back home in civilization, with the rest of humanity. We may've been lost on this island, but I found myself in you. And I'm never letting you go. Not now. Not ever."

His lips land on mine and I feel traces of tears on his face as his mouth moves with passion, an indisputable underscore to the emotions he's just laid bare at my feet. My hands reach up to cup his face as I pull back, breathing hard, and stare into his eyes.

"Beck."

"Violet."

"...Let's go home."

His eyes glitter down into mine, full of love, and I feel my breath catch as he grabs me by the hand and, together, we run full-tilt toward the bonfire. Toward our future.

"*CUT!* That's a wrap!"

Sloan's voice rings out when we hit the end of the beach. Out of breath, both Grayson and I bend over to clutch our knees, winded after our fifth time running headlong down the sandy stretch. We filmed the actual fire-lighting yesterday up on a nearby cliff, while Sloan's drones got sweeping shots of us from above as the dry pile of wood burst into flames higher than my head. Which means... we're done.

For the day.

For the week.

Forever.

The thought catches in my throat. I feel like I might choke. When I straighten back to full height, I find Grayson staring at me, looking a bit strangled himself.

"That was it. The last scene on the island." I see his Adam's apple bob. "Can you believe it?"

I shake my head. My eyes are watering — I tell myself the tears stem only from the emotional aftermath of Violet and Beck declaring their love, but it's not very convincing. The line between my character's feelings and my own have become irreparably blurred. Standing here, staring at him, my heart is so full it might explode.

"I..." I swallow. "I just can't believe it's over."

"I'm sure they'll drag us back into the studio at some point, to re-shoot something. Sloan is a perfectionist. It's not over yet."

"Right. But our time in Hawaii..." My voice gets quiet. Maybe it's odd, but I feel more like Violet than ever. The scripted lines I've said over and over all day are haunting me.

I don't want to leave. This is my home now. You're my home.

As soon as we leave, it'll all be over.

You'll go back to her. And I'll be alone.

Grayson offers me his hand. "Come on. Let's walk back."

I lace my fingers tightly with his, saying nothing but squeezing hard. When we arrive, hand in hand, at the other end of the beach, the entire crew is clapping and cheering. Sloan steps forward, eyes misty behind his glasses.

"Well done, you two. Tremendous work." He hugs me with surprising force for such a small man, and whispers quietly in my ear. "You, my girl, are a bright star. Thank you for bringing Violet to life so beautifully."

"Thank you for giving me the chance," I murmur back, before he pulls away and engulfs Grayson in a hug.

I'm trying not to cry, but it gets harder when Wyatt steps into my path. The way he looks at me — like I'm something remarkable and rare — is almost too much to handle, right now. He says nothing as he steps close and sweeps me into a bear hug that lifts me clean off my feet. I drape my arms around his shoulders and tuck my face into his neck as he swings me around in a dizzying circle. His mouth finds my ear, after a moment.

"Didn't I tell you, baby?"

"Tell me what?" I say, laughing as salty tears drip against his skin. "You tell me lots of things, old man. You'll have to narrow it down."

"I told you I was going to change your life." His voice gets rough. "I just didn't know you were going to change mine, too."

His words hit me like an arrow to the heart. I try to speak, but all that comes out is a squeak of air as I struggle to keep from blubbering like a little girl who's missed her afternoon nap.

He sets me down gently, but doesn't move away. His eyes are so steady, so deeply sincere as they hold mine, it simply makes my tears flow faster. His big hands cup my jaw, thumbs wiping away rogue teardrops as they trickle steadily down my cheeks.

"Don't cry, baby."

"I'm not crying," I lie.

His lips twitch. "You remember what else I told you the first day we met?"

"That your therapist says you're emotionally distant and damaged?"

"Well, yes, that too." He laughs. "But also that I thought you were going to be perfect for this project. Better than anyone we'd considered casting before."

"And?" I lift my brows.

"Well, I still think if we'd gotten one of the Olsen twins—"

I smack him.

He grins.

"Be serious, Hastings."

His grin fades a bit. "You don't want me to be serious, baby."

"I do!"

"You sure about that?" he asks softly. My heart starts pounding faster at his tone.

"Of course," I say lightly, disarmed by his sudden shift in mood from teasing to intent. "If I wasn't sure, I wouldn't have asked."

"Fine." He leans closer, blue eyes on mine. "You were the best Violet I could've asked for. The best Violet anyone could've asked for. You were perfect — *are* perfect. Katharine..." The guard he always keeps over his eyes drops, just for an instant, and I see a flash of a man so serious, so intense, so hopelessly contrary to the playful friend I've dismissed him as for the past three weeks, it makes my mouth go dry.

He leans a fraction closer and the celebrating crew around us goes suddenly mute, out of focus, until all that's left is this beautiful Viking, towering over me speaking words I'm not sure I want to hear.
"I don't know how to go back to a world where I don't see you every day. I know this is the wrong time to tell you, but if I don't say it now, I might never get the chance again. Katharine—" He cuts himself off before the words can escape him.
"What?" My heart flips inside my chest. My tears flow faster. "Wyatt, tell me—"
"There you two are!" Harper screams, shattering the moment as she bounds up to us. "It's over! I can't believe it. In fact, I refuse to believe it. I think we should stage a boycott. A sit-in. A riot. We'll just stake out the place and make the damn producers keep paying for at least another week in paradise as reciprocity for all the Oscars we're about to win them."
Wyatt stares at her. "And by *those damn producers* you mean me, correct?"
"Naturally."
"Sorry. No can do." He steps carefully out of my space. "We have to get this footage into post-production as soon as possible, if we want to have it ready in time for the winter festivals."
"Well that just *sucks*." Harper sighs heavily. "Kat, next time you get us one of these gigs, try to make it last at least a month, okay?"
I roll my eyes. "Yeah. I'll do my best."
"I have to go catch up with Sloan — I'll see you guys later." Wyatt winks and walks away, shoulder brushing mine as he passes. The strangest sensation comes over me as he leaves — that I should stop him, say something to him about that look in his eyes a few moments ago…
I swiftly dismiss it.
It was just a moment. Hell, maybe I imagined it.
No.
He's never looked at you like that before.

As the crew moves in around me, overflowing with warm words about the film and kind wishes for the future, I reach up and touch the spot where his shoulder brushed mine with light fingers, wondering why real life can't ever be as simple as a movie script.

***

Harper and I are wearing our grass skirts and coconut bras, knee-deep in the ocean with rum drinks in our hands. Drunker than sin, we sway and shimmy to the distant music piped through the resort's outdoor lounge speakers. The rest of the crew is up at the pool bar, doing shots to celebrate our last night on the island. Even typically buttoned-up Trey is letting loose — I saw him slurp down three tequila shots before he and one of the lighting crew guys disappeared like giggling teenagers to make out against a palm tree in the ever-lengthening afternoon shadows.

Wyatt is babysitting Sloan who, for once, has forgone his god-awful green juice in favor of something slightly less healthy. Two rum drinks and he's practically under the table, telling inebriated stories about his long Hollywood career to anyone who'll listen. Annabelle, looking sour as she sips her vodka soda and texts rapidly on her cellphone, watches the festivities unfolding around her like a prom queen stuck at band practice. If her nose gets any higher in the air, she'll get altitude sickness.

It's not the official wrap-party, of course — that's not till next week. Apparently, it's a formal affair at Wyatt's estate up in the Hills, and everyone will be there: the full cast of extras and flight crew from the plane crash scenes, our costume designers, set builders, and the rest of the production staff who stayed behind while we flew to Hawaii.

Harper's phone rings in her hand. She stops swaying and squints down at the screen. "Oh, crap."

"What? Who is it?"

"Greeeeeeeeeg," she wails drunkenly.

"Don't answer." I take a generous sip from my straw. "Boys are stupid."

"TRUE!" She shrieks, pointing aggressively at me with her drink. A dollop of mai-tai sloshes over the side of her cup into the ocean. She watches it fall, face twisting into a pout. "What a *waste*."

"Harper, it's an open bar," I point out, taking another large sip. "You can get more."

"There is not enough rum in the *world* to make me want to talk to Greg." She tilts her head to the sky. "Why am I with him?"

"I don't know, honey."

"He's not nice. He never takes out the trash unless I nag him. He leaves toothpaste gobs in the sink. AND!" She points at me again, sloshing more rum. "He has a really, really, incredibly small penis."

"Harper!" I gasp, giggling.

"Don't laugh," she says solemnly. "This is serious. I don't give a hoot about that whole *it's-not-the-size-of-the-ship-it's-the-motion-of-the-ocean* shit. You know who started that rumor? *Men.* Men with *small ships*, if you catch my drift, sailor."

I dissolve into giggles again.

Her phone chimes in her hand for the third time.

"Oh, for fuck's sake!" Stumbling a bit, she rears back and hurls her smartphone as far as she possibly can out into the ocean. I watch it sail through the air and plunk into the depths with wide eyes, hissing her name in a low voice.

She looks absolutely thrilled with herself.

"TAKE THAT, YOU TOOTHPASTE-GOOP MONSTER!" she screams at the top of her lungs, chugging down the rest of her cocktail and twirling round in happy circles that splash water in all directions.

Shaking my head at her ridiculous, drunken antics, I suddenly catch sight of someone standing on the beach, staring at me. With a start, I realize it's Grayson.

"Hiya, honey!" I call happily, feeling my face stretch

into a grin as I rush toward him. I shimmy my shoulders so my coconut bra cups clank together. "If you're looking for coconuts, you came to the right place."

His lips twitch as his eyes flicker down to my chest. *God, he's gorgeous.*

Just the sight of him brings me up short. He's wearing black jeans and a tight gray v-neck. There's a day's worth of scruff along his jawline and a duffle bag slung over one muscular shoulder.

Wait. Back up.

"Why do you have a duffle?" I ask, tilting my head at him. The grin falls off my face. "Are you leaving?"

He nods. "Yeah. I have to get back."

"Oh... right now?"

"Yeah." He shifts from one foot to the other in the sand and shoves his hands deep into his jean pockets. "I wish I could stay, but I have a commitment to another project. My agent just called, he said they need me back ASAP. I have a ticket out of Honolulu in two hours."

He's lying. We both know it.

"But..." I suck in a breath that does nothing to steady me. "It's our last night. We're all leaving tomorrow afternoon on the jet. Can't you stay, just for the party? It's only a few hours..."

"No." He clears his throat. "There are some things I have to take care of."

I'm not sure if it's because I'm drunk or genuinely devastated by this shift in his demeanor and his plans, but suddenly there are tears filling my eyes.

"Hey," he whispers, voice softening. "Don't cry, Kat."

"I'm not," I croak stubbornly. "I just thought..."

"What?"

"I thought we had more time. One more night together. One more morning. The whole flight home..." I swallow my tears, trying to get ahold of myself. "I was counting on a few more hours of paradise with you."

"I know. I'm sorry. Listen... I'm no good at long goodbyes."

Then don't leave, I think miserably.

He extends his hand to me but I stay knee-deep in the water where he can't reach — not unless he wants to ruin his expensive shoes and soak his jeans. My hula skirt is plastered to my legs as the waves crash around me. Their rhythmic pounding against the sand is the only sound I hear as I stare into Grayson's eyes, thinking this can't possibly be the end. A reckless, selfish part of me wants to beg him to stay; the rational, sane part of me realizes he's already made up his mind about leaving.

I'm weak — I beg anyway.

"Don't go," I whisper in a small voice. "Don't leave me."

"I'll see you in a few days," he tells me, eyes holding mine. "We'll have re-shoots, I'm sure of it. Plus, the cast party, then the press tour, then promotional interviews, and the film festivals... Trust me, over the next few months we'll see so much of each other you'll be sick of me. I promise."

"But it won't be the same."

"You can't be sad, Kat. Not after all the fun we've had together."

"Why can't I be sad? You're leaving and it sucks." I bite the inside of my cheek so I won't cry again. "I don't understand this. I don't understand *you*."

"What don't you understand?"

How you can walk away so easily, when the thought of saying goodbye to you is killing me.

"Any of it," I say, jerking my chin higher. I see Harper hovering awkwardly in my peripherals, not sure whether to stay or go.

"Just come here," Grayson says softly, eyes beckoning. "Would you, please? Things always make better sense when you're in my arms."

Because I always give in, when I'm in your arms...

"No."

I don't want to go to him. If I do, he'll kiss me. And when he kisses me, I can't think clearly. Can't see straight.

Can't do anything but cling to him as my limbs dissolve into water.

His eyes narrow. "You're being ridiculous."

"And you're being an ass."

"Look, my plane is leaving in an hour. There's already a car waiting to take me to the airport. I can't do this right now. Not when you're drunk and irrational."

"Don't call me names." My brows tug together. "Me being drunk has nothing to do with this, and you know it."

"We'll talk when we're both home." Grayson runs a hand through his hair, looking exasperated. "Don't blow this all out of proportion. If I could stay until tomorrow, I would. Don't you trust me?"

I don't respond, because I can't give him the answer he wants to hear. Not without lying.

"Kat." There's a pleading note in his voice. A week ago — hell, two days ago — hearing it would've brought me to my knees. Now, I just stand there frozen, staring at his mouth as it forms words I don't understand. "I'll see you soon."

There's that phrase again.

See you soon.

"Fine," I whisper into the fractured space between us. "I'll see you soon, Grayson."

We stand there, separated by five small feet and an entire goddamned chasm of miscommunication.

"Fuck it," he mutters finally, tossing his duffle down on the sand out of reach of the waves, striding into the water so his shoes fill with water, and yanking me into his arms. I make a small sound of protest, but it's swallowed up as his lips claim mine in a crushing kiss.

This kiss — this last, goodbye kiss — is hauntingly similar to our first. Ankle-deep and angry.

His lips are harsh, hard against mine. There is no compromise in the way his teeth and tongue dominate me. No tenderness or devotion. It is a clash of contrary interests and misguided feelings. It is desire laced with damage.

His hands cup my cheeks, pulling me closer, and I align my curves against the hard planes of the chest I've come to know so well, and we devour each other with the sun sinking at our backs — a boy made of stardust and selfishness; a girl filled with fire and fury at the world. We are a tangle of emotional wreckage, two broken messes thrown together, trying to navigate something we can barely comprehend.

I feel something shatter within me, as his lips leave mine. I look up at him, panting through swollen lips, and stare into those gorgeous green eyes that have held me spellbound for weeks, and know, deep inside myself, that nothing will ever be the same between us if he turns and walks away from me right now.

Don't go.

Please, don't go.

His eyes hold mine for one, two, three long beats... and then he releases my shoulders, strides out of the water in his sodden shoes, grabs his bag from the sandy shore, and leaves it all behind.

The hotel.

The island.

The movie.

Me.

***

I'm drunk, but it doesn't do anything to numb the pain radiating out from the left side of my chest. Back in my villa, I rip off my stupid grass skirt, toss my coconuts onto a nearby chair and stumble toward the bed, tears blurring my vision.

I burrow beneath sheets that still smell like him and curl myself around the pillow where he once rested his head, and think maybe, if I just lie here long enough, the ache inside my soul will fade from something unbearable to something slightly more tolerable. Something that lets me haul in breath without feeling like my ribs are splintered, that allows me to close my eyes and see only the darkness inside my eyelids instead of the memory of his face as he leaned down to kiss me for the first time on a deserted stretch of sand under a whole galaxy of stars, his big hands cupping my jaw and his thumbs tracing small warm circles on my cheeks.

It's ironic, in a way, that when he spent the night with me for the first time — a massive tangle of blanket-hoarding limbs, taking up too much space and stealing all the pillows — I'd rolled my eyes and huffed indignantly. Now, in the absence of his hulking frame, the bed feels vastly too large. I'd give anything to go back to those easy, empty nights before he crawled into my sheets and under my skin.

The tears flow faster.

I'm not even sure why I'm crying — maybe because this feels like an indisputable ending. But can you really call it an end when we'd barely even started? Can you call it a break up if you allow yourself to be broken? If you are a willing accomplice in your own destruction?

I'm not sure. All I know is, I am mourning something that was never mine. I am Violet, afraid to leave this island, afraid that he will slip through my fingertips like a ghost as soon as reality sets back in.

And he is *not* Beck, I realize with horror, hugging my pillow closer. He will not offer reassurances, will not make promises he has no intentions of keeping.

He is Grayson Dunn.

The movie star.

The sexiest man alive.

Hollywood's golden boy, with a million-dollar car and an endless supply of beautiful women at his beck and call.

Somehow, it was easy to forget all that while we were here, as far removed from Hollywood as you can get. Somehow, I managed to convince myself that two passion-filled weeks with me in paradise would be enough to change him.

But people don't ever change. Not really.

And the saddest part is that I *knew* it — I was fully aware of who he was, of the dangers of getting too close, of handing over my heart on a silver platter and expecting him not to shatter it to pieces. I knew, and I let myself fall anyway.

I am the only one to blame, here.
I am the reigning queen of bad decisions.

The hardest truths to swallow are the ones that contradict the lies we've been telling ourselves. When you're in denial about someone's intentions, when you've spent days or weeks or months or years making excuses for their inactions and inadequacies, it's damn near impossible to dig yourself out of the delusional hole you've burrowed into, like an ostrich with its head buried in the sand.

I've been lying to myself about him for so long, I can barely see straight anymore. I have inflated our relationship in my mind so far past the point of return, I counted even his indifference as intimacy and his distance as desire.

What the hell is the matter with me?

Perhaps I am simply that self-destructive, that incredibly masochistic, to align myself with such a man against all reason and common sense. Perhaps I'm even more messed up than I realized.

Or maybe I knew all the shitty things he'd do to me, in the end... and I fell in love with him regardless.

Maybe love isn't something you can control, or talk yourself out of just because it's not convenient.

Maybe Grayson is a choice that was never mine to make.

Harper comes in, eventually. She's slightly more sober as she lies down at my side and strokes my hair, murmuring all those soft, sweet things best friends say when a boy breaks your heart.

He's an idiot.
He'll come around, you'll see.
He's just scared of commitment, he's not scared of you.
Don't give up on him just yet, honey.
Maybe someday he'll see the woman you are, and be the man you need...

The problem is, there's another voice inside my head. A vicious voice with years of practice at making me feel inconsequential. This voice is far harder to shake off, and far more believable than Harper's heartfelt reassurances.
Who the hell do you think you are?
You're nothing.
Nothing.
Nothing.
Of course he saw that.
Of course he left you.
When the voices grow too strong, when the pain gets too intense, I mercifully tumble over the edge of consciousness, like Alice down a rabbit hole.

I dream of green eyes and crashing waves and solar system socks and cracked chess boards. And when I wake in the harsh light of morning, there are already tears on my cheeks.

CHAPTER FIFTEEN

"I can't feel anything when I use one of those."
- *A pull-out-method advocate.*

I watch Hawaii shrink into the distance as the jet ascends, wondering if I'll ever be back again. Wondering if there will ever come a time when I can walk a white sand beach without thinking of me and Grayson and Violet and Beck and this whole twisted mess we've made.

I'm sober — mostly — and my tears have dried. I will not waste another moment weeping, today. My mascara is far too expensive for that.

I sip a mimosa to stave off my hangover and fall into a fitful sleep on the couch for most of the flight home. The hushed sound of Wyatt and Harper murmuring back and forth wakes me a few minutes before we land in LA.

"Is she okay?"

"She's still sleeping."

"No... I mean, is she *okay*..." He pauses. "With Dunn leaving."

"She will be."

"It's like Helena all over again. He'll never learn." I hear a deep sigh from Wyatt. "Christ, if I didn't need his pretty face to promote this movie for the next six months, I'd bash it into something unrecognizable."

"Wyatt! I've never heard you talk like that."

"Yeah. I'm not generally the beat-down sort. But in the case of Grayson Dunn, I might make an exception."

Hearing those words makes my lips twitch into a smile. Wyatt Hastings is incapable of passing up an opportunity to flash that protective streak.

"I just hope she doesn't start to spiral." Harper sounds nervous. "Kat can get pretty self-destructive, when she's feeling low."

"How so?"

"In the past, she's had some bouts of depress—"

I choose that moment to sit up, startling them both into silence.

"Are we there yet?" I ask breezily, as though I haven't been eavesdropping on their private conversation about my emotional damage.

Wyatt smiles at me. "Wheels down in ten minutes, tops."

"Great. I'm starving." I stretch my arms over my head and feel my back crack. "Definitely need a burrito or three, as soon as we're back in the city. It's been far too long since I visited my favorite taco truck."

Wyatt laughs.

Harper mutters something about a bacon cheeseburger.

When the jet lands a few moments later, we disembark in numbed silence. I think we're all still stunned that it's finally over, that we're actually home.

Wyatt walks us to the town car waiting at the curb in front of the private terminal. He hands our duffle bags to the driver, slips him a tip, and faces me with a stern expression on his face.

"You call me if you need anything. I mean it, Katharine. Anything." His stare lingers on the dark circles beneath my eyes. "And get some rest. You look like crap."

"Thanks, old man." I hesitate a beat, then step into his chest and hug him tight.

"A hug?" he says, sounding shocked as his arms close around me. "From the self-proclaimed hug-hater?"

"Shut up." I squeeze him tighter. "Thank you. I mean it. *Thank you.* For everything."

"Don't get mushy on me, baby." He clears his throat roughly, trying to sound nonchalant. Releasing me, he turns to Harper and lifts his hand. She jumps to high-five it. "Bye, Harper."

"We'll see you at the cast party on Monday, right?"

His lips twitch. "I assume so — it's at my house."

"Oh. Right. Seeya there!"

I hook my arm with hers and drag her into the waiting town car. Exhausted from the trip, we lean back against the leather seats and stare out our windows at familiar streets lined with palm trees and gridlocked with rush-hour traffic. LA looks too bright, too busy, too bursting with life after the natural, unadulterated beauty of Hawaii. I can't help thinking, given the choice, I'd pick white sand beaches and green sea turtles over flashy designer stores and double-decker tourist buses any day of the week.

When we pull up outside Harper's apartment, she pauses with her hand on the door lever.

"What's wrong?" I ask.

"Time to break up with Greg," she mutters lowly. "Wish me luck."

"Luck." I squeeze her hand. "Hey. Just remember — toothpaste gobs."

She steadies her shoulders. "Toothpaste gobs. Got it."

"Life is too short to be with someone who doesn't make you happy."

She looks over at me as she digests my words and her eyes go soft. "Do me a favor?"

I raise my eyebrows.

"Try to remember that advice applies to your own life, too."

I blow her a kiss as she steps out of the car, takes her duffle from the driver, and heads inside with a melancholy wave and a flash of purple hair.

Being back inside my crappy condo is a bit surreal.

It's not exactly a climate-controlled villa on the beach with unlimited room service. Looking around at the thin coat of dust on my particleboard furniture, listening to the sound of my neighbors screaming through the thin wall, I realize, with a start, that it's the first time in almost three weeks I'm really, truly alone. No Harper to sunbathe with, no Sloan to hear feedback from, no Wyatt to run lines with.

No Grayson to make love with.

I drop my duffle on the floor without bothering to unpack, walk straight upstairs to my bed, and collapse into it with a groan. My phone is mocking me with its utter lack of messages from a man I'm not even sure I want to hear from. My houseplants are dead and withering in their pots by my window, after far too long without water. The stale air is suffocating me.

Or maybe it's the solitude, I'm choking on.

I attempt to turn on the AC, only to discover the unit has stopped working. When I pull open the sliding glass door to the balcony off my bedroom to let in the breeze, I spot my beat-up Honda sitting off-kilter in its spot out front, with not one but *two* flat tires.

There's not a speck of food in my refrigerator, but it looks like I won't be driving to the store to restock anytime soon. The thought of calling a tow truck and dealing with a mechanic is too much to handle, at the moment.

Stomach rumbling, I climb under my duvet and squeeze my eyes shut, wishing I had something — anything — to distract me from thoughts of Grayson and the fact that he hasn't called, though he must know I'm back in LA by now.

We'll talk when we're both home.

I'll see you soon.

As I drift off to sleep with my phone tucked beneath my pillow, I can't help wondering if there's a statute of limitations on those words. At what point does *soon* become *never*?

***

The next morning, I wrestle a wonky-wheeled cart down the dairy aisle, wondering how I always seem to pick one that's malfunctioning. It's a hidden talent —

much like my ability to only ever buy overripe avocados and continually purchase gross substitute sunflower butter instead of chunky peanut, by accident.

I sigh as I pass through the produce section, where hand-drawn chalkboard signs proclaim ORGANIC in bold white script above the locally-sourced lettuce. Smaller, discreetly-placed placards declare CONVENTIONAL LETTUCE in plain, passive aggressive lettering. Apparently, writing "normal goddamned produce" would be too straightforward.

In most parts of this country, they'd congratulate you for just buying vegetables; in California, they'll judge you heavily if you don't buy the right *kind* of vegetables.

The meat section is even worse.

All natural, hormone free, gluten free, antibiotic free chicken, bathed in the tears of free-range alpacas and massaged twice daily with a deep-pressure shiatsu technique to ensure maximum flavor and tenderness.

I spend more time trying to decipher bullshit on the labels than actually putting things in my cart. I can't help but think grocery shopping should not be this difficult.

By the time I reach the checkout aisle, I'm half-starved and feeling snappier than usual. I haven't eaten since the muffin I scarfed down on the flight yesterday, followed by a wholly unsatisfactory dinner consisting of a stale granola bar I discovered in the dark recesses of my cupboards last night.

I glance at my phone as I wait impatiently for the cashier to ring up the customer ahead of me. No new messages. Harper's cell is at the bottom of the South Pacific, somewhere. Wyatt's busy in post-production. And Grayson...

I scroll down through my contacts and find his number. He's still saved as *Jake From State Farm*, which should make me laugh but instead makes me feel sort of hollow. I reprogram it to GRAYSON DUNN while waiting for my turn at the register, resisting the urge to send him a text message. I will not succumb to the clingy, crazy impulses he's inspired... No matter how much his silence is killing me.

I load my items onto the revolving belt with more force than necessary, knocking over a stack of bubblegum in my haste. Looking up, I find the teenage cashier peering at me with wide brown eyes. Her face a perfect picture of shock.

"Sorry," I murmur, feeling foolish as I scramble to re-stack the scattered gum. "Under-caffeinated and overtired."

"You're Kat Firestone." She sounds awed.

I freeze with the last pack of gum clutched in my hand. "What? How could you possibly know...?"

Her finger lifts to point at the magazine rack of tabloids directly behind me. Whirling around, I see my own face glaring from their glossy covers.

The first one I focus on features a picture of me in pigtails on the set of *Busy Bees*, a young Grayson hovering in the background. I don't know how they found out about our history or where they got that picture of us, but it's clear someone has been spilling my secrets to the press.

FROM CHILDHOOD CRUSH TO BIG SCREEN ROMANCE: KAT AND GRAYSON'S STAR-CROSSED LOVE STORY! INSIDERS CLOSE TO THE COUPLE TELL ALL...

Insiders.

What a load of bullshit.

Rolling my eyes, I glance at the magazine on the rack beside it and feel the blood drain from my face. The picture they've used on the cover is bad enough — messy hair, pouty expression, zoomed in so far you can see my individual pores — but the headline is what stops me in my tracks.

The letters are bold, blood red.

WHEN KAT'S AWAY, HER MAN WILL PLAY... GRAYSON SPOTTED IN INTIMATE MOMENT WITH EX-LOVE, HELENA PUTNAM! EXCLUSIVE PHOTOS ON PAGE 12!

I feel my heart stutter inside my chest as I see the picture inset beside the close-up of my face. It's grainy and dark, taken outside a nightclub, from the looks of it. But it's definitely Grayson — I'd know him anywhere. I've memorized the exact shape of his shoulders, committed the precise scope of his build to memory.

He's unmistakable — even out-of-focus, holding another girl's hand and shielding her from the camera flashes.

Helena.

My heart begins to pound as I attempt to think of a good reason for him to be out with her, mere hours after he landed back in the city. I tell myself that he probably needed to see her for something work related... remind myself that these tabloids are full of lies and misleading stories... reassure myself that there's no possible way the man I've fallen for could be so unbelievably cold as to cut me out completely and go back to his ex without so much as a conversation...

None of it sounds very convincing.

"That's you on the cover, isn't it?" The cashier's voice is a squeak of excitement. "Have you really met Grayson Dunn? Are you really dating? Is he, like, actually that hot in person? Or *hotter*?" The questions pour out of her so fast, I'm not even sure she's breathing. "Is Helena really pregnant? Are you going to kick her ass? No offense, but you're pretty dainty and my friend Mary Beth said she saw Helena on Rodeo Drive once and she was, like, over six feet tall. She used to be a model, you know."

"Thanks for the reminder," I murmur.

"Anyway, watch out because I bet she could, like, totally kick your ass. Even if she's pregnant. Maybe *especially* if she's pregnant — all those crazy hormones in her system... I would not want to be you, right now." She starts scanning my groceries. "Actually, that's a lie. I'd kill to be you. Just tell me if he's a good kisser. Please? I read this interview with Helena a few months ago and she told the reporter he was, like, *amazing* in bed."

I bite my lip to keep from screaming, snatch the closest three tabloids from the shelf, and slam them down on top of my package of paper towels before I can change my mind. "I'll take these too."

She squeals again. "I knew it! It *is* you!"

The whole time she's bagging my groceries, she babbles on about Grayson and Helena and how absolutely *glamorous* it must be to have my life. The sound of my pulse roars in my ears, tuning out her words. I clutch the magazine so tight my fingertips turn white, staring down at the pixelated photograph of the man I spent the past three weeks falling in love with, taken less than two days ago outside a nightclub.

His first night home. His first night without me.

"Maybe this is lame," the girl says, flushing red as she passes me my receipt. "But do you have any advice about how to make it in Hollywood? My dream is to be an actress, like you."

I take the thin paper from her grip and shove it in the back pocket of my faded cut-off shorts. Hooking my grocery bags around my forearms, I look from the hopeful girl to the blurry picture of Grayson and feel my eyebrows pull into a scowl.

"My advice?" I laugh bitterly. "Find a new dream. Hollywood will break your damn heart, kid."

Her crestfallen expression chases me out the sliding automatic doors, all the way through the parking lot. It's a long walk back to my place, but I barely care. My feet move on autopilot as I flip through the tabloid with numb fingers, looking for the story about Grayson and Helena. I'm so focused on the magazine in my hands, I don't see them staked out between the row of cars until it's too late.

Camera flashes explode from all directions.

"*KAT!*"

"*KATHARINE!*"

"*MISS FIRESTONE!*"

"*CAN WE GET A SMILE?*"

"*LOOK THIS WAY!*"

"HAVE YOU SPOKEN TO GRAYSON SINCE THE SPLIT?"

The magazine tumbles to the ground. I throw my hands up to cover my face as they press closer, coming at me from all sides. I try to push my way through the crowd, but there's no way out. I'm completely surrounded.

"KAT!"

"TELL US ABOUT GRAYSON!"

I hunch into a protective crouch, curling in on myself like a wounded rabbit surrounded by wolves.

"HAVE YOU SEEN HIM SINCE HAWAII?"

"DO YOU HAVE A PLAN TO GET HIM BACK?"

My eyes are watering and my ears are ringing — I'm practically blind from the constant flashes. Their shouts and questions never cease. I'm starting to feel claustrophobic.

"HAVE YOU SPOKEN TO HELENA?"

"DO YOU KNOW ANYTHING ABOUT THE BABY?"

I search desperately for my keys in the depths of my purse, fingers colliding fruitlessly with lipsticks and gum wrappers and a million old receipts. Someone jostles me from behind, *hard*, and I topple forward against the pavement. When I hit the unforgiving asphalt, my grocery bags fly from my grip, sending apples and canned goods rolling in every direction.

My palms and kneecaps shred like cheese against a grater. I cry out — more in disbelief than actual pain. I've dealt with the paparazzi before, that night at Balthazar, but they weren't nearly this frenzied.

No one helps me to my feet. They don't even stop shooting. If anything, their fingers press down faster on their shutters.

Click, click, click.

They don't see me as human at all. To them, I am a zoo animal. A SeaWorld orca. A spectacle to be photographed and exploited.

I'm attempting to scramble back to my feet, knees trickling blood down my bare shins into the tops of my favorite boots, when the sound of a scuffle cuts through the din. A giant man in a suit I've never seen before shoves two paps out of his path like they're made of paper. He's *huge*, probably six-foot-five, and handsome in a tough, body-builder kind of way with his icy blue eyes and close-cropped hair.

I open my mouth to ask who the hell he is, but the words never make it past my lips as he swoops in, scoops me into his arms, and carries me through the crowd toward a waiting black SUV.

"What— *hey*!" I struggle against his hold, relatively certain that I'm being kidnapped.

His low voice rumbles overhead. "Mr. Hastings sent me as security, ma'am."

Wyatt.

My thrashing stops abruptly. Before I know it, I'm settled safely behind tinted glass in the passenger seat of a massive black SUV, the kind you see in motorcades and secret service details. The paparazzi are shooting pictures of the car, but their fervor seems to have cooled a bit, now that I have backup in the form of my massive, suited protector.

He rounds the hood and climbs behind the wheel. He doesn't even look over at me — he just starts up the engine and peels out of the lot. After a moment of silence, I clear my throat.

"So... thanks for that."

"Just doing my job. If you want to thank someone, thank Mr. Hastings. He's the one who hired me."

"When?"

"My retainer started the moment your plane landed last night."

"But... I didn't ask him to... It's not his responsibility..." I shake my head to clear it. I'm stunned that Wyatt set this up. I can't imagine hiring a full security detail is standard practice for every actor who works on one of his movies...

"If I can speak freely..." My new bodyguard's voice

261

drops lower. "When he hired me, Mr. Hastings mentioned you might not have had adequate time to enlist your own security yet. I think he was worried something like this might happen if you went out on your own in the meantime."

"And if I didn't go out?"

"I've been watching your building, making sure no one bothers you."

"I can't believe Wyatt didn't tell me about this."

"Mr. Hastings wanted me to be discreet. I wasn't to announce my presence unless something happened." He pauses, hands tightening on the wheel. "If I'd done a better job, nothing *would've* happened."

"It wasn't your fault. I'm totally fine."

His eyes dart to mine. I see them drop pointedly to my hands, which are crusty with blood and dirt from my fall. He reaches into the center console, pulls out a package of pre-moistened tissues, and hands it to me.

"Thanks," I murmur absently, wincing as I extract a pebble embedded in my aching palm.

"No problem, Miss Firestone."

"It's Kat."

He nods, but I get the sense he's still going to use my surname whenever addressing me. The air of professionalism and formality surrounding him is irrefutable. He's probably only in his mid-twenties but his deadly serious demeanor lends him an intimidating sense of maturity.

He takes a left. It's not lost on me that we're heading toward my condo… despite the fact that I never told him my address. Apparently, my anonymity has expired. It was only a matter of time before the paparazzi found out where I spend my nights, where I do my shopping…

I sigh heavily.

He looks over at me, brows raised in question.

"I suppose this means they know where I live," I mutter, jerking my thumb back in the general direction we came from.

He nods. "It would probably be best to stay somewhere else, for a few days. And also to think about moving permanently to somewhere with security. A gated entrance. Closed-circuit cameras."

"Seriously?"

"Permission to speak frankly?"

"Always."

"Right now, anyone off the street can walk up to your front door and bother you. I did a quick sweep of your townhouse exterior, earlier — it has cheap, crappy clasps on the windows and your doors wouldn't withstand even the most amateur of lock-pickers. Basically, it's a nightmare for anyone who needs basic security measures."

I swallow hard. "I didn't realize."

"Of course not. This is new to you." He turns the SUV into my condo parking lot and pulls up to the curb, eyes scanning for hidden paparazzi members in the bushes by my door. "If someone jumps out at us with a camera, I'll handle it. You just focus on getting inside. Pull your curtains closed and make sure all the windows are locked. Even your balcony — it's not so high off the ground that someone couldn't scale the drainpipe and try to gain entry that way."

I nod as if his words aren't giving me heart palpitations. As if the idea that someone would go to such lengths to invade my privacy isn't totally foreign to me.

"Would you say that's likely?" I ask in a bland voice. "Someone trying to break in?"

"Hey." His serious gaze meets mine. "Don't worry. It's my job to keep you safe. What happened earlier aside... I'm quite good at my job, Miss Firestone."

"I don't doubt it."

"Here." He reaches into his jacket pocket and pulls out a sleek black business card. It's blank except for a small row of letters that spell out MASTERS and a phone number.

"Ready?" He reaches for his door handle.

"Wait!"

He pauses.

I haul in a breath. "You never told me your name."

"Kent Masters. Most people call me Masters."

"Masters," I echo, sliding his card into my purse. "Nice to meet you."

His lips twitch in the merest hint of a smile as he steps onto the curb and comes around to let me out. Masters hovers behind me like a shield as I approach my front door and slide my key into the lock. Once inside, I collapse on my couch and stare at my bleeding kneecaps, attempting to take stock of my new reality.

I was just recognized in public by a teenage fangirl.
My face is on the cover of every supermarket tabloid.
A mob of paparazzi attacked me for photographs.
My groceries are lying abandoned in a parking lot.
I have a badass bodyguard to protect me from harm.

I guess those things prove I'm not a Hollywood nobody, anymore. That I've finally "made it." But I must say... life as a *somebody* is officially weird.

After checking all the doors, windows, closets, and shadowy corners, Masters leaves me to go sit in his SUV, keeping watch and doing whatever it is that security details do.

Scanning surroundings. Cleaning weapons. Brooding in a smoldering, sinister manner.

I look around, feeling strangely exposed. Maybe I was away in Hawaii too long — my home doesn't feel much like home anymore. Granted, it was always more shit-hole than sanctuary... but whatever relative peace or security I used to feel between these four walls has evaporated. Each time a car rumbles by outside my windows, I have to fight the urge to take cover behind a wall or under a table.

It's definitely time to start looking for a new place.

I pull open a real-estate app on my phone and begin browsing for listings in my neighborhood, automatically ruling out several places with rents I can't afford. I click on a nearby studio, grimacing at the pictures of the water-spotted ceiling and old-fashioned radiator, and scroll down, wondering if it wouldn't just be better to stay where I am. The nicer neighborhoods are out of my bartending-tip budget.

But... I'm not living on a bartender's budget anymore.
The realization shouldn't be surprising. I knew, when I signed on to the *Uncharted* project, I'd be making more in one paycheck than most people make in their entire lifetime. But knowing and believing are different creatures. It still doesn't feel real.

I wander over to the stack of mail that accumulated in my time away. There's no check from AXC amidst the junk pamphlets and card-stock coupons. A pang of foreboding shoots through me as I realize exactly where my check must be...

In the clutches of an acrylic-nailed monster.

I pull Masters' card from my back pocket and dial his number. He answers on the first ring.

"Miss Firestone? Is everything all right?"

"Yes, I'm fine," I assure him. "I was just wondering if you could drive me somewhere..."

***

Cynthia's home in Manhattan Beach is just as I remember it — immaculately cleaned, impeccably decorated, incredibly cold. There is no feeling of *home* here. No warmth. Despite the sunshine pouring through the many skylights overhead, walking through the front door is like stepping into an ice box. Even the amazing water views off the large deck cannot make up for the chill of my mother's presence.

She sits perched across from me, back stiffer than an ironing board. Avoiding her gaze, I stare at the glass coffee table between us. There is not a single speck of dust on its surface.

The room is entirely silent except for the rhythmic patter of her acrylic nails against the wooden arm of her chair. I wish, suddenly, that I'd forced Masters to come in with me instead of encouraging him to wait in the car.

It's clear Cynthia is enjoying this — wielding power over me again. Forcing me to come to her, a stray begging for scraps.

My eyes move to the writing desk against the wall. There's a familiar photograph sitting in a frame on the surface. I flinch when I recognize Grayson and me on the set of *Busy Bees* — the same photograph featured on the front of the magazines in the supermarket earlier...

My gaze flies to her as realization boils through me.

"It was you," I whisper in a stunned tone, fracturing the silence.

Her eyebrows arch. "Excuse me?"

"You were the *exclusive insider* who gave the tabloids details about me. About my life. My history with Grayson."

"Of course," she admits with a scoff. "Don't look so outraged, Katharine, you'll give yourself wrinkles with that scowl."

"You gave them quotes about me. Photos..." I shake my head. "That's private! How could you do that to me? You're supposed to protect me!"

"I'm supposed to *promote* you," she corrects.

A horrified expression contorts my features. Of all the things she's done, this may be the worst. Betraying my secrets to the press... ruining my privacy... Hell, she's probably the one who told them where I shop for groceries.

"Don't look at me like that." Her eyes narrow. "It was good publicity."

"I don't give a shit. It wasn't your place to talk to them about anything!"

"I wouldn't have to spin sweet stories about your childhood if you'd been able to keep control of things. You should thank me — without the stories I gave them, the only thing they'd be saying about you is that you've been dumped. That you're a *loser*. Two weeks in the spotlight and already old news."

My hands curl into fists. "I haven't been dumped."

"Oh, really?" Her lip curls. "When was the last time you saw Grayson Dunn? Has he called you, since you got back here? Come by your apartment? *No*."

I bite the inside of my cheek to stay silent.

"You haven't been spotted together since Hawaii. And I heard he flew back early." Her voice is smug. "If I had to guess, I'd say he's already forgotten you. That he's gone right back to the man he's always been — drinking and drugging and whoring around with other women."

"That's not true!"

"Isn't it, though? I know all about him and Helena Putnam."

"You don't know anything," I snap, wishing her words didn't have such power to wound me. "You don't know him."

"But I know men," she says coldly. "And men — especially rich, famous men like Grayson Dunn — are good for two things: orgasms and alimony."

"You're sick."

"No, Katharine, I'm honest." She tilts her head. "Did you truly believe he'd ever be loyal to you? That he could love you?"

Her questions are an indisputable echo of my deepest fears. They tear at me like knives, slicing me straight to the heart. Because, in truth, I *had* believed it — that he could love me back. That he could be loyal.

It isn't just another fling.

I am more than a notch in his belt.

And yet... he hasn't called. Hasn't once reached out. I feel the absence of him in my life like a physical weight. A wound that will not heal, torn open a little wider with each hour that passes without hearing from him.

He is hurting me without lifting a finger. He must know it.

He just doesn't give a shit.

"What a pity... you love him. I can see in your face that you do," Cynthia says, lips pursing in disapproval. "Reckless, Katharine. Very reckless. You *never* listen to me.

How many times have I told you, always pick someone who loves you more than you love them? How many ways did I explain that caring more means you have less power?"

My eyes prick with tears I'll never allow to fall in front of her. "Love isn't about power! That's what you don't understand — what you've *never* understood."

"How perfectly naive," she murmurs. "Darling, I'll let you in on a little secret — everything in the world is about power. Sex, fame, lust, success, money... and love. *Especially love.* When you love someone, you give them all the ammunition they'll ever need to destroy you."

She's right, a horribly familiar voice whispers from the back of my mind. *You just don't want to believe it. You just don't want to admit you've already lost him. You lost him the moment the movie wrapped.*

I pull in a deep breath and attempt to compose myself so I don't cross the room and strangle her with my bare hands. When I speak, my voice is shaking with the effort to remain in control.

"I'm leaving. I want my check. *Now.*"

"I suppose you do." Her smile is calculating. "But I think I'll hold onto it for a bit longer."

"You can't do that." I grit my teeth. "It's my money."

"And I'm your agent. I negotiated your contract. I can do whatever I want."

"Cynthia, I'm not playing this game anymore." I rise to my feet, cross my arms over my chest, and stare down at her. "You've got two choices — you can give me my money and step away from my career of your own accord, or you can refuse to give me my money and I'll fire you, slap you with a massive lawsuit, and take this house and every penny in your bank account."

I see a flash of anger in her dark blue eyes. Her voice is suffused with faux maternal indignation.

"Oh, that's *so* nice. You ignore me for weeks, shut me out of every aspect of your life, then come over here and make heartless demands." She gets dramatically to her feet, like a soap opera star — all breathy outrage and flashing eyes. "Is this any way to treat your mother?"

"You're playing the mother card? Really?" I snort. "That's funny, since you've spent the past two decades telling everyone you were nothing more than my agent."

"So, this is the thanks I get for nearly twenty-three years of supporting your career?"

"I'm pretty sure the massive chunk of money you got from this movie deal should be thanks enough, actually. What's the going rate for your services, these days – fifteen percent? Twenty?"

She acts as though I haven't spoken. "And now you're going to fire me. After all I've done. All the years I've put in. The countless hours I've spent getting your career off the ground, the sacrifices I've made…" Her voice quivers with barely-leashed anger. "I've been the best agent you could ever ask for."

"But you weren't supposed to be my agent," I say softly. "You were supposed to be my mother."

"You were always *so* dramatic." She scoffs.

"And you were always so cold." My voice gets even quieter, but there's no missing the sincerity of my words. "Now, give me my check before I get my security detail to come in here and *make* you give it to me."

Biting back the scathing words on the tip of her tongue, she whirls around with her taloned hands curled into fists. Her stilettos click against the hardwood floor as she crosses to her writing desk and pulls an envelope from the top drawer. I don't move as she approaches, extending it toward me.

"Here."

I reach out to take it, but her grip tightens on the check. We stand with the envelope suspended between us, playing tug-of-war over the key to my financial freedom, and I recognize the fear in her eyes, just below the contempt and frustration boiling at the surface. She knows, as soon as I have this money, I won't need her any more. The success she pushed so hard for has, ironically, made her irrelevant.

"I have only ever wanted what's best for you," she hisses, leaning into my face. "If I pushed you too hard, it was only because I knew you could be great. You can hate me for challenging you, but we both know without me, you'd be nowhere. I saw your potential and did everything in my power to make sure it was fully realized. I made the rest of the world see it too. If that makes me a monster in your eyes, so be it. I have no regrets."

I stare at the woman who made me pirouette in front of the mirror until my toes were bleeding through my ballet slippers. The woman who woke me at four in the morning to stand in line at open-call castings for parts I never wanted. The woman who bought me a spray-tan machine instead of a bicycle for my eighth birthday. The woman who padlocked the refrigerator before auditions so I'd look thinner. The woman who scoffed when I revealed her ex-husband had made a pass at me. The woman who gave me everything I'd never asked for and withheld the only thing I'd ever wanted.

Love.

"You aren't a monster," I say softly. "You're nothing at all."

I rip the envelope from her hand, turn my back on her, and walk out of her life for good.

***

I stare at my phone. The blank screen stares back at me.

No call.

Three days since I left the island behind, and with it all my hopes for us.

Three days since I let him strip me bare for the last time, body and soul alike.

Three days since I whispered secrets beneath sheets as his lips skimmed my temple.

Three days since I felt myself falling, sinking, a ship caught up in a sea of limbs and lust.

My sails weren't strong enough to hold me on course.

Grayson Dunn doesn't do commitment.
My keel wasn't steady enough to keep me from capsizing.
Grayson Dunn will never be what you need.
He kissed me like a wave against the shore, eroding my defenses with the brush of his mouth. The caress of his palms against my shoulder blades pulled me in like a piece of driftwood without a tether. I felt myself sink under his thrall as he sank into me beneath thousand thread-count sheets in a dim, humid hotel room.

He's probably fucked a thousand other girls, girls just like me, who thought it meant something because he said *it's different with you, babe* with his mouth tugged up in that half smile and his green eyes drooped at half-mast as his fingers slowly worked at the buttons of my blouse.

He talked about our future, and held my hand in his, and stroked my hair as we fell asleep intertwined, and for a little while, I let myself believe it was more than just sex for him.

The sad part is, I knew better and I let it happen anyway.

How many times have I told myself to judge a man by his actions, not his words? Words are pretty, useless things — butterflies behind glass. You may feel warm and bright as you stare at their beauty but you'll walk away empty and cold, clutching nothing but the painful realization that you never really had anything at all. You never even got close enough to touch those fleeting gossamer wings.

The blank screen taunts me.
Still no call.
Something ugly stirs to life in my stomach, claws its way up through my chest cavity with razor-edged fingertips. His silence is the sharpest knife; his indifference is the keenest weapon.

I have grown so used to constant contact, to the instant communication of my social media generation, that I have lost any ability I once possessed to be comfortable in my own company. An hour without a text message is an eternity. A day is unbearable. A week is tantamount to torture.

Worse is the itching of my hands to check the gossip site headlines, the stream of Instagram pictures he's posted, the online social network where we added each other as "friends" the first week of filming. I can barely leash the restless, self-destructive longing to log online and stare at the words *last active 23 minutes ago* beside his profile picture and pretend they don't leave me gutted. To see the last three photos he's tagged in are with girls — all blondes, all beautiful, at some club downtown. To feel that final, delusional shred of hope that maybe he dropped his phone in a toilet or accidentally left it in a limo or just didn't see my *'Hey! I'm home. Where are you?'* messages yet, slip away like a handful of sand on the wind.

He's an asshole.
You deserve better.
Why hasn't he called?
Why do you still want him to?

I hate him for reducing me to this. This needy, pathetic creature flailing between emotional extremes like one of those wacky inflatable tube men they set up outside car dealerships to catch your eye as you speed past on the interstate. Air-dancers, they call them — fifteen feet tall, fluorescent yellow, wavering this way and that at the mercy of the winds.

Spineless.

My phone buzzes on the pillow and my heart gives a great leap inside my chest. I fumble for the phone in the darkness, dragging it close enough to read the illuminated name.

CYNTHIA

The hope disintegrates so fast it makes my lungs ache. I throw my phone across the room in frustration, out of sight, where it can no longer provoke me. I won't look at it anymore. Cynthia's words earlier echo in the darkness.

Did you truly believe he'd ever be loyal to you? That he could love you?

I am disgusted at my own weakness when, not five full minutes later, I drag myself over to retrieve my phone from the floor and place it carefully back on my pillow, so I won't miss it if it buzzes with an incoming call from him. A familiar voice mocks from the deepest corners of my mind, especially piercing in the total silence of my bedroom.

You are the most pathetic girl who ever lived.

I press my fingertips hard into my temples and resolve to delete his number so I won't be tempted to reach out to him again. To change the name GRAYSON DUNN in my phone to something like GIANT DICKHEAD so if, in the off chance he does deign to communicate, I'll remember what an asshole he's been for waiting three days and — I glance at the clock on my bedside table — fourteen and a half hours to text me. I tell myself to remove him as a friend online, because surely we cannot be anything akin to friends when he has made me weep and rage and stand in front of my floor-length mirror pinching the thin layer of fat that rolls over the waist of my size-two jeans, wondering whether a few pounds would've made any sort of difference in his obvious ambivalence, or whether, if I'd looked more like one of his models, I would've lasted longer than two weeks on his ever-rotating roster.

I do none of these things.

Phone clutched between flattened palms, like a prayer to a god I don't believe in, I curl up in a ball beneath my favorite blanket and squeeze my eyes shut.

I hate him.
I hate him.
I hate him.
Because... I think I really could've loved him.

It doesn't matter that he didn't — couldn't — love me back.

Or, it *matters*... but it doesn't change anything. His indifference does not alter my attachment. His lack of love does not mitigate mine. The sad fact is, I gave him my loyalty when he never asked for it. I spent weeks falling for someone who never gave a shit. And there's no cure for that. Not even time.

It's past midnight when I walk outside my condo and knock on Masters' SUV window. He rolls it down, taking in my tear-stained face with curious eyes.

"I need you to drive me one more place." I sniffle and wipe my nose with my shirtsleeve. "But I promise, tomorrow, I'm buying myself a new car and you won't have to take me anywhere ever again."

"Get in," he says quietly, no questions asked. No complaints.

I do.

"Where are we going?" he asks, starting the engine.

"Malibu."

I swallow hard as I give him Grayson's address, but it does nothing to dislodge my heart, which is stuck firmly in my throat.

CHAPTER SIXTEEN

"Do you believe in soulmates?"
- A man who will undoubtedly get in your pants before the night is over.

He pulls open the door, wearing nothing but a thin pair of black boxer briefs. I can tell from the way his hair is sticking up that I've woken him.

"Kat?" He blinks at me blearily, as if he can't fathom why I'm standing on his doorstep at one in the morning. "What are you doing here?"

"Can I come in?" I ask.

He holds the door wide and I step inside, hugging my arms around my body as if they might somehow protect me from the emotional wreckage about to be inflicted.

The door closes. It's so quiet I can hear my own heartbeats. I look at him and I know, before he speaks a word, that everything is different.

This is not the man who kissed me on the beach, who fucked me under the stars. This is an unrecognizable stranger, someone whose motives I cannot comprehend.

We stand in his huge, high-ceilinged atrium, not touching. Staring at each other like we don't know each sloping curve of each other's bodies, like we haven't seen each other's every imperfection at three in the morning when the whole world is silent and still except for the soft, secret noises we make beneath the sheets.

The silence stretches on. He hasn't said a word yet, and I'm already blinking back tears.

"What's going on?" he asks finally. "Are you okay?"

"No," I say. "I'm really not."

I watch his throat work as he digests that. "Tell me what's wrong, Kat."

"I...." My voice breaks. I can't finish.

His eyes are sad as he takes a tentative step closer. "Do you want to sit down?"

"Not really."

"Okay."

I stare at him, every perfect part of him, and despite everything that's happened between us, there's still a part of me that cries out at the sight of his green eyes and strong jaw and dark eyebrows, whose shapes I've traced in the darkness. There's still a desperate piece of me that yearns to run into his arms and beg him to love me back.

I ignore it, steeling myself for the reality of my situation.

"Tell me what's wrong, Kat," he says eventually, the sleepy haze clearing from his eyes. "Tell me why you're here."

"Grayson..." My eyes fill with tears as I say his name. "Everything is wrong. You. Me. Us. The whole damn world."

His eyes narrow. "I don't know what you mean."

I scoff brokenly. "Of course you know. How could you not know?" My hands fly out from my sides as I gesticulate, and with that small lapse of control I feel my whole facade of togetherness begin to unravel. "You disappeared on me. And I thought, maybe, I could just let it go. I thought I could let you slip away without a protest, but I can't. I won't." My hands curl into fists. "I deserve an explanation. I deserve a conversation, after everything that happened between us back in Hawaii."

"I know." His voice is quiet.

I blink. "What?"

"I know — you deserve more than this. I'm sorry. None of this has been fair to you. Shutting you out. Not calling you back. The stuff with Helena..."

"It's true, then?" I feel my heart skip. "About you and Helena? About the... the *baby*?"

"Kat..."

"God, it's true." My eyes focus on the ceiling, to keep my tears from falling.

"No! No. It's... Look, things are just really complicated for me right now. I need some time."

"Uncomplicate it for me," I suggest. "Explain it to me. Give me a chance to understand."

"It's not that simple. There are things you don't know."

"Are you back with her?"

"I'm not back with her. I was never *with* her. We were just..."

"Just fucking?" My voice cracks on the word. "Right. Because that's what you do. That's your thing, huh? With her, with me. No emotions. No commitment. Just physical. Just *fucking*. Right?"

"That's not fair, Kat."

"*Fair*? Don't talk to me about fair, Grayson. None of this is remotely fair to me."

He runs a hand through his hair. "What do you want from me?"

"I don't want anything *from* you," I whisper. "I just want you! That's all I ever wanted. You're the one who changed things between us. You're the one who stepped away." My voice is a plea. "I just want things to be like they were, back in Hawaii."

"They can't be. Things have changed."

"What's changed?"

His eyes are tortured. "Look, while we were there, while we were away from all this bullshit — the press, the paparazzi, the parties, the past — I thought, maybe, things could be different. That *I* could be different. For a few weeks, I wanted more than anything to be the one for you. To be the standup guy who holds your hand and keeps his word and always comes through. But I think we both know... *I'm not that guy*. I don't think I'll ever be that guy, Kat. No matter how much either of us wants me to be."

The tears start to trickle from the corners of my eyes. He watches them fall, looking horrified.

"Don't cry…" He moves toward me. "God, I don't want to hurt you. I'd never want to hurt you, Kat. Don't you know that?"

I step back, arms held out to stop him. "Don't."

"What can I do?" he asks. "What can I say besides I'm sorry? How can I make this better for you? The last thing I ever wanted was to make you sad."

"It's a little late for that," I snap.

"That's not fair, Kat. You knew what this was. You know who I am." He runs his hands through his hair. "I can't be the guy you want me to be."

"I never asked you to be anyone except yourself."

"You didn't have to ask, Kat. I can see it in your eyes, every time I look at you. I can sense it in every breath you take. I can taste it on your lips. And it kills me, to know that I'm hurting you."

My tears fall faster. "So, instead of hurting me by being with me, you're going to break me completely by cutting me out of your life?"

"I'm not cutting you out. I couldn't do that, even if I wanted to, with the film premiere coming up…"

"*Wow.*" I cry. "What a gentleman."

"That's exactly what I've been trying to tell you. I'm not a gentleman. I'm no good for you, Kat. This, right here — you at my door in the middle of the night, heartbroken and hurting? — *this* is why I only do casual." He sighs. "You and me… there's nothing casual about us."

"Maybe *I* can do casual," I whisper recklessly.

"You can't. You're not built that way."

I don't argue, because I know he's right.

He steps closer, making me flinch back. "This thing, whatever it was that we had — it was beautiful. And I don't want to ruin it by trying to force it into something it's not." His voice softens. "I don't want to erase all those moments of joy with anger and bickering and bullshit. That's what happened to my parents. My grandparents.

My aunts and uncles and friends and cousins and every damn person I've ever met who's ever tried to make a serious relationship work."

"So, what? We see each other from now on and just… act like strangers? Like none of it ever happened?"

"I don't know," he murmurs. "All I know is, if we keep this up, I'll ruin it. No question."

"How do you know?"

"I feel so fucking guilty just being near you. I feel like I've let you down, because I can't be the guy you fell for in Hawaii. Maybe someday, I'll feel differently. Maybe someday, I'll be ready. But right now…"

"Don't!" I cross my arms over my chest to hold myself together. "Don't you say that to me. *Someday* is an empty promise. *Someday* is a lie you tell girls you blow off, to make yourself feel a little better."

"Kat…"

"You know what?" I ask, staring at him. "I came here for answers. You gave them to me. They just weren't the answers I wanted." It's an effort to keep my voice even, I'm crying so hard. "I appreciate your honesty. I'll be going now."

"Kat, wait—"

I turn back to look at him, just before I reach the door. "Wait for what, Grayson?" My words are soft. "For you to change your mind? For you to be someone you aren't? For you to force yourself into a relationship you don't want?"

His mouth opens and closes again without a sound escaping.

"That's what I thought," I whisper. "I can't wait for you — I'll be waiting forever." I pull open the door, steady my shoulders, and speak to the darkness. "Goodbye, Grayson Dunn."

He doesn't follow me.

This is not a movie — there is no last minute change of heart, as he chases the SUV down his driveway barefoot, determined to win me back. The music does not swell. We do not ride off into the sunset together.

I ride home alone, weeping steadily, much to the horror of my bodyguard.

It's over.

End scene.

***

Useless tears sting at my eyes as I walk into the kitchen and pour myself a drink. It's not the first I've had today, but it *is* the only thing I've consumed. The bottle is nearly empty — I hate the thought of going out again, of leaving the small, safe sanctuary of my shit-hole of a condo and seeing his face plastered everywhere, mocking me from the checkout aisle as I wait to pay for my industrial-sized bottle of vodka.

OLD FLAMES REKINDLED? GRAYSON AND HELENA SPOTTED OUT ON THE TOWN!

THEIR SECRET ENGAGEMENT... SEE THE HUGE RING ON PAGE 32!

BACK TOGETHER FOR THE BABY? WE'VE GOT ALL THE DETAILS...

I finish my drink, feeling numb as the vodka swirls around my empty stomach.

Grayson.

I ache. I ache so badly I can barely breathe. There's a steady throb inside me, like a broken bone never set properly — a constant source of chronic pain that catches me off guard when I least expect it, sending me stumbling off balance and craving an escape.

But I cannot escape him.

Not in sleep, for he haunts my dreams, not in a bottle, for he is always there in the darkest corners of my mind and the alcohol thrumming in my system seems to welcome him to the forefront of my cerebrum like an old friend. He has ensnared me like a frail winged insect in a spider's web. All my struggles only serve to tire me out, to shorten my fight. Demise is inevitable.

It always was.

We once played chess with weather-beaten pieces at an old scratched board in the heart of my favorite park, as the sun faded out into a star-studded sky. Though I put up a valiant effort, we both knew it was only a matter of time until he outmaneuvered me, his rook moving more deftly, his mind making moves and countermoves so far in advance I had no chance of ever capturing his king.

Checkmate, baby.

I suppose that's the fundamental problem with the two of us — he's always played the game better. Whether chess or the endless contest of indifference we were engaged in, he had a clearer grip on the rules since the very first moment our orbits crossed, and he always knew exactly how to make me feel childish and unskilled.

I find some small, twisted comfort in thinking that perhaps we used each other. Him, for a glimpse into what it would be like to live a life entirely different from the one he'd been raised to desire, and me for the steady diet of angst and emotional damage that seemed to make me better, sharper, like a sword against a whetstone. I was his intellectual escape from a long parade of pretty, empty girls... and he was my drug of choice — unhealthy, probably lethal, but ultimately so addictive it was hard to turn away.

The problem, of course, with this theory of mutual exploitation, is that it is the deepest of lies. There was nothing equal or mutual about the way we used each other. I barely scratched his surface while he sliced me limb from limb.

There's no comfort in that. None at all.

It's strange, realizing something that meant everything to you meant next to nothing to someone else. That you cared more, invested more, loved more.

I was one of many. I was mundane.

The safety net. The safe bet. The sure thing.

The one you call after a weekend spent chasing other women, because you know she's so caught up in you she'll always answer the phone.

I am his Monday girl.

And Grayson?

He is the worst kind of faker — the kind so full of shit he actually believes himself genuine. He talks of dreams for a different kind of life, an authentic life, with a girl like me who would push him to grab the world by the throat and squeeze every drop from it.

But he never wanted me. Not really.

He craved the idea of me.

The potential of what we could be.

The sad, shallow truth is that, when it comes down to it, he needs his string of bimbos more than he ever needed me. He cannot relinquish the Grayson Dunn he pretends to be for the cameras, the news crews, the crazed fans. He cannot be the man I want, the one I saw a glimpse of as he made me see stars beneath a waterfall in the middle of a cloudless sky one stolen afternoon in paradise.

In rare moments with him on the island, I saw flashes of a man I would follow over a cliff, just to keep loving. Flickers of a man I would offer all my devotion, if he could just love me back.

But I cannot survive on flashes and flickers.

I cannot love him for his potential. It is not enough to live on, though the masochistic streak I cannot seem to suppress would tell me to keep trying, to cling to the possibility I saw lurking in his eyes until it killed me. To keep hold of that empty promise of *someday*, lovesick and starving on the crumbs of attention he tossed my way, until I was nothing more than a skeleton — no thumping heart, no vital organs. Just a calcified corpse of longing, waiting for the day he'd finally look at me and realize, *Fuck, I am killing her.*

The thing it's taken me far too long to realize, so long I have dwindled to nothing but bone strung together by ever-hopeful cartilage, silent except for the sound of the wind whistling between my vacant ribcage, is that he happily let me wither down to nothing.

His indifference was not an accident. He saw that his silence was killing me and did nothing to stop it.

I pour another drink and wash the taste of dashed dreams from the back of my tongue. I feel half-dead, but my broken heart somehow still beats. What a stubborn, senseless organ, to keep going when all hope and happiness are lost.

That is the cruelest death in the world: the death of hope. The utter destruction of a dream you carried close inside you, praying someday it might come true, even if you never let yourself speak such words out loud.

Alone in the silence of my shitty condo, crushed beneath the weight of my own reality, with Grayson Dunn out of my bloodstream and settled firmly back in his old life without me, I see the gravity of my own miscalculations.

I am not the Juliet to his Romeo.

I am not the lodestar around which he orbits.

I am not the trade wind by which he sets the course of his sails.

I am not essential or exceptional.

If I were a day in his schedule, I would undoubtedly be Monday. An afterthought to an otherwise exciting weekend. Something to simply trudge through on your way to better things ahead.

I was his Monday girl.

Shitty, really, since he was my whole damn week.

***

The knocking starts and doesn't stop until I've dragged myself out of bed and made my way downstairs to the front door. Yanking it open angrily, I find Wyatt on my doorstep, dressed in jeans and a thin sweater that shows off his impressive chest. His long bronze hair is pulled back in that messy-perfect way he always manages to pull off and his eyes are roaming my face like he's staring at a ghost.

I want to die on the spot.

I hate him seeing me like this — mascara stained and messed up. I've been drunk for two days straight. Harper would undoubtedly call this a *spiral*.

"Jesus," Wyatt mutters, taking in the sight of me. From his dark expression, I'm guessing I look even worse than I feel. "Katharine, when was the last time you ate something?"

"Are we counting vodka?" I ask, slurring a little.

His jaw ticks. "No."

"Then I don't really remember." I shrug, turn, and head into the kitchen, leaving the entry open so he can follow me in. "Don't worry! I'm on an all-liquid diet. It's like the master juice cleanse, only alcoholic."

"Christ," I hear him mutter as the door clicks closed. "When Masters called me and said I needed to come, I knew it was bad… but I didn't know it was this bad. *Baby*." His voice cracks as he stops in front of me, face a mask of concern. "What happened?"

I lean against the counter and wave his words away, trying to look put together. "Don't worry, Wyatt. I'm fine."

"Yeah, you look it," he says dryly. "Not answering your phone for three days. Drunk at two in the afternoon. Alone. Thinner than a damn rail."

"Oh, relax. It's not that bad."

"Katharine. Tell me what happened."

"No."

"Is this about Dunn?"

"Don't!" I yell, glaring at him. "Don't say his name. I don't want to hear his name ever again."

Wyatt sighs and presses his hands over his eyes, thinking about something. I take the opportunity to search for my glass, in desperate need of a refill.

"Oh, no you don't." He plucks the vodka bottle from my grip, unscrews the cap, and pours the remnants down the kitchen sink.

"Hey! I was drinking that!"

"You've had enough." He whirls around to face me. "Now, this is what's going to happen. You are going to get in the shower. When you get out, I'm going to make you a meal and you are going to eat every damn bite of it without argument. Do you understand me?"

Wyatt's never talked to me like this before. I blink slowly at him, trying to reconcile the gentle giant I know with this angry, glaring man before me.

"I said *do you understand me*, Katharine?" he hisses.

"Yes," I say quietly. "I understand you."

"Good." He nods, and I see some of his anger ebb. "Are you sober enough to shower?"

"Of course." I scoff, swaying lightly on my feet. "I'm totally sober."

"Uh huh."

"Look!" Arms held out at my sides, I touch my pointer fingers to my nose one by one like I'm undergoing a field sobriety test. "See? Sober."

"Get in the shower. Try not to fall and crack open your skull, please."

"Fine. I'm *going*." I roll my eyes, reach down, and peel my long-sleeved shirt up over my head. Tossing it onto a nearby chair, I reach for the button on my jeans and quickly step out of them, so I'm only in my bra and panties. I hear a sound from Wyatt, not quite a cough, not quite a groan, and when I look up I see he's staring pointedly at the floor.

"Katharine," he growls through gritted teeth, his voice pained. "Please, go get in the shower."

"I said I'm going!" I turn and walk toward the bathroom, reaching for the clasp of my bra and sliding it off my shoulders as I go. There's another cough-groan from the kitchen, but I'm too drunk to think what it might mean as I slide my underwear off and turn on the shower head in my dingy pink-tiled bathroom. Naked, I step into the tub, almost stumbling off balance as I adjust the temperature.

The world is spinning.

I sit down on the cold porcelain and let the hot water pour over me in a torrent. The heat feels good, radiating into my numb chest cavity. My dark hair is plastered down my back, hanging half over my face like a curtain. Knees curled up to my breasts, I wrap my arms around myself and lean against the side of the tub with my eyes closed. And for the first time in days, I sleep.

***

"*Katharine!* Fuck, baby, what are you doing?"

Someone is shaking me. Big hands are on my shoulders, under my armpits, lifting me from the tub. The water's run cold. I hear the valve shut off and open my eyes to see Wyatt, his gaze frantic with worry as it scans my face. I'm naked and freezing in his arms, water beading against my pruned skin like rain on a windowpane.

Shivering, I stare up at his beautiful features and attempt a smile with frozen lips.

"You're like ice," he growls, pulling me into his chest. It's warm and broad and comforting against my cheek. "Are you okay?"

"Fell asleep." My teeth are chattering. "Sorry."

His arms come around me. "Don't be sorry. It's my fault. I shouldn't have let you shower alone. I mean… I should've helped you… I should've called Harper to help you."

I press closer to him, eyes closed. I rub against him like a cat, seeking warmth. "Mmmm."

"Christ." His voice sounds like he's in pain again. "You're going to kill me."

I feel his hands flex against the naked skin of my back. I hear him suck in a ragged breath as he grabs a towel off the nearby rack and wraps me in it.

"There," he rasps out. "That's better. Now…"

He scoops me into his arms and carries me into the living room, setting me down on the couch and tucking a blanket around me as soon as I'm horizontal. He crouches by my head, brushing the wet strands of hair from my face, and stares at me with those eyes that seem to see everything but demand nothing.

"Wyatt?" I say in a small voice.

"What, baby?"

"Will you stay? I don't want to be alone anymore."

He sighs and something unreadable flickers behind his eyes. "Of course I'll stay."

"Thank you."

"You don't have to thank me, Katharine. Just sleep. You'll feel better when you wake up. I promise."

With his words warding off the shadows that have held me hostage for the past few days, I close my eyes and drift off. Thankfully, this time, I don't dream at all.

***

He's gone, when I wake up, but Harper's there. The look on her face is of stark disapproval.

"You are in such deep shit, Katharine Firestone."

I sit up with a groan. I'm sober for the first time in days. My head is aching like someone's stuck a knife in my temple and twisted.

"Ouch," I mutter.

She hands me a glass of what looks like Gatorade along with two white tablets. "Drink this. Take these. You'll feel better."

I do as she says. Glancing down, I realize I'm still wearing nothing but a bath towel. My cheeks flame bright red.

"Oh, Jesus… the shower… the stripping… *Wyatt*…."

Harper's mouth twists. "Apparently, you put on quite the show, drunky."

"God, I was such a mess…."

"Yeah, he told me."

"What time is it?"

"It's about ten."

"In the *morning*?" I hiss, staring at the light pouring through my windows.

"Yep. Wyatt had to go to work, so he asked me if I could stay with you today. Good thing I got a new phone last night, or I'd never have gotten his message."

"He stayed all night?"

"Yep."

I moan, more embarrassed than I can remember being in ages. "He must hate me."

"I don't think that's even close to how he feels," she murmurs.

My eyes narrow. "What do you mean by that?"

"Nothing." She shrugs. "Go upstairs and put on some clothes. Wyatt ordered a whole spread of food for you, before he left. Pasta, bread, salad — basically the entire menu at *Mistral*."

I gasp. "I *love* Mistral."

"Good, because there's enough food here to feed an army and you're looking skeletal." Her frown intensifies. "I have no idea what you'll wear to the wrap party tonight. Everything in your closet is going to be loose."

"The wrap party is tonight?" I've lost all concept of time. "It's *Monday* already?"

"Yes. That's what happens when you crawl inside a bottle of vodka for an entire weekend."

I rise to my feet, feeling weak-kneed. "I'm sorry, Harper...." I swallow. "Things just..."

"Spiraled?" she finishes for me, voice soft. "I know, sweetie. And I'm sorry about Grayson. I know he broke your heart. I know he's an asshole. But if you let him break you... if you let yourself fall apart because of some douche-nozzle movie star who uses too much hair product... I'm going to have to kick your ass."

I feel the hint of a smile cross my lips.

She steps closer. "You look awful."

The smile fades. "Thanks."

She grabs my hand and squeezes. "Next time, if you need to fall apart, if you start to spiral... do me a favor? Call me first. I promise my phone won't be at the bottom of the Pacific. Okay?"

"Okay."

"Wyatt was ready to enroll you in rehab. I had to talk him into letting you come to the party tonight."

"One bad weekend doesn't make me an alcoholic."

"That's what I told him." Her eyes narrow. "Don't prove me wrong."

"I won't. I promise." I cross my arms over my chest. "I feel better, now. Honestly."

It's a lie, but she doesn't call me out on it. Her expression softens and she nods slowly. "Okay, Kat. Go pull yourself together. I'll reheat the food."

I turn so she doesn't see the tears and climb the stairs up to my bedroom, wondering how the hell I'm going to face Grayson again. How I'm going to survive not just tonight, but also a press tour, movie premiere, and a thousand photo ops with him at my side for the next six months. How I'm going to live in his world and pretend he hasn't shattered mine to pieces.

I guess I'll burn that bridge when I come to it.

CHAPTER SEVENTEEN

"I'M NOT CRAZY."
- *A psycho, stage-five clinger.*

"Are you ready?" Harper looks over at me in the back of the town car. "We can skip it. We don't have to go in there."

"No." I steady my shoulders and stare out the window at Wyatt's massive mansion in the Hills. It rises magnificently into the darkness, the front facade lit by ground-level spotlights. Urns filled with dancing flames line the driveway where we wait, watching people slowly filter in through the front door. "No, I'm okay. I'm good. I can do this."

Harper looks unconvinced.

She's wearing a gorgeous red cocktail dress that matches the exact shade of her freshly-dyed hair, which she's done up in an elaborate French twist. She styled mine in a half-up, half-down cascade of waves and braids that took hours in front of the mirror but perfectly complements the flowing, white Grecian-style gown she stuffed me into, evidently borrowed from a friend who works in the wardrobe department at AXC. I've been threatened with bodily harm, should I spill anything on it or lose any of the expensive pieces of gold jewelry clasped around my wrists, neck, and ears.

"Let's go," I say, calling thanks to our driver and stepping out into the driveway. Harper falls into step beside me, linking her arm with mine.

"Just breathe," she murmurs. "And remember how fucking fabulous you are. With or without Grayson Douchebag Dunn."

I smile faintly as the doors swing open and we step inside. My mouth gapes — if I thought the outside of the mansion was impressive, it's nothing compared to the interior.

"Holy shit," I hear Harper mutter. "That Hastings fortune is no joke."

"Apparently," I murmur, staring from the crystal chandelier hanging from the twenty-foot ceiling above us to the grand staircase leading to the top floor. We're engulfed by the crowd as soon as we step through the doors — people hugging us hello, calling greetings from the makeshift bar on the other side of the room. I see cater-waiters weaving through the mob, trays full of gourmet appetizers held aloft.

I don't see Grayson or Wyatt anywhere. Which is fine, because I have no idea what I'll say to either of them, when our paths inevitably cross. A waiter walks by with a tray of champagne flutes — I grab one, making Harper's eyebrows lift.

"Relax," I mutter, taking a tiny sip. "I'm pacing myself."

"Good," a steady male voice says from behind me. "Because I've already scraped you off the bottom of a bathtub once in the past twenty-four hours. Not looking to repeat that experience anytime soon."

I turn to face him, feeling a bolt of embarrassed electricity shoot through me when our eyes meet. He looks fantastic in dress pants and a fitted white button down, his hair slightly tidier than usual, pulled back in a bun with a black leather strap.

"I'm sorry," I blurt, after a moment of silence. "You have no idea how embarrassed I am that you saw me like that... I'm mortified."

"Don't be." Wyatt shrugs. "We've all been there. I understand."

I suddenly recall a different conversation with him, back on set in Hawaii.

Someday, you'll get your heart broken, and you'll understand.

I'm not wishing it on you. I wouldn't wish it on anyone.

I just know it'll happen at some point. It happens to us all, eventually.

"Hey," he murmurs, taking a step closer. His eyebrows draw together. "You okay?"

"Fine. I'm fine." I blink to clear the haze from my thoughts. "I just... I feel like I owe you. I *do* owe you."

"You don't owe me anything."

"But it's not just yesterday." I swallow. "Hiring Masters... making sure I wasn't alone..." I stare at him, wondering how I got lucky enough to have someone in my life who takes care of me, even when I don't deserve it. "You're always looking out for me, Hastings. Why is that?"

He shrugs. "Maybe I have a savior complex."

"Your shrink tell you that?"

"No, I figured that one out on my own."

I sigh as my eyes move from the massive chandelier over our heads, to the colorful art canvases on every wall, to the massive mahogany staircase bannisters that look like a dream to slide down.

"This place is amazing, Wyatt. Seriously... it's like a castle, or something. I can't believe you live here."

He grins. "You haven't even seen the best part."

"Are you going to show me voluntarily, or are you going to make me beg?"

"I wouldn't mind a little begging."

"Hastings."

"Oh, all right. Come on."

He grabs my hand and leads me away from the party, through a series of dark rooms, and out a set of sliding doors. We walk down an incredible terraced back yard, passing a pool, hot tub, and full tennis court, before we reach a landscaped pond. In the middle of it, a tiny white gazebo sits, connected to the shore by a thin walkway.

"Wow," I breathe.

He leads me out onto a wooden path, over the water, holding me steady so I don't trip over the long train of my dress. When we reach the gazebo, he releases my hand. We sit down a foot apart on the padded bench, looking out over the hills, and I feel my heart pounding twice its normal speed in the silence.

"It's beautiful." My voice is no more than a whisper.

I feel Wyatt looking at me. "And yet, not the most beautiful thing I've seen tonight."

My cheeks heat at his words. I meet his eyes and find them dancing with humor.

"Are you flirting with me, Mr. Hastings?"

"Of course not. You're far too young for me."

"Right. I forgot. You're… what did you say, the first day we met? Old enough to be my *cool uncle*?"

He groans. "I did not say that."

"You did," I insist. "I remember distinctly, because I've never had an uncle, let alone a cool one." I pause. "Let alone a cool, hot one."

"Now who's flirting, Miss Firestone?"

I grin and lean back, sipping my champagne with my eyes on the blanket of stars sprawled out over the LA haze. "Why did you bring me down here, Wyatt?" I ask softly.

He leans back, shoulder brushing mine. "I come here when I feel like things in my life don't make any sense. When everything's a mess, and I start to think nothing's ever going to be right again." He takes a slow sip of the scotch in his hand. "The world feels so small from up here, spread out under all these stars. Somehow, the idea that we're just one speck of dust in the great expanse of that universe over our heads makes everything seem more manageable." He sips again. "In the sum total of human existence, I'm just one person. There will come a time when no one remembers me, when everything that made up my life is gone and whatever problem I'm having that seems so monumental will cease to exist, even in memory.

Obliterated by time."

"And that makes you feel *better?*" I ask dryly.

He laughs. "Somehow, yes. Because it reminds me that life is what you make it. There will always be shadows and darkness, if that's what you gravitate toward."

"But you stay in the sunshine," I murmur, recalling a conversation we had, what seems like a lifetime ago.

"Exactly. Every day, you have a choice about how you're going to live your life." His voice drops lower. "Choose sunshine, baby. Always choose sunshine. You look so much prettier with light in your eyes."

We sip the rest of our drinks in silence as I stare out at the distant horizon. I'm not sure whether it's his words, working their magic over me, or simply the comfort I always seem to feel in his presence, but by the time our glasses are empty and we make our way back into the party, I feel more myself than I have in days.

Tonight, I'm choosing sunshine.

***

Grayson never shows up to the wrap party.

His absence grates on my raw nerves as the hours pass and things begin to wind down. I try to put him out of my mind.

Stay in the sunshine.

I finish my second glass of champagne while cornered by three crew members animatedly discussing the different mechanics behind the plane crash scene. I swap glasses with a passing waiter at the first opportunity, watching from the corner of my eye as a distracted Harper flirts shamelessly with Masters across the room.

The third glass goes down easy as Sloan gives a long-winded, watery-eyed speech about his deep delight in working on this film, and how proud he is of the art we came together to create.

By the time I finish my fourth glass, the party has mostly emptied out. Harper, buzzed and happy, pulls me into the bathroom with her. Her cheeks are flushed with the effects of alcohol and infatuation.

"He is *so* cute!"

"Who, Masters?"

"Kent," she murmurs dreamily. "But I'll let him be my master any day."

"Harper!" I giggle.

"What? I'm single now." She shrugs. "Truth be told, Greg and his teenie-weenie-peenie were not fulfilling my needs the past few months. But I have a feeling Kent is packing heat. And I'm not just talking about the gun in his holster."

"Go," I push her toward the door. "For god's sake, go. Get some. Call me after."

"I don't think he'll leave with me — he said he's still *on duty*."

"I'll have Wyatt talk to him." I shrug. "Seriously, the party is almost over anyway. I'll be fine for one night without Masters hovering."

She giggles and throws her arms around me. "You're the best."

"Not even close, but I'm glad you think so." I pat her on the back. "Now, go! Enjoy your night. If he won't leave, drag him down to the gazebo in the backyard. No one will bother you, out there."

"Genius!" she exclaims, heading off to find him.

I walk slowly back to the main room, startled to find everyone is gone when I get there. Harper must've found Masters, because he's nowhere in sight. There's no sign of Sloan or Wyatt. The bartender is packing up. Even the cater waiters are putting on their jackets and trickling out the door. I ask one of them if they've seen Wyatt, and she points vaguely at the staircase before heading out.

I slowly ascend the stairs of the empty house, careful not to trip on the train of my dress. I'm tired and somewhat buzzed from the champagne, but I still want to say goodbye to Wyatt before calling myself a car service. The lights upstairs are off, but I see a sliver of yellow spilling out beneath the crack of a door at the end of the hallway. I head toward it like the bugs I once watched flying toward the zapper-machine, not thinking about the potential repercussions of my actions. Not thinking about much of anything, except getting to Wyatt and feeling that warm, safe sensation I get whenever I'm sharing his space, breathing his air, feeling his arms wrapped around me.

He said to stay in the sunshine. He doesn't seem to realize he carries more light inside him than any distant star in the sky over our heads.

My hand finds the knob in the darkness. I turn it and the door swings inward easily.

He's sitting on the edge of his bed, a half-empty tumbler of scotch in his hand. His hair is unbound, falling around his face like a gleaming curtain of gold. His shirt is unbuttoned, exposing his broad chest in the dim light.

"Katharine?" he whispers, looking up when I step into the bedroom. "What are you doing here?"

The door closes behind me with a soft click that sounds like a bullet sliding into the chamber of a loaded gun. His eyes are hazy but so, so blue. Blue like the sky, blue like the Hawaiian waves.

He takes a sip of his scotch and rises to his feet, setting the empty glass on his bedside table. I've never seen him drunk before. It's a mesmerizing sight — solid, steadfast Wyatt Hastings, out of control for once.

"You should go," he says, not looking at me. His hands are braced against the wall. I can see the muscles beneath his shirt, bunched up with tension. Before I can stop myself, I'm across the room and my hands are reaching out, tracing the powerful planes with trembling fingers.

He goes rigid when he feels my hands on him.

"Katharine." His voice is rough. "Go. You have to go."

"Why?" I ask, still touching him.

He groans. "Baby, you can't touch me like that—"

I let my hands fall away. He turns his head to look at me, eyes at half-mast. They're stripped of all guards. I can see the desire in their depths, at war with logic and common sense and all the practical reasons that me being in his bedroom is a terrible idea.

"Baby, baby, baby," I whisper, reaching for the strap on my shoulder. "Always *baby*." I flick the strap; his eyes watch it fall and I see a muscle jump in his cheek. "I'm not a baby, Wyatt. I'm not a little girl." I flick the other strap and in one soundless instant, the dress falls to the floor. I feel the fabric pool around my high heels, but I never shift my eyes from his.

I watch them dilate as they move over my body, bare except for a white lace bra and matching thong. His nostrils flare. His hands tense violently against the wall and I get the sense he's a hairsbreadth away from completely losing control.

"Wyatt," I whisper, chest rising and falling rapidly. I reach for my bra clasp, flick it open, and let it fall to the ground. "I don't want to be a baby in your eyes tonight."

He pushes off the wall with a growl and grabs me. I see the savage expression on his face and think he looks like a Viking about to lay waste to a village.

I am that village, I realize as his lips come down on mine, hot and hard and nothing like I ever imagined they'd be, in the rare moments I allowed myself to envision this ever happening between us. *He's going to wreck me.*

And he does.

He practically throws me onto the bed, coming down on top of me an instant later and settling between my legs. I push off his shirt as his lips devour my neck, as his hands roam over my skin.

"God, Katharine," he groans as I reach down to stroke him. "You're killing me."

I grin against his mouth as I slide his belt buckle open. "Don't die yet," I murmur, pulling it from its loops. "We're just getting started."

A growl rattles from his throat.

His hands move roughly — I hear a ripping sound and then my lace underwear is simply gone, torn to pieces like tissue paper. I've never seen him like this — so savage.

So intense.

His hands are rough as they move over my bare skin, igniting something inside me I've never felt before.

Never, in all my time knowing him, did I think there would be such passion with Wyatt. Friendship, yes. Even attraction. But the raw, brutal, reckless way he's making me feel... Not in my wildest dreams did I ever consider it would be like this between us.

When he's finally naked, braced over me with lust in his eyes and his hair falling down around his face like a sheet of gold, I wrap my legs around his waist and slide my arms around his back. He's looking at me with such a mix of heat and tenderness and sheer, heart-stopping *need*, it's hard to breathe.

I feel him poised at my entrance, waiting for permission to ruin me.

"Wyatt," I breathe.

He pushes inside me, eyes never shifting from mine, and the whole world explodes into sunshine and starlight and something else, something I'm not quite ready to put words to, yet.

***

I wake the next morning, naked and tangled up in sheets that smell like Wyatt. He's not sleeping beside me. A glance around reveals he's not anywhere in the room.

Flashes of the night before play out in my head like a movie.

Wyatt's hands on my breasts as I squirmed on the mattress beneath his delicious weight.

Wyatt's mouth between my legs as my fingers fisted in his thick, gorgeous hair.

Wyatt's grin in the darkness as I bowed like a branch beneath his touch.

Wyatt's eyes burning into mine as he pushed into me with long, relentless thrusts.

Wyatt's name on my lips as I orgasmed again and again and again, until I thought I might die from the sheer bliss of it all.

I feel my heart beating too fast inside my chest. My emotions are more tangled than a spider's web.
I can't believe I did this.
I can't believe how good it was.
I have no idea what it means.
I have no idea what *he* thinks it means.
Sitting up, I clutch the sheets to my chest. It's hard to fathom Wyatt leaving me alone in his bed, after what happened between us.
Maybe he regrets it, I think, horrified at the prospect. *Maybe he hates me for coming here last night... for basically seducing him....*
I don't let myself look too closely at the feelings stirring inside my chest as I contemplate a world in which Wyatt Hastings hates me. I don't let myself wonder what this means — for me, for Wyatt, for Grayson, for the movie.
Throwing off the sheet, I rise and use the massive bathroom through the door on the left. I use a tissue to wipe the residual mascara from beneath my eyes, and brush my teeth with a dollop of minty white paste on the end of my finger, feeling slightly more in control as I walk back into the bedroom.
Still no Wyatt.
He can't even face you.
Leave. Now.
Before you make it worse.
Fearing the worst, I steady my shoulders, walk over to my discarded dress, and pull it on. My bra is nowhere to be found, and I'm in no rush to stick around. Not if he doesn't want me here.
I fish my cellphone from the depths of my small beaded purse and, in a hushed voice, call for a car service to pick me up. Clutching my high heels in one hand, I head for the door and slip into the hallway, trying to make as little noise as possible.
Just when I thought I couldn't make more of a mess out of my life...

I'm almost to the front door, almost to freedom, when I'm intercepted.

"You're leaving."

His voice is flat. Totally devoid of feeling.

I turn and see he's got a tray in his hands, a steaming stack of pancakes and two mimosas balanced on it.

"Wyatt—"

"So, that's what this was." He laughs, but there's no humor in it. "Just a one night stand you sneak out on in the morning, without even saying goodbye."

"No, Wyatt, that's not—"

"Just a convenient fuck, to help you get over Dunn. Is that it?"

"Wyatt, no! No, it wasn't like that—"

"What am I to you? Your fucking consolation prize?"

"*No!* No."

"Fuck, Katharine!" His curse rings out as he hurls the tray against the wall. I jump as the glasses shatter into a million pieces. Pancakes fly into the air, syrup puddles against the tile like spilled blood. He's breathing hard, completely out of control. His eyes are wild, but his voice is icy calm. "You know, I knew you were fucked up, but this is a whole new level."

I gasp. "I... I'm sorry, Wyatt, I..."

His eyes narrow into unrecognizable slits. "You might not love me, but I thought we were at least friends. Thought there was basic respect between us. That you cared enough to exhibit common fucking courtesy. But this..." He's staring at me like he's never seen me before in his life. "This is unforgivable."

I feel the fragile hope that bloomed inside me in his arms last night burst into flame and burn to ash. I stare at this man, who has protected me at every turn — from this industry, from my mother, from Grayson, from the paparazzi, and even from my own self-destructive tendencies — and see that I have done nothing but hurt him, have brought him nothing but pain.

I look at him and a million memories flash before my eyes.

Wyatt grinning at me and telling me he'd change my life.

Wyatt wrapping my freezing body in a towel and holding me close.

Wyatt keeping Cynthia away from the movie to protect me.

Wyatt handing me a bottle of water, telling me to stay hydrated.

Wyatt saying it would be a privilege, not a burden, to love one woman for a lifetime.

Wyatt laughing as he dunked me beneath the warm, salty waves of the South Pacific.

Wyatt pulling me from the depths of a drunken spiral and wrapping me in his safe, strong arms.

Wyatt making love to me, his eyes on mine the entire time, reverence and tenderness in their depths.

I stare at him, frozen in place, hit by a bolt of lightning as realization singes through me.

He loves me.

He has shown me in his every glance, his every touch, his every action. Unfailingly. Unobtrusively. Asking for nothing in return.

He has given me sunshine, but I have buried him in shadow.

While he has brought me joy, I have given him only misery.

I am a cancer. I am a plague.

I will kill anyone who gets too close.

My desolation is infectious.

My sadness is lethal.

"Wyatt..." I whisper brokenly. "Please, listen to me. It's not..."

"Just go." His blue eyes, usually so full of light, glitter with ice. "Just get out. I don't want to listen to you. Frankly, I can't even look at you."

With that, he turns and walks out of the room.

I stare at the empty space where he stood, at the syrup from our ruined breakfast leaking slowly across the floor, and I feel my heart, which I thought was already broken beyond repair, shatter into even more irreparable pieces.

CHAPTER EIGHTEEN

*"*I love you.*"*
- A glutton for punishment.

One month later…

I sit on the edge of my basin bathtub, in the glamorous bathroom of my brand new beach house, watching the seconds count down on the timer. It's the longest two minutes of my entire life.

I haven't spoken to Grayson since I left his house in the middle of the night.

I haven't spoken to Wyatt since the morning after the wrap party.

I have lost them both.

Sloan's assistant called this morning, to make sure I got the schedule they sent over. The movie press tour starts next week. I am filled with dread, at the prospect of seeing them.

Especially now.

The past month has been a blur of mind-numbing pain and mechanical productivity. I've kept as busy as possible, not letting myself think too much about the mess I created. If I did, I'd never make it through the day without drinking. Hell, I'd never get out of bed in the morning.

Harper's been a big help, keeping me on track. She and Masters — who she calls *Kent* in a dreamy voice every time she gets an opportunity — have made sure I don't spiral again. Between the two of them, I'm never alone. I never set my eyes on a bottle of alcohol, let alone my hands.

I don't protest their hovering. Left to my own devices, I tend to make questionable life decisions and fuck everything up beyond repair.

We put a serious dent in my AXC check, buying me all the accoutrements that match my new life as Katharine Firestone, A-list actress.

New house in the Pacific Palisades. New car that actually runs. New closet full of designer clothes.

Now, I have everything I've ever dreamed of owning.

Now, I have nothing at all.

I am utterly hollow.

I am twisted into knots.

I fell in love with a man who could not love me back.

A man I will never deserve fell in love with me.

Nothing makes sense. Nothing at all.

Especially now.

The timer on my phone beeps. I take a deep breath and stare down at the plastic stick in my hand. The tiny word on the screen fills me with more dread than I've ever felt in my life.

Positive.

To be continued....

THE**SOMEDAY**GIRL

THE GIRL DUET

PART TWO

COMING FEBRUARY 2017

ACKNOWLEDGMENTS

Thank you, first and foremost, to my readers.

As an author, it is always a risk to start a new series, to take on a fresh challenge, to do something *different* — different genre, different characters, different world to build piece by piece out of words and sentences and paragraphs.

Thank you for following me down new paths. For staying by my side when I decide to try something out of my comfort zone. I appreciate it more than words could ever express.

To my parents — thank you for being there with me for every moment of this process, from brainstorming to beta reading. I love you both so much. Sorry for all the sex scenes.

To my friends and family — thank you for understanding that sometimes, you won't see me for weeks at a time, and that doesn't mean I don't love you. It just means I'm writing.

To my Johnson Junkies — thank you for being a constant bright spot on social media, which is so often full of darkness.

And finally, to my dog Scout. I aspire to one day be the person you think I am.

ABOUT THE AUTHOR

JULIE JOHNSON is a twenty-something Boston native suffering from an extreme case of Peter Pan Syndrome. When she's not writing, Julie can most often be found adding stamps to her passport, drinking too much coffee, striving to conquer her Netflix queue, and Instagramming pictures of her dog. (Follow her: @authorjuliejohnson)

She published her debut novel LIKE GRAVITY in 2013, just before her senior year of college, and she's never looked back. Since, she has published six more novels, including the bestselling BOSTON LOVE STORY series. Her books have appeared on Kindle, B&N, and iTunes Bestseller lists around the world, as well as in AdWeek, Publishers Weekly, and USA Today.

Julie graduated cum laude from the University of Delaware in December 2013, one semester ahead of schedule, with two B.A. Honor's Degrees in Psychology and Mass Communications. She now hopes to put off the real world for as long as possible by writing full-time.

You can find Julie on Facebook, follow her on Instagram, or contact her by email at juliejohnsonbooks@gmail.com. Sometimes, when she can figure out how Twitter works, she tweets from @AuthorJulie.

For news and updates, be sure to subscribe to Julie's newsletter: http://eepurl.com/bnWtHH

Printed in Poland
by Amazon Fulfillment
Poland Sp. z o.o., Wrocław